Blank Spaces

The Legend of Jerusalem Walker

A novel by
Reid Matthias

ISBN   paperback: 978-0-6450472-6-4
          ebook: 978-0-6450472-7-1

This edition first published by A 13 in May 2022

Typesetting by Ben Morton

Publication assistance from Immortalise

Front and back cover photos by Greta Matthias

Acknowledgements

Full disclosure is appropriate, I think.

It seems strange to have to disclose something fully before a book begins. That's like accepting forgiveness before asking for it, and yet it feels necessary. As you meander through this book's adventures, I must tell you that *Blank Spaces* was written during the middle stages of the Coronavirus pandemic. For writers, this was a struggle. In the big picture of things, a minor inconvenience, but travel was limited to the online variety. Thus, in order to describe the places in this book, I was limited to two-dimensional images and websites which painted only half a picture.

Now, that is not to say, 'I'm sorry that this book will be most unfulfilling for you.' No, not by any means. *Blank Spaces* is a work of the heart dedicated to my most wonderful daughters, Elsa, Josephine and Greta who have been the source of so much curiosity in my life, and hopefully this book will be, for you, a source of humor, interest and a desire to have life *mean* something.

Back to full disclosure and the limitations of this book: since I've never been to any of the places described in this book, there will be factual inconsistencies of how things *actually* look. If you have ever been to these places (I don't want to spoil anything by revealing names), please be merciful and overlook the errors. With regards to historical figures depicted in this book, I have taken certain liberties making connections. These are fabrications for the story and shouldn't be viewed as fact, only *hmm, wouldn't that be interesting?*

I want to acknowledge the editorial work of two people, especially: Greta Matthias and Christine Matthias. Without their keen observations for both plot and structure, this book would fall into a *Well, that's a pleasant little story* mess, rather than a coming-of-age story that all of us, regardless of age or gender, can connect with.

Chapter 1 Across:
Cave in violently (7)

My name is Jerusalem Walker.

I am not normal.

Not in the normal sense of normal, anyway. I mean, I'm neither socially addled, nor do I have difficulties keeping my fingers out of my nose. It's just... well, my brain works at a different speed than others.

What I do have is a weird name. From this name, I have developed a deep sense of my own identity, one that is infinitely content to create new things inside my own head: new words, new phrases, new ways of approaching life. And sometimes they make me snicker at inappropriate times. Like the time Yugi and I were sitting in church and the priest steps up to the altar and starts to chant, but it sounds like a moan, like he was beginning to moo. The priest sings about as well as my dad does, and that's saying something. So, Father Benson starts mooing, and his first words are 'Lord, have mercy.' I looked at Yugi and whispered, 'Lord, if you don't have mercy, my ears are going to implode.'

Yugi quickly covered his mouth with one hand and his eyes started to pop out. He kept the laugh in until it started to leak through his fingers and then, when the tears started to form, he slapped the other one on top. Pretty soon, just when Father Benson was about to finish, and he raised his hands into the air above his head, I leaned back in to Yugi one more time and whisper,

Touchdown.

Yugi couldn't handle it and laughter burst out not from his mouth but from the other end. Unable to contain my own giggles, I leaned back into the wooden pew and ground my teeth. A few of the older ladies near us cast the death stare. You already know what they're thinking: *Why you little skidmarks, this is a holy place and you are defiling it. Go outside.* They turned their stares to my parents who were silently pleading for mercy from God who was located somewhere in the rafters of the church.

My father's face was upturned. I could see he'd missed a few whiskers alongside his trachea. They were jutting out alongside the rash by his Adam's apple. My dad's is so big I call it an 'Adam's melon,' but he never thinks that's funny.

He also didn't think laughing and farting in church was such a good idea either.

But what could we do? I'm fifteen years old and Yugi is ten. We're *supposed* to be like this.

Anyway, our non-normalness is my parents' fault anyway. Our 'difficulty to engage in social situations' is inextricably tied to the reason why I am called Jerusalem and my brother, Yugoslavia. My parents thought it cute to christen their children after the places where we were conceived. I thank God for many things, not only the fact that I am named Jerusalem and not 'Seedy Hotel Room.' I also give it up to the Big Guy upstairs because there was no third child. I'd hate to have a sister named Ho Chi Minh City.

Although Yugi was not *actually* conceived in Yugoslavia, they thought it would be better than writing 'Herzegovina.' Most people, my friends included, call me Jeri.

So this is me, and this is the way I talk. I like to daydream about all sorts of things; stories, ways to describe stuff. And I like my parents but...

I don't think they're exactly *normal* either.

Chapter 2 Down:

Relating to that which connects upper extremities to the anterior and lateral thoracic walls (8)

We need to clear one thing up before I go any further. There are two types of people in the world: those who do crosswords and stupid people. My mother, Beryl, thinks my proclivity for filling in 'silly little blank spaces with words from esoteric clues' is not something a normal teenager girl should be doing. The mere fact that she used the word 'esoteric' in a sentence, and I understood it, means that I'm on the right track... I think.

Some people, usually old people with a lot of extra time, work in their airless and tastelessly decorated kitchens, smelling of both cinnamon and mothballs, sitting behind gingham tablecloths spread across ancient oak tables, filling in the *small* crosswords from the Duncan Gazette. The clues are so easy, even Yugi (who has both insufficient attention and brain matter) could finish these. When I get a new crossword book, the first thing I do is have Yugi rip out all the answers in the back. Users are losers, I say.

Strangely, I do my best work in the bathroom. Sometimes, like today, Mom will knock on the door, two knuckles, *rap rap*, 'Jeri, get off the commode.' She thinks if she calls the toilet a commode it makes her sound smarter.

'Just a minute,' I call out, trying to push through the mental blockade for 26 across - *Insurer of Tina Turner's legs... second letter is an 'I'...*

'JERI!' Mom yells. 'Put the dang book down and finish your business, or you will be washing dishes for the rest of the day.'

I chew the tip of my pen - only troglodytes use pencils with erasers - and think past the excruciating noise my mother is making.

Lloyds. Of course. Lloyds of London.

'All right, missy, you asked for it.'

I open the door, crossword book in hand. I hadn't actually been doing a number two. I just do my best work in the bathroom.

Mom grunts and I see her face is a mask of frustration and resignation. Life is hard for her but I'm not sure why she is frustrated and resigned. We live in an idyllic neighborhood in Duncan, Oklahoma, a medium sized white-picket-fence kind of town. In fact, we have a white fence, but it's much taller than the picket variety. I wonder why it's called a 'picket' fence? In truth, the white has faded with grey mold and the lower third is mottled with the green lashings of our weed whacker. Home upkeep is not our forte.

I push past my mother and make my way to the kitchen where Yugi and my dad, Kevin, are perched on their stools like twin sphinxes. Dad is drinking coffee and staring morosely out the window. The glass is very dirty. A recent rainstorm has streaked it, but the ensuing winds brought Oklahoma dust and dirt and caked small lines across it. They look like worm tracings. Mom talks about cleaning the windows a lot, but I think it's a passive/aggressive way of getting one of the other Walkers to do it. I pretend not to notice.

Yugi is still in his pajamas even though he has to leave for school in fifteen minutes. The fleece pajamas are imprinted with the newest Disney movie, some kind of space-superhero-masterpiece, I'm sure. I have no interest in movies. They are for people who can't do crosswords.

Dad sighs and takes a sip of his coffee. It burns his lip, and he rubs it.

'Good morning, Jerusalem.'

'Dad, please.' My eyes speak volumes of disdain. 'I'd rather you not call me that.'

'But that's your name? I think it's beautiful.'

'I want to be called Jeri.'

'But why would you want such a normal sounding name? We want you to be special.'

'I don't want to be special, Dad. That's what they call kids who have intellectual impairments.' I pull the Rice Krispies from the cupboard. The cartoon characters who remind me how noisy the cereal is. *Snap. Crackle. Pop.*

Dad frowns and pulls himself from the stool. I can tell this is not the conversation he wanted to have this morning, but I am fifteen, and I have been establishing my boundaries and exit strategies for a while now.

'Okay, *Jeri.*' For some reason the way he says this hurts, but I choose to put all my mental energies into the snapping, the crackling and the popping. I pour the milk and listen. There it is.

Mom enters the kitchen after her morning ablutions looking slightly more refreshed and slightly less depressed. That's a good sign.

'What are you up to today?' She stands behind Dad to give him a reverse hug.

He is quiet then smiles through a dirty window at nothing and no one in particular, unless it's the lonely red cardinal twitching on the maple tree branch. I can see that the buds have transformed into small, tender leaves almost overnight. Our next-door neighbor, Donald Berry, would say, 'It's about fricking time.' Dongle Berry, as I call him, thinks that swearing is for the insecure.

'Same as always.' I watch, curious, because they never seem to get tired of each other. They are in love (whatever that means). It's a kind of deep-seated satisfaction with who the other person is and who they are becoming. I often wonder what that will be like, what my 78 Down will be like.

I suppose I should explain the next part of my abnormalcy with you. My favorite crossword in the entire world is a Saturday edition of the New York Times from 2020. It took me three months to figure it out, and when I finally filled in the last blank space, when the last word finally clicked in like a combination lock tumbler, I felt giddy with relief and accomplishment. After cutting the puzzle out of the paper, I laminated it at school. Carefully, I pushed a thumbtack through the upper and lower corners into the corkboard in my room. That crossword is surrounded by photos of my family and a few school acquaintances, glassy eyed friends unsure of where to look at the camera. Most appear startled, as if someone had clapped their hands in front of their faces just before the picture was taken.

Sometimes, instead of using the normal word, such as the one for 78 Down - *infatuation* - I just use the numeric symbol instead. Yugi likes it. Dad and Mom don't.

Now I've decided that my recollections and memoirs of life will use that crossword as a template for the things that I write. Of course, *infatuation* can be used in all sorts of situations, but a word like 'Lloyds' would be a little harder to insert into everyday writing.

'How about you?' My dad returns the question like a tennis ball. *Thwack.*

'Cleaning around the house. Then catching up with Dawn.' *Thwack*.

'When I get home tonight, do you think we could have a pot roast?' *Thwack*.

She searches his eyes and smiles, but there is a sigh festering just beneath, a putrid loathing of the routine which has taken them from the things they *used to do*.

When Kevin Walker and Beryl Adams were twenty-two years of age, life was their cracked mollusk. Kevin was about to finish college, with a BS in Social Work. Kevin's father, Walter, was *highly* unimpressed by Kevin's choice of career study. 'What the heck can you do with a BS degree in Social Work?' he would ask in his grumpy, old man voice, face reddened by indignation. 'You want to help poor people? I can fix 'em - tell 'em to get a job.' Needless to say, Grandpa Walt is not always the most popular person in the nursing home.

Dad was deaf to my grandfather's gruffness because he was completely 78 Down'ed with Beryl, a fellow classmate and graduate of the university of Oklahoma State.

When I look at the pictures of their graduation day, I am struck by their vivacity. Standing side by side, Kevin and Beryl are holding each other fiercely. My father is holding on to his mortarboard hat while the tassel flicks in his eyes. My mother is beaming - excruciatingly excited for the future.

As Dad relates the story, after graduation, Kevin and Beryl made a cultural and collective decision to travel together. Grandpa Walter informed Kevin and his 'lady-friend' that they were being incredibly irresponsible. 'Traveling around the world without jobs, without money, without *anything...*' he grizzled, shaking his thick, wrinkled forefinger at them. Now that Kevin and Beryl had freedom from parents, though, they could do as they *wanted*, not as they were *expected*.

Between the two of them, they scraped together a few thousand dollars of remaining scholarship money and sofa-cushion-petty-cash to fulfill their dreams of travel. After booking flights to Europe, they backpacked, hiked and slept in whatever accommodation could be had, just to SEE things, as my mother would emphasize with her eyes and hands. She wanted to SEE something and DO something. In those travel pictures, taken on an old Kodak camera with a pop-up flash, (sometimes Yugi and I still play with that camera to watch the bulb pop up like a Jack-in-the-Box) the grainy photos reveal a handsome couple, rosy cheeked and... and... well, 52 Across is the only word that comes to mind:

Vibrant.

Kevin Walker proposed for the first time in Denmark of all places. I guess it's not that Denmark *isn't* romantic, but my father leaned across the table at a place called 'Indre-missions Bible School' (they couldn't find anywhere else to stay) and through the haze of cigarette smoke, popped the question. Unfortunately, Beryl had been distracted by a particularly attractive Dane named Jens with blonde hair and a woolen sweater that emphasized his overdeveloped pectoral muscles. When Beryl asked my father to repeat the question, Kevin said, 'Never mind. We'll talk about it later.'

When that 'later' arrived, Beryl was much more receptive. As they laid out under the stars outside of Munich, it was getting quite chilly and Beryl shivered. Kevin moved closer. As they looked up into the vast emptiness of the unforgiving space, Dad rolled in and whispered, 'How about making this permanent?'

Chapter 2 Down:

'What, you want to move to Munich?'

Dad stroked her cheek tracing a path from the corner of her eye to her chin. 'Well, we can if you want to, but I was thinking about something else.'

'I bet you were.' She nudged him in the ribs with her elbow.

'I mean it,' he laughed. 'Do you want to get married?'

Mom's breath caught in her throat. They had been dating for two years. They seemed compatible. They loved each other, but marriage seemed so... final. So... heavy. For a few seconds she didn't respond, and my dad began to sweat. He wondered if he had made a terrible mistake.

'But how will we live? Where will we live? What are we going to...?'

'Beryl,' my dad silenced her, 'if I lost you, I would die a thousand deaths every day.'

When my mother tells me that story, I alternate between gagging, and thinking *oooh, isn't that cute?*

I don't think I'll ever find one of those.

I'd have to be normal.

Chapter 3 Down:
Neurotransmitter highway (7)

Cupping my yellow cereal bowl, I walk through the kitchen arch into the living room where our antique oak table lives. It's darkness and texture have been a constant in my life. Smooth top, ridges in the sides, it has a feeling of dependability and inerrancy about it. Underneath the tranquility of the eating surface are intricately carved knobs and spikes which served as the control room for my youthful submarine when I was younger. Sitting underneath, Yugi and I would plot a course far, far away to a galaxy far, far beneath the waves. To Vanuatu or Fiji or Bora Bora or any other exotically named island nation on Survivor, the two of us would raise a periscope, get a view of the surroundings and DIVE! DIVE! DIVE! into the tranquil submarining depths. No noise. No distractions. Only me and Yugi. We often dreamed of traveling, but my parents stopped once Yugi was conceived. I have very few memories of traveling with them before Yugi and strangely, my parents were averse to taking pictures even when we did.

I was four years old the last time *they* traveled abroad.

They dropped me and my toys at Grandpa Walt and Grandma Iris' house. My grandparents agreed insofar as that they would only have to look out for my basic needs. Grandpa Walt was insistent upon this - food, shelter, water – that's it. Doting love would have to be suspended until my parents returned. My dad threw up his hands and blessed his father who uncomfortably accepted his son's embrace. Grandpa Walt wasn't quite sure if leaving for an overseas vacation was such a responsible thing to do. 'Why couldn't they just travel around this country? There's no greater nation on earth than the U. S. of A.' He looked down at me as if I were a small alien and attempted to pat me on the head, but his hand just couldn't quite do it. He retracted it and crossed his arms.

While my parents were away, something strange happened. Grandpa Walt discovered that he didn't mind little humans. Even though he was gruff, he grew to appreciate the hourly tugging on his pants, 'Grandpa - read a book to me.' He would settle into his comfy, cushioned recliner, grunt twice on the way down, and allow me to clamber up over his legs (avoiding his German Jewels as he called them - once I kneed him in the gems and he didn't read to me for an entire day). We would sit there for an hour or two, my curly hair cradled into the place between his shoulder and armpit. He smelled of Old Spice and fabric softener. When he read, his voice would get lower and slower and eventually he would fall asleep. That is until I slammed my head into his chest to wake him up.

Grandpa and Grandma now live in a shared room at the Pine Point Retirement Acres. It's always weird to me why they have names like that as if somehow it makes it easier for the 'residents' (not 'inmates' as Grandpa Walt calls them) to assimilate to a new, differently-structured life. I suppose it's better than calling it 'Waiting to Die Geriatric Prison.'

I visit Grandpa and Grandma a couple of times per week. Their unit number is 64, which is ironically the word in my crossword for 'tranquil.' I love it when there are 'q's in words. It makes it so much easier.

Pine Point is a seven-minute bike ride from our house so I usually pedal there on Tuesday and Thursday afternoons. The nurses (or 'executioners' as Grandpa calls them) are pleasant and welcoming when I visit.

Grandpa is pretty much a 'right-here and right-now' kind of guy, and even though the right-here and right-now of Pine Point is not his idea of happiness, he is content to spend time with Grandma Iris who is now on the not-so-gentle slope of dementia. She has a few good days interspersed between the constant repetitions of questions, but they are getting farther and farther in between. Grandpa Walt sits in front of his bay window staring out into the vastness of the free world. Grandma sits beside him in her own chair, eyes flitting from here to there, a constant crease between her eyebrows; she is scared but doesn't know why. On her good days, she is frightened of losing the last vestiges of her awareness one synapse at a time. On her bad days, she can't understand why she is not in her pink party dress waiting for her parents to drive her to the skating rink.

My bowl of cereal continues to make delightful noises while I crunch away. I am tempted to pull a small crossword puzzle book from my pocket, but my eyes are distracted by movement next door. Dongle Berry is out in his front yard. *Puttering*, he calls it.

Finishing my cereal, I hear my dad call out that he is taking Yugi to school. My mom blows a kiss in their general direction, and I take this as my cue to drop my breakfast dish in the sink full of dirty dishes and hurry outside.

The day is boldly alight. Even though the sun drips honey from the sky, the breeze is chilly. I realize that I should have put on a jacket, but if I enter the house, Mom will demand assistance with an assortment of household tasks. Crossing my arms, I cover my thin pajama top and tiptoe barefoot through the yard towards the fence that divides Dongle's yard and ours. Where the Berry's have a manicured, trimmed lawn fit for a professional baseball game, the Walker's looks like the face of a seventeen-year-old boy, pockmarked with tufts sprouting in odd places.

Dongle is raking dead leaves from the ash trees on his side of the fence. It sounds like he is shaving the grass - *rick, rack, scritch, scratch* - slooooowly, methodically moving. It's as if he is on autopilot.

'Hi, Dongle.'

He turns slowly. Everything he does is slow. Brown eyes flicker with amusement and they drop down to my crossed arms and then to my tiptoed feet. 'Morning, Nosebleed.'

A few years ago, I saw him in the backyard and tripped as I approached him. I face-planted into the fence which resulted in a bloody nose. If I look closely, I can pick out the slat where the blood was streaked. 'Don't you ever get tired of playing with your grass?' I asked.

He grunts and rests his hands on the handle of the rake. Dongle used to be tall, but now he doesn't seem it. His grey hair is thinning revealing a glowing, pink, baby-butt color underneath. The skin of his cheeks has drooped giving him jowls which are webbed with tiny varicose blood vessels. He sniffs. 'Nope. Aren't you cold, Jeri?'

I think about pretending I am not, but it's difficult to lie to old people. 'Yes. Quite.'

'Maybe you should go back inside the house, then.'

'I don't want to do the dishes.'

He smiles and turns again to rake. *Rick, rack, scritch, scratch.* 'No school this morning?'

'Yeah, but I don't have any classes until eleven.' I sigh.

13

Grunt. 'Kids are soft these days, I'm telling you.'

'I didn't choose to have the morning off. That's just the way the schedule lined up.'

'What do you like about school? The boys, I suppose.'

Now it's my turn to grunt. '19 Downs.'

'What?' He stops his lawn shaving.

'19 Downs. In my crossword, 19 Down is the word 'cretin.''

Dongle shakes his head and peers over his trifocaled glasses at me. 'Where do you come up with these things? Why don't you talk like other kids?'

'You mean, why don't I speak normally and use the words 'like' and 'literally' and 'just' all the time?' He stares at me.

'You sound arrogant, is what you sound.'

'Just because I have a penchant for vocabulary doesn't mean I'm arrogant.' I spoke the word 'penchant' with the correct French pronunciation - *pen-shaw.*

'You sound like an a-hole.'

Score one point for Dongle for not swearing out loud. But really, does eliminating the two s's destroy the function of the profanity? It's the same when he says 'frickin' or 'dadgum.'

'No, Dongle, I am not particularly interested in boys and certainly the reverse is true also.'

'It's probably because you are smarter than all of them put together.'

I am pleased by his compliment and the blush warms me slightly, but my feet are getting cold. 'Perhaps.'

Dongle looks toward the back porch where his wife, Margery, is sitting with a blanket over her legs and two knitting needles clicking between her hands. They have been married for forty-seven years. *An eternity,* Dongle says. Dongle and Margery are both retired and both have difficulties acclimating to the life of leisure. Although they enjoy puttering, there is an edginess of an aquarium-bound barracuda about him.

'Kids these days, all they want to do is play video games and twiddle with their phones. Why, in my day, we all had jobs and chores to do. Work to be done...' His voice avalanches from geriatric indignation to a low mumble rumble of disgruntlement.

'Well,' I say, 'at least we aren't grumpy a-holes fixating on grass all day.' I smile and tap the cracking fence once. Dongle has already started laughing.

I walk back to the porch where Mom is watching me through the living room window. One of her arms is across her chest while the other is lifting a mug of steaming coffee to her lips. She sees me and blinks.

It's going to be a normal day.

Chapter 4 Down:
If you divide by 1, this is 0 (9)

After helping my mother finish the dishes, fold the laundry and work through the menu for evening meals, I ride my bike to school in hopes to stop in at Pine Point after the last bell has rung. As the breeze flows through my hair and across my face, I feel free.

The stolid face of the school looms over the well-tended lawns in front. A flagpole is planted in the center of the lawn. I park my bike in the rack and lock it up. Dongle said they never locked anything when he was a kid; he makes it sound as if they were never afraid of anything - but I know, yes, I do - they were always afraid of the Communists (which never took over) or the impending nuclear World War III (which never happened) or the oil shortage (which seems to be somewhat exaggerated). He suggests that my age bracket is afraid of everything, but especially weird stuff, things that can't be changed like Global Warming or Coronavirus or Murder Hornets. Dongle blames everything on the internet. He shakes a finger at me and says, 'In my day...'

Entering the building, I sign in at the front desk on the electronic scan pad. My photo ID shows a half-smiling girl with shoulder-length brown hair parted to the right side. A few zits are situated like lunar colonies on my face. The pinpoints of my eyes are blue and seem to reflect the light. I am not what one would call skinny, nor am I overweight. I have no desire at all to exercise. The thought of training for an athletic competition seems a monumental waste of caloric burn. I'd almost rather do the dishes.

Almost.

Mrs. Gaither thanks me for my attendance at school but she does not look up. She is tap-tap-tapping away on her computer, far too busy, so many tasks to be done by a receptionist, that she cannot possibly tear herself away to look at me.

By our lockers I meet my friend, Zara. We are the same age, but in different grades.

'You look happy,' she says.

'Yes.'

'What's going on?'

I pull my Physics book from my locker. The heft of it seems to pull me to the ground. 'I have exactly twenty-four days left of school.'

'Don't rub it in.' Zara leans against the locker to stare at me. She has an irritating, petite cuteness about her. Her small pug nose has a handful of freckles. Zara always wears blue jeans and a colored shirt, but the color of the shirt changes daily. She wears bright, neon tennis shoes which are completely out of line with her personality. When Zara smiles, which she does rarely right now because of her braces, she looks content, untouched by a world of anxiety and fear.

'I won't.' I close the locker.

'Don't you ever worry what next year will be like? I mean, you're like, only fifteen. That's literally, like, not even an adult.'

I squint at her, wanting to elevate her stilted vocabulary, but I need her as a friend. I don't have many. We found each other by cafeteria accident. We were standing next to each other in line waiting for watery macaroni and cheese and a ladleful of limp green beans. Simultaneously, we reached for the saltshaker and ended up scattering it across the counter. The lunch lady, Mrs. Benson, the priest's sister-in-law, scowled at us.

'What does my age have to do with anything at all?'

'Everything, Jeri, like, everything. You're going to be graduating, and just, like, leaving high school when you're fifteen and, like, you're going to college in the fall and all the people will be so much older than you and you'll be like scared, and like, um, yeah...' her inspiring words fell off Vocabulary Cliff.

'Zara,' I respond, turning slightly and tilting my head to signal that I'm about to go to class, 'why would you want to stay in high school if you don't have to?'

'Because it's like these are the best years of our lives. We're like young and free and beautiful.' She twirls in a small circle, eyes closed, innocent. I can see up her nose. It's not pretty.

'I plan on having an inordinate amount of fun mixing with the adults at college.'

'But, like, what about the boys...?'

'Like, what about them?'

'They'll be all graduated from high school..."

'And... so will I.' I back away from the locker.

'Yeah, but...' Zara is positioned in the middle of the hall, and as I leave her motionless form, paused in mid-*but*, it hits me that her biggest fear is being without me next year. She'll be in 10th grade and I will be in college. I lose a step in my stride, but these are the facts of life and the sooner we accept them, the quicker we'll move past the pain of change.

I sit through the first fifteen minutes of Physics while Mrs. Johnson struggles to maintain a full head of steam. What started out as a beautiful beginning to the year, moving from particles to electrons, has now fizzled into mindless videos and brain sucking homework. Sixteen minutes into the lecture, while Mrs. J. is scribbling furiously on the white board, I pull out a small pocket crossword book. The questions are far too easy, but so is Physics, and I'd rather do something that is more enjoyable. We have been working on pressures in fluid.

Yawn.

Cookie with twelve flowers on each side. I look at the puzzle - easy. *Oreo.* In general, crossword puzzles are really not about the size of one's vocabulary or even the limitations of one's general trivial knowledge. It is the ability to understand what the puzzle maker is trying to make you think. Wordplay is about outfoxing the creator, and I'm good at it. It just takes practice. For instance, I didn't know that Oreos had twelve flowers on each side, (I will remember it now, though) but the answer only has four spaces and there aren't very many cookies with four letters. Either way, it's just a matter of...

'Ms. Walker, is everything okay?' Mrs. Johnson has paused her whiteboard staining to turn and stare at me. She has a dark smudge on the fleshy part of her palm from the marker.

'Yes, Mrs. Johnson.'

'Would you care to enlighten us regarding the equation?' I look up at the board and my vision swims, the numbers, letters, Greek characters dance together in a logarithmic tango. Within seconds, I find that I already know the answer without knowing how I got there. Looking around at the other students in my class, eighteen-year-olds all smugly waiting for me to screw up and yet all fundamentally know that I already know.

'No, not really.'

'Ms. Walker, this is a Physics class, and the subject matter is highly important for your good grades.'

'Thank you, Mrs. Johnson.' Some of the class have begun to snicker and roll their eyes. A few boys in the back, boys with spectacles and braces, boys who spend more time playing computer games than addressing their hygiene, are nodding, their heads bouncing up and down in detached humor as if they are witnessing a particularly dehumanizing defeat of their favorite video game character.

'I would highly recommend that you refrain from crossword puzzles during Physics class.'

I want to be non-sarcastic. I really do. But there is something deep inside of me that is inordinately pleased with cutting small bits of emotional flesh from people. Little slices bringing about slow deaths.

'Thank you for the recommendation, Mrs. Johnson. I will write that little morsel in my personal journal.'

Mrs. Johnson's face turned beet-red and her curly hair seemed to tighten even more. Her voice lowers. 'If we weren't three weeks from graduation, I'd have you suspended.'

'My deepest apologies, Mrs. Johnson.'

Mrs. Johnson crosses to her desk and pops open her drawer. Taking a pen, she scribbles illegibly on a pink slip and rips it off the pad. I can see that a little piece of the corner is missing. That would be really annoying to have that chad hanging on the corner of a pad.

'Go to Mrs. Donnelly's office. Maybe she can see what's causing your anxiety to act out like this.'

I protest. 'I'm not anxious.'

'Get out! Go!' She slams the pink slip onto my desk. I stare at it. Even though her handwriting is suffering from a severe lack of control, I can still read the words:

J. Walker - disruptive in class. Needs a time out. Please keep her for the remainder of the lesson.

I sigh deeply and look at my crossword. *Yes! I know what seven across is too!* Closing my puzzle book, I stuff it and my Physics book into my bag. As I open the door for the room, I casually look back over my shoulder not entirely at Mrs. Johnson but towards her. I can't help it.

'P=3.71.'

Chapter 5 Across:
A mathematical statement (8)

I roll the pink slip up in my hand and rhythmically pound it into the other palm. An underclassman knowingly smirks at the piece of paper. He knows where I'm going. Mrs. Donnelly is the Guidance Counselor, but she is neither particularly good at guiding nor counseling. Instead, she desperately wants to love and to be loved, which precludes her from being a guiding light and an objective counselor. I have been sent to her a few times.

Mrs. Donnelly's office is decorated like a kindergarten room. Pictures of cuddly pets and soft pastels gild the walls giving off a cloying feeling that one is sitting inside a cotton candy ball. I am equally nauseated by her picture board with a felt dot that marks off an answer to the question: *How am I feeling today?*

Mrs. Donnelly sits behind the desk as I enter. Her large, transparent red glasses frame her plump face which has been distorted by make-up making her face look like a birthday cake. She smiles broadly at me. Magically, her face is transformed. She is obviously happy to see me, and then looks at the pink slip in my hand.

I raise my eyebrows and sigh.

'Oh, dear, is someone having a bad day? Come in and we'll talk about it.'

Speaking about my disappointment in Physics is probably the last thing I'll do considering the woman probably has never seen an equation more difficult than U + Me = Love heart.

'That's okay, Mrs. Donnelly. I'll just sit here until the next class.'

She pulls her face into a fake pout. 'Come on, Jeri. We'll have a little waggle of the chin.'

'No, really. I'm fine.'

'That's what they all say, dear, but when they see Mrs. D., I find out what the problem is quick-smart.'

There are all sorts of synonyms that any common person could pick out of the thesaurus for something to 'move rapidly,' but 'quick-smart' might be my least favorite. I dislike the situation even more now that she has said it.

I plop down in the chair and drop my bag on the ground next to me. She motions with her hand and eyes to a pea green bean bag in the corner. I shake my head and frown. I've got to get out of here quick-smart.

'Well, I guess I am a little worried.'

She leans forward as if she is about to settle in for a decent meal. Meaty forearms are flopped on the desk, hands tented. 'Tell me all about it.' Her eyes stray to a jar of Twizzlers.

'Okay.' I theatrically put my head down. I've seen enough drama in my school to copy it. 'I'm... afraid of... of... global warming and murder hornets.'

Mrs. Donnelly eyes seemed to have been magnified. I don't think she was prepared for that answer. Many who enter the friendly confines of the candy-coated office speak quietly about tests and papers and home life and relationships, but I might be the first one so ecologically minded.

'I... don't know what to say.'

'Tell me, Mrs. Donnelly, tell me everything is going to be okay!' I pretend to hitch in my breath as if I'm about to cry. 'The earth is warming, the poles are melting, dolphins are dying of plastic poisoning, and I have no

23

defense against stinging insects. For God's sake, I'm allergic to bee stings!'

I'm not, but I know she won't look in my file.

'I feel like my life is pointless - if Fiji is swallowed by the sea, if the polar bears can't swim to the mainland, if the otters - Oh, Lord, help the otters...' I begin to fake-cry into my hand.

'There, there, Jeri. There, there.' She reaches towards me.

'What are we going to do, Mrs. Donnelly?' I whisper. 'Do you think that because of my anxiety, I could be released to go home and work through it? Maybe I could do some color-by-numbers or take my dog for a walk?'

I abhor color-by-numbers and we don't have a dog. We had a hamster once. Dirty, noisy thing.

'Of course, Dear. I'll call your parents and let them know you are on your way.'

Thinking quickly, I lean in close to her. I hoped that she couldn't tell I hadn't been crying. 'That's fine, Mrs. Donnelly, but can I talk to my mom after you do? In private?'

Mrs. Donnelly pushes her glasses up on her nose and sniffs. Nodding slowly, she reaches for her pistachio green office phone. 'Number?'

I give her my mom's cell phone and within seconds, I hear the buzz of my mother's voice on the other end.

'Yes, hello, Mrs. Walker? This is Donna Donnelly at Duncan High School. Yes, well, I'm just calling to let you know that Jeri has had a little bit of a rough time at school this morning.' She paused and I heard my mother speaking. 'Mmhmmm. Yes, well we were thinking of sending her home to take a personal day to deal with some of her...' My mom interrupts.

I leaned forward. 'Can I talk to her, please?' Mrs. Donnelly looks over at me, then at her desk, then at me again. Mom was really going after it.

'Yes, I see, well, would you like to talk to her?'

Silence. My mom is thinking about it. Then a response. Mrs. Donnelly hands the phone to me. 'I'll just be outside the office, dear.' Heavily, she pulls herself out of her chair and grunts as she stretches her previously inert legs. I hold the phone to my ear but wait for Mrs. Donnelly to leave before I uncover the receiver with my hand.

'Hi, Mom.'

'Jerusalem Jean, what is going on?'

'There's something seriously wrong with that woman.'

'Jeri.'

'Yes, Mom.'

'What did you do?'

'You know, nothing, really. I'm just sick of high school. The inanity, putrid pools of puberty, everyone is drowning in stress with no lifesaver in sight.'

Silence. 'I have no idea what you're talking about.'

'All my work is finished. I'm going to get straight 'A's and they are worried about whether I'm paying attention to a YouTube video. Pointless, Mom. Pointless.'

'What did you say to Mrs. Donnelly? Why is she so worried about you?'

'She shouldn't be worried about me, Mom. She should worry about herself. The woman is a walking heart attack.' Discussion averted.

'Jeri.'

'I know, Mom, I'm supposed to be nice. But it's so hard. Some people make it so difficult.'

'We'll talk about it when you get home.'

I pause, aligning my plan of attack. 'I was thinking about going to visit Grandpa and Grandma at Pine Point. Is that okay.'

I could almost hear my mother sigh of relief. 'Yes, that would be okay.'

'Thanks, Mom. You're the best.' I'm surprised that I mean it, but I don't think she believes me.

'Be safe.' Mom hangs up the phone and I quietly replace the handset in the cradle. Softly, I open Mrs. Donnelly's Twizzler jar and pull out one of the sticks. I ball it into my hand.

I walk out the door and find Mrs. Donnelly waving to middle school students at the end of the hallway. Her face is lit up like a Christmas tree.

'Okay, Mrs. Donnelly, everything is cleared up. I'm on my way home.'

'That's good, dear.' She holds up a finger and taps it on her temple. 'I have to write you a release note for the front office.'

Glacially slow, she scrapes past me back into her office where she pulls a pad from her neatly arranged desk. I can see that her cursive is neat, almost childish, and inside the capital 'D's she has placed smiley faces.

'Thank you.' I quickly snatch the paper from her hand.

Within minutes, I'm standing in front of Mrs. Gaither again who is still tap-tap-tappety-tapping away on her computer. I hand her the note. She scans it and looks up quickly at me.

'You haven't been here long? Are you sick?'

I shrug. 'No, just have an allergy to the fustian.' *25 Down - Pompous speech or writing: Fustian*

Mrs. Gaither frowns. 'I didn't know that was a thing. Do many kids have it?'

My eyes are half-lidded. 'Unfortunately not, Mrs. Gaither. Unfortunately not.'

Chapter 6 Across:
Momentous occasion (11)

Exiting the school, I make my way to my bicycle. It is shimmering in the warm afternoon sun. Dark green, it seems to glint malevolently, like a Venus flytrap, but I know that my Schwinn bicycle is entirely friendly. We have been together a long time. Her name is Gershwin and I love her.

After popping the end of the Twizzler into my mouth, I pedal slowly and easily down the asphalted streets. Cracks rise from nowhere and yet Gershwin knows to avoid them. Various people mill along the avenues. Most are young to middle-aged women clad in active wear and wearing makeup and jewelry. It seems so disconcerting: exercise clothes and mascara, but who am I to judge, really? My sense of fashion is fairly limited to blue jeans and whatever t-shirt isn't lying on the floor in the morning. As I enjoy the ride, I eat the Twizzler, hands-free, manipulating it with my lips until there is only a small segment left.

The front desk attendant at Pine Point, bedecked in her maroon scrubs, glances up guardedly as I enter the nursing home. When the Coronavirus hit, all nursing homes became centers of suspicion; lockdown was essential and every person who entered the doors, whether parent or priest, was considered a potential mass-murderer. Because the disease seemed to be particularly virulent and deadly among the older folks, the nurses were required to stand like military sentries guarding entrances with their lives. When she, Lisa, sees that it is me, though, she smiles and waves me forward.

'Hi, Jeri, no school today?' Her eyes are green and bright. She reaches out with her fancy thermometer to take

28

my temperature and quickly ascertains that I am not a 21st century Typhoid Mary.

'No, it was an early out.'

'Aren't you close to graduating?' Lisa returns behind her desk and stands with hands on her hips.

'Yes, just a few weeks away.'

'Must be exciting.' Lisa buzzes me through the door.

'Certainly is.'

As I begin to walk away from her, I can tell that she is still watching me. She, like most people, wonders if there isn't something a little *off* about me.

They are used to me here at Pine Point. I have been coming without parents for about five years. The first time I came by myself, they stopped me and asked if I was lost, but I confidently replied that I had come to pay homage to my grandparents. I thought this sounded grown up, but the nurses snickered.

As I walk the familiar corridors, one long right, one short left and another long right, I spot the artwork. Traditionally, they are lake scenes - quiet waters, silhouettes of dusking pine trees, a loon or two inserted into the background. It's strange, I know instinctually that these birds are loons, and that these pine trees are very much part of the northern landscape, but I have never been north of Missouri to see them.

Over the last years, I have continued to question my parents as to why they stopped traveling. My father waved his hand in the air brushing the question aside while my mother vaguely mentioning something about finances. When I ask Grandpa Walt about the places he has gone, he is quite proud to tell me he has never left the country and the farthest he had ever roamed from Duncan was a summer family vacation to Disney World. When I pressed him about that trip, he said it was a 'lesson from hell' about family togetherness.

I turn right for the last leg of my journey and find the hall clogged with old people and their walkers. Almost all of them look lost, as if they are searching the ground or walls or even through the windows for something *eluding* them. They wander aimlessly, blue-veined hands gripping their handlebars, shuffling, scuffling in their soft leather shoes, chasing something that no longer exists. They smell of decay and moisturizing cream. All these people have been *exactly* where I am now - a young person searching for my way in the world.

I weave my way through them and their walkers. Sitting in a small alcove on a cushioned high-back chair is Alfred Owens. He holds a cane between his legs and his hands rest on top of the crook as if he is about to pull himself up and go for a walk.

'Israel.' There is nothing wrong with his memory, only his hips. He is 93 years old.

'Lord Tennyson.' I curtsy and stand in front of him like a courtier.

'You're getting prettier by the day.' He taps his hand on the cane, one for each word of his sentence, as if confirming his statement.

'I think you're getting blinder by the day.' He laughs. Old people want to laugh.

'What are you doing today?' I ask him.

He shrugs a few times. His thin shoulders rise and drop quickly making his entire body quiver. 'Thought I'd take the Ford out for a drive today, maybe over to the ocean.' Alfred's eyes get a faraway dreamy look as if he can't stop the memory from clouding the present.

I know that he does not have his driver's license anymore. He's told me that many times, but the desire to *be* licensed has never left him. The little plastic card is the ultimate symbol of freedom. Suddenly, I remember that I have to do some practice driving when I get home this afternoon. Dad is taking me out for a spin in the Cadillac, or his term for our Toyota Camry - Camrillac.

Ugh.

I hate being taught things. I'd rather just figure them out myself, but with driving, that's not really an option.

'Well, I hope you have a good drive, Lord Tennyson. I'll see you later. I'm going to visit Grandpa and Grandma.'

Alfred is shaken from his reverie. He lifts a hand and bobs his head. 'You have a good time. Say hello for me.'

I know that he has said 'hello' multiple times to them already today, but that's how old people talk.

Without knocking, I push open Grandpa and Grandma's door. Today, Grandpa Walt is sitting in his chair reading a magazine. From the yellow border, it looks like National Geographic. Grandpa likes to look at the pictures. Far away from here.

'Hi Grandpa Walt.' I wave to him from the doorway. He drops his magazine in his lap and looks over his glasses.

'Jeri!' He says delightedly and waves me over. As I approach his chair, he puts an arm around my waist and I kiss him on top of his head.

'How's Grandma today?'

His lips purse and he inhales deeply. 'We're still kicking. A little early to be out of school, isn't it?'

31

I pull myself from his arm and head to their small dining area. There is a jar of store-bought cookies in the middle of the table. I grab one and relate the difficulty of the morning. Grandpa laughs at the idea of a guidance counselor - someone paid to sit in a school office to work with kids and their stress.

'So, Grandma's having a bad day then?'

He nods and looks down at his hands. Grandpa Walt would never say it, but he would not be in a nursing home if not for her. In his own mind, he is as healthy and strong as ever. Certainly, he could be out working in the garden or playing a round of golf, not that he's ever golfed before, but 'I could if I wanted to' he would say. Yet, he has chosen to live inside this wonderfully decorated prison. I asked him about it once, a brief, quick question, not wanting to offend him or even bring up a sore point. His eyes moistened which made me feel uncomfortable. 'I take you, Iris, to be my lawfully wedded wife, to have and to hold, from this day forward, for better or for worse, for richer, for poorer, in sickness and in health, to love and to cherish until death parts us.' His voice trailed off near the end, but I was amazed that he still had his vows memorized.

'She's using the facilities.' His eyes wander to the bathroom where the light shines dimly in the crack under the door. His voice lowers. 'It's been a hard day today.'

'What did you say?'

'Nothing, Jeri. Nothing really.'

For some reason I want to cry, but I can't, and I don't think Grandpa wants me to either. So I talk about things at home. These are the bits of info that he loves to hear - things from the outside. Grandpa listens and nods. He laughs at the things Yugi does and the way Mom and Dad relate to each other. I tell him about other things, church and school and the tulips and grass that are popping up.

Grandma comes out of the bathroom. 'Oh, hello,' she says merrily.

'Hi, Grandma.'

Her face tightens and she looks at Grandpa who fashions a smile. 'Isn't it nice that our granddaughter, Jerusalem, has come to visit us?'

'Oooh, yes,' she claps her hands once, daintily, and holds them in front of her heart. Grandma's face is transformed and even though she is struggling to sew my face and name together, she at the very least understands that I am someone significant.

Grandma stands awkwardly staring at Grandpa and me. It's as if she doesn't know the next step so she can only wait for someone to show her. I reach out for her hand and she looks at it, then accepts it. As I lead her to the chair, I am aware of how papery her skin is and how warm her hands are. It's so weird because her muscles still seem so strong, yet her mind is weakened.

'Jeri,' Grandpa says, after I have situated Grandma in the chair, 'what's the question of the day?'

We've been doing this since I've been little. I make up a crossword like question for the day and he answers it as best he can in a most convincing way.

I think for a moment, and then suddenly realize I've run out of foolish questions. The ones that I want to ask are for these times, these gradually-running-out moments. These are sands of time kind of questions. I don't need to know what or who, but why and how.

I swallow, unsure if Grandpa knows what I'm thinking.

'Why do we get old?' It escapes before I can take it back.

For a moment, Grandpa seems stymied, and then magically, he coughs once and starts to laugh - laugh as if he has never heard anything so funny in his whole life. At first, I think that he is crying, but soon, I join him uncomfortably as I look at Grandma who is also laughing. She has no idea what's going on but seeing him gasp and breathe deeply, holding his sides he sighs and says, 'Aahoooaa, oh that's great. I wasn't expecting that.'

'Uh, Grandpa, I really want to know?'

'You want the serious answer or the sarcastic answer?'

'I'd prefer the serious answer, but if you need to regale me with both, I'm happy for it.' I look at Grandma who seems to be intently waiting also. Her blue eyes appear happy, yet vacant.

'Okay, here's the sarcastic answer: we grow old so that we can complain about he way things used to be.'

'What about the serious answer?'

Grandpa reaches over to Grandma's hand and holds it. She covers it with her other hand. 'Growing old reminds us to love the journey, the people we're with and the ones we love. We remind ourselves to love every step of our youth.'

'What kinds of things should I be doing then, Grandpa, in my youthful age.'

His face relaxes and his eyes melt. 'Laugh, Jerusalem. Laugh at every chance you get. Don't keep any in reserve.'

Chapter 7 Across:
Charitable, not-for-profit (10)

Gershwin seems to have a life of her own and we fly through the streets of Duncan, Oklahoma. Because I live here, I am not particularly impressed by it, nor do I feel a true sense of permanence. Nothing about Duncan feels *grounding*. My guess is that when I move away, I will appreciate it more. It's like having a pet at home and you rarely pay attention to it until it is lying on the front step, tongue out of its mouth, dead. THEN you wish you would have played with it more. Not that I've ever had a pet before.

School traffic is swooshing around me. A few of my classmates open their windows and laugh at me. Water off a duck's back, I say. Their derision will be overshadowed by mine when I show up with a Ferrari, or something, as I'll be making my fifteenth million while they suffer through their no-insurance-paid-six-hour-shift at Johnny Bing Bing's, the local fast-food joint.

Truly, I have no idea what I want to do with my life other than fly away from Duncan. Some of my teachers, like Mr. Carlson, my Chemistry teacher, think that I should go into some kind of benevolent, world-changing chemical engineering enterprise, but I'm highly suspicious of philanthropic scientists - like the ones that make vaccines or drugs to eliminate certain diseases. You can't tell me that they aren't making a squillion dollars from pandemic fears. I bet *they* aren't donating *their* money back. It's like the athletes and celebrities who have been leeching off common people for years. I bet when they go to bed at night they aren't thinking, 'Let's see, how can I use my millions for the greater good of the community?'

35

Heck, I'm fifteen years old. What's the hurry? Ah, yes, there is a hurry if I want to leave Duncan. Unfortunately, there are rules about people my age attending college *BUT* I won't be able to stay on campus. If I can just get to know someone in Miami or Washington or New York. I don't even care if it's freaking Pierre, South Dakota...

I turn into my driveway just in time to see Yugi pulling himself from the Camrillac. He runs to the house and chucks his bag onto the front porch. My dad grunts himself out from behind the steering wheel. From this perspective, I can see that his hair is thinning. He's got a small round circle near the back of his head. It looks like the top of a golf ball poking through the turf. He hasn't seen me yet, so I watch him trudge around the front of the car and tap on the hood which covers the ticking engine.

We've had the Camry for as long as I can remember. It is an important piece of the Walker family history. Our first new car, as dad says, is now our first really old car. It has almost 150,000 miles on it, and it gags as it accelerates. You push down the pedal, then it pauses, makes a *gwaaark* sound and then leaps before it shivers. Dad, who knows nothing about cars - zero - says that it's the carburetor, but when I once asked him to point out where the carburetor is, he rolled his eyes and told me not to be a wise guy.

My eyes shift to the house. This is the only home *I've* ever known. It is a two-story domicile with one gabled window on the second floor facing the street. It is supposed to be white, but by virtue of a lack of cleaning, it is mostly dirty grey, just like our picket fence. When it rains, dirt streaks from underneath the siding and my dad invariably states that we're going to get that power washer out and clean off the house. That's the same thing my mom says about washing the windows. *We'll get to it.*

The detached garage is set back behind the house. The Camrillac is supposed to be parked in it. There are two cement tracks, overgrown with grass, which lead to the garage, but the car is never parked in it because the garage is full of used things. Used things that will never be used again but deemed potentially useful by either Mom or Dad but not both, so they quibble over what should stay or go - until they decide they'll just put the object in the garage (pronounced 'GAY-rahj' by my dad) and sort it out later.

I walk to the fence and open it, when suddenly the back door to the house opens and Yugi explodes from it. As if shot from a cannon, he hurtles down the steps, his face alight with satisfaction.

'Jeri!' he shouts as he almost trips on the last step and stumbles four steps before he rights himself. 'Jeri! You're never gonna believe this.'

'Tell me.'

'No. Guess!' His grin is as big as his face.

'No.'

'Aw, come on, Jer, just guess.'

I shake my head and close my eyes. 'Fine. You got an 'A' on your math test.'

'No!' He's still smiling.

'You have a new friend.'

'No!'

'You have found a new level for annoying me?'

'No!' The sarcasm went whooshing over his head.

'Just tell me, Yugi.'

'Okay, okay, don't freak out, but Dad said I could ride with while you're doing your driving practice this afternoon.'

37

My eyes widen. 'What?'

Yugi holds up his hands and starts to back away. 'That's the beginning of a freak out, Jeri. Come back from the cliff.'

'Oh, shut up, Yugi. You can't come.'

'Yes, I can. Dad said it was okay.' He's laughing again and turns to run back up the steps. 'I promise I won't say anything about your driving.' He makes it to the top step. 'Not much, anyway.'

'Yugi!' I shout and he stops. 'Tell Dad to come out here now. Tell him we're going to have words.'

Yugi snorts and throws open the screen door and then the storm door. I can hear him yelling in the house but there is only a muffled response from Dad. I look across the back yard and see Dongle resting his arms on the white fence, his chin is on his forearms. Dongle's grey hair is floating above his head.

'What are you looking at, Dongle?'

'I'm looking at you, Nosebleed.'

'What for?'

He grins, stands up straight and puts his hands on his hips. 'I'm just seeing if you're having a spaz attack.'

'Ha ha, very funny.'

'So you're going for a drive?'

'So it appears.'

Dongle looks back at Margery who waves but does not break from her knitting. 'What are you afraid of?'

'I'm not afraid of anything.' There is a noise, something banging and thumping in the house.

'Fearless, huh?'

'Yeah...' I jut out my chin. Both he and I know that's not the truth.

'Wanna bet?'

I pause. *Come on, Jerusalem, you can do this. Show him you're unafraid.*

'All right. What's the bet?'

He motions with his hand to his own backyard. 'If you have a spaz attack while driving, you rake my lawn for a month.'

'And if I win?'

'I rebuild yours.'

'My what?'

'Your lawn.'

'But how does that help me?' Who cares about the backyard? I'll be gone to college in a few months anyway.

'It might not, but it certainly will help your parents.'

I think quickly and sigh. Even if I freak out in the car, there's no way he'd ever know. I walk across the pocked lawn to him. Even as I traverse the expanse, I am aware that by not freaking out, it would certainly beautify the place.

I extend my hand to him over the fence and he grasps it, shaking it once. I look up into his watery eyes and I recognize a deep kindness.

'You're on.'

'All right. I'll need to change my clothes.' He turns toward his house.

'What for? Are you going to start digging up our lawn already?'

'Are you kidding?' He speaks over his shoulder. 'I wouldn't miss this for the world.'

At that moment, Yugi crashes through the door again and Dad follows slowly behind. My jaw has dropped and the blood has drained from my face.

Dongle turns and yells to my dad. 'Kevin, don't leave yet. I'm coming with!'

Dad raises his eyebrows. Yugi thrusts a fist in the air and exclaims a sharp *Yes!*

'Okay.' Dad looks at me.

I tilt my head back to gaze into the heavens. *Why am I surrounded by 71 across?*

Lunacy. Absolute lunacy.

Chapter 8 Down:
One who feeds alongside the highway (9)

I can't believe that we're doing this. Before I even approach the car, Yugi is sitting in the backseat, bouncing in the middle. Dad and Dongle wait by the front fender, both men caught up in a moment of camaraderie. They get along really well: Dongle gives advice - Dad ignores it.

Dad tosses me the keys and I promptly drop them. As I bend down to pick them up, I hear Dongle say, 'I hope she drives better than she catches.' To which my dad responds, 'Hope your life insurance is paid up.' This is all very funny, ha ha, these guys are hilarious, but I made a bet and I'm going to win it. Yugi pushes open the back door to let Dongle in and my dad sits into the passenger seat. Entering the car, I pull the seat far forward, (I am 5'4 and done growing) and adjust the mirrors. The car is old enough now that they still must be manually adjusted. As my gaze fixes first upon my own face, I can see the tension already, but then my eyes shift back to Yugi who is tapping away on the seat back.

'Put your seatbelt on, Yugi,' I say as I make sure the steering wheel is low enough.

'Absolutely, Jer. I don't want to end up bug spatter when you stop too fast.'

This is going to be horrible.

I glance at my dad who seems to be looking for something, whether in his pockets or even just finding his own seatbelt, but he's giving himself a pat down.

'What are you doing?'

'I'm trying to find my blood pressure medication.'

'I am not amused.' I respond with grinding teeth.

41

The Camrillac smells of vanilla, gasoline, exhaust and a hint of cheeseburger. These odors have been embedded in the fabric like fossils. I insert the key into the ignition and turn the engine over. It coughs once and finally, as always, catches its breath. My foot is on the accelerator which makes the Camry roar. Sheepishly I look at my dad who is crossing himself. Then, I look in the rearview mirror to see both Dongle and Yugi doing the exact same thing.

'Do you think Jesus really cares?' I ask.

'Do I think he cares about your driving?' Dad responds tapping his chest with one hand. 'Of course. But I don't want you to ask him to take the wheel.' He thinks he's funny but he's not.

After a few seconds multiple things occur simultaneously: the heater starts, but it's not a slow breeze - it's as if the car sneezed and caught its breath; the windshield wipers turn on - why they were on, I don't know because Dad just drove home and it hasn't been raining; and finally, the stereo starts with whirring sound until finally, Barry Manilow's tender voice croons through the speakers.

'All right!' Dad shouts exultantly and turns around to the boys in the back. 'Barry is my favorite.' He sings along with Barry about Lola and Rico. *At the Copa, Copa Cabana.* And then suddenly, none of them know the words and they start to mumble.

'Good Lord,' I say and put the car in reverse.

We drive slowly backwards and I look in both mirrors making sure that I am not getting close to hitting anything with the sides of the car.

Yugi looks out the back window. 'You're clear from here, other than the fact that I could crawl faster than

42

you're driving.'

'Shut up. Shut up. Shut up.'

'Don't freak out, Jerusalem,' Yugi says. I look at Dongle who raises his eyebrows.

'I'm perfectly calm. In my zone. No problem.'

I back out into the street, but unfortunately, I run over the curb. The Camry shudders and judders to a stop. Dad almost bangs his head against the window and the backseat is entirely quiet. I pull forward and park along the curb and take a deep breath.

'It's okay, sweetheart.' Dad notices my face which is pool of frustration and anger.

'Look, Dad, and the rest of you in the backseat. I know this seems like a joyride for you, but for me, this is my ticket to freedom. When I get my license, I can, and will use it, to drive to many places. This is the price of my freedom.'

'So...' Dad says slowly and lowly, 'you want us to knock off the jokes?'

I look at him without turning towards him. 'Actually, the opposite. I want to be in the most difficult conditions possible. I need to be able to concentrate through distractions, road hazards, et cetera.'

Yugi's mouth drops. 'Does that mean you want us to make fun of your driving?'

I close my eyes and nod. 'It does me no good to have you along and be pleasant passengers.'

'I'm not following you,' Dad says.

'Just keep doing what you're doing, and I'll make it.' I put the car in drive and we move towards the sunset. My passengers are shocked - they don't know what to say. Each of them, in turn, wants to say something funny, yet somehow, I've disarmed them. Their ammunition is useless when I don't react. Even when the Camrillac accelerates too

43

slow and then too fast and my brother fakes hitting his head against the back seat - no one laughs. I am left in deafening, beautiful silence, except for the sultry voice of Aaron Neville crooning to Linda Rondstadt about the only things he knows about love.

Fifteen minutes into my drive, I look in the back seat and notice Dongle staring out the window with a smirk on his face.

Thunk.

I slam on the breaks. Yugi looks horrified and he's pointing out the front window. 'Jer, you just hit...'

My adrenaline is pumping madly. Heart racing, I look over at my dad who is staring at me.

'What is it? What did I hit?'

'Well... it was small and had a lot of hair.'

'A dog? A cat? What was it?'

'I don't know, Jerusalem, maybe we should go look?' Dad's voice has raised a notch.

Before we can open the front doors, Yugi has exited the back seat and rushes around to the back of the car. Traffic slows and drives around us. When I say traffic, I mean half a dozen cars.

Yugi is standing near the rear bumper, his face a mixture of horror and delight. He points down to the ground, but I cannot hear what he says.

Dongle and Dad jump out from the right side and I pull myself from behind the wheel. We make our way to Yugi.

'Holy crap, Jeri, you ran that thing down.' He stops and looks up at Dad. 'What is it?'

Dad shakes his head. 'It's a possum, Yug. A possum.'

'Jeez, it's ugly.'

'Yeah, it is, Yugi. Ugly as sin.'

All four of us crowd around the roadkill. The varmint is splayed on the asphalt, blood trickles from its nose. Obviously, at least one, if not two of its legs are broken. I am heartsick. I feel like my arrogance has slain this poor, defenseless animal.

'Well,' Dongle starts, 'I can remember one time when I hit a racoon. Splattered all over the road. Must a dragged it for a mile. When I got out of the car, all that was left was a cute little ear hanging from my license plate.'

'Donald… please,' my dad says.

'I'm just saying. These things sometimes have a death wish.'

'Jeez, Jer,' Yugi says, 'they'll probably put this on your license, like a special letter or something, that you're a road killer.' He crosses his arms and shakes his head. 'A stone-cold killer.'

I don't know what to say. I've never killed anything larger than a frog before and that was in biology class.

'So, let's get back in the car.' Dad is looking around at the continued slow procession of cars which are craning to see what we've done. A few have paused to see the dead animal and then speed up. They were hoping for a human body, I think.

I find my voice. 'We can't leave it here, Dad.'

'Well, clear it off the road, then.' He stares down at me. 'You killed it, you clear it.'

'But Dad, it was an accident.'

'What difference does it make if it was premeditated murder or vehicular manslaughter?'

'Vehicular possum-slaughter.' Yugi cracks himself up.

'What should I do then?'

45

'Just kick it over to the curb. The scavengers will take care of it.'

I gag a little. This poor possum, slain by my own hand, or right foot in this case, must be taken care of. 'We should take it home and give it a burial.'

Dongle looks at my dad and smiles. 'That's a great idea, Kevin. You should pick up that possum and take it home with you. Weren't you the one who was talking about getting a pet for the kids?'

Dad frowns at Dongle. 'News flash, Donald. Pets are generally breathing and available for play. How many people do you think bring home roadkill for their children to play with? 'Look, kids! I've got a new friend for y'all. Here's Randy Raccoon or what's left of him! Just missing one ear and most of his intestines, but, have fun!'

Dongle laughs and hits his leg with his hand. 'That's a good one, Kevin. I like it.'

'Just be quiet! All of you!' I can feel my blood pressure rising. Freak out, spaz attack is just below the horizon. 'AAAGH! Can't you have a little respect?'

Yugi sniffs. 'I can appreciate that you've just proved all three of Newton's laws of motion.'

'What!?' In my rising hysteria, I am not thinking clearly.

'One. Objects keep moving unless something gets in their way. B. Net force and acceleration - dang, girl, you were really moving. And thirdly, uh, there was definitely an equal and opposite reaction to you nailing this poor possum - you smushed him.'

Freak out came calling.

'NOOOOOOOOOOO!' I rush back to the car and attempt to open the door. 'SON OF A B...'

Chapter 8 Down:

'Jerusalem!' My dad shouts and stops me in mid-swear. 'What's wrong?'

I begin to cry. 'I just frickin' ran over a possum, I failed my driving test, my brother is a total...'

'Careful...' Dad cautions.

'A-hole, and now I've locked the keys in the car!'

'What?' Dad moves back to the passenger door and pulls on it. It does not open and the car is still running.

Cars continue to drive by us, each passenger insistent on staring. 'Well,' Dongle says, 'maybe we should call the locksmith?'

'Good idea.' Dad pulls out his phone.

As we wait by the side of the road, a police officer rounds the corner, turns on his lights and pulls in behind us.

'Oh, great,' I say. Now I'm not only scarred for life, but I'm going to lose my learner's permit too. The flashing lights only slow the traffic down even more. Most of them are probably assuming it's a drug bust judging by the age and state of the car that is 'stalled' in the road.

The police officer puts his cap on and comes forward. He is tall and of substantial girth and carries a sidearm. His handcuffs are in a little pouch on his belt.

'Good afternoon.' He has a surprisingly high voice. 'What seems to be the problem? Are you broken down?'

Dad is about to respond when Yugi jumps in. 'My sister was driving and she totally splattered this possum and when we stopped, we all got out of the car, and Jeri must have hit the locking mechanism and then, we're locked out and now we're all staring at the squished possum and his face looks all mashed, like a little pig...' My dad grimaces but the police officer peeks around the back of the car.

'You're locked out?'

'Yes, the locksmith is coming. So sorry, officer.'

His eyes fall on me. 'You were driving?'

My heart drops into my shoes. I'm going to be arrested, charged with animal abuse. I'm not going to be able to go to college. I can only nod.

He smiles. 'You okay?'

I am surprised by the question. I expected him to start reciting the Miranda. 'Yeah, I think so.'

'It's not your fault,' he says. 'It happens all the time. Why, a few months ago, I nailed a squirrel and it wound up under the car in the chassis. About a month later I couldn't figure out what the smell was until I checked under the car and the back half of Rocky was hanging from my wheel well. Nasty thing.'

Dongle takes a step forward. 'See! See! It happens!'

The officer sees my green face. 'Well, I can see that you've got things under control. I'll probably just move on.' Shamefacedly, the officer retreats to his car where he removes his hat, turns off his lights and pulls around us.

'That was so cool,' Yugi exclaims. 'You almost got busted, Jeri, and he let you off the hook.'

Finally, my voice begins to work again. 'Look, everyone, I think we should take it home and bury it. It's the least we can do.'

My dad looks at me and Dongle. 'I suppose we could, Jeri, but I'm not touching it. Do you want to carry it home, Donald?'

'It's probably got rabies,' Dongle sagely responds.

'Fine,' I say, 'after the locksmith gets here, I'll put it in the trunk and we'll drive home. No one, and I mean no one, is going to say anything about this to anyone, not Mom, not Margery and not your stupid friend Jeffrey either.' Yugi holds up his hands in surrender.

Chapter 8 Down:

Five uncomfortable minutes of silence later the locksmith arrives and jimmies the lock. Noticing our disturbed demeanors, the locksmith says nothing even though he notices the possum. Quickly, Dad pays him by credit card.

I open the trunk and find an old cheeseburger wrapper from Johnny Bing Bing's. Knowing that this is going to be the most disgusting thing I've done in my life so far, I use the wrapper as a shield against the rabid fur of the possum. Dongle, Dad and Yugi have all taken a step back. The possum is warm and squishy and I gag. I drop the possum and the wrapper in the trunk and slam it shut.

We drive home, and when I turn off the car, silence surrounds us. We are not quite sure what to do next. I take a deep breath and pull the keys from the ignition. My father shrugs. Dongle raises an eyebrow. My brother grins.

And I get out of the car to do my duty.

After popping the trunk, I lean in knowing that the sight will be gruesome and yet it's worse than I could imagine.

Not only has the possum moved, but it is alive and well, all except for the fact that at least one of its legs is broken.

And it is pissed.

Chapter 9 Across:
Moving around in a regular pattern (11)

And so it came to pass that Maximus Walker, Possum Extraordinaire, became part of our family.

While the trunk is open, a yawning mouth exposing the hissing marsupial, his back left leg bent awkwardly, Yugi runs into the house. Dad and Dongle stand back watching the spectacle while I ponder the animal cornered behind the spare tire. He gazes at me through coal black eyes tucked in the depths of a snowy white face. His pink nose glints in the dimness of the trunk. Grey, spiky fur stands on end. I know that he is trying to make himself look bigger, a predator rather than, well, a possum. I am strangely drawn to his bravery. I know a little something about wanting to appear bigger than I am, scarier than I ever could be, needing others to see that I am a predator and not prey. Maximus' claws, white and sharp tipped at the ends of his black feet, appear as if they could do damage, whereas my weapons are words, dangerously pointed, daggers for disemboweling.

I hear voices in the house. Mom yells, 'Yugoslavia! What are you doing with those oven mitts?' I hear him giggling. 'Yugi! Answer me!' She does not sound happy.

Yugi bursts through the door and down the porch steps. His feet are flying and his hair is blowing in the breeze. He rushes up to me, out of breath.

'Is it still in there?'

'No duh,' I say and point. 'What's it going to do? Dig a hole in the trunk?'

'You never know.' He looks at the possum. 'I thought they were supposed to play dead, or something.'

'I think he's an aberration - one of the brave ones.'

Chapter 9 Across:

'How could you possibly know that?' Yugi asks.

'Deduction, my dear Watson. See how he finds a place to defend himself? Even when his leg is broken.'

'You're weird,' Yugi says and holds up the oven mitts.

I hold up my hands as if preparing for surgery and Yugi slides the pink mitts over them. I clap them together once, then twice.

'What in the world is going on out here?' Mom descends the steps quickly. She has crossed her arms in front of her chest. She approaches the trunk of the car and, without warning, shrieks and falls backward at the sight of Maximus. Dad catches her.

The noise scares the possum and, also without warning, Maximus falls over and plays dead.

'What is that?' Mom asks peeking around her husband's shoulder. 'It looks like a moldy rat.'

'It's a possum,' Dad responds as if it's the most natural thing in the world.

'Does it have rabies?'

Dongle leaned over to her. 'I asked the same thing.'

Mom looks at him as if seeing him for the first time. Her eyes shift to my father who shrugs. 'Long story.'

'But what is that thing doing in the back of my car?'

'It's about to be released into the wild.'

'No, it's not,' I say pounding the oven mitts again. Maximus' tongue lolls out of his mouth.

'What do you mean?' Mom asks almost hysterically. 'And... and... put those mitts away. I don't want rabies on them.'

I look back at her. 'You mean you want your daughter to pull it out of the trunk with her bare hands? You want rabies on my bare hands?'

Dad butts in. 'Wait a minute, Jer, you just said you're not releasing it into the wild. You're not going to kill it, are you?'

I scrunch up my face at him. His arm is around Mom. 'No, I'm not going to kill it. I'm going to take it into the backyard, put it in a box and nurse it back to health.'

'You most certainly are not!' Mom almost shouts.

'Yes. I am.' My face is set like flint. The real fight is no longer between woman and animal, but she-bear and bear cub.

'I swear, Jeri, if you put that... that... THING in our backyard, I'll... I'll...'

'No you won't, Mom, and I'll tell you why.' I approach my mother and I place my mitted hands on her arms. 'Because you are a kind and wonderful woman. Gentle with humans and beasts. I've already named him and you can't kill an animal that is part of your family. His name is Maximus. Maximus Walker.'

'Why did you call him Maximus?' Dad asks.

'Because he will be the greatest of all possums. He will be king of marsupials. He will be the prince of mammals.'

'Going a little overboard, Jeri? He's not Jesus.' Yugi has returned to the trunk where Maximus still has not moved.

Now is the time. The adults crowd in behind the kids and I slowly reach toward Maximus. Cute little thing other than the fact that he's really ugly. Gently, my mitts lift him. His limp body feels fragile. I have never had a pet before. Pulling him from the trunk like a pan from the oven, I hold Maximus in my arms. The adults take a step back, but as I turn to show him to them, Maximus opens his eyes and suddenly spasms. I try to hold on to him, but he leaps toward my mother who sinks to the ground. My dad attempts to catch her halfway but loses his grip. Mom falls into his legs and knocks him to the ground.

Maximus, taking advantage of the ambush, attempts to run, but his broken rear leg cannot handle the activity and he falls over right next to Mom's armpit where, as the adage goes, he turns possum and promptly passes out again. Dongle, unable to control himself, begins to laugh, deep, belly-throated guffaws. He is pounding his hands on his legs. Meanwhile, Yugi takes his phone out and starts shooting photo after photo of the drama.

These photos would become some of my greatest memories of all time.

There is Dad struggling to push himself up.

There is Mom unconscious to the wily animal curled up near her chest.

There is Dongle bent over laughing.

There am I, bemused and smiling, hands in oven mitts staring into a camera hoping that moments like these would come more often.

At this single, crucial moment, I realize that everything in life can change instantaneously: your mom can fall, your dad can stumble, your brother can capture you with one push of a button and even neighbors can become more than neighbors - family. It is a brief, fleeting thought, a butterfly landing on my mind and quickly alights, floating away, but I can still feel the touch of it.

I approach my mother and pick up my new pet who has yet to rise from his faint. My dad and Dongle are in the process of reviving Mom.

'Hey, Jeri, let's go make a cage for Maximus.' Yugi's face is alight with excitement.

'All right.' We leave the adults and walk to the backyard. The gate screeches open, and then swings back shut behind us. I carry Maximus towards the back side of the chain link fence.

'Go get the birdcage out of the garage,' I command Yugi. For some reason, my parents had thoughts of purchasing a bird, some kind of parakeet. Instead of buying the bird, they bought a cage and then had second thoughts about filling it. *Birds are noisy*, my mom would say. Dad then wanted to take the birdcage back for a refund, but Mom thought that it might come in handy someday. So they put it in the garage for just such an occasion as this. I'm not sure they were thinking about housing a possum, though.

Yugi opens the garage door manually. The handle wobbles but holds, and a large, crowded, dusty world is revealed to us. Crates, cardboard boxes, trunks, plastic containers all containing gathered treasures. On the shelves are antique electronic appliances collecting layers of soot: oscillating fans, toasters, even a dot-matrix printer. It seems like the chaos before creation. It just needs the finger of God to bring order.

As Yugi wades through the disarray, my eyes fall on dim labels. Each seems to be from a different country where my parents have traveled. I had no idea that they'd been to so many places. So many that they had not told us about.

Egypt. Madagascar. Russia. India. I frown. What memories are inside these boxes? Why are they in the garage? Why don't they talk about them? Why had I never noticed them before?

These questions echo in my mind until they are interrupted by Yugi's exclamation, 'Eureka, I have found it!'

Hoisting the cage above his head, he emerges from the detritus of dusty memories and into the light. I notice that the cage isn't very big.

Yugi opens the birdcage door and as gently as I can, I place my marsupial into the bottom. He lies there motionless and I wonder if in fact he has suffered a heart attack.

'Do you think we should take him to the vet?' Yugi asks as his face is pressed dangerously close to the cage. In my mind, Yugi and Maximus bear a striking resemblance around the eyes and nose.

'I forgot about his broken leg.' Turning away from the garage, we walk back past the Camrillac to where Mom, Dad and Dongle are recovering. Dad is brushing Mom's shirt and pants off. She's sees us coming and holds up her hands.

'Don't bring that thing near me!' Hysteria is very near.

'But Mom...' Yugi starts.

'Don't you 'but Mom,' me. That oversized rat is not a pet. It's a disease infested varmint.'

I snigger. 'You called it a varmint, like... Yosemite Sam.'

'It's not funny, Jerusalem. That thing frightens me.'

'It's just a possum.'

'I don't care if it's 'just' any furry thing. Take it somewhere and let it go.'

'But mom, its leg is broken. I broke its leg. The kindest thing we can do is take it to the vet and have it set. Then I'll let it go.' I really won't, but I'm hoping she'll grow to love him like I already do.

'No, absolutely not. We're not spending money on it.'

'His name is Maximus, Mom.'

'No, Jerusalem, his name is Unfortunate Road Damage. Go put it back where you found it. And for God's sake, burn those oven mitts.'

'Beryl,' my dad says gently as he puts his arm around her and pulls her in for a hug. 'Let Jeri do this thing. You don't have to go anywhere near it.'

'Maximus,' I correct, but Dad widens his eyes and frowns at me, mouthing the words, *Stop talking.*

Dongle coughs uncomfortably and mumbles something like, 'I think I hear Margery'... He turns to leave and then waves at me. He gives me two thumbs up.

'Okay,' Mom murmurs, 'take it away, do whatever you want with it.'

'Thank you, Mom.' I look at Dad. 'Can we drive to the vet?' Looking at his watch over my mom's shoulder, Dad tilts his head deliberating.

'If we hurry, we should be able to make it on time.' Mom isn't quite ready to let go of him. 'Did you want to drive with Jeri to the vet, or do you want me to?'

Mom eyelids lower. *Stupid question.*

Thankfully, the drive to the vet was much less eventful than the previous one. With furious intensity, I navigate the streets of Duncan focused on getting our furry pet some medical help. Yugi sits in the back seat, cage on his lap, hands on top. He stares down into the face of his long-lost brother. 'Jeri, Maximus is stirring. I think he's got an eye open.'

We arrive at the veterinarian as if we are bringing a medivac from battle. Opening the door to the clinic, we enter and I take the cage from a reluctant Yugi. Their bonding time frustrates me. This is my possum. Run over your own pet.

Chapter 9 Across:

Written in stencil on the door, we notice that the vet is closing in fifteen minutes. The waiting room is empty save for two lonely and forlorn humans clutching pet cages. A morose feline gazes out imperturbably at the world. The cat's owner, a woman in her fifties, has bright purple hair and brilliant red lipstick. Her eyes catch ours and drop to our birdcage where they open wide and blink quickly.

On the other side of the room is a human man holding a terrarium where a seemingly empty turtle shell resides in the middle of it. The man, bald with bushy eyebrows and a thin moustache, seems to be talking to the turtle, whispering something to it.

'Can I help you?'

The animal nurse sits at the front desk in scrubs.

'Yes, we'd like the vet to take a look at Maximus.' I hold up the cage up.

'Is that a...um...' The nurse can't quite finish the sentence.

'Yes, he is a possum.'

Her brown eyes squint at Maximus. 'I'll see what I can do.' The nurse pulls herself from the seat and I notice that she has a clump of fur attached to her shoulder. She exits through to the back where I hear yips and yaps through the cracked door. I can't hear exactly what she says, but I think it starts with, 'You may want to come out here and look at this.'

Moments later, both nurse and doctor, a youngish woman in her late twenties or early thirties, approach us.

'Hello. My name is Jenny. Who have we got here?' She bends over to look into the cage.

'His name is Maximus.'

Jenny laughs. 'That's a good name for a possum. Tough little fellow.'

'Yeah,' I hold the cage slightly forward.

Maximus is watching her closely. His ears are at full extension and his claws grasp the cage tightly. 'How long have you had him?'

I look at Dad and Yugi. 'About an hour.'

She grins. 'He's, uh... a... uh... recent acquisition?'

I nod.

'What do you think is wrong with him?' She moves closer to the cage and Maximus makes a strange growling noise, then hisses. Jenny smiles at him.

'I think his back leg is broken.'

The doctor does not look at me but examines his leg. I am grateful that she doesn't ask me how his leg came to be broken, but I can guess that she already knows.

'What's your name?'

'Jeri,' I say.

'Is that short for anything?'

'Yes,' I respond simply.

She puts a finger to her nose and taps it. 'I understand completely. My real name is 'Jentaria.' My parents did a real doozy on me.' She looks up at Dad who blushes.

I really like her now.

'Do you want me to take Maximus and see what I can do about that leg of his?'

Both Yugi and I nod at the same time. She looks at him. 'What's your name?'

'Yugoslavia.'

Jenny blinks about a dozen times and looks back to Dad again who is looking up and around at different corners of the room.

'Have a seat over there. I'll see if I can get him back on four feet in a jiffy.' She pauses and then leans closer into

58

the Walker family to whisper, 'Do you want me to see if Maximus has any... special diseases?'

'Yes, please,' my dad responds in with the same volume level, 'that would be very nice. But, Doctor...'

'Jenny,' she fills in and reaches out to shake his hand.

'Kevin.'

'How... much is this going to cost. We're kind of doing this for... catch and release.'

'Dad!' I say sharply.

'We'll see how much work needs to be done first, okay?' Jenny's eyes bounce back and forth between my dad and me. 'I've never actually worked on a possum before. Thank you for bringing him to me.'

I hand the cage over to Jenny. The nurse also appears curious.

'Hey!' the woman with the cat yells out. 'We were here before the girl and her rat!'

The nurse reveals a pinched smile. 'I'm so sorry, Mrs. Lambert. Your cat...'

'Peaches. Peaches!' The woman's purple hair bounces.

'Yes, Peaches can come in now.'

Mrs. Lambert's crimson lips turn into a frown. After two attempts at standing, she sets the caged Peaches down beside her and pulls her bulk from the cushioned chair. She presses out her blue, floral print dress. 'I shall go with Peaches. I am her parent.'

Two women and one feline move back into the animal area. As soon as the dogs see the cat, they begin barking. Peaches hisses. Mrs. Lambert puts the cage up to her lips and attempts to calm her savage beast which is jerking in the cage. Mrs. Lambert almost drops it.

The door shuts behind them.

Meanwhile, the man with his tortoise watches with sad, drooping eyes. What hair he has left is fixed in a combover. He looks strangely out of place in his brown suit with multicolored tie. Slowly, he makes an attempt at speaking, but his mouth only drops open and closes a few times before he stops and resumes his mute conversation with the turtle.

We make our way over to the opposite corner of the room where Yugi begins to look at nature magazines. Dad pulls out his phone and texts Mom. I search through the other literature to see if I can find a crossword, which I do, but it has already been half-filled-out by an obvious moron. A few of the spaces have been written in, scratched over and written in again and the answers are *still* wrong. It hurts my eyes to look at it.

The door opens and my heart leaps, but it is only Mrs. Lambert who has obviously been crying. Mascara has streaked her cheeks. Staggering, it appears as if she is about to fall over. The nurse raises her hand and is about to speak but decides against it. Shaking her head, the nurse repositions behind her desk and resumes typing.

'Excuse me,' I say quietly, 'but is my possum finished.'

The nurse looks up and nods. 'Yes, just about.'

'Can you tell me what was wrong?'

Without looking up from her computer, the nurse responds while typing. 'I'll let Doctor Jenny tell you.'

Now I'm worried. 'Does he have internal bleeding? Did she have to put him down!'

'Don't worry,' the nurse says as she hears the worry in my voice. 'Your possum will live.'

After what seemed a lifetime later, Doctor Jenny pushes open the door and there, in his little cage, is my beautiful, fixed pet. His eyes are dull, but I notice that he doesn't have a cast on his leg. He has *two*.

'Well,' Jenny says, 'Maximus is going to be uncomfortable for awhile. I had to sedate him to put the casts on, but two broken legs will take some time to recover from.' I can see my dad's mind calculating both the financial cost and the emotional cost at home.

'I'm afraid I have some bad news, Jeri,' she hands the cage to me.

'What is it? Is his back broken also?'

'No,' Jenny smiles, 'but *she* is not going to like the name Maximus.'

My eyes pop open. *You mean I have a sister?* I laugh and clap my hands. 'Well, *she'll* fit right in with weird names.' I look down into the cage and Maximus is staring up at me. She seems to be grinning from a drug induced stupor. 'You'll be all right Maximus. Everything is going to be all right.'

My dad clears his throat. 'So there's no threat of disease with our little friend?'

'Surprisingly, possums are resistant to rabies and many diseases. Not only will Maximus be a clean pet, but she'll be good for your kids if she eventually lets them touch her. Possums aren't generally that friendly. You know what else is interesting about possums?'

Dad's eyes widen at the doctor as if willing her to stop making the animal interesting. 'They do much better in the wild?'

Jenny laughs. 'That's most certainly true, but it sounds like Jeri is going to nurse her back to health.'

I don't see it, but I feel my dad's resignation.

'Possums can be bitten eighty times by rattlesnakes and survive. Supposedly, possums have helped to develop antivenoms.'

'Fascinating,' Dad responds uninterestedly as he crosses his arms. 'The next time we have a herd of rattlesnakes in our backyard, we'll throw the possum at them.'

Jenny frowns and smiles at the same time. 'And they eat ticks.'

'Well, great. Now we're safe to walk in the woods again.'

'Jeri,' Jenny puts a hand on my shoulder, 'it's actually not entirely legal to keep a possum as a pet. As long as you promise to put Maximus back in the wild when she is healed...'

'Of course.' I cross my fingers under the cage.

'Jeri, you'll have to get a different kind of enclosure. She'll need a tree, or bush, something to climb and hang from.'

'Thanks,' I respond. 'By the way, what should I be feeding her?'

'Whatever you find. I looked it up because even I didn't know. Small rodents, snails, frogs, birds, eggs, nuts, fruit, berries - pretty much whatever you can find.'

Yugi's eyes brighten. 'You mean he's a carnivore?'

'*She's* an omnivore,' I correct him.

'I can't wait to start digging up the back yard.'

'How much is this going to cost me?' Dad says softly.

Jenny types into the computer and waits for it to print. He looks at the sheet and his eyes shine gratefully.

No charge. Enjoy the ride. Good luck.

Chapter 10 Down:
What fresh cake should have (8)

The next morning, I am awakened by beeping. At first, I think it is my alarm clock, but soon realize that it sounds more like a truck backing up. I try putting the pillow over my head, but once awake, it doesn't matter. It is 7:30. On Saturdays, I like to sleep in, and 7:30 is ridiculous...

Then, I remember Maximus.

Hustling out of bed, I put on my slippers and pad down the hallway, past my brother's room and head down the stairs. They creak. Dad says that he will eventually fix them.

Mom and Dad are sitting at the kitchen table. Both have a mug of coffee cupped in their hands. Their heads are leaning in towards each other and they are talking softly.

'What's going on? What's that noise?'

'Is there something you haven't told us?' Dad asks.

I run to the front window. Dongle is reversing a trailer down the driveway. A load of rolled up sod fills the trailer.

What?

Without answering, I hurry outside. The air is fresh and I wish that I would have brought my coat. The pickup moves past me, but Dongle is too busy backing to notice. I return to my parents back through the living room.

'I don't understand.'

'Donald told me that you two made a little wager yesterday afternoon.'

'I didn't think he'd actually take that seriously.'

'What, exactly, was the wager?' Both my parents are staring at me intently.

'I... well... I didn't want to seem afraid about driving, and especially with Yugi in the car, and so he said if I didn't freak out, or have a spaz attack, those are his words, mind you, then he would do a makeover on our backyard, but if I did spaz out, then I'd help him manicure his lawn, and I didn't really think he would do it, and I kind of did freak out when I hit Maximus...'

Maximus. 'Maximus! How is he. I mean, how is she?'

'Your animal is fine.'

After we returned from the vet, we, Yugi and I, built a makeshift enclosure. We found a gigantic, old dollhouse in the garage, made from plywood. It was three stories tall and almost reached my height. After clearing it out, we dismantled the floors and placed Maximus in it.

'I'm going to see her.'

I run back upstairs to change my clothes. Hurriedly, I toss on a dirty, crumpled t-shirt and throw a sweatshirt over the top. I put on my tennis shoes, but leave the strings untied. Racing out of my room, I tear down the steps. Yugi has heard me.

'Jeri! What is it?'

'We've got a full day ahead of us!'

'Wait! What are you talking about?'

'We're going to build a natural habitat for Maximus. Dongle is here to help us.'

Without hearing his response, I rush back through the house, out the side door to Dongle's truck. He has finally made it to the end of our drive.

After shutting off his pickup, he opens the door and gets out. He is wearing thick tan pants, a flannel shirt, gloves and boots.

'Morning, Nosebleed.'

'Morning, Dongle.'

He reaches inside the truck bed and extracts lawn tools. After leaning the rakes, hoes and shovels against the truck, he grabs the wheelbarrow and lifts it over. Dongle is stronger than I imagined. This is not one of the cheap, plastic wheelbarrows either, but the metal version, dented and wood handled. He grunts as he lowers it to the ground.

'A bet is a bet,' he says.

'But I freaked out. When I hit Maximus, I locked the keys in the car, and we waited there alongside the road and...'

'Nosebleed,' he stops me. 'You did fine.'

'But all of this,' I wave my hand over the sod and the equipment, 'isn't this really expensive?'

He puts the tools into the wheelbarrow and pushes it into the backyard. 'Maybe, but you know what it will do?'

'Make our back yard look nice?'

'Yup. And when your backyard looks nice, then my backyard looks even nicer. And do you know what that means?'

'You can sit outside and not worry about how bad ours looks.'

'No,' he stops and turns around, motioning me to him with his gloved hand. 'My property value goes up. My house will no longer look as if I'm living next to a drug lord.'

Yugi rushes over to us, his face flushed with excitement. 'Dongle! What are we doing?'

'You're going to help me dig up your lawn.'

'Yeah!' Yugi fist pumps and then holds out a hand to Dongle for a bump. Dongle does not know what is happening, so Yugi grabs Dongle's hand and gives himself knuckles.

65

'What do we do first?' Yugi asks.

Dongle smiles and motions to Yugi with a finger for him to follow. Yugi bounces next to him and Dongle places an arm around his shoulder. The two exit the yard to the other side of the pickup where the handles of a machine are poking over the top.

I hear them chattering wildly, something about a sod cutter and loud noises, but my mind is now focused on Maximus. She has spent the night in the dollhouse and I hope that she is okay. I stride quickly to the back corner. The grass is full of morning dew and already the tops of my shoes are wet. I hate wet socks.

The dollhouse has cobwebs from top to bottom. Morning dewdrops cling to them like tears. I hear a scuttling inside the house and open it from the top. Maximus looks up at me from her place on the bottom. She cowers and hisses. Afraid and cornered again, she exposes her teeth. I see the needles, how sharp they must be. I realize that the impermanence of the cage places a future responsibility on me, and I feel sorry for her. As I reach down slowly, she backs even further to the corner cringing.

The back door opens and my parents come out. My mom stays on the landing while my dad descends. Crossing to Dongle and Yugi, Dad stands by the pickup and soon they are lifting the heavy machine onto the ground. It looks like a tiller, but it doesn't have the rotary blades in front. I focus my attention back on Maximus who seems to be looking for an exit, when suddenly, the machine starts up loudly. Maximus' eyes roll back in her head and she passes out. Of course, I now know this is normal, but it still is disconcerting. Then, without warning, a smell issues upwards from the dollhouse, something vile and freakishly off-putting. I place a hand over my nose - oh, God! Did she just die? I slam the doll house lid shut. While I feel bad for locking her back in the box in her current unconscious state, no one could withstand the force of that odor.

The boys now begin to cut the sod with the machine. Yugi trails behind, jittery, finding various treasure in the freshly scalped lawn. With each worm he finds, Yugi raises it to the sky thanking God for the generous gift. When he has a handful, he rushes towards me.

'Look, Jeri!' He shouts over the sound of the sod cutter. 'Breakfast for Maximus!'

'Yeah, okay.' I shout back.

'What's wrong?'

'Something happened to Maximus.'

Dad and Dongle have paused and are shouting at each other. Dongle gives driving responsibilities to Dad and turns around to go back to the pickup.

'Did she pass out?'

'Yes, but...'

'But what?' Yugi moves to the doll house and opens it up. 'Holy Shackleford!' He shouts and drops the lid again. 'What is that smell? Did she crap herself. Jeez, Louise!'

'I think she might be dead. That's a dead smell, right?' My heart misses beats. I had a pet for all of fifteen hours and now I've scared it to death.

'It's definitely an odor you don't want clinging to your clothes, that's for sure.' His tongue moves across the roof of his mouth and out through his lips a couple of times. His nose curls up. 'It kind of gets caught in your mouth. Yuck.'

I see Dongle pulling the pickup and trailer out of the driveway. Dad continues the slow, methodical process of stripping the lawn.

67

'What are we going to do, Jeri?' Yugi asks as he peers through one of the small windows of the doll house near the ground. Maximus is still lying on her side, tongue lolling out of her mouth.

I take out my phone.

'Are you calling the ambulance?"

'Shut up, Yugi. I'm going to Google her symptoms, see if there is anything that we can do.'

'Mouth to snout resuscitation, I bet.'

I give him the *look*, the one that means 'You're *this close* to getting your butt kicked.' I open the web browser and type in *possum's reek*. Sure enough, the first page to come up has a detailed forum about possums and their smells.

'It reads, '*When possums are cornered, they sometimes will play dead. Included could be an odor to give the impression that they have, indeed, died. This can last up to forty-five minutes.*"

'Great,' Yugi says. 'You've chosen the one pet in the world that will cause us to puke every time we want to get near it.

'It could be worse,' I complain loudly over the sod scalper, or whatever it is called, 'I could have hit a skunk.'

'I'm not sure that would be much worse.'

'Well, at least she's not dead.'

'Yeah,' he responds sarcastically. 'She only smells like it.'

Dad pulls up alongside us and turns off the machine. He has only been working for fifteen minutes, but a thin sheen of sweat glistens on his brow. He wipes it with his forearm leaving a streak of moisture and mud through his arm hair.

Chapter 10 Down:

'You guys all right?' He smiles. The exercise is good for him. Sitting behind a computer monitor, sitting in meetings, sitting *through* meetings, sitting, sitting, sitting. Rarely does my dad complain, but when he does, this is his primary gripe.

'Hey, Dad,' Yugi gestures with his finger, 'come over here and see what Maximus is doing.'

Dad looks suspiciously at Yugi - there is too much connivery in his son. Dad's eyes narrow as he walks over to the doll house. Yugi opens the lid quickly. Dad immediately recoils.

'Holy Moses.' Dad says as Yugi laughs and drops the lid. 'What is that smell?'

'It's Maximus,' I respond. 'One of her other protective measures.'

'Didn't think about that one when you decided which pet to run over?'

'Very funny, Dad. Where did Dongle go?'

Dad shrugs. 'He said he had an errand to run and would be back in about an hour.'

'Just wanted us to do the hard work, huh?'

'It's only right, I guess.'

For the next hour, as Dad and Yugi give the lawn a new scalp, I pick up various bits of twine, twig and trash. It's amazing how much is in our own backyard that we never seem to notice.

When my bucket is almost full, I walk to the trash bin with the red lid, and dump it in. At this moment, Dongle's truck is pulling into the driveway again.

He has two passengers with him.

Chapter 11 Across:
Relating to a career (12)

My eyes brighten.

It's been a long time since they've been to our house. Grandpa Walt and Grandma Iris are sitting shotgun across the front seat. Grandpa is grinning maniacally, hand on the safety bar above him while Grandma also seems very pleased with herself. She also looks frightened. Dongle pulls up next to the gate and turns off the engine. Both doors swing open and the men get out first. Dongle seems so young compared to my grandparents, but he is actually about the same age as they are. Grandpa leans back in and releases Grandma's seatbelt. She gives him her hand and steps out of the truck like Cinderella descending from her pumpkin. I drop my bucket and rush over to them.

'Grandpa! Grandma! What are you doing here?' I hug them both. Grandpa squeezes my shoulders.

'We've come to help.'

'But how did you know what was going on?' Dongle is smirking conspiratorially.

'We talked to your parents this morning,' Grandpa says as he escorts us to the gate, 'and they asked if we'd like to come over today.'

'But how can...' I look to Grandma whose face has turned to the sky, the early morning light reflects off of her skin. She seems to be glowing.

Grandpa frowns. 'We're not prisoners.'

'I didn't mean...'

His face softens. 'I know. I know, Jeri.' His voice lowers slightly. 'Occasionally, these trips are really good. We'll pay for it later, but still worth it.'

Chapter 11 Across:

The rest of the Walker clan converges on them. Dongle opens the gate for Grandpa and Grandma, but as they approach, Grandma's eye falls on our open garage door. Pulling up short, Grandma covers her mouth with a small gasp.

'What is it, Grandma?' I ask.

Her head shakes a few times, her lips tremble. Grandma places a hand over her forehead and mumbles to herself. I hear a few words, but they are gibberish. She takes a few steps towards the open garage. The darkness seems both inviting and frightening. Leaving behind her escort, Grandma pauses at the front.

'Grandpa, what's going on?'

'It's okay. Your parents have been housing some of our old things.'" He points toward the shelf containing all the old electrical appliances. 'See that up there?' I squint into the darkness. I follow his finger over the boxes, across the appliances and to the shelves. Treasures for everyone.

'I'm not sure what I'm looking for.'

'That old cooker. When we used to live in the country, we had a garden full of vegetables and good things. Grandma used to cook them and put them in jars.'

I look up into his eyes. Something isn't quite right.

'Come on, dear,' he pulls Grandma by her arm. She resists but eventually gives in to the urging and turns back to us. The cloud rolls back from her face and she smiles again.

That is very odd, I think.

Dad and Grandpa exchange a look, one that I am not used to. Perplexed, I follow them. Mom has now come out of the house. She smiles and waves to Grandpa and Grandma. After descending the steps, she approaches

Grandma and hugs her. 'Hello, Iris. Do you want to come inside for a cup of coffee?'

Grandma smiles and nods, but she looks at Grandpa. 'That's Beryl. She's our daughter-in-law.'

'Oh, that's nice.'

The two of them climb the stairs. Grandma's body has not failed her, only her mind, and she is able to ascend with ease. Mom has changed out of her robe and is wearing a sky-blue blouse and blue jeans. She looks fresh and content. As they walk together I wonder if perhaps this is part of Mom's great sadness - she's lost not only her mother-in-law, but a good friend.

Grandpa joins the rest of the men, and me, to stand around the sod cotter as if it's a '57 Chevy. Dongle points out the features of the machinery, and Dad nods, as if he, too, is a professional sod engineer. He's crossed his arms and kind of sways back and forth, rocking, true men talking about true man things. I roll my eyes.

'Grandpa,' I interrupt, 'I want to show you my new pet.'

He raises an eyebrow. 'You got a pet? I thought your parents didn't want to have one?'

'They didn't have much of a choice.'

My dad and Dongle laugh. 'All right, show me the beast,' Grandpa says.

Yugi giggles and both of us take an arm to pull him towards the doll house.

'That's a pretty strange doghouse,' he says.

'We don't have a kennel yet.' This sends Yugi into hysterics.

'Okay, Grandpa,' Yugi says. 'It's dark in there, so you have to put your face right down to see in there.'

Chapter 11 Across:

'Yugi...' I start, but Grandpa has already leaned over.

Yugi lifts the doll house lid quickly and ducks away. Grandpa's face turns white and he stands up. 'Oh, crap,' he says quietly and then starts to gag and cough. Yugi's paroxysms are funny, but I'm worried about Grandpa who gathers himself and looks back and forth between both of us. 'Is that a joke?'

'No,' I plug my nose and check inside Maximus' enclosure. 'Her name is Maximus. I hit her with the car last night.'

He blinks rapidly trying to understand.

'I broke her back legs and I didn't want to leave her to suffer on the road...'

'So... you've got a pet possum.'

'That's correct, Grandpa. Her name is Maximus.'

'Of all the hare-brained ideas...' His eyes shift to my dad. 'How much did that set you back, Kev?'

'The vet wrote it off as a new experience.'

'What are you going to do with it?' Grandpa asks.

Dad shrugs. 'We haven't quite decided.'

'You should have just finished the thing off.'

'That's what I said,' Dongle added.

I am thankful that Dad stands up for me. 'This is Jeri's choice. If she wants a possum for a pet, well, we'll all just have to put up with the sewage pipe smell.'

'Dad!'

'I'm just saying.'

Grandpa shakes his head. 'Well, you can swim in your own insanity, but I'm here to work.'

Dongle takes his cue and urges Grandpa to take care of the machine. 'Why don't you run the machine for a few laps.' Grandpa smiles gratefully.

73

For the next twenty minutes, Grandpa walks delightedly behind the sod-cutter. A permagrin is fastened to his face. For a man that has been cooped up, he does incredibly well, and the labor seems to loosen his joints. He looks ten years younger.

Instead of standing around watching him work like a road construction crew, I decide that I'm going to talk to Mom and Grandma for a while.

After entering the house through the back door, I step over a mound of clothes needing to be folded and walk to the front door where I can see Grandma and Mom framed in the pane of glass. Like a silent movie, the two women are silhouettes watching the street. It is hard to tell if they are speaking, but I sense that this is Mom's comfortable place. Grandma makes no requests of her. She does not impose her will or her needs. Grandma only desires to be loved and to be listened to.

As I approach, I hear Mom speaking, but I am astonished.

She is not speaking English.

I must have stepped on a weak board in the entryway, because my mother starts, and looks back. Sheepishly, she smiles over her shoulder and motions me outward to them.

I open the door and walk out onto the porch. The sound of the sod cutter is muffled here.

'Come sit with us, Jeri,' Mom says.

'What were you just talking about?' I ask as I stay put.

'What do you mean?'

'I heard you. You were speaking a different language.'

'I'm sure you misheard me.' Mom's eyes shift away.

74

Chapter 11 Across:

'No, Mom.'

'Well, whatever you heard... Grandma and I were just talking about the weather, weren't we?'

Grandma looks up at me trying to recognize who I am. She is nodding though.

'The guys are cutting up the sod and pounding themselves on the back as to how manly they are,' I explain.

'That's great. Isn't that great, Iris?' Grandma smiles and nods.

'Sit down, Jeri. Do you want some tea or coffee?'

'I'll go get some,' I say.

'Don't be silly,' Mom says - she never says that, *don't be silly.* It sounds silly coming out of her mouth, like she's a snooty English duchess.

'Thanks, Mom. I'd love some. Lots of sugar in mine.'

'As always.'

When Mom gets up, I pull up another wicker chair to sit on Grandma's other side. Somewhere beneath the surface of her dementia, she has finally clawed her way back to me. 'Oh, Jeri, you've grown so much! How old are you know? Are you ten yet? The years have passed so quickly.'

'What grade are you in?' She will ask me this at least a dozen times while I sit with her, and I know this is her attempt to control any one part of her world, but it also lets me know that she is desperately interested in making me feel comfortable. Grandma is inviting me into her ever-shrinking world and I am so grateful.

'I'm in twelfth grade, Grandma.'

'Already? My goodness, I remember when you were just a baby and we were living in... where was that?'

'We were living in Israel, Grandma, and you lived in Duncan. Out on the farm.'

'Goodness,' she says. 'What grade are you in?'

Mom swings the door open with her foot, but it bangs into her arm spilling the hot coffee. She jumps out of the way, but some of the coffee lands on the porch. I pop up and grab the coffee. Sitting down, we bookend Grandma. In conversational silence, we listen to the passing traffic and the chatter of birds. The breeze has picked up, so we are chilled. I look at Grandma's face - her eyes have a faraway look and Mom notices too. For some reason, Mom is mirroring it. *We can't always be where we want to be.*

'Tell me some stories of when I was born in Israel, Mom.'

She looks at me sharply. 'What kind of story would you like?'

'Something happy.'

Grandma smiles at Mom, waiting.

'Okay, let's see.' She leans back into her chair. 'It must have been when you were about two or three, we were living in the Christian Quarter. The air in Israel was awful. Smog hung in the air like brown clouds. Traffic was ridiculous until you got out of the city - Jerusalem, that is. When you reached the olive orchards, the world changed - it was beautiful and full of ancient stories.'

The tale she unravels for us, one of adventure and nostalgia, is not one I've heard before. I'm not even sure if it is autobiographical, but it is true for her at that moment. Grandma's eyes follow the story. She gasps when Mom speaks of me, as a three-year-old, wanting to climb a tree like the biblical Zaccheus. As she spins and weaves the tale, her face changes and becomes beautiful and expressive like the world she was describing. Instead of ending with a flourish, Mom's voice trails off and out.

'What happens next?' I ask.

Mom stumbles over her words, unavailable for comment. Grandma ponders me. 'We drive through the foothills, through the trees. The green trees.'

Mom reaches over to Grandma and grips her arm. 'That's nice,' she says, 'that you remember your days of driving across the state.'

Grandma frowns, confused.

I am too.

Chapter 12 Down:
A crafty approach (6)

I wake slowly. It is the day after graduation. It is ten o'clock and I have slept long enough. I can hear people outside and underneath my bedroom window on the front porch. I open the curtain of my window and look out into the driveway. My parents are talking in low voices. I can't quite hear what they are saying, but no one is laughing.

I put on some fresh clothes, not school clothes anymore, thank God, and move deliberately down the hallway and then down the steps. Yugi is sitting at the kitchen table. An ever-present droplet of milk dangles from his chin. He uses the spoon like a shovel. A book is held open by his left hand. It is a young adult novel, one that I've read many times, but I didn't realize that Yugi was old enough to read them yet, and yet I do.

I hope he doesn't graduate from high school early. It's a very lonely thing.

Just as I am about to go outside, the front door opens and Mom rushes in.

'What's wrong?' I ask.

'Nothing. Just some... things... that have to be taken care of.'

'What things?'

'Nothing,' she repeats.

'When do I get to be old enough to be let in on these 'nothings?''

'Not now, Jeri,' Mom brushes past me. Yugi looks up from his book but ignores the commotion to continue reading.

Frustrated, I leave Mom to hurry through the house and I go outside. Dad is talking to a woman and man. They are smartly dressed, which is odd for both the day of the week - Monday - and location - Duncan. They both wear sunglasses, like they are some kind of special agents. Dad's expression is one of resolve. He takes a deep breath and begins to walk along the side of the house. The visitors do not say anything but stand uncomfortably in the early morning sun. The man nods to me and then turns away. The woman does neither. She seems to be staring after my father.

The door opens behind me and Mom comes out again. She is clutching a manilla envelope in front of her. Hurriedly, Mom brushes past me and down the steps. After handing the folder to the mysterious duo, she takes a step back. They say nothing. My mom turns to me and says, 'Jeri, go back in the house.'

'I want to know what's going on.'

'Jeri!' She shouts, startling me. I have never heard her publicly speak to me like this before. I think she is afraid.

I trudge inside but immediately press my face to the dusty side window where Dad is returning from the garage. He is carrying a silver, rounded briefcase. Even from here, I can read the word *Madagascar* on its surface. I watch as the couple receive the suitcase. The man, stern, with a face of cut granite, sticks out his hand for my dad to shake, but Dad refuses. The woman speaks to the man and he nods. They turn away and walk to their large SUV parked in our driveway. Suddenly, I wonder if my parents are spies.

Are they?

No, that's stupid. My dad doesn't know the first thing about being observant. And yet... would he not be the best person to blend in? And my mom? Were they a spying couple? That would be so cool.

I go back to the kitchen where Yugi left his bowl and spoon on the table. He is walking away from me, head still buried in the book.

'Yugi.'

He ignores me.

'Yugi!'

'What?' He turns, perturbed

'Come with me.'

'Where are we going?'

'To the garage.'

'I don't want to. I'm reading.'

'I'll give you some of my graduation chocolate.'

He pauses, now interested. 'What are we doing?'

'Adventuring.'

We sneak to the back of the house, out the door and down the steps. Peeking around the corner we see Mom and Dad in concentrated discussion. Both have arms crossed, but Mom is covering her mouth with one of her hands. Dad stares down the street, his eyes following the diminishing vehicle, his voice hidden by the sounds of the outside world. Quickly, we slink to the garage and pull the door open. As always, it makes a loud noise. We check to see if they have heard us. They haven't. After entering the darkness, I tell Yugi to shut the door behind us. He looks at me strangely, but does as I ask, and within seconds of the shutting door, we are enveloped by a strange new world. Eventually, our eyes adjust. We are thankful for a small window in the back wall which allows a small amount of light.

Cobwebs cling between everything. Dust particles frolic in the rays of light penetrating the darkness. I feel like covering my mouth.

'What are we looking for?' Yugi whispers.

Chapter 12 Down:

'I want you to search for things from different countries, places Mom and Dad have been, or maybe even places they haven't told us about.'

'Like where?'

'If they haven't told us, how could I possibly answer that question?'

'Oh, yeah.'

For a minute, we let our eyes adjust to the dimness and then we investigate. I can't for the life of me understand why we haven't done this before. It's like my parents have a secret hoarding life we didn't know about. In the most general sense, there is organization: in the back left corner are odds and ends, old tools, the ball and peen of a hammer, a Bell jar full of screws, an oil drum, a couple of crusty paintbrushes. On the back shelves are small boxes. We open them and are surprised to find photographs, some black and white, ageless, captured unsmiling faces. Eyes surprised or vacant, they are unsure of what is happening, children and parents, men with long beards or handlebar moustaches. Some contain people in military uniforms.

Yugi discovers a small box that has bullets in it. For some reason, he is enamored by the thought of my parents owning a gun. My parents, not fastidious cleaners, would have continued to pile their belongs in and around the old, new layers compacting upon old until, through time and pressure, they've turned to diamonds. I half expect to find an old jewelry box, but unfortunately we did not. Or, not yet.

Suddenly, the garage door begins to slide open.

'Yugi,' I whisper. 'Hide.'

He ducks behind a stack of traveling cases, each with old fashioned faded brass clasps and a skeleton key lock. I dive to my right and cover myself behind a tarpaulin.

I peek through a crack in the tarp and see my mother and father silhouetted. His arms are holding the door up, even though the door will stay by itself.

'Do you think they will be back?' Mom asked quietly.

'I hope not.'

'Do we need to move them? Will they...?'

'I don't know, Beryl. It's like asking the sun if it will burn tomorrow. Probably, yes, but you never know.'

'I think we should hide them somewhere else,' Mom says and moves forward. Just a few steps more and Yugi will be exposed.

Dad scans the darkened garage. 'Let's just wait until it's dark...'

'Good idea.' They take a step back. Dad closes the door.

We wait for a few seconds and then emerge from our hiding spots.

'Wow!' Yugi whispers. 'That was reaaaaaalllly weird.'

'Yes.'

'What are they going to hide? Do you think it's a body? Who are they hiding it from? From the Commies?'

'I don't know, Yugi, but we're going to need some extra time to look through all this stuff.'

'Let's just do it now. We've got all day.'

'No,' I say. 'They'll get suspicious. We need to do it when they aren't around.'

'But what if they move *it* before we find out what *it* is?'

'I guess you and I are going to be staying up late tonight.'

'Yes! Can I bring my flashlight? Should I wear all black?'

'How about we figure that out tonight. Let's just get back inside before they start looking for us.'

Yugi surges forward, but as he does, he knocks a lamp stand. Fortunately, I catch it on the way down. The shade is made of cardboard and fabric. Tassels dangle and dance from the shade. And then I see something very, very strange and exciting.

There is money attached to the inside of the shade.

And it's not American.

After re-emerging into the bright world, we hustle back up the stairs and into the living room. Mom and Dad are in the kitchen.

'Where have you two been, and why do you look so guilty?'

Yugi's eyes open wide, and they plead with me to commit the perjury. 'Uh,' I stammer, 'we were playing with Maximus.'

Mom frowns. 'We didn't see you out there.'

'We saw you.'

'What did you see?'

I shrug. 'You went into the garage.' I pause and stare at my hands. 'What... who were those people?'

Both of my parents answer quickly and at the same time. 'Nobody.' 'Neighbors.'

'Are you hiding something from us?' I ask.

Dad frowns. 'Are you?'

I have to say it's probably much easier for an adult to lie than a child. Naturally, we have not yet had practice in subtle deceptions to distract from the real issues at hand.

83

For me, reading my parents' faces is much more difficult than deciphering clues for crosswords, and sifting through their intonations is fairly stressful. On the other hand, covering up my falsehoods is miserably hard because of my necessity for straightforwardness.

'What were the nobody neighbors needing from you? Are they FBI? National Security?'

'Don't be ridiculous,' Dad laughs nervously. 'They moved in over on... on... Sycamore, wasn't that right, Beryl?'

'Yes, yes,' my mother agrees quickly.

'Why were they wearing those outfits then?'

'What outfits?' My dad scratches his nose with a forefinger. He is either very agitated, or he has one heck of a hay fever flare up.

'Matching black blazers - men's and women's - Top Gun aviator sunglasses. I'm sure if I looked a little more carefully, they'd have those curly cord things dangling from their ears.'

'That's some imagination, Jeri.' Dad responds

I'm starting to get suspicious that I've strangely hit close to the target.

'You still haven't answered my question.'

'What was the question?' Dad asks.

'Dad!'

'Look, Jer, they're new to the neighborhood and they asked if we had some extra tools to borrow. I took one of the old briefcases, it just had some old files, out of the old garage and put in the old tools.'

'What?'

'We're just doing our civic duty.'

'All for the good of our new neighbors on Mulberry. How nice.' Mom spreads her hands and shrugs.

'Nothing is wrong.' Dad stresses.

Yeah right. 'Other than the fact that you just lied to us.'

'Jeri!' Mom is now frowning.

'You said they moved onto Sycamore Street, not Mulberry.' I stand up and walk out.

Chapter 13 Down:
Areas (8)

About nine o'clock, I slowly push open Yugi's door. Our expectations are that Mom and Dad will wait until ten or eleven in order to search for *it,* whatever *it* is. Yugi is almost peeing his pants with excitement. All of this seems surreal - we have partitioned the family into two sections. Two on two. Adults versus kids.

We leave the lights off, but Yugi is wearing his small camping headlight. I shush him and warn him not to turn it on. Even in the dim light I can see that he is disappointed. Yugi's room window looks over the back of the house. Our parents' bedroom is downstairs which gives them easy access to leave the house to go to the garage. What they don't know is that we went back to the garage and plugged in a small walkie talkie set and taped the 'talk' button down. We should hear anything that they say to each other. When ten o'clock rolls around, we begin to get bored. Yugi sits on the floor picking at his socks. Then he jumps onto his bed to tap the pillows.

At 10:27, there is movement below us. Yugi's head pops up like a prairie dog and he motions me over to his bed. We peer out the window into the darkness, our vision strained through the paned glass, hoping for movement. Thankfully, the moon is crescent and casting some glow. I can see that Maximus is sitting on the branch in her pen.

Muffled voices. The back door opens. Soft, creeping, creaking stairs and my parents appear at the base of the steps. They glance upwards - Yugi and I dive to the side where I knock my head against Yugi's bed head. Yugi gets the giggles. My death stare has no power in the dark, but I do punch him in the arm. Yugi retrieves the walkie talkie from his pajama pants. He turns the volume up just in time to listen to their conversation.

'Where is it, Kevin?' We can hear them shuffling the boxes and containers aside.

'The last time we looked for it, it was in one of these...' the word is drowned out by something they drop.

Come on, Parents! Speak clearly!

'Let's think, we've been here how many years?' Mom asks.

'Nine, I think. Yes, that's right. Yugi was one and Jeri was six.'

They stopped moving around.

'They are such beautiful kids, aren't they?'

'Yes,' Dad says, 'perfect specimens.'

'The time we had in Israel was great, wasn't it? And then, Herzegovina? Good times.'

'It seemed like life had so much more meaning then, you know? Now, masquerading at an advertising company, talking to executives, pretending to know what's going on? Not my fav.'

'Sweetheart, you are much more than a glorified receptionist. You get to handle other things, pass on the assignments.'

'But I want to be *doing* the assignments,' Dad responds fiercely.

'Wow, Kevin, I didn't realize you missed your old job so much.'

'There was excitement, freedom, risk, and you...' Dad stops.

'And I... what?' Her voice lowers a notch. I frown.

'You were so sexy back then.'

I look at Yugi and I can see the whites in his eyes. Suddenly, I have no more interest in listening to the conversation.

'And you,' Mom says, breathless, husky, 'I wanted to just eat you up when you'd come home from work.'

Uh oh.

It sounds like clothes are rustling. I want to put my fingers in my ears and sing, lalalalalalalala.

'Those clothes you wore that emphasized...'

'Emphasized what...?'

'Your assets.' Mom gets the giggles and then we hear kind of a slobbery sucking noise, some moaning. *Come on. Parents, please don't talk clearly!*

'What's going on? Is Dad hurting her?' Yugi is honestly worried.

'Pretty sure not, Yug.'

'Then, what is it?'

I shake my head. This is not what we had signed up for. I mean, I suppose I get it: it's dark, they are fumbling around amidst their old memories, they can't see their faces, how old they've gotten and suddenly they're locked in coital acrobatics. I shiver. *Yuck.*

'Dad must have... knocked his finger on something. He's probably sucking his thumb.'

'Mmmmmhmmm. Wow, Kevin, it's been a long time.'

'Beryl...' More strangling noise. Where is the frickin' mute button?

'Beryl,' my dad repeats. 'We should wait until we get back to the house. We have to find the...' His words are silenced again by a kiss - a long one by the sound of it, and they are both breathless.

'You're right. You're right. Hurry up, let's find it and get back inside.'

Chapter 13 Down:

I lift a prayer of thanksgiving to the Lord that I wasn't going to have to explain to my ten-year-old brother why there might be a possibility of having a brother named 'Garage.'

The minutes pass slowly. The garage door is open and we see two flashlight beams pass over various surfaces. Through their rummaging, they are quiet; their voices are muted and their passions held back behind a dam of necessity.

'Kevin, where is it?'

'I don't know!' He whispers. 'I don't know!'

Boxes are pushed around; shelves are reordered; the cooker must have been moved. Shuffling papers.

'Shine your light! Shine your light! I think I found it!' Mom's voice is exultant.

'That's not it,' my dad says dejectedly, 'but look there, it's a picture of us when the kids are little. Those faces! Everyone is so much younger.'

'The Weismanns; Chaim and Miriam. Weren't they wonderful? And their son, Simeon, just a few years older than Jeri.'

Suddenly, my parents are startled.

'What was that? What's that noise?' Mom whispers.

'It came from outside.'

'We need to go, Kev. We'll look again tomorrow night.'

Silence.

'Promise?' My dad's voice is full of mischief. *Gag me.*

They exit the garage and the last thing I hear is, 'Oh, it was just Maximus. He's just hanging from his cage.' *Her cage, Dad. Her cage.*

'Well, let's get back inside the house.'

The door closes and I see my parents making out in front of the garage.

Yugi and his nose are scrunched up in the moonlight. 'I didn't need to see that.'

'No, you didn't, Yugi. Neither did I.'

My parents finally break and head back into the house. I look over at Maximus who is clinging to her cage. She is looking up at me, I think.

She sees everything.

Chapter 14 Across:

*Relating to the northern states
of the Civil War (7)*

I am wakened in the middle of the night by a knee being forced into the small of my back. I want to scream. I fear something dastardly is happening, yet when I am able catch my breath and open my eyes, I see a maniacally grinning Yugi face hovering above me and to the left.

'Hey, Jeri, are you asleep?'

'What are you doing?' I shout-whisper at him and roll over to get away from his knee.

'I'm awake.'

'No kidding, Dipstick.'

'I wanted to wake Mom and Dad, but I didn't want to tell them that I could hear them in the garage.'

'Yeah, Yugi, we already talked about that. The walkie talkie is our secret. Why did you wake me up for that?'

He frowns. In the dim moonlight, he looks slightly scared. 'Because someone else is in the garage right now. I can hear them.' He turns the volume up on the walkie talkie. 'And it's not Mom and Dad.'

'What?' I grab the handset from him and turn it up a little louder.

Voices. Whispers. Scraping sounds in the dark. I'm surprised Yugi wasn't frightened out of his wits - this is the stuff of nightmares.

Nicholas. Have you located the package?

Negative, Lorenzo. This place is a Chernobyl.

Repeat?

A nuclear bomb has gone off in here. I think I saw on the same table half a rotted sandwich, a postcard from

Vietnam and a Grecian vase. Over.

'Who is that, Jeri?'

'It's the feds.'

'What?' Yugi questions excitedly. 'You mean like the FBI or the CIA?'

I nod gravely.

'But why are they in our garage? It's just junk in there.'

'Is it? I'm starting to think otherwise.'

'Are they looking for the same thing Mom and Dad were looking for?' Yugi's eyes bore into mine.

'I would guess so.'

'But why?'

'That's the hundred-million-dollar question, isn't it?'

Yugi hunches on the side of my bed. The streetlamp in front of the house casts dulling shadows across the front lawn and into my bedroom. The windowpane puts a crosshair on my brother's face and I want to move him.

'Should we go stop them?'

I frown. Every fiber of my being shouts - *That is utterly the stupidest idea you could entertain* - but I've watched so many movies where fifteen-year-old girls are supposed to be heroic and brave and invincible and armed with hand to hand combat skills or reaaaaallly good at shooting arrows, and I know that my best move should be to personally confront these federal officers wearing black (I assume) who are peering through night vision goggles (like duh, obviously).

'Yes, Yugi, we most certainly should stop them.' Thoughts of waking our parents, or even more appropriately, calling the police, have flown out the proverbial window. I put on my bathrobe, grab my Buzz Lightyear flashlight and slip on my Ugg boots. Yugi doesn't seem to care about adding anything to his ensemble. His excitement is too great.

Creeping across the hallway and down the stairs, we walk quietly towards the backdoor. We pause in the kitchen when the walkie talkie comes to life again. We are startled and turn the volume down to listen.

Nicholas, I think I've found something. There are five briefcases here. One is labeled Herzegovina, another Israel, Argentina, Poland and the last, Brazil.

Grab them all, Lorenzo. We've been in too long...

Copy that. Two minutes. Over.

I look at Yugi.

Yugi looks at me. His eyes are wide and alight. 'Come on!' He whispers.

Crouching down, we can see in the dim light a figure standing in the shadows of the garage.

'What do we do now?' Yugi whispers.

I shrug. I haven't thought that far ahead.

Suddenly, without warning, Yugi grabs my Buzz Lightyear flashlight, stands up and opens the door shouting, 'FREEZE SUCKERS! HANDS UP!'

'Yugi, what the heck are you doing?'

There is a violent noise from the garage. Like rats jumping from a burning ship, three figures clad in black explode outwards and begin running down the driveway. Yugi jumps down the steps and chases after them. He is giggling widely. I am five steps behind him watching him chase the masked marauders down our pitted driveway. They have briefcases in their hands.

There is a squeal of tires and a large black SUV screeches up to the end of our lane. Doors are thrown open and the thieves enter it like an FBI bobsled. With incredible speed, they slam the doors and scream away from the house.

Moments later, Yugi and I are standing in the very spot where the men left, staring down the street, at the 21st century DeLorean and its 1985 tracks.

Yugi is a grinning fool. 'That was fun.'

'That was stupid,' I counter. 'I thought we were going to just scare them a little bit.'

'Mission accomplished, Dude.'

There is a sound behind us. 'What in the world are you doing, kids?' My Mom asks as she touches our hair and our faces as if testing to see if we have been harmed.

'We heard a noise in the garage, and thought we should investigate,' Yugi says as he avoids Mom's touches.

'News flash, Champ,' my dad speaks into the fluid darkness, his face staring into the distance, 'it's not your job to investigate.'

'But...' Dad cuts Yugi off.

'No buts, Yugoslavia.'

Yugi is not sure whether to be proud or ashamed, so he remains quiet. A good choice, I think.

'Who were those people?' I ask quietly.

I can't see their faces very well, but the shadows are far darker than the night around us. 'How about we go back inside the house?'

'Shouldn't we call the cops?' I ask.

'Not yet,' Dad responds and puts a hand on Yugi's neck to gently drive him forward. Yugi slaps it away and runs to the house.

As we walk in my brother's tracks, I notice that I am standing between them. 'Should we be worried?'

Chapter 14 Across:

Dad takes a deep breath and sighs. 'Jerusalem, the world is full of worries, some are imposed on us, others we pick up and put in our own backpacks.'

'Which is this one?'

'It falls in both categories.'

'Are we safe?' I pause for a second and then add, 'Not in the philosophical sense, by the way, but is our house about to be stormed?'

'No, we are not going to be stormed, Jerusalem,' Dad states authoritatively.

'Whatever questions you have, save it for the morning Jeri,' Mom rubs the worry lines from her forehead.

'I have so many questions. Thousands. Gazillions.'

'We all do,' Mom counters.

'But what about the men in the garage? Who are they? Are they the feds? What were they looking for?' I protest.

'Tomorrow, Jeri. It's three in the morning.'

Once inside, Dad ushers both Yugi and I to the stairs which we climb reluctantly. We reach Yugi's room first and I wait outside as my dad tucks him in. I see Mom's shadow appear at the bottom of the stairs. In the thin glow from the kitchen, I can see that the worry lines have extended around her eyes to the corners of her mouth. Her brown hair is mussed and her robe is hitched up on one side.

'Why aren't we safe anymore, Mom?' I ask her from above.

She waves at me and shakes her head. 'You're safe with us, Jeri. We'll explain everything tomorrow.' Their vague non-answers frustrate me.

Dad exits Yugi's room and we walk the small corridor to my room. Usually, he just bids me goodnight with a smile and a blown kiss, but tonight, he enters. For the first time in a long time, he tucks me in. This is surprisingly comforting, something I never knew I'd missed.

'Just answer me this one question before I go to sleep. Are they really federal agents?'

He looked out the window and the same crosshairs that marked my brother are now on my dad. I've seen far too many movies to wonder if the little red dot is going to start dancing on his chest.

'Something like that.'

'Okay, now I'll try to go to sleep tonight, but tomorrow, we're going to continue.'

'Love you, Squirt.'

He hasn't called me that for a long time, and something about the way he says it makes me want to cry, like a piece of me has outgrown the rest of my body and it's trying to shed it. 'Love you too, Dad.'

Mom appears in my shadowy doorframe and stands next to Dad. She leans into him and I once again wonder how old people can put up with each other for so long. They've been married over twenty years. Some people get less time for murder, or that's what Dongle says.

Dad closes the door behind him; it snicks softly as he locks it tight. There is something comforting about the sound of a lock when you are on the inside. Unless, of course, you need to get out.

Chapter 15 Across:
After midnight but before mid-day (7)

I didn't realize how tired I was, but when the adrenaline wore off, I must have fallen asleep quickly. When I awake, the sun is mid-thigh in the sky, as Grandpa Walt would say. Throwing back the covers, I shove my feet into my slippers and dart out into the hallway. Yugi is standing by his doorway wearing camouflage. Binoculars are strapped around his neck and circling his waist is a toy gun belt. Holstered are two Roy Rogers six shooters and double strapped across his chest are plastic bandoliers. When he sees me, he draws his gun and shoots me.

'Sorry,' he says as he blows on the muzzle of the gun. 'I mistook you for a corrupt federal agent.'

I roll my eyes and walk past him. 'Don't let the parents hear you talking like that. They'll disavow you. Besides,' I make my voice mysterious, 'they might have been Russian spies.'

Yugi puffs out his chest. 'Like, duh svedanya, Commie. *I'm* a spy who won't talk, even under torture.'

'You'll just be Yugi. Just Yugi Walker.'

'Right.' He salutes me as I walk down the stairs. I hear the gun click again behind me. I know he's double tapped my back.

Mom is in the living room folding laundry. She is humming as if nothing happened the night before.

'Good morning,' she says cheerily.

I frown. 'Was everything last night just a dream?'

'What do you mean?'

'You're down here folding clothes.'

'What did you think I'd be doing - assembling rifles and making defense plans for our house? I think Yugi is

97

handling that side of things.'

'No, I just...'

Suddenly, Dad appears in the back door window. He opens it and steps through. He, too, seems quite cheerful.

'All right. What's going on? You guys are acting like it's a beautiful Tuesday in May and everything is nice outside.'

'It *is* a beautiful Tuesday in May,' Dad says as he strolls through the living room and plants a kiss on Mom's cheek.

I just want the truth. 'So, are we ready to come clean then?'

'Yes, but I assume you'll want to have some breakfast first.'

My stomach immediately growls. I fix myself a bowl of cereal and sit at the kitchen table. I watch my parents silently finish the laundry and put it in the correct piles to be retrieved by the correct people. After finishing my cereal, I put the dish in the dishwasher and stand before them, arms crossed.

'I'm ready.'

They nod. 'Yugi, come down,' Dad calls out. This is met by thunderous movement in the stairwell. Seconds later, the camouflaged youngest Walker is leaning against one of the beams in the living room. Both of his hands rest on guns.

'Come on, let's sit down.'

Formally, we sit in pairs across from each other. My parents are positioned separately although their hands are connected in the middle. Yugi and I watch them and wait.

'Let me preface today's discussion by saying that your mother and I never lied to you, we just didn't reveal the whole truth of things.'

'Semantics, Dad.'

'Be that as it may, there are things that children don't, and shouldn't know. At the end of our tale, you may ask questions. Not before. Agreed?'

We nod. Yugi takes a pistol from his hip and places it on his lap pulling the trigger absentmindedly.

'Jeri, as to your question from last night, no, we most assuredly are not safe. Not anymore.'

My heart falls. I thought for sure he was going to serve a few parental platitudes. *We'll make it through, kids. Just let us handle it. This too shall pass. Don't worry, we've got it under control.*

'What is it, then?' Even Yugi has stopped his gun fixation to listen intently.

'There are some very powerful people out there who never stop looking for things,' Mom says. All the sunshine is gone from her demeanor and her voice is quavering.

'You still haven't told us anything.'

Dad leans forward and sighs. 'I never expected this conversation would take place so soon.'

'Go on,' I urge.

Dad closes his eyes and begins the tale.

'At the close of World War II, many Nazis were beginning to abandon ship. You've heard of the Nazis, right?'

'Like duh, Dad,' Yugi says and fingers the hammer on his six-shooter.

'Good. When the war finished, the Allies captured many high-ranking Nazis. After the Nuremberg Trials, many, including Frank, Göring, Rosenberg, Streicher were executed. Then, there were the cowards who committed suicide. Hitler, Himmler, Bormann and Goebbels. But some Nazis managed to escape along a ratline, or an escape route for criminals, which was a route from Europe to South America - or, in some cases, even to the United States. The leader of Argentina, Peron, was a Nazi sympathizer and allowed these monsters to enter his country with their stolen treasures.'

'Very few in the U.S. were paying attention to escaping Nazis. The new enemy was Russia. But the *real* enemy, though, was always the Nazis. An estimated ten thousand Nazis escaped to places like India, Madagascar, Yugoslavia, Israel and Argentina.'

Those were the same cases that we saw in the garage!

Dad nods. 'You've already filled in some of the blanks.'

'But you're not a spy, are you Dad? You're far too young. I mean, you weren't even born until the late 1970's.'

'No, I'm not. But you do know this person.' He looks at Mom.

'NO!' I gasp. 'Mom?'

She shakes her head. 'It's not me.'

'Who is it then?'

Dad's lips tighten. 'Grandma.'

Our mouths drop open. 'But...' I stammer, but I can't say it. *Grandma has dementia!*

'If you think about it, it's a perfect cover. Back in the 70's, Grandpa and Grandma lived a life of travel. Moving all over the world, they pretended to be the ideal, bumbling American couple from the south. You can't see that in Grandma now, but her mind was so keen, so nimble, she could see everything and hear everything and be anyone.'

Yugi's feet start rocking. 'What, you mean like Jason Bourne? Grandma is Jason Bourne! That is sooooo awesome!'

'But Grandpa always says that they've never traveled anywhere.'

Dad shakes his head. 'As much as he might have wanted to tell you, there was no way he could.'

'So, he lied to us?'

'Think of it this way, Jeri, he covered up things to protect us all.'

'But...' I don't know what to say next, 'this is unbelievable.'

'Jeri,' Mom finally speaks, 'have you ever seen a photograph of you and the grandparents when you were little? Have you never noticed that our house is strangely empty of 'grandparent pictures'?'

'That's because we were living overseas. They couldn't travel to us.'

'That's right, because eventually, we became part of their cover story. Grandpa was never really comfortable with it.' Mom's voice falters, but she plows on. 'He was afraid that they would connect the dots.'

'Can we back up a minute?' I ask. 'When did Grandma start spying?'

Mom speaks instead of Dad. '1969. She told me about it once. On the way to her college Sociology lecture, a professor sidled up and asked her if she was interested in international politics. Grandma replied that she didn't care about politics, but she was interested in making the world a better place. After the scare of the Cuban Missile Crisis and constant tensions around the world, she wanted to be part of peace.'

'The man spoke quietly to her - she called it spy talk, out-of-the-corner-of-your-mouth-while-smiling talk - and asked, 'What do you know about Argentina?' Grandma shrugged and said, 'Not much."

"How would you like to go there?"

"I'm only nineteen. I'm a woman. What would I be doing?"

'The man smiled at her, knowing she was already hooked. 'Let's just say there are a few people of interest in South America that hold information the American people would be interested in."

'Supposedly, Grandma looked at him and said, 'I'll be ready by Spring Break."

'What did she do then?' I am hopelessly trapped in the story already.

'In April of 1969, Grandma took her first plane flight from Dallas to Mexico City and then on to Santiago. Flying with her was her 'handler,' or trainer. For the next two weeks, they posed as a young, nouveau rich American couple, in love and high on life. Traveling into the black side of the hills, they took pictures of the countryside while simultaneously peering through the gates of notorious war criminals' homes. Only once did Grandma say they were close to being caught. 'It was the most frightening and exhilarating moment of my life,' she said.'

'How did Grandpa feel about her double life? I mean, did he ever find out about it? Did he ever meet her handler?'

Mom and Dad share a look. Then, Dad replies. 'He knew all along. He *was* her handler.'

'Holy moley.'

Yugi is now dancing.

'It's a lot of information to take in, I know.'

Chapter 15 Across:

'In 1973, Grandpa and Grandma got married. The CIA told them that if she went through with marrying Grandpa, she could be fired, or demoted, but Grandma knew that they were bluffing. By 1973, four years after she had begun her investigation into Nazi ratliners, Grandma had unearthed an astounding amount of information about the Nazis. She had a way of blending into any situation and any place. Her ability to learn languages was second to none. Her mind was so quick that she needed only seconds to understand both surroundings and outcomes.'

'Grandpa, for his part, was the one who prepared the path for Grandma - he made the connections, greased the wheels for her entry into very tight situations. He purposely put the love of his life in places where she might not have come out alive.'

'The adrenaline kept them afloat through the 70's and when I came along in '75, my interruption gave them perspective on what was most important in life. We moved back to the U.S. for the first ten years of my life, when suddenly, without warning, a man showed up at our house. He had a briefcase in his hand. I noticed two things: the first was that it had a three-digit combination to open it, you know, kind of like on a bike lock, and the second was that the briefcase was chained to his wrist.'

'When I found them, Grandma was crying and Grandpa had his head in his hands. I asked them what was wrong, but Grandma only mumbled, 'We have to go back.' Little did I know that within two days, we would be on a plane to Germany, where I would spend the next four years of my life. On November 9, 1989, the Berlin Wall was torn down, but nobody knew Grandma's role in instigating the protest and the chaos that ensued. I thought my mother was a cleaning woman and my father, a janitor.'

103

'After the Wall fell, my mother shifted to Israel to continue her search for missing Nazis. What she thought had finished twenty years before was just beginning.'

'Keep going,' I encourage.

'In 1999, after living in Israel for ten years, I finally met your mother.' He looks down sheepishly.

'Wait a minute,' I can't hold on any longer. 'I thought you guys met in Denmark, at some Bible School?'

Simultaneously, they both shrug and lift their hands in almost the same way. 'Sorry, that is one slight untruth that we may have used as a cover.'

'Cover? Cover! Our whole life is a lie! You mean, you guys are spies too?'

'Kind of.' Both of our jaws drop.

'Okay, very funny,' I say. 'Let's take a few steps back from the edge.' I wait for them to start laughing, but they don't. 'Wait, you're serious?'

Yugi has dropped his gun and is clapping excitedly. 'This is so AWESOME!' he shouts. 'We're a bunch of spies!'

'Yugi,' Mom shushes, 'not so loud.'

'Not so loud! Mom! You've just told us that everything we know about life has to be relearned - actually, just learned. We have to erase you as a housewife and Dad as an ad-man.'

'I know this may be a little hard to accept,' Mom accedes, 'but with the current turn of events in the garage, we need to have you in the know.'

'Tell us the truth, the whole truth and nothing but the truth.'

Yugi puts a hand on my shoulder. 'You can't handle the truth.'

I glare at him.

Chapter 15 Across:

'Your dad and I met at a nightclub in Jerusalem. He was a dashing twenty-four-year-old with a broad smile and a beautiful American accent. For a few months we dated, went dancing and enjoyed the nightlife, but there was something mysterious about him. I didn't know, and he didn't want to tell me, that he had been recruited by the CIA in the same way that his mother was.

'We fell in love - that part has always been true - but your dad was told he would have to make a choice. Recruit me or leave me. Eventually, Iris and I began to work together, but I didn't know the full extent of her clandestine activities. I had no idea that Grandma was the Queenpin until much later - till it was almost too late.' Mom's hands worried in her lap.

'Dad and I got married in a Christian ceremony in Jerusalem in 2003. My parents were not thrilled with the turn of events, of course. As Jews, they were concerned about a mixed religion marriage.' She glanced down at her hands and stopped them. 'Because of our life in the American and Jewish Secret Agencies, I haven't seen my parents in fourteen years.'

'Whoa, Mom, I'm trying to catch up here, but did you just say that you are a Jewish agent?'

She nods.

My world spins. 'I think I'm going to be sick.'

'That's fine, dear,' Mom says. 'Just go to the bathroom.'

I hold my stomach and the wave of nausea passes. 'This can't be true. It just can't be. You guys are far too normal.'

'We are now,' Mom says, 'but when you were born, we were very different. Life was completely unpredictable.'

'You guys continued to do your spy stuff even while we were little?'

Dad nods. 'I was a stay-at-home dad.'

'A stay-at-home-super-agent dad,' Yugi counters.

'Did you really go to Yugoslavia then?'

'Yes, kids, you really are named after the places you were conceived. While Grandpa and Grandma stayed in Israel, Mom and I followed a lead. It was a dead end, but we... well, we got you, Yugi.'

'Yay,' he claps his hands lightly.

'But when did all this spying activity end?'

My parents look at each other, worry etching their faces.

'And that, Jeri, is where we'll have to stop. That story is not for your ears. Not yet.'

When I hear them say that it feels like opening a crossword and finishing all but the very last answer, not because I couldn't fill in the blanks, but because there are no clues. They've been left out.

'Oh, come on! You've told us everything so far.'

I scan the living room and wonder if anything we have is real, or if it's just a prop in someone else's life. There is an old clock - they've told us that's from Mom's parents. Highly suspicious now. An antique china cabinet, a corner piece, holds floral patterned dishes and plates. Mom has never cared much about using them. Yugi is waiting patiently for me, thumbing the hammer of his pistol. His feet are swinging against the sofa. I can safely assume that the blanket underneath of us was not made by Grandma Iris.

Spies don't crochet.

'First,' I put my right index finger on my left, 'is there anything in our growing up years that you've told us true?'

'Yes,' they say simultaneously and then point at each other for the other to go first.

'We love you very much,' my dad says, 'and that will not change. Your welfare is our highest priority.'

I stare at them implacably. 'You don't get brownie points for that. Question two.' Next finger. 'Who were those guys and what were they after?'

'Technically,' Yugi interjects, 'that's two questions.'

I glare.

'They are from the Directorate of Operations - CIA.'

My comprehension is redlining.

'And the reason they are here is because they are searching for something. They think we have it.'

'Why aren't you telling us? Is it nuclear secrets or something?'

Mom's laughter seems forced. 'No, it's nothing as dark as that.' I waited. 'Grandma found some inconsistencies in Nazi records. It shocked her - they were generally so fastidious about their documents. Because of her eye for detail, she caught it. A manifest of stolen goods - many were recovered and returned. It was one of the world's most famous pieces of art - Raphael's *Portrait of a Young Man.*'

'Does Grandma have it?

'Nobody knows,' Mom says truthfully, 'but if Grandma had it, I'm sure she would not have stored it in our garage... or,' she smiles ruefully, 'at least we hope she didn't.'

'You mean you don't know what's in the garage?' I ask.

'In a general sense, yes,' Dad responds, 'but when we arrived in Duncan, most of Grandpa and Grandma's life was put in the garage; all their old photos and things. Most of them are junk, we think.'

'Weren't you curious?'

'We'd been in the business so long, and leaving like we did...' she stops short and looks at Dad whose head shakes fractionally, '...we wanted to put that life behind us and take care of you two.'

'Getting back to this painting: I know who Raphael is, but how much would it be worth today, ten million?'

Dad points upwards.

'Fifty million?'

Another point.

'One hundred million?' I ask incredulously and he nods. 'For one painting.' Yugi has already Googled the picture and his face wrinkles up.

'One hundred million for that? Jeez, it looks like he couldn't figure out if it was a girl or a guy.' Yugi snorts and shows me the phone. 'Look at the guy's hat. It looks like he skinned a cat and put it on sideways.'

'It used to hang in Poland.' Mom responds. 'A Prince took it to his home as the Nazis invaded. Somewhere along the line, Hans Frank, one of the Gestapo heavyweights found it and 'loaned it' to the Hitler Museum. Eventually he took it back and put it in 'his' castle.'

'Wawel,' Dad inserts. He pronounces it *Vavel.*

'That's the last anyone saw of it. When the Russians overran Poland, there's a good chance it was secreted out of the country. Hans Frank, the last 'owner,' was one of the Nazi war criminals tried and executed. He didn't reveal the location before he was killed.'

'And you think Grandma found it?'

'Well, there's a chance she was on the trail until...'

'What? Just tell us.'

'We can't, Jeri. Not yet.' Dad's voice pleads with me.

I switch tacks. 'How much of this does Grandpa know? Can't we just ask him?'

'We certainly could ask him,' Dad responds, 'but unfortunately, this mission was done outside normal channels. He might not even know.'

I'm beginning to put the pieces together. 'So whatever is in the garage is what the CIA was looking for. They want the Raphael.'

'We think so.'

'Why would the CIA want a painting?' I ask.

Dad puts his head down and sighs. 'Why do they do anything? It's always about control. That painting could grease a lot of palms to make things easier in Europe and the Middle East.'

'Last question for now.' I lead forward too. 'The guys in the garage last night - we heard them find something, cases with names of countries on them. Do you remember what they were, Yugi?'

'Yeah, they said, 'Nicholas, I think I've found something - cases with Israel, Argentina, Herzegovina, Brazil and Poland.''

Mom and Dad look at each other knowingly.

'What?'

'They obviously didn't find anything then.'

'What do you mean? It sounds like they got away with exactly what they wanted.'

'Do you think Grandma would have put the notes and information in labeled cases? Seems like a pretty poor spy who puts a bullseye on what can be stolen.'

109

'Aah,' Yugi and I respond at the same time.

Mom's face frowns. 'Wait a minute, kids. How do you know what they were saying?'

It's our turn to be shamefaced.

Chapter 16 Across:
Link (10)

Dad opens the garage door. His face is a mixture of pride and disappointment. I can tell he is displeased by our actions, but mingled with amazement that we, his offspring, are able to hide our actions as well as they. I see his jaw twitch as he lifts. Mom stands well behind the opening door. Her arms are crossed. I stare, wondering about all the things I've ever seen and ever heard from her. I feel the foundations of my soul quiver, and suddenly it feels as if I can understand something of what it's like to be told that you're adopted.

But now I also understand the subterfuge that adoptive parents go through when trying to conceal the fact that someone else didn't *want* you. I think it's better to be truthful from the get-go - that's what I think now, but really, would it have been any better knowing sooner? As I stare at my parents, I have to figure out if I can possibly adopt *them*.

Uncomfortable silence envelopes us as we gaze into the garage. Although some ambient light illuminates the front, most of the interior is shrouded in darkness. Mom is squinting and I think I can see some Israeli blood in her. This, of course, is a lie - I know nothing about what an Israeli should look like. Duncan does not have a Jewish district and I'm not sure I could pick an Israeli out of a two-person lineup. My brain continues to roil and seethe, a tumultuous sea of thoughts crashing onto the shores of my conscious reality. *If she is Jewish, that makes me half-Jewish. I'm a Jewess!* Certainly, now that everything has fundamentally shifted, we could enter the garage and our parents could turn to us with a big smile, clap their hands together and shout, 'Just kidding!'

'How is it that you don't have an accent?' I ask Mom.

She smiles and fidgets. We will have to get to know each other again. It will take a long time for me to trust deeply again. Not just her - anyone.

'To be honest,' that word takes on new meaning, 'it took a lot of practice. Your father was disciplined in making sure that I - we - could hide in our new home without suspicion.'

'But it's just an accent,' I say. 'Lots of people have accents.'

Her eyes harden. 'An accent is an open door to suspicion. Always.' Something about her words chill me.

'Was your family impacted by the Nazis?' It's so strange for me to be speaking about 'her' family, as if they are not part of me.

She seesaws her hand. 'Yes, no, yes.' She paused to see Yugi and Dad watching her also. 'None of my relatives were in Europe at the time, but my parents did talk about watching Jews returning to Israel when the State was born.'

Yugi and Dad move into the garage, but I hesitate. There is so much more I want to know about my mother. 'Did you ever want to tell us the truth?' I ask quietly.

My mother's face slowly crumbles, her hands fall to her sides and tears form. She reaches for me, a new mother seeing her daughter for a second time, wrapping me in her arms. I allow the embrace - maybe that is not the right word - I *accept* the embrace as down payment on future hope. She is shaking, but not crying. She smells like strawberries. I can feel her hair across my face and it makes my nose itch. I can't withhold the urge, so I break and scratch furiously around my nostrils. She pulls back and wipes her eyes with the palms of her hands.

'Come on,' she says and tugs at my upper arm, 'let's see what kind of treasures we can find in here.'

There seems to be a threshold to everything: love, connection, truth. Once one steps over it, life cannot, and should not, be the same. The Garage, with a capital 'G,' is now the threshold. The line dividing light and darkness is blurred, and there is a distinct crack, where the door consistently closes, that must be crossed to see and understand. As we step into the delumination, I feel a shiver of apprehension, much like a snake must feel when shedding its skin.

'Hey, Jeri!' Yugi cries out from the depths. 'You got to see some of these things! Look at this!' He holds up an ancient iron, heavy and rusted. 'Dad says this is how people used to iron their clothes. So cool!'

He bends down and I have this vision of Oscar the Grouch digging through his trashcan, bits and pieces flying up and around. Dad is in the far-left corner quietly searching through small boxes. Something has caught his attention. A photograph. 'Look, Beryl. It's a picture of Mom and Dad. Argentina, I think.'

I wonder why I've never really searched the Garage before. The untidiness, dust and rat droppings have something to do with it, I would guess, but still...

There are boxes and stacks of things in front of me that will need to be examined. Yugi excavates the mounds of artefacts and stacks them somewhere else. *Well, it should go faster, but with Yugi assisting, probably not.*

'What exactly are we looking for?' I ask my parents.

They don't respond. Still mesmerized by the photograph in front of them, Dad stands with his arm around Mom's shoulders. I shake my head. I wonder if something will jump out at us, or maybe, if we're really lucky, Grandma will have rolled up Raphael's portrait into a tube and labeled it, 'Interesting Artwork.'

Until lunchtime, we sift through old letters, papers, and relocate lamp stands and suitcases. Mom hefts a box and sets it on a small table. She wrestles with the clasps on the wooden box until they pop open. I stand next to her. Our eyes adjust to the box's darkness and I can see both paper and objects randomly positioned. The inner lining of the box has eroded and bits of silklike material lie on top of the contents. We pull out the objects first: a cast iron pencil sharpener in the shape of Atlas carrying the world on his shoulders. I unearth a snow globe from beneath a pile of papers. It is beautiful, a scene of a German village. There is a steepled church, a market, children playing with hoop and stick, a dog is in mid-bark and runs beside the children. Houses of white and wood, Tudored beams, support a decorative line of homes. I turn the crystal ball upside down and the snow falls upwards. I read the label on the bottom - *Ulm, 1988, Weihnachten.* Although I wasn't born until 2007, 1988 doesn't seem that long ago - or, at least it doesn't *sound* that long ago - but it is. It's a lifetime and so many things have changed. My mother's eyes have become snow globes themselves, frosted and full of stationary memories. *Why?*

Mom takes the globe from me and loses herself in the snow. I begin to sift through documents and photos. Thoroughly uninterested in wordy documents, I look through the pictures, old, color-drained sepia containing faces, fedoras and sunglasses. The clothes, starched and jaunty, seem frozen in time, while the people with bleached and scraggly hair, are staring out over an ocean. I turn the photo over and am happy to see that whoever had the photo developed, wrote 'San Diego' on the back. Scrutinizing the photo, I don't recognize any of the faces, but I find a strange longing for a time I never lived through. What would life have been like in the 1970's?

I lay the picture to the side and thumb my way through the stack on the bottom. These are landscapes with small figures. It's as if the photographer is less interested in the people as the location. Unfortunately, the places are not written on these, but it is certainly not San Diego. Tall, leafy trees overshadow a hacienda-like house, its arches are an entryway into a fountained courtyard. The buildings have terra cotta tiles on the roofs. A solitary German Shepherd is peering to its right as if sensing danger. It's tail sticks straight out behind it.

Mom has begun to go through my pile. She has a bemused expression; obviously she recognizes some of the people in the pictures. She turns them over as I did. Similarly, she is irritated that they are not labeled.

Suddenly, I am surprised and excited. *There is a book of crosswords*! I reach into the box and retrieve it. Carefully holding it in my hands, I show it to Mom. She cares nothing about it. I take the crossword book back into the light, holding it like the Dead Sea Scrolls. I can't believe in the collection of all the junk, there is a pink Barbie crossword puzzle. I'm disappointed to see that it's been used, but perhaps there are a few in the back that haven't yet been filled in. *Maybe it's Grandma's book!*

Gently, I touch the front cover. Barbie is lying prone, crosswords in front of her. She is wearing a pink, orange and yellow shirt, and her hair is held back from her eyes by an orange headband. I wonder if I would have looked like that in the 70's.

115

The yellowed pages reveal a sharp mind, or at least someone adept at cheating. As I page through the book, there are only a few blank spaces. Oddly, though, they aren't entire words, just individual squares. Whoever filled it in is obviously a bad speller. As I peer closer, I marvel at the fact that they did a great job of persevering. Without thought, I squat down next to Maximus's cage almost sitting on an aloe plant. When Maximus makes a sound, I remember that I've accustomed myself to filling my pockets with Maxisnacks, fruit, vegetables or other delicacies. Unlike Yugi, I haven't yet lowered myself to putting worms in my pockets.

I lift a slice of desiccated apple over my shoulder and I hear Maximus crawl over to retrieve it. Reaching through the wire, she grabs it and proceeds to munch. I take a piece myself and eat it. Looking back, I realize that Maximus has not retreated to the other side of the fence but seems content to be near me. I put the book down, stand up and open the lid. Maximus gazes up at me, remnants of apple still in her clawsy paws, her jaws stilled. I reach down to her. *Why not?* I think to myself. Sooner or later, we'll have to see if she'll trust me enough to put herself in my hands. Maximus recoils slightly at my extended hand, but then relaxes once I let her sniff my fingers. For whatever reason, she turns her head slightly and I scratch her behind the ears like last night. Her fur is not what I'd call silky smooth, but the coarseness of it reminds me that not all animals, just like not all people, have skins that are good for touching.

My hand moves to her back which, surprisingly, she allows me to stroke. At the base of her tail, I find myself slightly disgusted by the pink root. As I move farther down the tail, I notice that she doesn't like that as much. She pulls it away from me and I go back to scratching her head. Just to test, I reach in with my other hand, and put my hands around her middle.

Too far. She nips at my hands. Maybe next time. I go back to petting her head which she likes.

Yugi's face pokes out from the Garage. 'Jeri, you got to come here and see this!' He sees me petting Maximus and his face lightens. 'When did she start letting you do that?'

'Yesterday.'

'Awesome. Now, get over here. I have to show you this.'

'Bye, Maximus.' After picking up my Barbie crossword, I roll it into a scroll, put it in my back pocket and walk back to the Garage.

'Okay, okay, this is really cool,' he says. 'You've got to see some of these pictures. There's some real-life Nazis in here. Dad recognizes some of the pictures, you know like Hitler and his funny moustache and chubby Göring.'

'And then, and then!' His voice is rising to crescendo, 'Look at this!' Yugi pulls out an Iron Cross. He holds it up in front of my face.

'Yeah, neat.'

'Neat? Are you joking! This is amazing!'

'Yugi,' Mom chides him. Even in the dim light of the Garage, I can see that her face has turned ashen. 'That belonged to a mass-murderer.'

He drops it as if it had suddenly turned red hot. 'Which one?'

'They all were.' Something about her lowered voice is spooky.

'Is it fair to throw them all into the same company?' I ask.

117

'Was it fair to throw all of my people into incinerators?' Her voice is edged with chilling anger.

'I'm sorry, Mom.'

Her face softens. 'It's not you.'

Dad holds up a picture. 'This came from a manila envelope containing roughly fifty pictures of the same guy but from different locations. This one is obviously World War II - here is one much later in life, on a beach somewhere.' The photo is of an older man, shirtless, a tuft of white hair seems pasted to the center of his chest. He is staring into the camera with a strange, twisted smile on his face. A small gap separates his top two teeth. He doesn't look like a monster - just an average old man who happens to be sunbathing. Beside him are two boys and a woman. The boys appear to be about ten years old. The woman is blond and bright eyed. She is smiling broadly while the boys, their mops of blond hair looking scraggly from salt water, have freckles everywhere - almost like twin Alfred E. Neumanns from Mad Magazine.

'Who is the man?' I ask.

Dad's jaw is tightened.

'What's wrong? Who is it?'

'The Angel of Death.'

Chapter 17 Down:

The code to which all knights adhere (8)

Whatever light was in the Garage seems to have been sucked out.

'Who is that?' Yugi whispers.

'Josef Mengele.'

'Why is he called 'the Angel of Death'?'

Dad leans against the bench behind him. He can't seem to take his eyes off the pictures. 'He was a German doctor. Auschwitz. Birkenau. When you hear about human experiments, you'll hear Mengele's name.'

'Is he still alive?' I ask.

'No, thankfully. He must have been born near the turn of the 20th century. I heard a rumor that he died somewhere in South America. Uruguay, maybe.'

'Is that his son?'

'I don't think so. Maybe this was a son or grandson.'

'Do you think he was one of the Nazis Grandma was following?' I stare at the Nazi's face with interest.

'Since his picture is in with Grandma's files, I'd say it's a good possibility.'

'Dad,' I put my hand on his arm, 'do you think Mengele and the Raphael have anything to do with each other?

'As of this point, anything is possible.'

'Except asking Grandma for help.'

'No, that won't be possible,' he replies.

After lunch, we empty the Garage, dust everything off and bring it inside the house. Yugi, tired of crawling through the past, pretends to stand guard at the Garage door. He is still wearing his matching pistols, and his bandoliers which give him a humorous, though menacing, look. Through it all, Maximus watches the Walker family tote this chaotic history into the house. Every half a dozen trips or so, I stop back by her cage and stroke her. When she sees me coming, she anticipates the attention. Late in the afternoon, I stop and try once more to lift her. For the first time, she lets me. As I bring her close to my chest, I can feel her claws gouging into my arm. Her tail has wrapped around my elbow and I can feel her heart beating wildly. As I bring her to my chest, I see her eyes begin to roll back.

'Maximus, easy girl.' My soothing words seem to have an effect until Yugi recognizes what is happening and he runs over.

'All right, Maximus!' He shouts. She faints and the predictable, overpowering odor issues forth.

'Uuuuugh, Yugi! Why did you have to do that?'

Yugi runs away screaming at the noxious scent. I gag. 'Oh, Maxi...' I almost vomit and drop her as gently as I can on the floor of her pen.

When I walk into the house, both Mom and Dad sniff. Yugi grabs his nose and points at me.

'It wasn't me. I was holding Maximus - let that sink in for a second; I was holding my pet possum - when Yugi comes screaming at me. I can't blame Maximus. If I was her, I'd probably fart at him also.'

'Jeri...'

'What? It's Yugi's fault.' He is already laughing and hiding behind chairs shooting imaginary Nazis and calling them 'Dirty Krauts.'

By dinner time, the entire contents of the Garage are scattered across our living room. After dinner Dad and I check the Garage one last time. There is nothing on the back bench; nothing on the side shelves. We even tap the floor to see if anything might be buried.

'Hello?'

A disembodied voice stands on the threshold. We can see him, but he can't see us.

Dongle.

'Hey, Dongle,' I say.

'Well, it looks like you all have been busy today.'

'Yup. It looks a lot different, doesn't it?'

Dongle peers around the space. It smells distinctly of dust and motor oil.

'Do you want to come in?' I ask.

'Don't mind if I do,' he says and crosses the crack. I watch his feet, dirty work-boots encrusted with labor. One of his laces is undone. He scuffs across the length of the garage to the back. Like a building inspector, Dongle touches the 2x4 supports. Naked nails protrude. He ponders his hand, now full of dust, and brushes it against the leg of his pants.

He grunts as he stares up near the ceiling. 'Huh.'

'What is it?' I ask.

There is something strange in his expression. I follow his eyes to a darkened niche. There is nothing in the space, but there is certainly something in his eyes.

'Nothing, Jer.'

'What?' I'm intrigued.

'It's nothing.' He walks back towards the light.

'Wait,' my dad calls out, 'is there something I can do for you?'

He smiles and shakes his head as if clearing the cobwebs from a memory. 'I just wondered if maybe we shouldn't be watering your new sod. If you don't water it every day for the first few weeks, you're going to end up

121

with very expensive straw.' The implication was that because Dongle had paid for our upgrade, he was hoping to keep it looking like an upgrade.

'Good idea,' Dad says. 'Jeri, why don't you hook up the hose and get to that.'

'Right, Dad.' I cross into the outdoors dragging Dongle with me. He is still pondering Dad who has one hand on his hip and one scratching the balding golf ball on the back of his head.

As we enter through the gate to the backyard, the muted, setting sunlight reveals the beauty of the new grass even if it's in strips. For as long as I can remember, our backyard has been a forlorn wilderness, spiky thistles and powdery dandelions. I remove my sandals to step into the holy place. I look at Dongle's boots and raise my eyebrows. He shakes his head.

'Dongle, I have to show you something.' We walk to Maximus' cage where the possum seems to be having an early evening siesta. I produce a piece of dried orange. She climbs the screen, sniffs it and decides that it would be a delicious afternoon repast. Clinging to the cage with her lower legs and tail, she gnaws on the fruit.

'I'll be danged,' Dongle says. 'It's almost like you got a real pet there.'

'Watch this.' I desperately hope that Maximus will let me pick her up. Opening the cage, I reach in and pat her head which signals, hopefully, that I am going to pick her up. She is resistant - her claws catch on the cage - but eventually she releases them and quivers her way into my arms.

'Wow,' Dongle says with true amazement, 'you're the Possum Whisperer.'

'Yes,' I whisper.

Chapter 17 Down:

We both stare at the animal who is looking back and forth between us. I am grateful that she has not tried to leap off my arm either. It would be devastating for her to escape now.

'I suppose we'd better water the lawn?' Dongle's statement sounds like a question, but it's not.

I pat Maximus' head and try to put her into her cage. Instead of accepting her captivity, she claws her way up my arm and curls around my neck. My skin feels like a pincushion, but this is the kind of pet that I always wanted! A living neck warmer!

'Maybe you should put that thing back in the wild before one of you gets hurt.'

'No,' I say fiercely.

Dongle raises his hands in surrender. 'All right. All right, don't get testy, Nosebleed. I'm just saying that I think keeping a wild animal might not be such a good idea.'

'As you can see, Dongle, she is not wild.'

He harrumphs and we walk back to the watering hose. Dongle grabs the hose while I turn the spigot on. Walking back over the edge of the sod, Dongle puts his thumb over the end to create a pressurized spray. We are quiet for a few moments, an old neighbor and his young neighbor. Dongle doesn't allow me to water the grass. Whether this is some archaic sense of chivalry or a distrust that I could get the job done, I don't know. Maximus watches the proceedings over my shoulder. 'Dongle, where were your parents during World War II?'

'That's quite a question. What makes you ask?'

'I... well... my favorite subject in high school was World History and I find the stories fascinating. I'm assuming you weren't old enough to have lived through it.'

123

He laughs. 'I'm a child of the 50's, my dear girl. My parents, though, were directly in the middle of it. My dad enlisted in the army in 1942, just after Pearl Harbor. My mom worked in a factory until some of the men returned from the war.' The phrase, *some of the men*, seemed to have struck a chord.

'Did your dad fight anywhere?'

He nods and looks to the west. The sun, a searing white lightbulb casting yellowish rays across the landscape, is resting just above the generational oak trees. Their silvery leaves shimmer in the sun's gaze. 'Yes, Europe.'

'Was it horrible?'

'Yes,' he responds simply.

'Did you ever join the military?'

His jaw clenches and the water spurts out suddenly as if he had squeezed the hose too tightly. 'Yes, Nosebleed, I spent a few years in the forces.'

'Vietnam?'

He doesn't respond and I don't push. We are quiet for a little while longer.

'Dongle, do you think there will ever be a world without wars?'

'I would guess there's about as much chance of that happening as your little furry friend there becoming a superhero.' Maximus seems to be grinning.

'The world needs more superheroes,' I say.

Chapter 18 Across:
Skewed and unrecognizable (9)

It is a gorgeous day. June and me - we get along very well. Yugi is bouncing around outside my bedroom door. I can hear him as plain as day. 'Come on, Jeri. Come on!' His voice is plaintive, antsy.

For years, Mom and Dad have been taking us 'into the sticks,' as they say, so that we can splash around in a local watering hole. The land belongs to a friend of my dad's, but he opens it up to town kids during the summer. The insurance alone must be extraordinary, but Garland Grant has made millions in the 80's investing in oil. Most days, Garland sits with the parents, lazing along the shore with a long piece of grass dangling from his mouth. Garland enjoys the company; the parents enjoy the entertainment, and the kids enjoy being kids. The Pond is a little oasis situated in the isolated countryside outside Duncan and the echoes of shouts and laughter remain embedded in the surrounding woods.

'Hold your horses,' I yell out to Yugi. I glance in the mirror. I'm far too insecure about my body to go traipsing around in a bikini. Even though I tell myself that I don't care what others think of 'my look,' I do care. I don't have the idealized teenage girl body for swimsuits. My shoulders are a little thick, my belly-button seems to have a safety airbag around it and my hips, well, they'll probably come in handy someday. My one-piece swimsuit is sky-blue with strings around the neck. I tie them up and, as always, put a t-shirt over the top and denim shorts to cover the lower half. I lean in close to the mirror and notice a zit that's about to give birth right between my eyes. *Great.*

'JERI!'

'Yugi,' I shout through my teeth, 'I swear, one of these days...'

'Come and get me,' he laughs and pounds on the door.

I throw open the door and he shrieks like a little girl, but he cannot run because he's already got his swimming flippers on.

'Good Lord,' I mutter as he scrambles away from me to the railing and rounds it. Halfway down the stairs, his flipper missteps and his feet slide out from under him. The impact is heavy, and he rolls to his side and down to the first level. I can see that he wants to cry or moan, but he sees me standing above him, an avenging angel smugly watching over him with karmic humor. I laugh.

Mom sees him lying at the foot of the stairs writhing. 'I told you, Yugoslavia, if you wear those stupid things in the house, you're going to hurt yourself.'

'I'm not hurt,' he whimpers.

'Come on, kids,' Dad yells from the back door. 'Let's go!' He, too, sounds impatient but happy.

Just as I am making my way down the stairs, I remember that I wanted to take my Barbie crossword puzzle book with me. Retracing my steps, I hurry back to the room and grab it. Curling it up, I stuff it into my back pocket.

'Jeri!' Mom calls up the stairs. Everyone is impatient.

'Coming.' I race out of the room and down the stairs again. Mom is standing at the base, hands on hips. She looks like she wants to be smiling, but cringing is probably a better word. Yugi's flippers are slapping across the kitchen.

Mom pretends to push me forward and out the back door. I reach the back stairs where Yugi is descending slowly, but suddenly, his feet go out again and he splays at the base of the stairs writhing again.

'Yugi!' Mom rushes down to him. He is holding his butt and I cover my grinning mouth with my hand. Yugi looks like a true fish out of water. Now having fallen twice, he must be in pain, but still, he refuses to take off his flippers.

Dad opens the car window and encourages us to hurry up. Yugi is rubbing his butt and duck walks to the car. I look to my right where Dongle is standing by the fence a wry smile is attached to his face. He is leaning on his garden hoe.

'See you later, Dongle,' I shout out with a wave.

'Enjoy your time at the Pond, Nosebleed.' His hat is pushed back on his head revealing a reddened face.

'We will.'

Yugi is scowling when I shove into the back seat next to him. The excitement has faded from his face and his arms are crossed. Stubbornly, he has still refused to take off his flippers. They are forced under Dad's seat.

Twenty minutes later, we arrive at Pond Lane. Garland had the road renamed after he generously donated to the town recovery benefit after the flood. Pond Lane is a pathway to Eden. Lined with flowing willow trees, it feels as if we are floating. Their soft greenness is in contrast with the brilliant blue sky above them. Even at this time of morning, heat shimmers above and around the road. It seems like this place should be a mirage.

Gravel crunches underneath our tires as we drive down the lane. Dad is humming and tapping the steering wheel. Mom is quiet, her mind somewhere else.

Last week, we visited Grandpa and Grandma. It was very hard to look them in the eyes. Grandma was distracted and fidgety. She mumbled and sniffed. Deceiving Grandpa, well, maybe 'deceiving' is not the right word, *misleading* him, made me feel uncomfortable. Weirdly, it feels as if there is a wedge between us now, an invisible wall that has risen from the ground.

Dad pulls the car into the parking area. In the shade of a gigantic oak tree, we open the car doors. For the third time, Yugi's flippers trip him up and he splats onto the gravel. He screams not in pain but frustration and finally, I laugh out loud. His face is full of fury when he sees me. Pointing at me, he snarls which makes me laugh even more. Dad tells him to settle down. A voice calls in the distance.

'Yugi!'

His eyes perk up and his face morphs immediately into joy. The voice belongs to one of Yugi's best friends, Richard. Little Richard, I call him. He is a year older than Yugi, but six inches shorter. Little Richard has a very high voice and the skinniest body I've ever seen. Richard eats like a horse, but it gets burned up faster than it goes in.

Yugi walks as fast as he can towards Richard and within moments, Richard and Yugi are in the shallows. Their lily-white torsos are blinding. Within days, though, they will turn brown as the dried mud around them. Even from this distance, I can see that Richard has his snorkel gear on also. I shake my head. It's not like they can see anything under the water anyway. When so many people are swimming, the mud is constantly stirred up, yet the boys don't really care.

Dad takes the lawn chairs from the trunk while Mom gathers the towels and blankets. I take the picnic basket and we walk the last thirty yards to the shaded edge of the Pond.

Chapter 18 Across:

Already, there are a few dozen parents rimming the edge and more than fifty kids splashing and shouting in the water. On the far side, a few girls have gathered to throw their towels onto the grass and are slowly roasting themselves like Christmas turkeys. Oil has been rubbed into their nubile bodies which glisten like butter. Their wings have been pushed up over their heads. Bikini straps have been undone. Of course, this communal baking has been done for the male eyes on the shore and in the water. A handful of high school boys stand in the shallows pretending not to watch the sunbathers. I shake my head unsure if I am jealous or disgusted.

'I'm going to the shade,' I tell Mom.

'You should get some sun today. You've been cooped up for most of June.'

'Okay.'

The parents have situated themselves in small groups under the trees on the right side. Dads, resplendent in ubiquitous Hawaiian swimsuits, have congregated slightly apart from the women. They stare out over the water, sunglasses on. They don't seem to be talking much. Nearby, a group of mothers has gathered and they are clucking away, emphasizing words with hands and faces.

On the opposite shore, near the sunbathers are the young boys and girls who have actually come to play in the water. Yugi and Little Richard ignore everyone else.

As I survey the surroundings, I am acutely aware that I fit in with none of these groups. Although I would enjoy more mature conversation, I do not want to listen to the mothers, nor do I want to sit in silence with the fathers. I have no interest in sunbathing and Yugi's group is far too young for me. I am an outcast.

129

Grabbing a chair from dad, I walk to a place in the shade but very close to the edge of the sunlight. If I want to warm up, I can move five feet. If I want to get in the water, I can wade and return. After opening my chair, I sit and immediately bounce up. I've forgotten that my crossword puzzle is in my back pocket. Retrieving it, I place it in my lap.

As I survey the scene, I feel the slight warm breeze that brings the summer scents to my nose. Water, even muddy water, has a pleasant, delicious odor. The trees rimming the Pond rustle slightly and the voices of happy people ring out. I wonder if there are other places like this on earth, places of peace and joy. I wonder if it is like this in Israel.

I've thought a lot about what we've discovered in the last month. I wonder if life will ever be the same, or even go back to normal.

Yugi throws Little Richard into the air. Richard is laughing and shouting loudly as little boys do. Yugi seems not to have a care in the world. Mom and Dad are lazing idly. My mom has reclined her chair and seems to be asleep. My dad converses with Garland. Garland's sunglasses are pushed down onto his nose. Smiling, Garland listens and guffaws with laughter.

I open the Barbie crossword puzzle. I have enclosed a pen inside it, but as of yet, I haven't filled in any of the clues. If this was my grandmother's, I am reticent to mark it in any way. These thoughts from her own mind seem important for me to keep in situ. As I have leafed through the book many times already, I know that I could fill them in easily and quickly, but something holds me back.

Poor spelling is rampant but it hasn't seemed to affect the outcome of solving the crosswords. Some of them are completely done, but others have random blank spaces. Grandma seems to do as I do when solving: she puts a little slash through the number when finished. I am pleased about this. About one-third of the way into the puzzles, I notice a difference. It's not startlingly different, just different. Instead of slashing through the numbers, Grandma has slashed through letters in the clues themselves. I wonder if Grandma is writing something in code. She's a spy! Of course! I write down the clues where she has crossed them out.

46 Across: *Goldsmith's* The _____ of Wakefield
70 Across: *Kissin' makeup?*
80 Across: *Item on a rod*
109 Across: *Charlatan*
11 Down: *Subject of the biography* Wired
18 Down: *Raises one's spirits?*
81 Down: *They're called on account of rain*
83 Down: *Deride publicly*

I quickly scribble down the letters which have been crossed through – LAECSIHI.

Obviously, it is an anagram. I've seen the *Da Vinci Code*. My brain is running on a cup of adrenaline. Is it possible that Grandma and I have a connection across the decades?

I am not quite as used to working through anagrams. My first thought is that I've written them down as they appear in the clues. I try in numerical order disregarding the direction – SILAEHIC. Uh, no. For a few moments I try to pull a Robert Langdon and rearrange them in my head, but the best that I can come up with is *chilaise*. I take my phone out and find that there is a town in France named 'Chilaise.' I scribble this name in my book.

Now I go back to the beginning of my Barbie book and look over every square inch. I notice that the puzzle number 6 has been circled, but none of the others had. As I leaf through the book, I begin to notice spelling errors and spaces, but they don't seem to have any significance as of this point. I make a few notes near the front of the book including the word 'Chilaise' and keep moving.

Pg. 6 circled

Blank spaces in puzzles 4, 24 and 32 - two on each page.

'Hey, Jeri.' I jump and look up quickly. It's Mom. I hadn't heard her approach. 'What are you doing?'

'Just looking at the crossword puzzle book.'

'Oh, that old thing.' Mom holds her hand out and I give it to her. 'Is it finished?'

'Almost.'

Mom looks at the cover and laughs. 'Barbie. It's hard to believe she's been around so long.'

'I think there might be some clues in here...'

'Jeri,' Mom chides, 'we're supposed to be relaxing today.'

'I am.'

She playfully taps me on the head with the rolled-up puzzle book. 'You're working.' As she hands the book back to me, her hand rests on the back of my hair. 'Or worrying.'

'I'm just fascinated.'

'My little Jerusalem,' she says affectionately. 'There was so much that happened during World War II. Most of it awful.'

'Why can't we let it go?'

Chapter 18 Across:

'I don't know, Jer. I just don't know.'

We are both quiet. 'Why don't you get in the water for a while,' she says.

'Maybe for a little while.'

'That's a good girl,' she heads back to her people.

I strip off my t-shirt and shorts and amble down to the water. When I cross the indistinct line between sun and shade, shore and water, into mud and mayhem, I find that it is a pleasant experience. I'm not sure why I don't take advantage of swimming more often. With amazement, I feel the warmth of the sun canceled by the chill of the water in a visceral tug of war. I cross my arms over my chest. I feel as if everyone is watching me, an ugly duckling, trying to enter the water, that has of yet exchanged pin feathers for wing feathers. The reality is: *no one* is watching, and *nobody* cares but me. I edge deeper into the waist-deep water. Raising my elbows like wings, I stand on my tiptoes. Each inch is a cold needle into freshly submerged skin.

I take a step back thinking it best to accustom my way into the depths when suddenly, I am hit with a tidal wave. My back feels as if I have been stabbed by a thousand knives and the adrenaline to retaliate rushes to my mind.

Yugi and Little Richard are standing side by side laughing uproariously. Obviously, they have been waiting for just this moment and their smiling faces peer out from behind their snorkeling masks. I can see bits of mud and algae in their teeth.

'You little a-holes!'

Yugi flexes one of his biceps in front of his chest. 'Eat this, Eva Braun.' His voice is distorted, pinched, because of the mask. He sounds like he has a plugged nose.

'Why you little....' He and Little Richard fall backwards into the water and splash away. Because I am still cold from my dousing, I can't follow them quickly. Now submerged, Yugi extends his arm like a periscope and raises his middle finger.

I gasp. *The little worm! I'm going rip that snorkel out of his mouth and I don't even care if I pull out his teeth.*

Pull out his teeth.

Blank spaces where something used to be or should be.

Holy Sacajawea.

Chapter 19 Down:
To describe a hermit (8)

I rush back to my chair, grab my towel and dry off quickly. I look over at my mother who is frowning at me. She holds up her hands to her sides, palms up and mouths the words, *What's wrong?*

Shaking my head, I quickly put my shorts and t-shirt back on. In the shade, it is cold and I begin to shiver. Adrenaline or cold is indistinguishable. My swimsuit soaks quickly through my shorts and t-shirt. At this point, I don't care. I sit back down in my chair and wrap my towel around me. Hunched over, I page through the book to puzzle four.

46 Down: *Mettle for a medal winner.* The included letters are v_lor

54 Across: *Prepare to advance after a sac fly.* I have no idea what a 'sac fly' is, I imagine something to do with an insect, but the letters shown are ta_up

Even though I know nothing about sac flies, I can intuit that the letters are an *a* and a *g. v*alor and *tag up.* None of the other letters in the alphabet seem applicable for both words.

Rapidly, I work through and find that the other unfilled spaces in the book are like this:
Puzzle 4: A and G
Puzzle 24: A and R
Puzzle 32: E and G

AGAREG

The letters swim and just like I ordered the numbers in Physics class, suddenly the astonishing answer floats in front of my vision.

Garage.

I cover my mouth with my hand. My heart beats wildly. We have cleaned everything out of the Garage and it is now in our house. But this little word coded into my crossword puzzle book is evidence that we are on the right track. I wonder what was in the Garage - is it another coded clue or is it something more obvious?

I return to the other letters, *chilaise*. That doesn't make sense. If Grandma wanted to leave us a clue, it seems like it would have to be something different.

I puzzle over the letters and when I look up again, I see that other Pond patrons are now unpacking their lunches. I check my phone and see that it is almost 12:30. We've been swimming - or at least here - for over three hours. I put the Barbie book to the side. When I got up the last time, the answer came to me. Perhaps it would happen again?

Mom and Dad are watching me as I walk towards them. Mom's eyes hold mine as Dad reaches into the picnic basket and retrieves a peanut butter and jelly sandwich for me.

'Are you having a good day?' she asks this as if genuinely wondering whether I am.

'Yes,' I say slowly. 'And you?'

'Delightful.' Mom's friend, Mrs. Claussen, stops her prattle as I approach. Her eyes casually take in my appearance. I can see the disdain. It's not that she doesn't like me, but I don't fit her physical standards.

'Beryl,' Mrs. Claussen starts talking again and puts a hand on Mom's arm, 'she's getting so mature.'

I roll my eyes. I hate it when adults speak as if you aren't present.

'Yes, Debbie, Jeri just graduated from high school a few weeks ago.'

'Oh, my, how wonderful. You must be so pleased, Beryl.' Debbie says with syrupy fakeness.

'Of course. She finished top of the class, too. Straight 'A's.'

'Congratulations, Jeri.' Mrs. Claussen pulls her sunglasses down on her nose, as if to get a better look at me. Then, she pushes them back up. 'Are you going to go to college next year?'

'I haven't decided what I'm doing yet for sure, but that would certainly be at the top of my list.'

'What are your first choices?'

'I was thinking about Mid-America.'

My mom looks up at me, shocked. 'Oh,' Mrs. Claussen can't quite hide her sneer. 'My Jimmy went to Stanford last year,' she responds haughtily, 'but the professors were so mean to him that he had to come home. Poor thing.' She shakes her head. 'These universities are so arrogant. My Jimmy just thinks in different ways.'

'What's he doing now, working at Johnny Bing Bing's?'

Mom is about to scold me, but Mrs. Claussen answers first. 'Why, yes! Have you seen him there? They make the very best French fries.'

Mom's mouth snaps shut.

'Thanks for the sandwich.' I return to my chair. As I go, I can hear the adults behind me, their voices lowered, like mooing cows, talking about nothing. *Just chewing cud. Moo moo. Chew my cud. Huuurgh.*

While I walk back to my chair, I am strangely irritated by the young people and their nubile movement and their coquettish laughter and their hormonal village dances; I wish I could be one of them. One of the girls sees me in my shorts and t-shirt, my sandy brown hair pulled back, and she squints, unsure if I'm real or. I have always been invisible to them, the beautiful people.

Sometimes I think my parents wonder if I'm happy. Because of my natural solitary nature, I draw away from crowds and social opportunities. I think they blame themselves.

I make my way back from the water's edge to my chair. The wind has blown my towel from the back, and it lies in a heap on the ground. I walk over to pick it up. The Barbie book has blown open to the last page - the answer boxes are there, filled in, everything in neat order. On those pages, there is no imagination, no curiosity, no working out - just black and white, yes or no. Maybe that is why I don't like looking at the answer boxes. Everything else in my life, in my mind, is supposed to be black and white, already filled in. I just want the process to be more fun than simply seeing the answers.

I sit back in my chair and cover myself with my tattered towel.

I'm not sure when it is that I fall asleep.

Chapter 20 Across:
Has the same effect (10)

I am roused by a tap on my shoulder. My dad is standing over me holding two chairs.

'Hey, Jer, I think we're going to get going. Do you want to come with us?'

I clear my eyes to see that most people have retreated from the water and onto the shore. A few shivering little ones have towels wrapped around their torsos. Their lips are blue and their teeth are chattering, but they seem happy.

My mouth tastes weird, like something is stuck to my teeth and cheeks. I run my tongue over it and find partially chewed peanut butter. I stretch from my curled-up position and feel the blood flood in my face. After lifting myself from my chair, Dad brushes off the seat and folds it up. I follow him to the car where Yugi is tenderly hopping across the gravel in his bare feet. His trifecta of wipeouts this morning hasn't dimmed his enthusiasm at all.

Mom and Dad have decided that we will eat out for the evening, which is a real treat. My parents view eating out as an expensive vanity, so when we do, we kind of feel guilty about it. After driving back into Duncan, my dad pulls the car into the parking lot of Johnny Bing Bing's. I look at Mom who is smirking.

A young man at the front, Kyle, is wearing a striped shirt with suspenders. A button is affixed to his chest with the oh-so-clever slogan, *'Bein' a Bing Bing.'* The mascot is a bean, which doesn't make any sense to me at all, but neither does fast food.

We ask for a booth, so Kyle guides us between wooden stationary chairs and tables where grossly overweight families have gathered.

'Why are we eating here?' I ask. 'Why can't we eat out somewhere nice?'

'What do you mean?' Dad responds with faux indignation. 'This is my kind a joint.' He feigns a New York accent.

Soon, an identically clad server approaches our table and I see that his name is Jimmy. He is tall and pudgy. His hair is lank and greasy. It has probably absorbed the oil from the French fries.

'Are you Jimmy Claussen?' I smile at him.

He frowns. 'Yes. How did you know?'

'We were talking to your mom at the Pond. She's very proud of you.'

'Yeah, right.'

'No, really. She is so proud of you. She said you did the right thing in coming home from Stanford. No match for Duncan, is it?'

He sighs. 'What can I getcha?'

Yugi pipes up first. 'I'll have two Bing Burgers and a Boppity Boppity strawbingy milkshake.' Jimmy writes it down.

'I'll have a Stanford salad... I mean, a Caesar salad.' His face turns red.

'Jeri,' my mom cautions without looking up from her menu.

'I'll have the fish bangs,' Dad says and hands the menu back to him.

'And I'll have a piece of pepperoni Bingnanza,' Mom says.

Soon, Jimmy returns with our orders on a brown plastic tray. He carefully sets the drinks and then places our food in front of us. I can smell that he has tried to disguise

140

the smell of the fast food with cologne, but the mixture makes my stomach lurch. I grimace and he notices.

'Just let me know if you need anything else.' He says this in a way like it is the last thing in the world that he wants to happen.

We watch him walk away from us and then Dad asks, 'What was our favorite part of the day?'

Yugi launches into a minute by minute, play by play of his day with Little Richard. All details are considered both necessary and crucial. With great glee, he details the soaking of his sister but fails to mention the extended middle finger. I stick my tongue out at him. Jimmy arrives with the check soon after Yugi stops speaking. We have only been dining for ten minutes, but Bing Bing's wants to keep their patronage moving, I guess. That's why it's called fast food.

'How about you, Jeri?'

'I found something interesting today.'

'A boy?' Dad responds with a smile.

'Let's not start that again.'

'Sorry. So, what is it?'

I produce my crossword puzzle book.

Yugi drops his head onto his forearms. Some of his hair falls into his catsup. 'Ugh, those stupid crosswords,' he mumbles into his lap.

I ignore him. 'Doesn't it seem really strange to anyone else that a 1970's puzzle book is in the middle of all Grandpa and Grandma's relics? I mean, it makes no sense to have pictures of Nazis, an Iron Cross, foreign money plastered onto a lampshade, and then a Barbie book? Right?'

'I guess I hadn't really thought about it,' Dad says with mouth full of fish bangs, which are, as far as I can tell, the equivalent of hamburger - all the leftover bits ground up, deep fried and slapped onto a desiccated bun.

'I was paging through the book and I began to notice a few strange things.' I opened the book and showed them my notes.

Mom leaned forward. Her eyes opened wide. 'Garage?'

'Interesting, isn't it?'

By the time we finish our meal, it's almost nine o'clock. The drive is short. We all feel slightly nauseous after consuming Johnny's fare, but nothing prepares us for when we turn onto our street.

There are flashing lights outside our house.

Police.

And an ambulance.

As we pull up outside the house, a police officer holds up his hand to stop us. Dad rolls down his window. 'What's going on? Tell us! This is our house.'

The police officer shines his flashlight through the windows. He sees us kids in the back but doesn't smile. 'Sir, if you could step out of the car, please.'

'But officer...'

'It would help me, sir, if we could speak privately.'

'I want to hear this too,' Mom says and unbuckles her seatbelt. My parents meet them in front of the car. Yugi and I watch as the officer explains something in the headlights. Mom covers her mouth, frightened.

'What's happening?' Yugi's face is white.

'I don't know, Yug.' I look at the house - there are lights on inside. Someone must have broken in.

Mom and Dad return to the car and the police officer allows us to park in our driveway.

'What happened?' I lean forward between their seats.

Face hardened, Dad's jaw jumps and rolls as he clenches his teeth. Mom has tears in her eyes. 'They've broken into our house.'

'Did they take anything? Is our stuff gone?'

'I don't know yet, but that's not the worst of the news.'

'Oh no.' I am worried at the tears in Mom's eyes.

'Dongle tried to stop them.'

'He's not dead, is he?' I can feel hysteria rising.

'Thankfully, no, but he's been stabbed. It's not bad, but he is very shaken.'

Poor Dongle. I can feel my own tears forming. I don't want to cry, but I can't help it.

Our house has suddenly become an imposing figure. Its character has turned from welcoming residence to a foreboding entity. A few police officers stand near the front door. One is writing a few things down on a notepad. Across the street, a crowd has gathered to watch.

Mom puts her arm around my shoulder and pulls me towards her.

We follow Dad and Yugi to the back of the house and I suddenly remember Maximus. Running past my brother and dad, I open the back gate just in time to see another police officer coming out the back door. She is clad in a dark blue uniform and her hair is tied up tightly in a bun. She smiles at me, and I point to the cage and she nods.

The smell is back: she must have passed out when all the excitement occurred. Now that she's alert, when she sees me, she climbs up the fence. I lift the lid and pull her out. Immediately, she runs up my arm to my neck. We are both, I think, comforted by the closeness.

I turn my gaze to Donald's house. The Berry's lights are on but no one is there. The ambulance sits halfway between their house and ours. The police officer from the front approaches us again. He stares at the possum on my shoulder but does not say anything.

'Mr. and Mrs. Walker, we just need to get a statement from you.'

Dad nods and we all walk to the house together.

'We were at the Pond today. We left at nine o'clock this morning, ate at Johnny Bing Bings and just returned.'

'Do you have any ideas about the break in?'

'No,' Dad responds sternly.

The officer gestures with his pad at the back door. 'The glass was broken and they entered there. Your neighbor, Mr. Berry, must have heard the commotion and came over to investigate. His wife called the police when she couldn't find him. We will have someone come to clean up the... clean up in a few moments.'

'How bad is it?' Mom asks.

'He was stabbed in the thigh and beaten. Thankfully, no major blood vessels, but he's lost some blood.'

'Is he still in the ambulance?'

'Yes,' the officer nods, 'but he's being taken to the hospital for observation. We'll get his statement tomorrow.'

Dad and Mom both nod gravely.

'Can we go in now?' Mom asks.

He nods and takes a deep breath. 'It's a depressing world when nice people like you get taken advantage of.'

'Thank you, officer.'

The police have mostly cleared out of the house when we ascend the back steps. Not all the glass has been swept up. It crunches under our feet. As we hit the top step, I've completely forgotten that Maximus is still on my shoulder. 'Can Maximus come inside, Mom? Just for a little bit?'

'I suppose,' she replies distractedly.

Mom leads into the living room, but it's not just a mess. It's a disaster.

All the stacks are gone. All the documents. All the photos. All the notes. Everything that seemed to be foreign has been removed. The only things that are left are the objects from the garage, but they have been broken or shattered. The appliances have been smashed, the lampshade is ripped and the money is gone. Even my old doll house, ironically, a Barbie house, is in multiple pieces in the corner.

A true sense of violation overcomes us all.

And then anger.

I can see my Dad's wrath. I can see my Mom's rage. And I feel it palpably.

These people will pay.

Chapter 21 Down:
Infamous (9)

My intention had been to sift through piles of Nazi war documents and photos, but instead, I hop on my bike and ride. I feel intensely disoriented. What was, as of a week ago, just a normal, small-town existence for me, has been turned every which way, upside down and sideways. Our home, which housed a decent family of four, and one possum, is now a shell of immaculate deception. I am not as distressed about the break in as I am the break from reality.

I stop at Pine Point and drop Gershwin on her side. The nurse at the front door greets me. 'Hi, Jeri.' She is surprised. I can read it in her eyes. 'I heard about your house last night, or I saw it on the late news anyway. Is everyone okay?'

'Yes, we're okay.'

'Did they catch the people who did it?'

'Not yet.'

'I hope they do.'

'Thanks.'

Cleared at Checkpoint Charlie, I make my way down the hallway, right-left-right. Mrs. Williams is forcing her way down the middle oblivious to any other walkers. She has a half-smile on her face - I think. Mrs. Williams had a stroke quite a while ago, and even though she's relearned how to walk, smiling has posed the bigger problem.

'Good morning, Mrs. Williams.'

She looks at me as if trying to place my face. She cannot. 'Hello.' She continues on her journey, but I can hear her mumbling to herself. I feel sorry for her - for all of them. This menagerie of humanity once vibrant, now not. The healthy come to wander between the cages, some bringing food, staring, pointing, but they can leave. When they are released from captivity, something amazing happens to them. They come alive. I love taking Grandpa out for a walk, so I'm going to invite him out of the confines today. Maybe we'll walk up to the cafe.

Grandpa is in his chair in the bay window when I enter. Grandma stands by the bookshelf mumbling. She smiles when she sees me, but it's a frown at the same time. Grandpa Walt stirs. Maybe it's a draft of air from the open door, or a noise from the hallway. Either way, his eyes pop open.

'Hi Gramps.'

'Jeri.' His eyes are full of happiness. 'I'm glad you came. I was worried about you.'

'You were watching the news last night?'

'I wanted to call you, but I still can't figure out these bloomin' cell phones.' In his hands is an archaic cellphone. 'I am supposed to be able to text you, but I just can't quite get my mind around it.'

'Don't hurt yourself, Grandpa.' I approach my grandmother slowly to hug her. It's very much the same way I approach Maximus. Too quickly and I might scare her, and her claws might come out. We tentatively embrace. I feel her tremble. Through muscle memory, she encloses me in her arms and hugs me tight. This is the longest she has hugged me in ages. She still doesn't let me go. I can't see her face.

Finally, I pull away from her. Her face is blank, but tears have formed in the corners of her eyes.

Grandpa says her memories are leaking when that happens. His eyes are also moist. Something about this moment seems pivotal.

'Grandpa, do you want to go for a walk and get a cup of coffee?'

His eyes light up and he rubs his hands together. 'Oooh, that sounds good.' He checks Grandma who is now staring out the window. 'Iris, I'm going to go get Stacy and she'll sit with you. Jeri and I are going out for a little bit.' She doesn't respond.

After Grandpa extricates himself from the chair, he puts on his Velcro walking shoes. I ask him if he wants his cane, but he flushes that suggestion away with a swipe of his hand. We enter the hallway where Grandpa finds a nurse, informing her that he would like to go for a walk.

After signing out, we leave Pine Point through the front doors. My grandpa tilts his head towards the sky and closes his eyes. He looks like a prisoner of war released from captivity.

We walk slowly; our conversation travels at the same speed. I ask him about Grandma, which I think is frustrating for him. Everyone asks about her.

'She's fine. How about you? Was anything stolen?'

I pause. How should we proceed? Do we forge ahead? The great reveal?

'Yeah. Most of the stuff from the garage was taken.' He is startled. He tried to cover it, but it was too late.

'The news said that they broke into the house, not the garage.'

'All the stuff from the garage was in the house. We were sorting it.'

'What? Why would you do that?'

'We were protecting it. I think some other people thought it was more valuable to them than us.'

I can tell there are so many things that he wants to ask, questions are written on his face and behind his eyes.

His walking pace quickens. 'Why did you bring them inside?'

'Because the garage was broken into about three weeks ago.'

He stops.

'Grandpa, tell me what's going on. What are they looking for?'

'I don't know what you're taking about.'

'Grandpa...'

'I can't.'

'Why not? Why can't you tell me?'

'Because you're a child. You're... innocent in all of this... you always have been.'

'What does that mean?'

'Jeri,' Grandpa puts his hands on my shoulders, 'this never should have happened. Any of this.' He motions around the city of Duncan. 'We should have been more careful, but...'

My heart is racing. 'But what?'

He takes a deep breath and holds it. He can't hold my eyes and turns away from me. 'Let's get our cup of coffee and talk about what we can.'

The last few blocks pass in silence. I can tell that Grandpa is attempting to formulate a plan for what and how much he will tell me. As we enter the cafe, the door jingles above us. I don't like coffee, but I'll drink it if I have to.

We sit at a far corner table, and I wonder if this is the way it was fifty years ago for spies: recessed corners of cafes staring out into busy streets, the enemy, unseen and unknown, perhaps just seats away.

I sip my coffee and cringe. Even with the sugar, the bitterness puckers my face. I can't understand how people can drink more than one of these per day.

'You don't have to drink that, you know.'

'I will,' I say. I want to be an adult - adults drink coffee and pretend to like it.

'Was anyone hurt?'

'Dongle tried to stop them. They stabbed him. He's okay, but shaken.'

Grandpa's jaw flexes just like Dad's. I see Grandpa as an older Dad now.

'Who is trying to do this, Grandpa? You know, don't you?'

'Jeri...' he starts then stops. 'It's such a weird world. It always has been. I don't know where I can start.'

'The beginning. Please. I only know part of it.'

'What do you know?'

'The men who came to our house a few weeks ago were agents of some sort. They broke into our garage and took some briefcases.' I can see him smirk slightly. 'My Mom smirked too.' He stopped.

'After they broke into the garage, we decided to bring everything in and sort through it in case there was something that could help us understand.'

'Did you find anything?'

'I'll get to that in a second,' I say. 'Mom and Dad told us about your... previous occupation. I can't believe you've been able to hide it from us all these years.'

He leans into me. 'It's not because we wanted to deceive you, Jeri.'

'I can appreciate that. But as of yesterday, we were surrounded by tons of World War II stuff. Everything was so jumbled, but Mom pieced together some things about Mengele,' Grandpa uses his hands to quiet my voice, 'and a very famous painting.'

He looks surprised. Real surprise. 'What?'

'Yeah, on one of the documents, there was a missing painting - a very famous one - by Raphael. The last anyone heard, it was in the possession of a man named Hans Frank.'

'Nasty man. Horrible.' Grandpa's distaste is obvious.

'I looked it up. He was the former Governor General of Poland. He had a hand in Auschwitz, Birkenau, Treblinka.' He nods. 'Frank sent the Raphael to the Hitler Museum, but eventually had it returned to him, and why not - it's a Raphael.'

'Hmm.'

'Why wouldn't Grandma tell you?'

'I wasn't always told the finer details of her missions.'

'It's pretty impressive what you and Grandma got up to. All over the world - even South America.'

'What do you know about it?'

'Only that you took Grandma there to hunt Nazi war criminals. Who were you looking for?'

His face eased. It seemed as if the division between us was being torn down, brick by brick. *Mr. Walker, tear down this wall!* 'Any of them - all of them. Rauff, Stangl, Schwammberger. No one could understand why they were being protected. First Argentina, then Chile.'

'Who were you and Grandma looking for most? Mengele?'

He nods. 'Mengele was considered the top prize, but any of them would have been a close second.'

I made a mental note to investigate some of these others.

'We actually found Mengele's ranch. We couldn't get close enough to learn too much, but we saw his face.'

'We saw the pictures. He had a few children, didn't he?'

'Yes, a son from his first marriage, Rolf, who supported him his whole life. We were in Brazil when Rolf visited. That was in 1977, I think. We were on the beach pretending to be tourists.'

'Where was Dad? He was already born, wasn't he?'

'Yes,' Grandpa said shamefacedly, 'he was on the beach with us. He completed our disguise. To my great shame, we took our son within twenty yards of the Angel of Death - Josef Mengele.'

'What happened next?'

'After Mengele died, we moved to the U.S. to raise your dad, here in Duncan. It's the house that you now live in.'

'What?' I'm flabbergasted. 'You lived in our house!'

'This must all be shocking for you, I'm sure.'

'Yes,' I say.

'The government gave us that house. Until the time we moved to Germany, that was our home and the garage was a convenient storage spot.

'And now we come to find out that it's not the German Fascists but American Fascists who break the law.'

Grandpa frowns. 'You have to understand, Jeri, governments don't do things willy-nilly. There are many other spinning plates which affect everything else. The common public sees almost nothing. Imagine if the American people knew everything that was going on in the government. There would be chaos.'

'Maybe we need some chaos.'

'Don't be naïve, Jeri.'

Chapter 21 Down:

My hackles raise. 'For what purpose is the CIA breaking into our house to steal documents and photos from decades ago?'

'I don't know, Jeri,' his voice is calm. 'My job is, and was, not to know, but to act.'

'I need you to act now, Grandpa, before anyone else gets hurt.'

His face reddens. 'I can't.'

'Yes, you can. You have to. It might be Yugi or me next.'

Grandpa's breath catches. 'Don't say that.'

'What is it?'

His voice lowers to a whisper. 'That's how we ended up back in Duncan after Europe.'

'Tell me, Grandpa. Mom and Dad won't say anything...'

'Jeri...' he pleads, 'if I tell you, bad things could happen. I'd never forgive myself. They told us if we ever...'

'Who, Grandpa, who is it?'

He sighs. 'The Neo-Nazis.'

'What are you talking about?'

'Jeri, we had to get out of the business because Grandma made a mistake. A large one. That's why we are here in Duncan, in a nursing home.'

'You're not making any sense, Grandpa. What mistake did she make?'

He sighs. 'Let's go to the park.'

We sit in the park. Grandpa leans back on the bench but we no longer look at each other. As I survey the surroundings, I look for Neo-Nazi spies, but all I can see are

Duncanites eating ice cream cones and wandering around the village.

'Tell me, Grandpa.' I speak without moving my lips in case anyone is looking through a telescoped camera.

'What are you doing?' He asks.

'I don't want anyone to read my lips.'

'Good Lord, Jeri, you've seen too many movies.'

'Isn't this how spies communicate?'

Finally, he laughs. 'If they really wanted to listen in, I'm pretty sure reading lips would be last on the list of methods.'

'Go ahead. I'm ready for the whole story.'

'This will take a little bit of time and I don't want to stay away from Grandma too long.'

'Okay.'

'In 2012, we were living in Europe; you guys were in Herzegovina; Grandma and I were living in Poland.'

Poland! That was one of the piles!

'Grandma's dossier on Nazi war criminals was enormous, but we were running out of time. Most of the monsters had already died. Some of their children were still alive, but you can't prosecute them for their parents' crimes. Many truly hated their parents. Others deluded themselves believing their fathers were completely innocent. The stories we could tell...'

'When we moved to Poland, we'd been in espionage for thirty-five years. I thought to myself, *This is the last time.* Grandma and I were in our 60's. Lots of things in the business had changed, and to be honest, I could tell some things were going on with Grandma.'

Grandpa's eyes shift slightly and he looks at his hands. They are shaking. 'One day, when we were living in Warsaw, there was a knock at the door. Grandma had been

154

investigating some connections with Treblinka, the notorious concentration camp near the eastern border of Poland. When the knock came, I was surprised. Nobody really knew we were there. Through the keyhole I saw Grandma looking frightened. When I opened the door, she was shoved into me. These four skinheads began speaking in German and shouting at us to stand up, 'Stand up! Faster or we will kill you!' Grandma was crying, sobbing, her head was pressed into my shoulder.'

"You are American spies!' He shouted.'

"No, no, we are an old couple here visiting family.' I said.'

"She told us,' he pointed at Grandma.'

"She told you what? What is it?'

"She told us that you work for the American government. You are looking for Nazis."

"That's ridiculous."

'The man punched me in the face - this is while Grandma's face was in my shoulder - and we both fell to the floor. The Skinhead kicked Grandma in the back.'

"Stop! Stop! We're an old couple. What do you want?"

'His expression was pure hatred. 'We followed her to Treblinka. She was talking to people she shouldn't have."

"She is confused.' I said.'

"She told us that you are after Mengele."

"Who?"

'He kicked me in the ribs and I felt one of them break. 'Herr Mengele is a hero. If you continue, we will destroy you.' And then he stopped and put his face closer to mine, 'and your family - your son, his wife and their children."

'Then the leader said, 'Either you leave the country and take your family with you, or we will kill all of you. Do you understand?''

'I nodded. I couldn't believe they didn't kill us.'

'After trashing the apartment, they left. Grandma kept apologizing. They had kidnapped her and tortured her.'

'So you had to leave Europe because they threatened us?'

Grandpa nodded. 'Your parents never wanted you to find out about that - they didn't want you to look at her differently. It's not as if they could tell you that she was a spy, either. It was a convenient tale for us to blame living at Pine Point on dementia. But it is also a way that they keep an eye on us. If we try to leave, something happens to you guys.'

'But Grandpa, something is happening to us. The CIA broke into our house, remember? Shouldn't we try to fight back? I mean, Mom and Dad are like spies, right? They know how to blend in and hide. Isn't that how they were trained?'

Grandpa smiles and shakes his head. 'Because they had you two, and wanted to keep you safe. Your dad was a dispatch officer - ran the phones. Nothing like what Grandma was doing,'

'Wow,' I say. That's all I can say. We live in Oklahoma because Grandma got dementia and broke under torture. If that hadn't happened, we might still be in Europe. 'Grandpa, can I ask you a question.'

'I don't think it makes any difference now.'

'Did Grandma have a codename or something, you know like The Jackal or something like that.'

Grandpa began to laugh. 'You know what, she did. But it was just something that the Agency called her. Not really a codename.'

'What was it?'

'Barbie.'

My heart stops. 'What did you say?'

'Barbie. She was a stunning blond woman with a 1970's figure and a computer for a mind. For different assignments, we would dress her a different character or profession. She was an amazing actress. Sometimes when she would come home at night, I didn't know who she... Jeri, what's wrong?'

I reach to my back pocket. My Barbie book is there. I pull it out and Grandpa's face turns white.

'Where did you get that?'

'It was in the bottom of one of the trunks.'

'Why do you have it?'

'You know how much I like to do crosswords.'

He is speechless, but regains his voice quickly. 'That was Grandma's'

'How do you know?'

'Because I've seen it before - a long time ago.' He studies me. 'It's not just a crossword, is it?'

'I don't think so, Grandpa. The spaces write out the word 'Garage.' Was there something else in the Garage we are supposed to find? Do you think it was taken away?'

'I don't know,' he holds his hands out for the book. I give it to him. 'I hope not.'

'But what is this book trying to tell us?' I show him the spaces and the crossed-out lines.

'Good Lord,' he says. 'I know how to decipher this, I think.'

'How?' My heart is beating hard.

'We have to go back to the nursing home. I've got something to show you.'

Chapter 22 Across:
Energizing (11)

We enter their room, breathless. Grandma is standing by the bookshelf. Grandpa approaches, kisses her on the cheek and reaches behind her to grab some crossword puzzle books. 'She loves these things just like you do.'

We sit down at the table. Grandma decides to join us, but her eyes are locked onto the books.

'I think you should take these with you.'

'But Grandpa, I still have so many questions.'

He shakes his head and looks at the ceiling and around. I get his meaning. Someone might be listening. This isn't old person paranoia.

'I will.'

'Can I see your crossword puzzle one more time?' I hand it to him. 'You can tell it was hers,' he says.

'How?'

'Look at the front cover.' He points to the title. 'She's shaded the word 'Barbie' and put a slight line through the 'w' in the word 'crossword.' Can you see that?'

'I saw it, but it didn't mean anything until today. Do you think Grandma was trying to reveal something in this?' I look at her. She is smiling at me.

'I hope so.'

'All right, Grandpa, I'll give it a shot. Thanks for the great talk.' I stand and hug him and then repeat the process with Grandma. Her face is vacant but beautiful.

When I get home, I see that my mom is on the phone. My dad has gone to work, whatever that means now. Yugi is in the living room either attempting to, or pretending to, fix some of things that were broken in last night's theft. He looks up at me and sniffs.

The crossword puzzles are recent ones. It appears that Grandma may have been attempting to exercise her mental memory by stimulating it with word games, but I can see by the lack of completeness, she is struggling.

Opening the first, I leaf through until astonishingly I see that there is one page with cross-outs like my Barbie book.

36 Across: *Greek who introduced the question-and-answer method*

40 Across: *Disappear like Alka Seltzer tablets*

53 Across: *More than off-color*

77 Across: *NBC show based on a Thomas Harris novel*

89 Across: *Precipitous*

7 Down: *Roman poet*

12 Down: *Lobster portion*

45 Down: *Pope after Sergius II*

80 Down: *The Big Easy briefly*

r e r b r m o o e

In numerical order: m o r e o r b e r. *More rober? Broomerer?*

These don't seem to make sense. It is as stumping as the Barbie book. I take out the second book and repeat the process.

21 Across: *Prince Andrew's title*

34 Across: *Go between*

54 Across: *Linger*

35 Down: *Memorable mission*

160

Chapter 22 Across:

37 Down: ~~Trespassed~~
64 Down: ~~Armorial~~ bearings

e g g o t l

Finally! A word! *Toggle* But what does it mean? And it makes no sense to the other crosswords. What's the key? Where is the primer?

'What are you doing, Jeri?' Mom asks

'I'm looking at crossword puzzles.'

'You mean you're solving them.'

'No, I'm looking at them.'

Her interest is piqued. 'Where did you get these two?'

'Grandpa.'

'When was this?' She is suspicious already.

'This morning. Mom,' I hold up my hands, 'don't be preemptively angry. Let me explain.'

'Jeri, we talked about this! Why are you dragging them back into it!'

'Grandpa told me. About everything. How Grandma spilled the beans and almost got us all killed.'

Mom's face turns ashen. 'He shouldn't have told you that.'

'Why not? Why can't I know these things? I'm old enough to know. I want to help.'

'It's not about age, Jeri, don't you see.' She tenderly rests her hands on my cheeks. 'You and Yugi are the most important things in our life. We're happy here, aren't we?' It's as if she's asking the question to herself as well as me.

Are we?

'Look,' I mirror the hands-on-cheeks gesture to her, 'life hasn't really turned out like any of the Walkers would

161

have preferred. Frankly, I think life owes us all a great big IOU. Grandpa and Grandma didn't deserve to end up in a nursing home; you guys couldn't travel; Yugi and I missed out on our history. Come on, it's genetic – it's in our blood. Grandma was only a few years older than I am when she went to Argentina for the first time.'

We both remove our hands. 'I'd say there is a big difference between a nineteen-year-old in the 60's and a fifteen-year-old in the 21st century.'

'That's unfair, Mom.'

'What about Yugi? He's only ten.'

'Have you seen him, Mom? As much as I hate to say it, he's as quick as I am. He just has to be *focused*.'

'HE'S TEN YEARS OLD! I don't think you're getting this, Jeri. Maybe if you guys were at least five years older - at least.'

I am quiet, not quite wanting to add the next sentence, but we've already alit on the shores of Full Disclosure. 'Why were our lives worth risking when we were little and not now?'

Mom's mouth hangs open and then flops back and forth with *ung buah ahyuh* sounds. Eventually, she shakes her head. 'I don't know what to say. I just think the difference now is that we could control you when you were small and now we can't.'

'Especially Yugi.'

She laughs. 'No, especially you. You have a gift, Jerusalem, a power about you. You've always had it. It scares me and inspires me. But if we're going to do this, we *must* harness that power. Use it for good and not to go out on your own - like pedaling over to Grandpa and Grandma's without telling us. Got it?'

'Understood.'

'Now,' Mom's voice is shaky, 'what else have you found in the crossword puzzle?'

I show her my work and the words spelled by putting together the crossed-out letters. She sits beside me and I begin to read the clues out. 'Maybe there is something in the words themselves?'

'*Greek who introduced the question-and-answer method.*'

'What is the answer?' Mom asked.

I shrugged. 'If I knew how many spaces there were and...'

'Oh, Jeri, just open up to the answers in the back of the book.'

Oh yeah, like duh. I flipped to the solution and quickly get the answers to the clues, and I put them side by side in a graph.

36 Across: *Greek who introduced the question-and-answer method*   Socrates

40 Across: *Disappear like Alka Seltzer tablets*   Dissolve

53 Across: *More than off-color*   Lewd

77 Across: *NBC show based on a Thomas Harris novel*   Hannibal

89 Across: *Precipitous*   Steep

7 Down: *Roman poet*   Ovid

12 Down: *Lobster portion*   Claw

45 Down: *Pope after Sergius II*
Leo IV
80 Down: *The Big Easy briefly*
Nola
21 Across: *Prince Andrew's title*
Duke of York
34 Across: *Go between*
Agent
54 Across: *Linger*
Dally
35 Down: *Memorable mission*
Alamo
37 Down: *Trespassed*
Invaded
64 Down: *Armorial bearings*
Heraldry

And my Barbie book

46 Across: *Goldsmith's The _____ of Wakefield*
Vicar
70 Across: *Kissin' makeup?*
Lipstick
80 Across: *Item on a rod*
Towel
109 Across: *Charlatan*
Liar
11 Down: *Subject of the biography* Wired
Belushi
18 Down: *Raises one's spirits?*
Toast
81 Down: *They're called on account of rain*
Cabs

Chapter 22 Across:

83 Down: *Deride publicly*
Pillory

None of the answers seem to fit together. Yugi whistles as he looks over our shoulders. He hums a non-melodious tune, tonal fidgeting, and it annoys me. He sniffs again.

'I don't know,' Mom says. 'Maybe there is nothing.'

'There's got to be something here.'

Yugi points to the book at the scratches. 'Maybe it's not the letter that's scratched out, but where it's positioned? Have you tried the location of the scratched-out letter and transferred it to the answer? I mean, if you've already done the crosswords, it would be easy to pick out the letters you needed.' He keeps humming.

I'm astounded. Why didn't I think of that?

We try the shortest one first. F A L M I Y. Disappointed, I see that doesn't work either.

'Try doing it in numeric order of the clues.' Yugi says.

I'm not convinced, but I do it anyway. Suddenly, a word is revealed.

Family.

'Yugi!' I exclaim. 'You're a genius!' I try to hug him. He definitely does not like that and pulls away from me.

'I know,' he cringes while retreating.

'Do you want to do the next one?' I ask him.

'Sure.' He completes the second puzzler from Grandpa.

ILOVEWALT.

Mom's breath sucks in. A tear comes to her eye. Grandma is speaking from beneath her illness. She loves her husband and her family.

Oh, Grandma. God bless you.

Finally, the last puzzle. I'll take this one myself. The Barbie book is open in front of me and I am aware of how excited I am.

I write it out.

My Mom and I look at each other. We are astounded.

Chapter 23 Down:
What comes before a main? (10)

The Camrillac rumbles into the driveway and my dad steps out of the car. As he ambles to the house, we watch him through the front window. His face is tense and excited. Yugi knocks on the window and smiles. As he opens the door, Yugi rushes and pounces almost bowling my dad over.

'Dad! I figured it out!'

'What is it? What did you figure out?' He is dragged into the kitchen where Mom sits at the table. Her face is in her cupped hand. I bounce back and forth between my feet.

'Come on, Dad!'

'All right,' he says after he sets his briefcase on the counter, 'lay it on me.'

I describe my morning's journey to Grandpa Walt. At first my dad has the same reaction as my mom and wants to chastise me, but by the end, he waits with bated breath for the big reveal.

'And? So where are we going?'

'The clue reads, 'Back Wall.' Combined with the other clue in the crossword puzzle book, it must mean there is something in, or on, the back wall of the Garage. Come on, let's go look!' Yugi and I race ahead of our parents who walk swiftly behind us.

Yugi and I wrestle with the Garage door. Eventually, it gives way, and we race to the back wall. After searching every inch, we knock on the 2 x 4's, we search for hollow recesses, anywhere that might contain something that Grandma might have hidden. Frustrated, we repeat our inspection, but we can't find anything.

'It has to be here.' I feel an impotent dejection. 'But what are we supposed to be looking for?'

'I don't know,' Dad says. 'If only Grandma would have said, 'There's a secret key in a magic box behind the wall.''

I gasp. *Behind the wall.*

'Dad, that's it! We're looking on the wrong side of the back wall. What if it's on the outside?'

He raises an eyebrow.

We race around to the outside. The wall has white/grey siding all the way up to the eaves. Where the eave joins the top, there is a gap, but there not much space. Dad lifts Yugi up to push his hand into the dark holes, but even Yugi is hesitant about putting his hand into things he can't see.

Where is it? What are we missing?

I run back inside the house and get my Barbie book. We must have missed something.

Is it the circled number six? Could it be that easy?

'Dad, lift me up to the sixth hole from the left.'

'Did you find something?'

I hope so.'

We walk to the left side and count under the eaves to number six. Dad grunts loudly as he puts me on his shoulders. I slap him on his head. He's faking it, I know, but it's been a long time since he's carried me on his shoulders.

I reach up to the empty space and cautiously stick my hand into the hole. Unfortunately, Yugi thinks it would be hilarious to shout, 'AAAAAAAGH' at that moment and I shriek. Dad almost drops me.

'Yugi, you imbecile! Why can't you just grow up?'

He giggles but sees that no one else is laughing. He pouts and goes to Mom who puts an arm around his shoulders.

'Don't comfort him,' I say. 'He needs to learn that not everything is a joke.'

'And you,' Mom responds, 'have to learn that some things are funny.'

'Can we hurry?' Dad insists. 'My shoulders are beginning to spasm.'

'Take me back to that hole.' Once again, I reach in. I feel around inside and then farther back, just at the edge of my reach, I feel an object. 'There's something here!'

I wrap my hand around it and pull it out.

I have no idea what it is.

But Mom and Dad do.

Dad tries to let me down to the ground gently, but his legs are about to give out. As he bends the last distance, I am dropped unceremoniously and tumble to the ground. Yugi laughs and looks at Mom for permission to continue doing so. She smiles, so he does. I hold the object up in front of them.

'What is it?'

'Let's go in the house, shall we?'

The object is a small box about six inches across. It is very dusty and looks quite old. It is pistachio-colored with a yellowed label. Grandma has written on it, *Barbie's Memories.*

We sit at the kitchen table, four heads staring at the little box. I push it to Dad who shakes it open. It looks like an old movie camera reel.

'What is it, Dad?'

'It's called a microfilm. They came in very handy back in the 70's. You can cram thousands of documents and photos onto these things and they last forever - much longer than flash drives or computer hard drives. When the computer has gone the way of the dodo, these bad boys,' he taps the reel, 'will still be around.'

'Is that like spy film?' Yugi asks.

'That's exactly what this is.'

'But how do we look at it?' I ask. 'It's not like we can plug it into a USB port.'

'We're off to the library tomorrow, kids. That's one of the beautiful things about living in Duncan. I'm sure we can find a dusty, unused microfilm reader.'

'What do we do tonight then?' Yugi asks.

Mom and Dad share a look. 'We tell ghost stories.'

For the first time in forever, we make dinner together. Yugi and Dad work on the appetizers, Mom on the main meal and I on dessert. In the small kitchen, it seems like chaos, but in the midst of the noise and confusion is a delicious confluence of smells, lemon and myrtle, almond and cinnamon. There is laughter and singing. Dad stands behind Mom, hands on her hips, tasting the broth over her shoulder. Yugi is wearing a much-too-large apron even though his part in cooking is done. Life seems pretty good.

After dinner, Mom locates a photo album, one that I've never seen before.

'This was the only vacation we ever took there, wasn't it?'

The mood changes. 'Yes,' Dad says slowly.

'It's time to tell the rest of the story.' Mom's face is a mixture of excitement and trepidation. 'If you want to stop, we will, but there is no sugar-coating this.'

When the grandfather clock chimes midnight, I am surprised. Mom's stories of horror were told in a clinical, passionless way. Due to Mom's heritage, the stories of mass-murderers of her people ('Our people,' Dad corrected her), we felt an intense connection to the story. When they spoke about their time in Israel with generations of Holocaust survivors, they were overwhelmed.

I asked my parents what the word 'Holocaust' actually meant. I've only ever heard it used with regards to World War II extermination camps.

'The Old Testament,' Mom says, 'is about *our* people.' She stressed the word 'our' which made Dad smile. 'There are swaths of writings about the correct sacrifices to be burned for God.'

I was beginning to see.

'The word for the whole burnt offering, not the ones cut up into pieces, was '*olah.'* The Greek translation of the whole burnt offering was a mixture of two words *holos* - whole and *kaustos* - burned.'

'Oh, no,' I began to understand.

'It wasn't just that individuals were burned up in the crematoria across Europe, but the whole Jewish community was on the verge of incineration. Every Jew was affected somehow.'

'They must be very angry.' Yugi's whispered.

Mom nodded. 'Back in the 1950's, after Israel was 'granted' nationhood status, one of the great problems was that the world was in danger of purposely forgetting what happened during the Holocaust, so the new state of Israel created the Mossad - the equivalent of the CIA. One of the Mossad's goals was to track down high ranking escaped Nazis. Some Nazi officials, like Eichmann and Mengele, either fled or were helped to escape to South America.'

'Wait a minute,' Yugi stopped her, 'why would they be *helped* to escape to South America?'

'Because these men carried with them certain useful 'talents' for dictatorships. Imagine Argentina getting

171

their hands on a man who had invested a lifetime torturing people for information.'

Yugi shivered.

'By 1960, much of the world was shifting away from the Holocaust and beginning to think about things like racial relations. The plight of the Jewish survivors faded. Irael did not want these men to escape justice, so they hunted them down for their crimes against humanity.'

'Did they find them all?' I asked.

'No,' Mom responded as she handled the mug of hot chocolate in her hands. 'Not all, but some. In 1960, Adolf Eichmann, the architect of the Holocaust, was kidnapped from Argentina and flown back to Israel for a trial.'

'Why didn't they just... uh... eliminate him in Argentina?' I asked.

'Some things,' Mom's voice trembled, 'need to be publicly executed before they can be privately finished. Eichmann's trial was a media sensation. The gruesome stories told by survivors and victims of the concentration camps were fodder for a world that couldn't quite believe that a government could be so inhuman.'

'Once Eichmann was convicted and sentenced to death, they hanged him. Immediately after his body was cremated - a beautiful irony - they dumped his ashes in a bucket, put it on a boat and drove past Israeli international waters where the Mossad unceremoniously dumped his remains in the ocean. Then, rinsing the bucket out, they drove back in.'

'Wow,' I whispered. 'That's quite a story.'

Chapter 23 Down:

After they tuck us in, I cannot sleep, so I creep down the hallway to the top of the stairs. Thankfully, I avoid the creaking step. From here, I can hear their lowered voices.

'Are we really thinking about doing this?' Mom asks.

'Do we have a choice?'

'There's always a choice, Kevin.'

'Not making a decision is still a decision, right?' Dad's voice sounds harsh.

'What should we do?'

'Maybe we should call them.'

'Who?' Mom asks.

I lean in closer, but the board creaks. Silence ensues and I know they are listening for me. I hear one of my parents get up from the sofa and walk towards the stairs. As silently as possible, I race back to my bed and throw the covers up and over my head. No one comes to check on me. But as I lie in the darkness of my bed, I wonder: *Who are they going to call?*

The Duncan Public Library is, in my opinion, an architectural disaster. It looks like a toddler has been playing with Legos and put it together with cylinders, rectangles, triangles and squares. Two white columns stand sentry behind us as we wait for the doors to whoosh open.

At 9:30, the doors are unlocked, and we stream in with the other morning readers and Wi-Fi users to the lighted atrium. To our right are the book rooms. To the left are rows of tables, both circular and triangular, with hard plastic chairs. We approach the front desk where a young woman, decked out in a DPL striped shirt and dark blue pants, greets us with a wide smile.

'Can I help you?'

'Yes,' my dad leans on the counter, 'I was wondering if the library has a microfilm reader.'

'A what?' I smirk. It's one of my pet peeves when people pronounce the word 'what' as if they are say '*hoowat.*'

'Microfilm.' Dad extracts the film from the pocket of his pants.

She accepts it from his hands. 'I don't think so. I mean, this must be like, really old. Like *hoowat,* from the 80's?'

'Do you think you could find someone who could tell us whether the library has a machine?'

'*Hoowat,* like an old person?'

Dad grinds his teeth. 'Yes, if age has anything to do with it.'

'Give me a minute, please.'

The girl, Dana, according to her nametag, picks up the phone. After a few *ahuhs* and *yeps* and one *for sure,* Dana lets us know that her supervisor will be with us shortly. Dana goes back to tapping away on her computer, completely disinterested in the family standing in front of her.

An identically clad woman to Dana, Sherry, approaches us. Although she is probably in her sixties, she has dyed her hair sky blue. It looks like cotton candy. Yugi stares at it and I nudge him with my elbow. He frowns up at me.

'Can I help you?' Sherry asks.

'Yes, ma'am,' Dad says. I've never actually heard him call a woman 'ma'am' before. 'We're looking for a microfilm reader.'

Her face lights up. '*Hoowhy* yes! Lord have mercy, it's been a long time since someone has asked for one. Come on, y'all, follow me.' We traipse after Sherry who leads us at a brisk pace.

We approach a room with a rectangular window in the door. After retrieving a key, Sherry unlocks it and pushes it open. 'Nobody ever uses this anymore. I've often wondered if we should just get rid of the thing. It's so large and bulky, but now I'm glad we didn't.' She flips on a light and leaves the door ajar. 'Now, do you know how to use one of these things?'

'Why, yes, we do, Sherry. Thank you,' Dad responds.

'Ya never know. I just thought I'd ask. Well, y'all have a good time with the machine. Just let me know if you need anything.'

Mom has already situated herself in front of the machine. Sherry sniffs and looks up at Dad and grins. 'The only people who know how to use these things are spies, ya know. You're not spies, are ya?'

Dad puts a finger to the side of his nose. 'That will be our little secret, Sherry.' Sherry laughs, or snorts, I'm not sure which, and whistles softly down the hallway as she leaves.

After opening the correct program, mom forwards the reel through the reader which copies it to the computer.

'Now, we wait.'

'How long?' Yugi asks.

'Judging by the length of the film, it could be an hour or two.'

'Do you mind if I do something else?' I ask.

'Go ahead.'

175

For the next hour, I browse websites about Eichmann, Mengele and Hans Frank. Eichmann, strangely, slipped right through the hands of the Allies and escaped into the countryside at the end of the war. He worked on a few farms, a grain and poultry farm before being rat-lined to South America where he assumed a new name, Ricardo Klement. Eichmann lived in a small box house in the middle of nowhere. From the picture, it looked like a way station at the end of the world. Behind the house, a dilapidated shed sat somewhere between erection and implosion. A clothesline, like a superimposed garroting wire, was hung between two rickety poles. A knee-high fence bordered the exposed, treeless property. I wondered, just briefly, how such a man as this could have ended up in a hovel like that.

For what seemed hours, I stare at the greyscale photos: Eichmann appeared to be a normal looking man, not a mass-murderer. I'm not sure what the visual prerequisites of a mass-murderer should be, but there seems to be a disconnect in my internal logic that a skinny, generally good-looking man with kind eyes, a thin nose, strong jaw and clean-shaven face could be a master of extermination. I try to conjure up feelings of hatred for him, but I don't have a true connection to him or the people he killed. His life and death mean nothing to me, except now they are indelibly tied to our mystery.

Mengele, on the other hand, has a demented glint in his eye. There is something about that little gap in his teeth and his beady expression. It seems like if he just looked at you, you would feel violated. I researched his 'experiments,' especially on twins, and I now find a stirring of hatred. Sources report that he lived out his days in Paraguay and eventually died in a swimming accident in

176

Brazil. He, too, lived under an assumed name: Wolfgang Gerhard.

Mom texts me to come back to the microfilm room. They are just packing up when I get there.

'What did you find out?'

Yugi is holding a magnifying glass up to his eye and approaches me. I swat him away.

'There wasn't as much on it as we thought. That will make it easier for us, I think.'

My parents let me drive home. We stop at the Chinese restaurant takeaway. Carrying the little white boxes with metal handles, we exit the Ka Ching and drive home. Mom spreads a blanket on the ground and the Walker family settles in for lunch. I retrieve Maximus to eat with us while Yugi checks our food with his magnifying glass looking for God knows *hoowat,* then eventually allows us to eat after giving us the okay.

'What I don't understand,' I say as I pass a piece of green pepper up to my shoulder where Maximus grabs it and begins to noisily gnaw it in her teeth, 'is how these high-ranking Nazis could have escaped with such ease. How could the Allies not have known who they were?'

'I don't think you should give Maximus your pepper,' Yugi says, 'it's full of SMG.'

'Like duh, Yugi. It's MSG. I'm fine, so she's fine.' Even so, the next bite I give her, I lick it off first. Yugi grimaces.

'It's like this, Jeri,' Dad says as he expertly engages his chopsticks to shovel rice into his mouth. It is hot, so he opens his mouth, says *aaahaaha* and blows while covering it with his wrist. He swallows and tears come to his eyes. 'It should have been easy,' he continued. 'The SS men all had numbered tattoos on the inside of their left arms. In

177

Mengele's case, though, he was so vain that he did not want to mar his body, so there was no tattoo. Eichmann, though, had his removed thus making his identification more difficult.'

'Crazy,' I say.

'These two men, Eichmann and Mengele, were considered after Hitler's inner circle, the most despicable men on the planet. It's a real tragedy they weren't found earlier.'

'Let's take a look at what you found on the microfilm today.'

Mom boots up the computer and we scroll through the photos. Excitingly, it seems like everything is in code, or at least in puzzle form. Except for one note.

One note.

Dear Whoever You Are,

I assume the book has guided you to me, so let it continue to do so. One never knows what kinds of numbers and words one might find inside.

In my house, one finds all sorts of things.

I also assume that you are on the yellow brick ratline I was, but if not, I suggest putting this small piece of history safely back where you found it and go about your business.

Now, to work...
Just follow the path. Follow my prints.
Visit the White Man to the first leg of the journey.
He will bring your case before the court.
The White Man will speak of the hotdog man whose story will send you to the second leg.

Chapter 23 Down:

The connection made between the hotdog man and the 'foul' man who fled.
> *There you will find the Angel beneath the Cross.*
> *At that intersection, the union place...*
> *You will find me.*

Finish the book, where I was unable. Pieces of me still remain.

> *Love,*
> *Barbie.*

'Well, that's certainly weird.' Mom's eyebrows are knitted. 'I suppose you should go get your Barbie crossword book.'

Maximus and I run into the house to grab it. I have stuck it between my mattresses.

As Maximus readjusts on my shoulder, I see that Yugi is eating the remnants of my lunch. It's not that I'm still hungry, but the principle of the thing. I snarl at him, but he leans away and finishes the last piece of my chicken.

'Okay, now what?' I hand the book to my mom.

'We should fill in the missing letters, shouldn't we?'

'I guess we could, but maybe we should wait. That seems like it should be the very last thing.'

Dad pulls the laptop closer to him. 'From first glance, it looks like the book will give us a few things. Why did Mom write, 'You'll never know what kinds of numbers and words?' It seems very strange to focus on numbers in a word puzzle book, doesn't it?' I nod.

He continues. 'What interests me is that strange little quip, 'In my house, one finds all sorts of things.' Considering that Grandma and Grandpa lived here, maybe

179

there are other things inside the house that we haven't found yet.'

I reach up and scratch Maximus behind her ears. She snorts. 'But where? Do we have to tear up the entire house? It could be anywhere.'

Yugi laughs.

'What's so funny?' I ask. He has sauce on his face.

'You didn't read the clue very well.'

'What do you mean?'

'I mean,' he says slowly, over-exaggerating the words, 'you didn't read the clue. You filled in a space that wasn't blank.'

I look at Mom and Dad who are both staring at Yugi.

'Enlighten me, Yoda.'

'Come on. Am I the only smart one here? You guessed that this is Grandma Iris who has written this, so you inserted her name. But, she didn't sign it 'Iris Walker, or LW, or anything that has to do with Grandma - we just filled that in. But read it again - 'You never know what you might find in my house.' It's not Grandma's house, it's Barbie's house - a Barbie house.'

I'm shocked. 'Whoa, Yugi, you might be right.'

'We can tear up the house. Yeah!'

Yugi and I race inside. Still piled in the corner are all the physical things the CIA did not take including the iron, the crockpot and, unsurprisingly the Barbie house.

I set Maximus on the floor. She is not particularly happy to have carpet beneath her toes. Her gaze is accusing, as if I've abandoned her. Apologizing, but not deviating from my course, Yugi and I descend upon the Barbie house. It is made from white, pink and light blue plastic. It folds open and reveals a three-story house. The ground floor consists of a living area with walls painted pink. Photos of Barbie's relatives, her parents, maybe, and a painting of a dog - a poodle - are on the walls. The kitchen has a sink and fixed cupboards, but all the furniture has been removed. The second floors are bedrooms, each with wooden floorboards and cinched pink curtains pulled back away from windows. Although it is a little worse for wear from the thieves' ill-treatment, a few pieces have broken off, it is still in decent shape.

Mom and Dad stand behind us as if it is Christmas and we are unwrapping presents. Dad's arm is around her waist and she is leaning into his shoulder.

'What did the clue say again?'

'*In my house, one finds all sorts of things.*' I respond.

We search diligently but cannot find anything on the walls or under the floorboards - no secret compartments. I humph. 'I thought you'd be right, Yugi.'

He continues to fuss over the house. 'We can't expect that everything is going to be easy. If Grandma is a super spy, she can't make it too simple for the likes of kids.'

'The odds are,' Mom says, 'she might have expected Dad or I to find it. It would have been great if she would have just given us a key to a lockbox.'

'You found something?' I ask Yugi. I move towards him as Maximus climbs up my back and digs her claws into my shirt to pull herself back up on my shoulder. 'Ouch! Maximus!'

'She just wants to see my triumph.' Yugi is smiling.

'Go on, what did you find?'

'I'm trying to figure out these clues,' he says, 'and it feels like Grandma, or Barbie, is hiding in the obvious.'

'We're waiting,' I say impatiently. Maximus looks impassively at Yugi who reaches out to scratch her. She bares her teeth at him and hisses. 'Good girl,' I scratch her cheeks.

'I'm thinking of the words right before, '*One never knows what numbers and words one might find inside.*'

'I didn't see any words or numbers inside the house if that's what you're inferring.'

'Think,' Yugi says, 'not just inside the house, *inside* the house.'

'Not following.'

Yugi turns the house on its side. 'See any numbers?'

'No,' I say, 'there are just two streaks on the bottom of the wings.'

Smirking, Yugi points to them. '*One* never knows what *one* might find inside. These are 'ones.' And my guess is that if we unscrew these little babies, we're going to find something inside the plastic.'

Yugi jumps up to get a screwdriver and returns quickly.

Dropping down to the floor, Yugi unscrews the exoskeleton of the house and sure enough, hollowed innards reveal an empty space.

'Is there anything in there?' I ask excitedly.

'Yes,' he his face scrunched up, 'but it's not what I was expecting.' He reaches into each hole and pulls out two objects.

I can see why he is confused.

It's a blackened arm of a Barbie doll and in the other, a Barbie mirror.

'That's it?'

He shakes the house. 'That's it. Kind of sick if you ask me.'

Chapter 23 Down:

I take the objects in my hands.

Grandma, what in the heck are you trying to tell us?

The rest of the afternoon we spend outdoors scrolling through the other documents and photos. Some of them don't make sense at all. It looks as if Grandma, or Barbie, or whoever has gone on vacation and taken photos of the most random things. Sometimes it's as if she accidentally snapped a picture. There are a few photos of people. Grandpa appears in a few - he looks very young and handsome. My dad as a young man, early teens, appears in many photos. His hair is long and his face is framed by large, plastic rimmed glasses. In some, he is flexing, but his arms are very skinny. Yugi is almost an exact replica of him.

We sift out the random ones, partial faces, partial objects, blurry images, spotted with black, and placed them in a separate folder. We look more carefully into the ones with people and places which are clearer. 'Who are these people?' I ask.

Dad squints as if this will help him see better. 'I don't know. I mean, I've seen a few of them and I remember a few, but these photos are taken in multiple decades. There are some from both Germany and Israel here.' He points tenderly to Mom's face on the screen.

'Well,' Mom says as she stretches her arms above her head and then twists her back. It pops. 'I think we should call it a day.'

'Good idea,' Dad agrees. 'Let's pack this away and go for a little walk.'

Both Yugi and I complain about this. Walking is not a form of enjoyment for us. The parents always walk

183

quickly, always swing their arms and always chat, chat, chat, words, words, words, about things that don't really interest us.

'Come on, you two, we'll walk up to the ice cream shop and grab a treat.'

Yugi is up before Dad finishes his sentence.

After putting Maximus back in her cage, I close the lid and walk back to the blanket. I reach down for the plastic bag that has the Barbie arm and a mirror in it.

Why is the arm black? I wonder. *And what does the mirror have to do with anything?*

Chapter 24 Down:
Captivate – regarding clues (8)

My dreams are filled with intrigue: silhouetted men and women creeping stealthily down darkened alleys, bright lights shining from headlights, blinding me. I cringe and reach up to shield my eyes. Maximus is dashing out in front of the car, protecting me. I run to her - too late. The car smashes into her and veers, but she is thrown upwards, higher and higher into the air. She looks like a flying rat. On the way back down, she is transfigured and becomes an amputated Barbie arm. I reach out to catch her, now *it*, and I am appalled and angry that Maximus is now dead and I'm left with Barbie's right arm. Her fingers are blackened still and her...

I gasp as I wake up. My mind is itching. Something I haven't been able to grab onto, but now that sleep has given me free access to my subconscious, I put the pieces together.

Barbie's arm.

Blackened fingers.

Fingerprints...

Follow the path. Follow my prints.

How could I have missed this? As we were scrolling through all the photos this afternoon, it didn't connect with me that we were supposed to follow the prints.

I check my phone. It is 4:12 a.m. No one else is awake. I won't be able to get back to sleep until I investigate that which woke me up.

Pulling back the curtains, I look outside. There is a crescent moon to the east illuminating our street, but the sun won't be far behind.

185

Padding down the hallway, I softly make my way down the stairs cringing as I go. There are so many creaking boards which, in the dark hours of the night sound like rusty iron grates opening and shutting.

My parents have left the computer on the kitchen table. Next to it is the bag with the Barbie arm and mirror. I open the computer and boot it up. While the computer boots up, I grab a pen and piece of paper. Then, I color Barbie's arm, well, her fingertips, with ink and imprint on the page. In the dim light of the computer, I can see the five small dots.

I smile. *Barbie's prints!*

The desktop is full of icons, but I find the folder I want. It is not the folder of people and faces we know, but the haphazard ones.

Opening the folder, I expand the pictures into a slide show and magnify them. When Yugi had his magnifying glass out earlier today, I should have looked at all the pictures a little closer. Those that we had summarily set aside had five distinctive small black dots somewhere in the picture.

Five fingerprints.

The ones that don't, I close out and put back into the folder, but these... now I see what has happened. Grandma has taken one photo and turned it into six; she's done that twice and if I print these two sextets out, I think we'll have a better idea of...

'What's going on?'

I almost jump out of my skin. Because I've been staring into the screen, the light has night-blinded me.

'Is that you, Dad?'

'Yes, Jeri. Do you know what time it is?'

'Yeah, it's about 4:30.'

'No, it's sleeping time. Jeri,' he says exasperatedly, 'you can't be fixating on this. You're going to get sick.'

'But Dad...'

'No, Jeri.'

'But Dad!' I say louder. 'I've figured it out.'

'What?'

I lift the Barbie arm. 'Fingerprints.'

'Where?'

Pointing at the screen, I look up into his face. He squints. 'I'll be darned. What are the pictures of? They seem to be random.'

I copy and paste them into a document and arrange them so that the entirety of a face appears. It is a flash-surprised face, eyes open wide, frightened as if caught doing something illicit. And yet, there is a tinge of humor around the mouth, a slight upturned smile. Like someone caught making a joke.

'Oh my sweet jeepers.'

'Who is it, Dad?'

He stands and pushes a hand through his hair. The faint glow across his body is eerie. Is he my dad or a specter?

'That's Chaim Weismann.'

'I heard you say his name the other day, but who is that?'

'Chaim,' he says distractedly and paces slightly in the dark. 'Chaim - he and Miriam were two of our closest friends. They basically took us under their wings and made us feel welcome, always.'

'Were they spies?'

Dad's eyes are open wide. 'I... I... they weren't, but I don't really know.'

'How old would you say he is here?'

'I've never seen this picture before, but it's much newer than the other ones. He looks maybe in his late thirties or early forties? When we left Israel, Chaim and Miriam were still in their late twenties. I think Grandma is giving us an idea of where to begin.'

'Where, Israel?'

'Yes.'

'But how can you tell?'

'*Visit the White Man to the first leg of the journey.* White Man...'

'Weismann,' we both say together.

Okay, so sleeping is out of the question. Dad and I sit in front of the computer staring at the strange clue sheet.

'We've got a few of these done already,' Dad whispers trying to keep his voice down.

'Yes.'

'*One and one - check.*' The numbers on the bottom of the Barbie house.

'*In my house...*' Barbie arm and mirror. 'We haven't figured out the mirror yet.'

'That's okay,' I respond as I bite the tip of the pen.

Dad points to the next part of the screen. '*Follow the path. Follow my prints.* So we'll follow Grandma's path and Barbie's prints - Check.'

'*Visit the White Man to the first leg of the journey.*'

'Why doesn't it say, 'Visit the White Man *on* the first leg of the journey?'

'I'm sure it will mean something to us at some point.'

188

He leans into the computer again. 'What about the other sextet? What is that one?'

'It's hard to say. It looks like an attaché case.'

'Dad, does this mean we're going to Israel?'

'I don't know, Jeri. Optimally, that would be great, but we have a few things working against us.'

'Like what?'

'Well, money, for instance. We could scrape some funds for Mom and me to get there.'

'Whoa, wait a minute. Are you saying that you're going to leave Yugi and me here? That's not fair! We're the ones who have been figuring out the clues. You can't do it.'

'Jeri, quiet!' He hushes and glances towards his bedroom. 'It's only been fifteen minutes since we - you - figured out the clue. It's just...'

'Don't say it, Dad. Don't say that it's too dangerous. That's so cliche.'

'Sometimes cliches are all that we have, Jeri.'

'Not this time. It would be much more dangerous to leave us here. Why, the CIA could kidnap us and hold us for ransom.'

'Jeri! Don't even mention that.'

'Then take us with. Let's go back to Israel.'

'We'll talk about it.'

'I've heard that before.' Parents can be so frustratingly predictable with their pallet of responses for all situations in life. 'You guys say, 'We'll talk about it,' which means your minds are already made up; you're just going to plot how to coordinate your excuses of why we don't get what we want.'

'Now, Jeri, that's not entirely true.' The way he says it means he knows that it is *entirely* true.

'We'll talk about it as a family - vote on it if we have to,' I say.

'It would be split down the middle.'

'Not if Maximus votes.'

'Only human votes will be counted.' Dad pours coffee grounds into the filter. He shuts the top of the coffee pot and flips the switch to start the machine. In a few seconds the bubbling sound starts.

'The voting rules have not been established yet,' I counter.

'Oh, Jeri, please.'

Mom and Dad's bedroom door cracks open and a sleepy face appears in the crack. Mom is squinting against the bright light.

'For goodness sake, what are you two doing out here at this hour?' Mom enters the kitchen light and tightens the robe's belt around her.

'I figured out where we're going next.' I smile at her sleepy face.

'Really?'

'Yup. We're going to Israel.'

'Excuse me? I thought for a moment you said Israel.'

'I did.'

Mom gasps as she approaches Dad. 'Kevin...'

His eyebrows arch. 'I don't know how to explain it.'

'Tell me what happened.'

I do, but she can't quite comprehend what has just happened. She studies the images on the computer, the Barbie arm, the picture of Chaim Weismann - it's overwhelming. 'That's quite a turn of events.'

'Indeed it is.' Dad has filled up another mug of coffee and hands it to Mom. He raises his eyebrows to me. I shake my head.

'It's been so long. So many years... We would get to see my mother and father. The kids would finally meet their Israeli grandparents.' Mom is speaking to Dad, but it's me who exults.

'Yes!' I shout triumphantly. 'Take that, Dad! Three votes to one.'

'What are you talking about?' Mom asks.

I point to Dad who is peering over his coffee mug. 'Dad's trying to keep Yugi and me here in Duncan while you two fly around the globe on a treasure hunt. He says it would be far too dangerous.' I mock his voice.

'He's probably right.'

'But he might be wrong...'

'There are so many logistical things that we'd have to think about like...' Dad's voice fades into mental wandering. I hear things like 'someone to watch the house' and 'pay the bills,' and 'What about Grandpa and Grandma?' But my imagination and hopes have already boarded the airplane.

Dreams of travel have always been part of my life. I hear about other kids in my class flying to Mexican resorts or once-in-a-lifetime-trips to Europe, and here I am, fifteen years old stuck in Duncan my whole life.

I surface back to reality as Dad implores me to be reasonable. 'Do you see, Jeri? All these things would have to happen if all four of us were to go.'

'Yes, and Maximus would have to be taken care of.'

'There is that. You'll have to find a gamekeeper.' He motions with his cup towards me as if he is lifting a toast.

'Dongle will do it.'

'Dongle?' Dad responds with incredulity. 'He's just out of the hospital.'

Now I'm getting frustrated by his excuses. 'It's not like we'll be leaving tomorrow, Dad.'

'Be that as it may,' Dad says slowly, 'you, Jeri, don't know the first thing about logistics for an assignment like this.'

'And you do?'

'Yes, as a matter of fact. This is what I've been doing for twenty years.'

I was silent. He did have me there.

'All that I'm saying, Jeri, and this is a reminder again for you, is that we would not be going on a family vacation. Sightseeing will not be an objective and the odds are, we might be stirring up a hornet's nest. We already know the CIA is after something or it could be something far worse.'

'Or better,' I counter.

'You're not listening, Jeri.' His voice is frustrated.

'So what do we have to do to prepare for this mission.' I liked the sound of that. *This message will self-destruct in five seconds.*

Dad shakes his head and looks to Mom for help.

Mom walks to the desk and pulls out a pad of paper. 'First, we need to locate Chaim and Miriam. We can't use normal channels, just in case our emails are being monitored. Jeri, maybe we'll use one of your emails.'

'No problem.'

'We'll have to get together some gear for the trip.' Mom studies Dad whose head is hanging with resignation.

'What kinds of things?' I ask.

'A few new phones, a new credit card.'

Chapter 24 Down:

'Let's put the brakes on a little,' Dad says as Mom scribbles her list. 'There's a little thing called *money* that is in short supply.

'We'll figure it out.' Her face has hardened.

I glance out the kitchen window. Even though it is only five-thirty, the early morning summer sun has made an appearance above the eastern horizon. Pink clouds have reacquired their normal white and grey color. The sun's glint squeezes between the branches of our front yard trees. This dawning of a new day is a turning point in my life. And I am very excited.

Chapter 25 Across:
RSVP'd first (9)

I am quite sure, positively sure, that I have never been this excited in all my life. Certainly, there have been moments of expectation, restless anticipation before taking a test, or even sitting behind the steering wheel for the first time. But nothing compares to what I am feeling at this exact moment. Inside my guts, right down in the middle, is a flurry of activity. A few butterflies have spread their wings and are testing the currents next to a colony of bats circling my belfry.

My mom tried to calm me down about an hour ago with ineffective words, but I can't stop smiling. I can't stop moving. For Yugi, this is his normal *modus operendi* - literally bouncing - until my Dad tossed him outside to 'guard' the luggage in case someone came to 'steal' it. I went to chat with Dongle. He looks much better. It's been six weeks since the attack and the purple around his eye has gone. He still complains a little about the itch in his leg.

As we talked, he kept looking at the house as if it's a living thing. He asked me a couple of times where we were going, to which I responded that our family was going on a much-needed vacation. It was summer, I just graduated from high school, my parents had been planning this for a very long time, blah blah blah. It's not as if I was lying. I mean, it *is* summer, and I *did* graduate, and six weeks *does* seem like a very long time to me. In those six weeks we bought flights from Tulsa to Dallas to Amsterdam to Munich to Tel Aviv. All those places sound so incredibly exotic and romantic - not that I was looking for romance, certainly - but I couldn't wait to breathe the air, to hear the sounds, to *see everything.*

Chapter 25 Across:

When I told Dongle we were going to Amsterdam, he frowned and cocked his head to the side. 'Now why in the world would you want to go there when there are so many wonderful *American* places to check out?'

Dongle agreed to watch Maximus for me. I can't say he was overly thrilled by the idea, but his good nature and my pleading won him over. He assured me that he would not, in fact, cuddle the creature at any time, to which I nodded thankfully and said, 'That's probably for the best.' I introduced him to Maximus' dietary plans. He rolled his eyes and responded, 'The stupid animal is going to get what comes off my table. If he doesn't like it, he can starve.' To which I responded, '*She* will eat many things but don't give *her* any sweets.'

I look out the back window where Yugi is standing beside Dongle's Yukon. Dongle is driving us to the airport and because he is 'dang well sure not going to drive that hunk of junk there and back.' Dongle was pointing to the Camrillac.

The Camrillac is in the empty garage and I feel kind of sorry for it. Dad has asked Dongle to drive it around the block a few times just to keep the battery charged. Dongle grumbles, but I think deep down he really feels honored to be asked. He has always been a helper and he likes us kids.

As I study the Camrillac and its advanced age, I am reminded of our trip to Pine Point last week. Grandma was not doing well so Mom volunteered to sit with her and Yugi while Dad and I took Grandpa for a walk. After a cup of coffee and a brief explanation about what had happened, Grandpa leaned in. When Dad gave a brief rundown of our itinerary, Grandpa looked envious and worried.

'Be careful, Kev.'

195

'I will, Dad.'

'These people, they don't mess around.' Something in his eyes told us that he was scared and not altogether certain that my parents were doing the right thing in taking us kids with them.

'We'll watch our backs.'

'You realize,' Grandpa said gravely, 'that none of this matters much if something happens to any of you.'

We both nod.

'Is there anything else we need to know, Dad?'

Grandpa took a deep breath. 'Yes.' He reached into his pocket and retrieved an envelope. 'Inside is information about a special account.' He tapped it. 'There is two hundred thousand dollars in there. It is untraceable.'

'Dad!' Where did you get that kind of money?'

'Doesn't matter,' Grandpa pressed the envelope into Dad's hand. 'Remember, don't use credit cards. As much as possible, don't use your phones or the internet. Don't let them track you. Hide, blend in - you guys will be good at it.' He looked at me. 'Right, Jeri?'

'Absolutely, Gramps.'

'Now,' Grandpa said resolutely, 'you'd better get going and find whatever it is that Grandma wanted you to find.' He touched his pocket for his phone. 'I'll send an email with a few names of people who might provide some assistance if you get into any trouble.' He retrieved his phone and typed slowly for a few seconds. He is not good at it. Then, he looked up at us, smiled and put the phone away.

Dongle and Yugi see me at the top of the stairs.

'Jeri, are they almost ready?'

Chapter 25 Across:

'I don't know, Yug, I think so'. They've done the 'final' walk through for the fourth time.

'Tell them to hurry up.'

'Yeah, right.'

After descending the steps, I can see a strange look on Dongle's face.

'You okay, Dongle?' I put a hand on his shoulder.

'No problem, Nosebleed. I hope you guys have a great time.'

Mom and Dad speak loudly as they exit the house and approach us, the impatient ones. 'Donald,' Dad says, 'thank you very much for helping us with this.' He extends his hand and drops the house keys into Dongle's. 'Watching the house, driving us to the airport, taking care of the animal... All above and beyond the call of duty.'

'Well,' Dongle grumbles falsely, 'I needed something to do, I guess. I can make sure your lawn stays alive too.'

Mom approaches him, grabs his face in her hands and kisses him on the cheeks. 'You're a good man, Donald.' I snort when Dongle's face turns all red and splotchy.

Yugi cringes. 'Yuck.'

At the Tulsa airport, Dongle pulls to a stop in the unloading area. Yugi pushes me out the door into traffic. Mom, not for the last time I'm sure, warns her son about his behavior. We unpack our bags and bid our neighbor a fond farewell. He looks like a man who is about to lose every good thing in the world.

Dongle gets back in the car and without waving, enters traffic and speeds away. Yugi hurries towards the front doors of the airport, his backpack riding like a jockey on his back. Dad frustratedly calls him back which he summarily ignores. From a distance, we can see him standing by the entrance of the airport, wide grin on his face, tapping his foot impatiently and waving to us. The rest of us dutifully tow the luggage behind us. I feel the weight of my own backpack on my shoulders. I have been chosen as the passport carrier and crossword bearer. My parents are both jubilant and frightened. It's been a long time since they've done any of this stuff.

We check our baggage, pass through security and find ourselves sitting at the gate. Yugi positions his video game controller in front of him and is animatedly killing something. Mom and Dad sit across from each other in very uncomfortable chairs with armrests. There is not much talking in the airport - I'm surprised by this. People should be excited about the prospect of flying, to be going places, far away from the mundane to the exotic. They should be standing by the windows like the toddlers, faces inches away from the glass, hands pressed against the pane staring out at these modern miracles of physics.

As the minutes pass glacially, I stroll up and down the terminal corridors. One woman, I see, has a small pet carrier. I wonder what kind of animal is in it. Probably not a possum. Her platinum hair and makeup are done to perfection. Large hoop earrings dangle from her lobes. Her lipstick is kind of a blueberry maroon. I've only worn lipstick a couple of times, and it just seemed to get stuck in my teeth.

She is wearing a white cashmere sweater. It's fuzzy - it reminds me of my pillowcase which is falling apart. Her pants are skin-tight - I mean, I think I can actually see her flesh beneath them. To top it all off, or should I say 'bottom' it all off, her shoes, clunky things with four-inch corky heels, seem highly inefficient for walking through airports. Even as I judge her, I still find that a piece of me is jealous. She takes out her phone and types something in, probably a Twitter update, but it's hard for her, because her French tip fingernails get in the way.

Our outbound plane is twenty minutes late. For Yugi, this is the worst possible scenario. Twenty more minutes of excruciating waiting. Almost maniacally, after ditching his video game, he paced in front of the windows talking to himself. Once, I got close to him, and heard him practicing what he must think is a Jewish accent. He's very creative, I'll give him that.

We don't really know how long we'll be gone. Part of this unknowingness makes me uncomfortable, but the other part is exhilarating and wonderful. It's like making it all the way to Christmas without Yugi partially unwrapping all the gifts and sending an 'anonymous' email telling me what's in the boxes.

The inbound passengers stagger up the walkway. I wonder what kind of adventure they've just had, whether a vacation or just a work trip. Some of them look excited to be home, others are yawning as if this day, or this part of their life, is going to need an extra shot of something to get going.

Yugi is still bouncing. His backpack follows the backbeat rhythm and he glances to Dad whose eyes are focused ahead of us. Mom's arms are folded over her chest holding her book.

Unfortunately, the four of us cannot fit into the same row. Thus, Mom positions me and Yugi into the row behind them. He has a window seat as does Dad. Mom and I are shoved into the middle seat. On my left is a bored looking older woman wearing a navy-blue shirt. She has dander problems. She smiles. Red lipstick is stuck to her teeth.

'How're y'all doin' today?'

Add halitosis to her medical report. Either way, I'll be looking in Yugi's direction whether I want to or not.

'Fine.' I put my headphones in my ears. I have no music playing, but this should be a signal to the old woman that I don't want her breathing on me. Yugi tugs on my arm and points to the wings. *Those flimsy things are supposed to keep this battleship in the air? Holy cripes.* I'm excited to go, but it's too bad we couldn't have taken a cruise to Israel.

We taxi down the runway and I have now progressed much farther up the nervousness scale. The airplane taxis to the last corner and then, the plane slows. *Is something wrong? Are the engines burning? Can we crash while we're on the ground? Why have we s...?* Suddenly, the plane lurches forward and accelerates at warp speed. Yugi looks at me with eyes as wide as saucers. At this point, we are going faster than I've ever been before. The road below us seems to be getting noisier, a roar, and suddenly, there is no noise. The plane lifts slightly. *Oh God, forgive me for I have sinned!* My stomach drops. If I was Maximus, I would have gassed the plane already.

There is a large thud and then two more. *What was that? What was that!* The old lady turns to me and says, 'Those'r just the wheels being put away. Are you okay?' She asks me. 'Because if you are, you can stop cutting off circulation in my hand.' I notice my left hand has unconsciously vised her wrist. I release quickly and apologize, but the smell of her breath has made me very, very nauseous. We keep going up. Farther and farther. Yugi points excitedly as we tuuuuuurn, *O God, O God, why have you forsaken me?* we're now approaching the clouds, soft and fluffy, like toilet paper, and then...

Turbulence.

Chapter 25 Across:

Yugi recoils from me. 'What's wrong, Jeri? You're moaning.'

My eyes are wide and horrified. I think of all the things that can go wrong beginning with the fact that I HAVE NO CONTROL OVER WHERE THIS FRICKIN' AIRPLANE IS GOING! There is a mile long drop to the ground. If the doors blow out now, we'll all be sucked into the air and die for sure. What if the engines fail? What if the turbulence is so great that it shears one of the wings off? Or both? I peer over Yugi's body and it appears that they are shimmying out of control. Is that a loose bolt?

'This is fun,' Yugi says and claps his hands underneath me. I want to slap him.

'Yugi,' I say through gritted teeth, 'holdmyhandholdmyhandholdmyhand!'

'I'm not holding your stupid hand. Stop being a baby.' He reaches over and slaps my face slightly. I hear the woman next to me snort. Now, I'm angry.

'Yugi!' My blood is boiling but at least my anger has replaced the sick feeling in my stomach.

Yugi reaches forward and taps Dad on the shoulder. 'Dad, Jeri's going to puke.'

Dad whips around in the seat. 'Are you?'

'No,' I say, but the mere thought of it makes me feel kind of ill. The woman next to me seems to be leaning away from me already.

'If you need to, there's a small white bag in the seat pocket in front of you. Just open it up and...' he pantomimes the vomit bag opening and makes a *blaaagh* sound.

Now I can't stop thinking about it. Am I going to get sick? We hit a bump. I grab the arm rests again and scan the rear of the plane. I'm trapped. The seat has become far

201

too small. There's no way to get out and even if I did, where would I go? We're in a flying death-cylinder two miles in the air. I look around. A rising panic has begun in my chest which lays siege to my brain. The cabin is imploding. *Is that a change in engine noise I hear?* The flight attendants are beginning to mill around the seats. Some people have pushed a button above them which makes a *ding* sound. The attendants look unconcerned and quite happy to serve the passengers. Do I push the button?

'Jeri,' Dad says, 'it will pass. Deep breaths. Breathe, Jer. Think of something else.'

Easy for him to say. He's done this before. But this is entirely new to me.

'Yeah, breathe, Jerusalem,' Yugi says as he curls up into the window as far away from me as possible. 'And don't puke on me.'

'Shut up, Yugi. Shut up. Shut up! Just let me think.'

Yugi goes back to looking out the window at the cottony clouds beneath. From this distance, it looks as if you could dive out the window and bounce onto them. *That's right, Jeri, nothing to be afraid of. Everything is nice and blue and comfortable outside.*

I close my eyes and put my head back against the seat. I try to imagine anything else, anything at all, Maximus, Grandpa and Grandma, cheese and crackers, a friendly-faced-Jesus flying the airplane, but the only thought that comes to my mind and keeps repeating is:

This is only the first leg.

The first leg.

What does that phrase mean? Why did Barbie write, 'Visit the white man *to* the first leg?' My mind stutters. How many legs of the journey is Grandma going to take us on? I think of Grandma and her amazing history that I've never known before. The photos on the microfilm, the pictures with her in them, of a beautiful woman with high cheek bones and brilliantly lit eyes accentuated by long eyelashes. Her hair, beehived on top of her head, reveals a high and proud forehead. Long shapely legs slither from the bottom hem of her dress. She would be the epitome of a Hollywood female spy, and yet this is my grandma, Iris Walker. And my Grandpa Walt. How can you have a spy named 'Walter?' That's like naming your cat Xylophone - it just doesn't seem to fit. He was young and handsome. In his photos, he seems tough and hardened, not weak and feeble like now. Do I really know him?

My thoughts continue to drift and without knowing it, I have relaxed slightly. The plane has leveled and tilts back slightly. I open my eyes and notice the woman next to me is reading a magazine. Yugi's face is pressed against the window. Suddenly, I know I'm going to make it. It's just a bus ride in the sky.

Unfortunately, the descent, which is new to me, is far worse than the take off. There's something about going down that is more frightening when I think to myself, *We're going down.* Descend is the right work. I repeat that. Not going down. Descending. I've used that word so many times in my crosswords. We approach the clouds and Yugi watches me, not the clouds. He reaches forward and pulls out his puke bag from his seat pocket and hands it to me. I snarl at him and smack him over the head with it. He laughs.

Yugi becomes the altimeter and tells me how low we are getting. I'm pretty sure he has no idea the exact amount of air between us and the...

Oh my God, something just clunked. The wing is dancing again. The engines begin screaming, roaring louder. *Are we on fire?* I look around and it seems that no one else is similarly scared.

'That was just the wheels being put down,' Halitosis woman says.

'Why are they being put down now? Is something wrong?'

'No, dear, we're just about to land.' She points out the window.

'One hundred yards to impact,' Yugi laughs maniacally.

Crapcrapcrapcrapcrapcrap. My entire body tenses and prepares. What was that crash position the stewards showed us? Curl up in a ball and smush?

'Twenty yards. Almost there. Almost there.' Yugi's voice intones like a rebel pilot in Star Wars.

Suddenly, the plane touches the ground, crunch, and then a very loud growling noise. 'What's happening!' I yell out over the noise.

The woman grabs my arm. 'It's the brakes! It's the brakes!'

We slow down. I am sweating. Yugi is grinning. Somehow, we are still alive.

Chapter 26 Down:
Carefully consider (6)

Well, I can officially check a few career choices off my future list. Certainly, aviation and flight attending will not have my name on the manifest.

The flight from Dallas to Amsterdam was nine and a half arduous hours. Nine and a half hours of my life in the air. I was thankful, though, that the larger plane afforded more physical comfort, although psychological ease was still far out of reach. Even more, Mom and Yugi switched seats so that I didn't have to sit next to him. The long flight had movies to watch so I could attempt to focus on something besides what was happening underneath my feet. For the most part, thankfully, that flight and the one into Munich were much less eventful than the one into Dallas.

We descend into Tel Aviv. I study the countryside with Mom leaning over my lap. I turn slightly. She is crying.

'Are you okay?'

She nods and sniffs. Her smile is forced. 'Someday you might understand what it's like, to be far away from the place where you grew up and then suddenly, unexpectedly, you're there again.' She wipes her eyes and leans back in her chair.

I am quiet.

'I spoke to my parents last month. I was afraid they wouldn't want to see us because I haven't allowed them to meet you. It's just one of the consequences of the life we decided to lead. But I was wrong about them. They're very ready to see all of us.'

'Have your parents ever seen pictures of us?'

She nods and beings to cry again. 'Every time I talked to them, I showed them pictures of you.'

'That's good.'

Mom puts her hand in mine. 'You've grown up so fast and missed out on so much. Thank you for understanding.'

After alighting, which was once again not particularly pleasant, we wait by the luggage carousel. Yugi is very tired. I think he watched movies the entire time we were airborne. Dad, too, seems to have packed extra baggage under his eyes.

We find our luggage and haul it through customs. Israeli border patrol, dark and brooding men and women with brown eyes and dark hair, stand watch. We're no longer in Oklahoma, that's for sure.

The customs agent checks our passports and we rush through as a family - the Walker family, world travelers. I have been in four countries in the last day. That boggles my mind. The U.S., Holland, Germany and now Israel. It would not be a stretch of the imagination to say that I'd never really been in four different counties in one day before, but four countries?

As we exit the gates, Mom scans the crowd. Grandpa and Grandma Klein are supposed to be picking us up. It's weird to think about those names. I hear a cacophony of languages spoken around me. The unintelligible words, Arabic, then English, Hebrew, of course, some Greek, maybe, resonate throughout the airport. Through me.

Suddenly, Mom gasps. I follow her eyes to a sign written in English. *Welcome to Israel, Walker family!* The sign is written in a rainbow of colors. The holder of the placard is a matronly woman with dyed brown hair. She is smiling and crying. The woman shoves the sign into the chest of the portly man beside her. Holding her mouth with one hand, she shoves her way through the crowd towards my mother, arms open. The two blubber and carry on while the rest of us follow. Dad approaches the man with the sign who is also holding two light jackets. He has thinning grey hair and a thick moustache. His eyes are a deep brown and have laughter lines in the corners.

'Shalom, Avram,' my dad says warmly.

'Shalom, Kevin,' he responds kindly.

'Kids,' my dad says, 'this is your *Saba* Klein. 'Saba' is the word for 'grandfather.' And that is *Savti.'*

'I didn't know you spoke Hebrew, Dad,' I say.

'Only a few phrases. Most people here speak many languages.'

'How many do you speak?'

His eyes sparkle. 'A few...'

Yugi has introduced himself to his Saba Klein while Savti pulls herself away from Mom and crushes me to herself. 'Your name,' she says in thickly accented English, 'is so, so beautiful. Jerusalem.' She pronounces it *Yehrushalehm.* It's sounds much more beautiful in Hebrew. 'It means, 'Place of peace.'

I smile while suffocated by her embrace. Finally, she pushes me back and goes after Yugi. 'Yugoslavia,' she intones. 'That's quite a mouthful.' Yugi accepts the grandmotherly attention with good grace, but I can tell he does not want a second helping.

'Most people would say he's a handful,' I add. He sticks his tongue out at me.

'Handful?' Savti grabs his arms. 'He's skinny as a rake. I must fatten him up some.' She holds his cheeks in her hands. Gradually, he is able to disengage himself from her. 'Come. It's time to go home. Avram, their bags.' Like a general giving orders to a private, Savti snaps her fingers and points to our baggage. I am happy to take my share, but my dad tells me that it is culturally better for the men to carry the load. This annoys me, but I allow it to happen.

We walk outside into the steamy afternoon air. After packing our belongings into the car, we crush into the back seat. The car, designed for five but now packing six, is uncomfortable. Yugi sits between Mom's legs which squishes me in the middle. Savti is in the front passenger seat speaking far too quickly in Hebrew. Even my mom seems to struggle. Saba reaches across the car and touches her arm. 'English, *Eema*. English. The children do not understand.'

'My English is not good,' Savti says.

Mom leans over to me and translates. 'It's traditional for people who have been separated to give news about relatives. Grandma is just telling me about my cousins in Jerusalem.'

'How many do you have?'

'Dozens.'

'What else did she say?'

Mom smirks and looks over my head at Dad who is staring out the window.

'She says that we will be having a party tonight. Lots of friends and family coming over. A real Jewish celebration.'

Yugi's face lights up. 'Does this mean there will be lots of food?'

'Yes - far too much.'

'Count me in,' he says as he yawns.

'I'm tired, though,' I respond.

Chapter 26 Down:

'Try to sleep on the way. It's only about an hour, but that will tide you over...'

She must have said 'until we get there,' but I'm already asleep on Dad's shoulder.

We arrive at the Klein house around 6:00. Already, a crowd has arrived. My grandparents' home is a three-story sandstone unit with shared walls. Mom is glowing when we arrive. Savti calls out to everyone in the neighborhood to come meet her daughter and grandchildren. She grabs both Yugi and I by our waists and presses us close to her considerable hips.

Gawkers come out from across the street to see what the commotion is. Each person has dark hair, dark eyes and olive skin. They are beautiful. Someone inside the house has turned on some music. It sounds a lot like American dance music. The front door opens and a young man pops out. His arms are raised up and out from his head. 'Aaaaah, Beryl!' He cries and rushes to her. A stream of Hebrew issues from his mouth and they hug and bounce up and down.

Dad and Saba extricate the bags from the trunk of the car and lug them to the house. We follow Mom, and who we assume to be a long lost relative, up the stairs. Strange and exotic smells emanate from the open door and waft under our noses. I'm now very hungry.

The house is dimly lit. We walk through a narrow hallway where shiny white tiles reflect light from beneath us. Corridor walls are adorned with photographs of young and old people, mostly family settings, stylized representations of life caught in the crosshairs of a particular moment. I am caught by the scrubbed clean faces of people I don't know: Saba and Savti, relatives, friends, ghostly figures of people I've never met yet somehow always hoped for. As we continued towards the light in the backyard, Mom points out some of the people to me. Her face is more excited than I've ever seen. In this moment, she is above life. Their names, foreign and unfamiliar, flow like water over my tongue: Yosef, Daniel, Eitan, Yael, Adele, Shira. Each name connected with joyful, happy faces seem to overwhelm my senses, but thankfully, they are gentle with me. We near the end of the hallway and I feel reborn into a new life. When Mom throws open the sliding glass doors, what was once a muffled sound is now boisterous and noisy. I am greeted by all-consuming sensory waves, smell and sight, aural and textural. I am a stranger in a strange land.

As we stepped into the backyard two of the girls, Shira and Maya, approach me.

'Hello,' the one called Shira speaks. Her voice, husky and low, is beautifully accented. Her eyes, luminous, almost glowing, are alive and excited. I can't quite figure out if she's a relative or an angel. 'It is so good to have you here. We have been waiting for you to arrive. Maya and I,' she points to her sidekick, 'we are look to forward meeting you.' She shakes her head. 'No, we are looking forward to meeting you.'

'Thank you,' I say.

'We are your cousins.'

'You are sisters?' I ask.

'No,' Shira giggles. 'We have different parents.'

'What is it like,' Maya finally speaks shyly, tentatively, aware of the difficulty conversing in a second language, 'to live in America? Is it full of movie stars and basketball players?'

Chapter 26 Down:

'No,' I laugh. 'Not many movie stars but basketball is pretty popular.'

Now, after meeting two of my cousins, it seems that this is the alternative reality that I always wanted. At first, I am overwhelmed by the throng, the sheer numbers of people who have gathered. Strangely, Shira and Maya treat me as if I'm a rock star. They introduce me to some other young people, Moshe and David, who are a few years older than we. A set of adults call us over and I am introduced to them. Interspersed with English is the submachine gun rapidity of Hebrew. No one but me seems to miss a thing.

'Do you want something to drink?' Maya asks.

'Yes, that would be nice.' She runs off to get refreshments. As we are waiting, a tall and lanky boy with a shock of curly brown hair, raises a hand to me. He has a cute smile, more like a grin - it bends off to the side. I look around to see if he is waving at me. He nods and laughs.

Shira leans in and whispers. 'I don't know him that well. I think he is a friend of your family.'

'What's his name?'

'Shime.' She pronounces it *Shimeey*.

Shira motions for Shime to come over. He speaks to his friends and nods to me. They approach us casually, like a dance - very different than the boys at the Pond. He has intense brown eyes. Shime must be a few years older than I.

'Hello,' he says. His voice has the teenage male scratch.

'Hi.' *Hi? That's all you've got? Can't you just be cool. Like, Hi?*

'I'm Shime and you are Jeri.' He pronounces my name *Yehri*. I think I'm in love.

211

'That's right.' I swallow hard. He probably sees that. *Be normal, Yehri, be normal.*

'You have flown from America? Where in America are you from? How long did it take to get here?'

I give him my background. For some reason it feels like one of those speed dating things. As he listens, his brown eyes never leave mine and I kind of get the same feeling inside me as before we were taking off in the airplane. He is a complete 77 Across. *Hunk.*

Shime's friends and Shira begin to converse in Hebrew so Shime draws me away slightly. 'What are you doing in Jerusalem?'

'We've come to visit my Saba and Savti.'

He raises his eyebrows. 'Oh, you speak some Hebrew.'

I nod. 'As of right now, I know two words: Saba and Savti. I just learned today.'

He laughs. It's kind of staccatoish, rapid, not what I expected. But really, what did I expect?

'I will have to teach you,' he says.

You can teach me all sorts of things, I say with my eyes. *Good Lord, Jeri.* I mentally slap myself. *What the heck are you doing?*

'I can teach you many things,' he says.

Holy Moley. Can Jewish people read minds? 'Uh, okay.' *Get ahold of yourself. You're acting like a teenage girl. I am a teenage girl!* Shime watches me while I finish my internal dialogue.

'How old are you?' He asks.

'I'm almost sixteen. Two more months. And you?'

'I am eighteen.'

An older man. How delightful.

Chapter 26 Down:

Maya shows up with our drinks and, distressingly, Yugi makes a sudden appearance at my side. I try to ignore him, but he is pulling on my sleeve.

'What?' My impatience is evident.

'Mom and Dad want us to meet some more natives.'

'Later,' I say through clenched teeth.

'Dude, what's wrong with you?' He looks around the crowd at the much taller humans and his eyes settle on Shime. His eyes close slightly and he smirks.

'Hello, my name is Yugoslavia. What's your name?'

Shime shakes his hand and laughs. 'Shime.'

Yugi giggles. 'In English, shimmy means to do this.' Yugi starts wiggling his butt which makes the others laugh.

'I'm so sorry.' I can't remember any other time I've been this embarrassed.

'Don't worry about it. He's a funny kid.'

I grab Yugi by the arm and pull him away. 'What in the world was that? Are you trying to ruin my life in multiple countries?'

'Like, duh.' Yugi pulls himself from my grasp and I follow behind him slowly.

Mom is hugging someone who I can only describe as an older version of Wonder Woman. She is tall and long-limbed, her black hair is streaked with white, her eyes are golden brown and the strong jut of her chin seems to add to her beauty. They are both crying and laughing at the same time. The man standing behind her is shaking Dad's hand furiously; it's as if they are long lost brothers.

Mom, while still hugging the woman, motions for Yugi and me to hurry to her. Even as I approach, my eyes cannot disconnect with the beauty of these two people.

213

'Jeri,' Mom says putting a hand on my shoulder while keeping the other on Wonder Woman's arm, 'this is one of my best friends in the world and certainly in Israel - Miriam Weismann.'

'Hello,' I respond hesitantly.

'Jeri,' Miriam calls me *Yehri* also, 'it is so nice to meet you.' She turns to the man behind her and touches his shoulder. 'This is my husband, Chaim.' His name sounds so strange coming out of her mouth, like she's got a fishbone in her throat - *Hckhkhime.*

'How do you do?' I say.

Yugi snorts. He's been eating something. 'How do you do?' He repeats. 'What, are you suddenly in the Sound of Music?'

I smack him quickly in the stomach which unfortunately makes him spit out whatever he's been eating. Mom is severely displeased. 'Jeri,' she says sharply and motions with her eyes, eyebrows and head at the Weismanns in a kind of *stop-embarrassing-me* movement.

'I'm so sorry. My lovely brother and I, we enjoy moments of tormenting each other.'

Miriam laughs and winks. 'I still enjoy tormenting my brother,' she whispers conspiratorially. I can't help but like her already. 'I think you have met our son already - Simeon.' She points and then waves. Shime waves back.

Oh heavens. We're going to have beautiful children, I think. *Stop it, Jeri. Stop it.*

'Yes, we did meet briefly. He's very nice.'

'Nice?' Yugi laughs. 'You were droo...' I pop him again. He bends over and makes a *waaaahuunh* sound.

'Jeri!'

'Sorry, that was preemptive. Habit.'

214

Chapter 26 Down:

Miriam is still laughing while Chaim tries to hide his smile. 'Really,' Mom says, 'the kids are never like this. They must be tired.'

I pretend to yawn. 'Oh, yes. Very tired. Okay, well, I'm going back to the young people again.'

As I turn, Chaim's voice rings out behind me. 'Nice to meet you, Yehri. We're glad that you are going to be staying with us a few days.'

Slowly, I rotate my body. 'I'm sorry. What did you say?'

Chaim bows slightly. 'We are very happy that you'll be staying at our house. We have so many things to talk about.'

I nod.

Yugi has recovered enough that he is about to say something smart, but my evil eye stops him short.

'I'll see you soon, then.'

I approach the teenage group and I see that Maya and Shira are chatting with Shime and another boy I haven't met. Immediately I feel a weird sense of jealousy, which is odd because I've never, *ever* had feelings for a boy before, but then again, I have never seen a boy in Duncan who looks like *that*. What is this weirdness? Why do I feel as if I'm at the zenith of a rollercoaster and the bottom is just about to fall out? This is what happens in romance books and movies, not in real life.

'Yehri,' Shime eyes are fastened on mine. 'We have some questions about America.'

We talk for a while and I feel a warm sense of acceptance that I've rarely felt before. They asked me about my high school experience and when I told them that I had recently graduated and that I was quite mathematically minded, the other boy, Moshi, quizzed me about calculus.

215

The surprise on his face was all the reward I needed when I answered all of his questions. He didn't know that girls had the right kind of brains to understand.

Someone clinks a glass behind us. It is Savti. She speaks in Hebrew, but Miriam stands next to her to translate. There is such a dissimilarity in appearance and yet the identical strength of the women is unmistakable. Where Miriam is tall and stately, Savti is short and stocky, but their eyes carry the same gravitas. Savti invites Saba up who also speaks with great happiness.

'*Shalom*, friends,' Miriam translates, 'what a beautiful night to have our family together. It has been many years. The Klein family circle has been stretched all the way to the United States but remains unbroken. Now,' Saba says as he puffs out his chest, 'we are very, very proud to have our Beryl back and her husband, Kevin.' Saba struggles with 'Kevin' and it comes out sounding very much like Chaim's name. 'As most of you good Jews know, beryl was one of the twelve stones placed on the priest's breastplate. It was a precious adornment near his heart.' Saba's voice breaks. Emotion washes over him and Savti steps in. She is about to say something when Saba laughs and controls himself and moves her back again. Everyone laughs. 'And now, our precious Beryl and Kevin have brought back two more jewels with them which will forever adorn our Klein house: Yugoslavia and Yehrushalem.' He claps his hands together rhythmically which incites the entire crowd to clap with him. Seconds later, music starts with the same rhythm as the clapping, and amazingly, spontaneous dancing breaks out. People link arms, clap, laugh and shout, *Mazel Tov!*

I am spun about by various people, by Maya and then Shira, another boy named Eli and finally, I see Shime twirling near me and then towards me. Our eyes connect, he is smiling, I am smiling, his hair is flowing, mine is stringy. Just as our arms are about to connect, Yugi pops up between us and wiggles his eyes. 'Ba da bing, ba da boom.'

Shime laughs at my brother, but I am furious. 'Come on. Let's dance,' he shouts.

Never have I been more relieved in my life to dance.

As the night wears on, exhaustion clings to the horizon of my consciousness. I am aware that consistent new stimuli, wrapped in a shawl of adrenaline, has kept me awake far longer than I should have been. I have never eaten directly from a roasted animal - until tonight. I have never attempted learning words in another language (other than Spanish which doesn't seem to really count) until tonight. I have never understood the desire to have others notice me and want to be included in their group - until tonight. Now that I have experienced these new things, I can safely say I want them to keep coming.

Glancing around the backyard of my recently discovered grandparents' house, I see an explosion of emotions and senses. I can't quite get my head around the fact that Saba and Savti Klein have always been in existence. Savti is standing next to Mom and Dad. She is grasping onto Mom's arm as if she is afraid the dream will float away into the night air. Saba stands back like a grinning emperor. He has raised his wine glass in countless toasts tonight and for the first time I finally understand the Prodigal Son's father, or Prodigal Daughter in this case. To love a party like this is to love life itself.

217

Suddenly I have cousins, aunts and uncles, distant relations, people who love different things which makes life infinitely more interesting. We talk about school and politics and the struggle of being Jewish in the Middle East.

Yugi has found a few young boys and girls to play with. One of them brought a soccer ball and they have been playing in the front yard. When he comes back in to get a drink of water, his hair is sticking up at odd angles. The sweat is a disgusting natural gel.

I have watched Mom throughout the night, and even from this distance, I can see that she has been needing this for a long time. She looks entirely alive. To be with her people, to bring her family to her people, to have us all experience a break. This, for her, was a deep breath after swimming underwater.

Dad, for his part, is social, but wary at the same time. He knows that our trip to Israel is not a vacation. I suppose it is a holiday from routine, but he knows that sooner or later he must lever his family from this to move onwards and outwards seeking the path which his own parents set him on.

As the night wears on, I find myself shimmying closer to the handsome young man who has captured my amorous attention. He is a specimen that I've never experienced before; an intelligent young human who poses a challenge for my previously unchallenged male perceptions. Maybe it is me, maybe it was my desire to leave Duncan, that I can't see desirable characteristics about young males in my hometown. Maybe I just wasn't ready to think about partnerships and, yes, romantic attraction. I want to tell myself, *stop being so melodramatic*, but I don't. If this is going to be a once-in-a-lifetime thing, well then I'm going to feel once-in-a-lifetime things. I think Maya and Shira see me drooling over him and they smirk.

Shime towers above me. It's not just his height, but it feels like his width and breadth of experience living in 21st century Israel overshadows my own cloistered experience. To live in a nation that is constantly in conflict, internal and external, a land destined to struggle and claw for every moment of its existence - this makes people grow up very quickly.

Finally, long after the sun sets and the party lights go on, the meat has been trimmed from the carcass, the music has been turned up louder, Shime reaches for two glasses of wine. He hands me one. I hesitate. I've never had a glass of wine before, not for legalistic or Puritanical reason, but I just haven't grown up with it. Wine isn't the drink of choice in the south. I smile and take it from his hand.

'*La Heim,*' he says and takes a sip.

I repeat the toast and it sounds funny - like saying his dad's name - and I take a sip. The red wine is delightfully fruity, but it also leaves kind of a furry taste on my tongue. Chalk up another new experience.

I wonder if my parents, or older people in general, remember what it feels like to fall in love for the first time. I'm not saying I'm in love, that would be preposterous - no one falls in love at first sight except in the movies - but I feel this strange weirdness, a longing. Something in my cells, something deeply embedded in my human DNA, is yanking me from adolescence into the vast, agora of adulthood. As I look at him, yes, I can't help but think he's beautiful. He has dimples in his cheeks when he smiles, and his teeth are perfectly white. I want to stay here for a long time.

Even as Shime and I dance, I spot my parents and notice that they have a sense of comfort about them. If I ask my dad what my mom was wearing, he would shrug and look, but if I were to ask him what she was feeling, I know, beyond a shadow of a doubt, he would describe her to a 't' without looking at her. And my mother, it's almost as if my dad is a magnet for her and she can't quite help being pulled in his direction. Her elbow seems to be perpetually bent and pointing towards him. Often her head turns just to see how close he is standing. Is that love? Or is it just convenience?

The night passes far too quickly. At eleven o'clock, Yugi approaches. 'Jeri,' he says, 'it's time for you to stop dancing with your b...' I throw him a significant, brother-beating, warning gaze. 'It's time for you to stop dancing, dear sister, so that you can get some sleep.' Mom and Dad who are motioning for me to come over.

'I have to go.' I say to Shime.

'If you're going, then I guess I will too.' My heart continues dancing while my body stops.

'Gag me,' Yugi murmurs.

Miriam smiles at me when I approach. 'We'll drive your parents if you're willing to ride with Shime. We didn't know how much luggage you were going to bring, so we brought two cars.' She smiles knowingly at me. Can she tell? I am so excited, I feel nauseous.

'What about Yugi?'

'He's staying with Saba and Savti. They only have one spare bedroom and I'm pretty sure you don't want to share a room.' Both Yugi and I feel twin nightmares fade before our eyes.

Simultaneously we both held up our hands in front of us. 'No thanks.'

Chapter 26 Down:

Many of the revelers seem content to continue partying, so we bid them farewell. I find that I am hugged a million times by a million strangers and yet it seems perfectly normal as if I've been doing this for years. Savti squeezes me hard and kisses my cheeks. Saba bends his cherubic face to mine and repeats Savti's kiss. Savti's eyes are wet with happiness.

I am incredibly nervous as I walk with Shime to his car. As of this point in my life, I am certain of only a few things: One - nothing like this has ever happened to me before and B - I am sure that I want to be normal. Just for one stinking night. I don't want to think about crossword puzzles; I don't want to worry about my brother, which I immediately do - *Dangit!* - and I don't want to be awkward.

While I ponder these very things, whether because of my tiredness or poor eyesight, I don't see the crack in the sidewalk. It would have been much better if I would have just fallen flat, just gone down in a heap, but no, no, Jerusalem Walker stumbles on a crack and then for seven more steps tries to readjust. My feet *fwap fwap* lurching forward like a Pelican attempting to take off from the water. I look so ungainly, so entirely out of control, and my mind is spinning with horror because my mind says, *Just give up and hit the ground* but my body refuses to endure the physical pain. Good Lord, after seven steps I finally run out of grace and faceplant into the grass.

So much for love at first sight.

Shime attempted to catch my arm after the third or fourth *fwap*, but my flailing was too wild for him to help. As I slam into the ground, he is immediately beside me. I don't want to look up at him. I don't want him to behold my embarrassment. I just want to lay down and cry.

221

I can feel his hand on my shoulder. 'Yehri, are you okay?'

'No.'

'Is anything broken?'

'My dignity.'

I roll over. My hair ends up in my mouth. I spit it out and I see his concerned face. 'Well, let's put it this way: I wanted to make a good impression on you and let's just say I made an indent in the grass instead.'

He attempts to translate what I'm saying. I can visually see this - his mouth is moving over the English words. Finally, his translation is transformed to understanding.

'I...,' he says and then smiles and starts to laugh, 'I will never forget this moment with you.'

'That makes two of us.'

I can hear that his laugh is not one of ill-humor, but genuine kindness. He is glad that I am not hurt. 'And,' I continue, 'it could have been worse. I could have done this exact same thing in front of everyone else.'

'Well, at least we get a few moments to ourselves.' He sits down next to me.

I smile wryly at this. He reaches over and plucks a blade of grass from my stringy hair. My arms have carpet burn from the grass and they itch, but there is no way I'm going to complain. It is dark in the street and our faces are only dimly lit by streetlamps. I sense there is something going on inside his head that he can't quite speak of.

Slowly, Shime puts a hand up to the side of my face. I feel electricity spark. *What in the world? Is he going to do this? I mean, we're on the ground. I've got gravel rash and grass stains. Shut up, Jeri! Shut up!*

Chapter 26 Down:

'You are very pretty.' The simplicity of his statement and its obvious detachment from reality is humorous and I smile.

'So are you.' *WHAT! YOU JUST CALLED HIM PRETTY!* 'Uh, I mean, you're gorgeous. Wait, wait, handsome?' *Jeri, normal. Find normal. Just once. Locate it* deep *inside you.*

'Thank you. Any of those words will work.'

His hand is still on my face, and I reach up and touch it with mine. Suddenly, without understanding how or why it happened, I pull on his forearm. Fortunately, he recognizes what I want, what I DESIRE, and he leans in toward me. *Do I keep my eyes open? Do I close them? What do I do? It's not like this is the first time I've been kissed. Remember Derek Davis in seventh grade by the water fountain, you know the one with the braces - that was very awkward. Jeri! Stop it!*

I go with eyes closed. This is going to be beautiful.

'Hey, Jeri! Nice job.'

Yugi.

We break away quickly and with more fury than I've ever felt in my life, I see Yugi standing in the doorway of Saba and Savti's house grinning from ear to ear. He is waving at us like Forest Gump, one hand on his hip, the other painting the sky. I am about to unleash an unprecedented verbal attack when Shime puts a hand on my arm. He shouts in Hebrew. His voice rings out with frustration. My brother's face falls and he looks scared. My mouth drops open and I look back to the door. Yugi has disappeared inside the house.

'What did you say?'

'I told him he was very funny and that he was a nice little kid.'

'Really?'

Shime smiles. 'Yeah, why not. It's all in the tone anyway. And, he does seem like a nice little kid. But, I don't think he'll be interrupting us again.' *Again? This won't be the last time he'd have a chance to interrupt us!*

'Come on. Let's go. I'll take you home.' Shime leans back and pushes himself off the ground. After he stands, he reaches down to help me up. I place both of my hands in his and I can feel his strength as I almost float into the air. I feel almost weightless.

If not for the crash landing and my stupid brother, I'm pretty sure I've never been this happy before.

Chapter 27 Down:
One who designs buildings (9)

When I wake up, I am decidedly confused. I have no idea where I am. The bed in which I have been sleeping is foreign to me. There is no window to my left nor is there my brother's annoying voice or antics outside my room. Suddenly, memories of last night's amorous adventures enter my brain and I flush. Was I just about to kiss a gorgeous boy with a crazy sexy accent last night?

I push back the covers, sheets and a handmade quilt. Light glows around the edges of an accordion blind covering the large window at the foot of the bed. There is a desk with books and pencils in one corner. A few pictures are tripoded on top. Floral-patterned wallpaper camouflages the pictures, but when I look closely, I see the obvious younger faces of Chaim, Miriam and Simeon. The photo seems to have been taken about five years ago. Tall and sinewy, almost pathetically thin, Simeon's body has stretched like bread dough. In this picture, he has both glasses and braces. Chaim is shading his eyes with a hand as he stares toward the photographer while Miriam seems to be posing. *Wow, what a body she has!*

For a moment, I reflect on my own body. I have not filled out, but I have noticed, even in the last six weeks or so, that I've shed some baby fat. By no means am I slender and certainly not buxom. I hope this is not a problem for Shime. It has never been an issue for me before, but now it seems strangely important for someone else to think that my body is beautiful.

I yawn and wrinkle my nose. My breath reeks. I can taste the remnants of lamb, rosemary, lemon and a hint of red wine. I run my tongue along the top of my mouth. It sticks. In desperate need of a toothbrush and a shower, I open the door.

Shime is standing in the hallway. He looks at me and smiles.

How many different ways can I strike out? I touch my hair. Honestly, it feels like a rat's nest filled with leaves and twigs, which, if I think about it, it probably is filled with leaves and twigs.

'Uh, hi,' I say completely conscious that I might be the most underwhelming young woman he's ever seen in his life.

He smirks. 'Hello.'

'I... well... I'm sorry that I have to knock your socks off with my incredible beauty this morning.' I can still smell my breath. I hope he can't. 'What time is it?'

'About noon.'

'Oops.'

'You must have slept well. Our parents have been up for quite a while talking very loudly.'

'What have you been doing?'

'I went out to get some groceries. I waited for you for a while, but I assumed that you needed to sleep.'

Dang it. 'Yeah, sorry about that.'

'Next time.'

'So, what's the plan?' I ask.

'I think we'll find you something to eat and then talk to the parents.'

'Yes,' I say. We've come to the pointy end of why we're in Israel. I hope we don't move too fast. I'd like to spend a little more time in Jerusalem. 'What are we talking about?'

'Nazis.'

'What have your parents told you?'

He pauses for a moment and then smiles again. 'Get dressed and come downstairs.'

Forty minutes later I arrive freshly scrubbed and dressed. My cheeks feel rosy, fleshy - somehow new. Miriam and Chaim are in the kitchen making lunch. Mom and dad are huddled with Shime at the table telling stories about Yugi and me. I hope, I hope, I hope they are not pillorying me in their stories. Parents seem to enjoy embarrassing their children, but I am quite good at doing that myself.

'Good morning, Yehri,' Miriam says. The spatula in her hand is dripping with oil. It splatters onto the floor.

'Wow, that smells amazing.' Fish and salad, lemon and pepper. My stomach grumbles loudly.

'Thank you,' Miriam says and flips one of the fish over onto the sizzling griddle. 'Go sit down and I'll bring lunch to you.'

Near the end of the meal, Chaim pushes his plate further out in front of him and rests his forearms on the table. They are very hairy. 'Tell us about your parents, Kevin.'

Dad, finishing his last mouthful of food, takes a drink of water and then leans forward seesawing his hand. 'My dad is doing pretty well, although he certainly feels trapped in the nursing home.'

'And your mother?' Chaim asks quietly.

'She's fading. I think she still recognizes us, but our names sometimes escape her.'

'She is a wonderful woman,' Miriam says as she reaches out to touch Dad's arm.

'Yes, she is.'

There is an uncomfortable silence. It is as if Grandma's presence is in the room and that memory is overpowering.

'What was she like when you knew her?' I ask.

Chaim smiles. 'She was like a movie star. I used to think that a woman as beautiful as she could not be a spy. She was so good at her job; she could become anyone. I remember that. One time she was supposed to be a fat laundrywoman in the house of a diplomat. This was before fat suits, so she stuffed her clothes and put on a dirty launderers outfit. I remember dropping her off and watching her assume the identity - she slouched and then walked like a very fat person, legs bowed out, arms swinging away from the body.' He chuckles.

'You know what's funny?' Dad interjects. 'Until we talked this morning, we had no idea that you and Miriam were involved in any of this stuff. Nice job of hiding it.' Chaim looks guilty, but Dad brushes it aside and reaches beside him to retrieve the computer.

'Mom led us to a microfilm.' Dad points to the screen. 'There was a lot of distraction from old photos but they were necessary to hide a dozen pictures. These,' he points at the twelve, 'are what brought us to you.'

'I don't understand,' Miriam says.

'Mom seems to have left you something. Something important.'

'What was it?'

Dad's face hardens. 'As far as we can tell, the location of something that will help us to follow the trail of some pretty serious Nazi war criminals.'

Chaim squints. 'These photos are of me,' he says incredulously, 'but how did you sift them from the others? How do you know that your mom was leading you to me?'

'Because of this.' Dad retrieves the amputated Barbie arm from his computer bag.

Shime snorts. 'What is that?'

'It is the arm of a doll, but more importantly, the name of the doll - Barbie. That was Mom's nickname. Barbie.'

'But why is there an arm?'

'Because of this...' Dad takes out the written printout of the clues.

Dear Whoever You Are,

I assume the book has guided you to me, so let it continue to do so. One never knows what kinds of numbers and words one might find inside.

In my house, one finds all sorts of things.

I also assume that you are on the yellow brick ratline that I was, but if you are not, I suggest putting this small piece of history safely where you found it and go about your daily business.

Now, to work...
Just follow the path. Follow my prints.

Visit the White Man to the first leg of the journey.
He will bring your case before the court.

The White Man will speak of the hotdog man whose story will send you to the second leg.

The connection made between the hotdog man and the 'foul' man who fled.

There you will find the Angel beneath the Cross.
At that intersection, the union place...
You will find me.

Finish the book, where I was unable. Pieces of me still remain.

Love,
Barbie.

'We've figured out that *my prints* are actually Barbie's prints - the photos we needed to put together she stamped with this Barbie arm.' Dad showed them the blackened fingers and then pointed to the screen. 'Her prints were in a crossword puzzle that led us to everything else. Jeri is an amazing crossword solver. We never could have done it without her.'

Shime looks at me admiringly. I blush.

'Now,' Dad continues, 'the letter reads, 'Visit the White Man to the first leg of the journey.' Your picture came up when we connected the dots, fingerprints, I guess. Did Mom give you something a long time ago?'

Chaim thinks for a moment. 'Not that I know of. That's very clever, though, the fingerprints.'

'Did she take you anywhere? To a courtroom? Any place where judicial activities take place?'

'No, but maybe it's near where Eichmann's trial was held?' He scratches his head.

'That's a good idea,' Mom says.

'Can you tell me about Eichmann?' I ask.

Chaim's jaw sets, hardened. 'Eichmann was considered the 'Architect of the Final Solution,' and unfortunately, he was a very good architect. After the war, he was captured by the Allies but somehow slipped through their fingers after almost being caught in Germany.

'To South America, right?' I ask.

230

Chapter 27 Down:

Nodding, Chaim continued. 'Eventually, the Mossad planned a mission to kidnap him from South America.' Chaim leaned back in his chair. 'In 1960, there was a celebration to which the State of Israel was invited. Generally, there were no direct flights from Israel to Argentina - sixty years ago the flight would have had four or five stops. But the Mossad saw their opportunity, their one shot to take him. If they could kidnap Eichmann and get him onto the delegates' plane, they could go without notice.' Chaim took a drink of water and then held up a finger waiting for the swallow to hit his stomach. 'Everything was going swimmingly - they practiced and practiced the kidnap at their rented house. They followed Eichmann to and from work - he always took the same bus. Always.'

'Except...?' I insert a question knowing what was coming.

'Except the night of the kidnapping. In the weeks leading up, Eichmann's routine never varied. But on the night of the kidnapping, Eichmann, for some reason, changed buses. The Israeli spies didn't know whether to abort or keep waiting, but the plane was supposed to be arriving the next day and they would leave the day after. The leader of the team made the decision to stay. Eichmann showed up on the next bus an hour later. As he began to walk the small lane to his house, one of the agents asked for help - the only three words he knew in Spanish. Eichmann nervously backed away and they jumped him. His screams were loud. This was not how they had practiced it and as they stuffed him into the car, they truly hoped that this was indeed Eichmann. Imagine if they'd kidnapped the wrong man?'

'They took him back to their safehouse. After hours of interrogation, Eichmann finally admitted his identity. To the end, though, he denied responsibility for any part in the Holocaust, only that he was following orders. How these Mossad agents didn't kill him right there was a testament to their strength.'

'That's quite a story. Sounds like a movie script,' I say.

Miriam's smiled derisively. 'It gets even more stressful. Unfortunately, their departure was delayed a week. They had to keep Eichmann under wraps at the safehouse for seven more days. They had to do everything for him, and I mean everything, so that he wouldn't commit suicide or attempt an escape. When the plane finally did arrive, they smuggled Eichmann onto it drugged and in the guise of a drunk flight attendant. They waited on the runway until it was their turn to take off, but just as they were about to power up, the control tower stopped them. For forty agonizing minutes they waited. The navigator got up and volunteered to see what was happening. The pilot told him if he wasn't back in ten minutes they were going to take off and attempt to outmaneuver the Argentinian air force.'

'With two minutes to spare, the navigator returned to the airplane and said that something had gone wrong with the manifest and they were free to go. They were supposed to stop in Brazil, but decided to attempt to cross the Atlantic non-stop. They landed in Morocco on fumes.'

The Weismann family smiled. 'The rest is beautiful justice. He was tried and after fifty-six days hanged, cremated and dumped in the ocean.'

I can't help smiling either, but part of me is feeling slightly uneasy, off center. How is it that I can feel good about another human's death?

'What about these other things?' Simeon points to Grandma's clue. "*The White Man will speak of the hotdog man.*' What does that mean?'

'We don't know yet.' Dad's eyes are on Chaim.

'What is a 'hotdog'?' Chaim asks.

'It's like a sausage,' I say, 'but not quite as good. Thinner.'

At one point in the afternoon, we move from the kitchen table to the living room. Dad connects the computer screen to the television and we sort through photos, letters and what precious few documents are included in the microfilm. Both 'hotdog man' and 'foul' man confuse us, but I'm trying to use my crossword brain to think of different meanings. Hotdog. Hotdog. Ace? Hotshot? Arrogant? 'Foul' could symbolize something that smells as well as someone whose disposition is off.

Angel beneath the Cross. Were there angels at Jesus' crucifixion? What were their names? Why is Cross capitalized? Is it a location not an object?

Each of us in pairs, type in combination after combination of phrases and synonyms for hotdog and foul. After each search, notes are taken and compiled. Time has flown by, and as we look up at the clock, suddenly we realize it is almost dinnertime.

We order pizza for dinner and make plans for the following day. I sit next to Shime, probably too close, but who cares. When in Jerusalem, be Jerusalem.

In the middle of the night, I wake up sweating. My sheets are wet and my hair feels as if I've taken a shower. Darkness surrounds me. It feels tomb-like. Still. I search for my phone. 3:30. The light hurts my eyes and I shut it off quickly. Unfortunately, I am wide awake now. I have more than half a mind to walk down the hallway to peek into Simeon's room.

I lie back in bed and stare into the darkness. It is normal, I think, for any normal person to imagine various scenarios about the future. But, my realistic nature keeps butting in. *Be serious*, or *This is just a casual summer fling. Everyone has them. When you leave, you'll both be back to square 1 or at least 2.* I don't want to be serious. I want to imagine. I want to pretend. In my heart, I know that I'm still a teenager, but...

I hear movement in the hallway and my heart beats faster. Is he sneaking down the corridor? Should I pretend to be asleep? How should I arrange my hair?

A muffled cough in the outer doorway. It's my dad. How disappointing. I return to dreaming.

We stand in the parking lot of the Jerusalem District Court. It is a weekday, yet the cars, Japanese and German mostly, ironic, I think, fill the lot. The day is warm and humid. There is honking, yelling, whistles, the general commotion of trucks and buildings. I smell exhaust and fried food. Yugi has decided to stay with Saba and Savti which is a blessing.

The Jerusalem District Court looks like Gotham City Hall. It is made from sandstone; there are no curves, nothing delicate. It is built for justice. Surrounding the premises is a black metal gate which I am sure is a preventative measure to stop terrorists from bombing it. A few guards stand menacingly scanning the crowd. Covered from head to toe in protective gear, these men and women look as if they could tear me to bits with their pinky toes.

Chapter 27 Down:

Chaim looks at my parents. 'It says that I'm supposed to '*bring your case before the court.*' What case? Is it a physical case or judicial?'

'I don't know, Chaim,' my mom says. The guards' eyes follow us. At the security checkpoint, we wait while our bags are searched then walk through a metal detector. I am nervous. This is nothing like home, not even at the airport. It's almost as if they think that the building *will* be attacked, not *might* be.

Inside, we see photos from the Eichmann trial. They are black and white taken from above. A glass cage, if you will, is positioned to the left of the photo. Inside the cage, Eichmann sits passively, expressionless. His bespectacled eyes seem calm, as if he believes that he's going to be set free. The courtroom is packed. At the front of the room, three judges sit high above the proceedings.

From the perspective of the photo, it's hard to see faces very well. The judges' expressions are clouded in darkness, but even from a picture, it is easy to feel the tension in the room. Almost everyone is leaning forward, straining to hear, straining to hate the man in the box.

Just as we were about to pass on, my eye falls on something - something that triggers another idea.

One never knows what kind of words and numbers one might find inside.

Words and numbers.

Case number 40/61. Could it be?

I ask Dad for my crossword puzzle book. I look at each of the puzzles that had empty spaces: 4, 24, 32. Then, I cross check the number 40/61. Only puzzle 32 has it. The answers are 'players' and 'peace.'

I hold the book up to Shime. 'Do these words mean anything to you?'

235

He looks at them and shrugs. 'Well, kind of. The Peace Players are Jerusalem's NBA basketball team.'

It doesn't hit me for a moment, then all the pieces click. 'Holy moley, Shime.'

'What?'

'We're not supposed to begin the leg here. We're supposed to find the Peace Players.'

'I'm not following you.'

'*Bring your case before the court.* It's a basketball court.'

His eyes open wide. 'Are you sure?'

'Look at Grandma's note: *One never knows what kinds of words and numbers one might find inside.* Numbers and words. Of these that have blank spaces, 32 is the only one that has both 40 and 61. It's too much of a coincidence that the name of the basketball team, which plays on a court, is the clue?'

'You're right.' He looks at me with incredulity. 'You are very smart.'

'Thank you.' I beam.

We race to the adults who are lost in time.

'Mom,' I whisper. She doesn't look from the photo she is studying. 'Mom,' I say more intently, 'I think I've figured it out!

She looks at me sharply. 'Really?'

'Yes.' I show her. She takes the crossword puzzle in her hands, looks at it and then back up at me.

'Where do the Peace Players play basketball?' Mom asks Shime.

'At the YMCA.'

'Where is it at the YMCA?' Mom asks.

'I don't know, but we should check it out, don't you think?'

236

Chapter 27 Down:

Quickly, we exit the court. I am not altogether upset to be shoved into the backseat with Shime.

We drive through dense traffic and make our way to the YMCA. Needless to say, it is not what I expected. I assumed that it would be very much like YMCA's in the U.S., utilitarian, blocky things with lots of windows showing off a pool and a waterslide. Instead, the Jerusalem YMCA is humongous and looks very similar to the District Court except for the immense spire at the front. It is called the Three Arches YMCA; it's a hotel and resort all mixed into one. The wings of the YMCA look like synagogues. They have rounded cupolas on top.

'Why is it called Three Arches?' I ask Shime.

'Inside the hotel, there is a decorated area with three arches. Many people come to take photographs of it. The hotel is quite an impressive place.'

'Do you think my grandma would have stayed there?'

'There's a good chance.'

'Now,' Chaim says, 'how are we going to do this? What are we looking for?'

Strangely, everyone looks to me which makes me nervous. 'Well, I suppose we're looking for a case, or a box, that will have something in it.'

'How will we know which one?'

I raise my eyebrows. 'My best guess is it will be by a number or Barbie's fingerprints will be all over it.'

We enter through the door at the base of the spire. The entry is immaculately clean where people mill around taking photos or lounge on furniture. We wait in line at the front desk behind two very tall boys who appear ready to play basketball. Finally, we approach the desk. A fit looking woman speaks to us in Hebrew. Shime translates for me and we pay for entry. The woman arches her eyebrows at the six people who are entering without any kind of exercise clothes.

The boys, Dad, Chaim and Shime, enter the men's locker room and the girls, Mom, Miriam and I, on the other side. We search the lockers searching carefully for any 'fingerprints.' When all have been checked, I begin to feel nervous that I've brought everyone on a wild goose chase. Chaim texts Miriam to say they haven't found anything.

We meet them back in the foyer and then walk through the rest of the building toward the basketball courts. The gym is hot and smells of sweat and something else, deeper, a dense smell, like something has been polished, whether the floor or seats. We wander along the seats scanning carefully for any Barbie marks, but there are none, not even seats 40 or 61. I'm beginning to despair. How is it that we can't find it? This should have been cut and dried. *Grandma, help us!*

'Maybe it's already gone?' Dad says. 'That would be a real bummer.'

'It's got to be here!' I stubbornly respond.

'How about we check in the hotel, too.' Shime has his hands in his pockets. He now looks much younger.

'Let's just go back to the front desk one more time.'

We stand in front of the woman again. Her brown eyes are inquisitive and curious. 'Tell me what you want me to ask her,' Shime says.

The adults are standing back. Now it's just me and him. 'Ask her if there is any lost and found.'

Smiling the woman nods. Obviously, she speaks English. 'Yes,' she responds, 'is there something specific that you are looking for?'

I lean on the counter. 'Yes, a case.'

'How big? A suitcase?'

'No, no. About this big,' I make the size with my hands, but I have no idea. It's simply to see if there is anything in the lost and found. 'It would have been here a long time. Years.'

The woman frowns. 'Generally, if something is lost we attempt to call the owner, and if it isn't claimed, it is either thrown away or sold. The proceeds are used by the YMCA charity.'

Frustration. 'What about security boxes. Do you have those?'

Nodding, she points over our shoulders. 'Behind you. There are about one hundred boxes.'

'Are those cleaned out?'

'Yes, but not if the rent is paid on them.'

'Are there any which have been rented long term, say, over ten years?'

Wanting to be helpful, the woman types into her computer and moves her finger along the screen. 'There are a half dozen or so. May I ask why?'

'My grandmother, who used to live here in Jerusalem, left us a message that she left something in one of the boxes for us, but she has dementia...' I let the words trail off.

The woman frowns. 'I don't know that word.' Shime translates for me. 'I'm sorry,' she says. 'Let's see,' she peers intently at the screen, 'box numbers 7, 19, 32, 67, 81 and 83.'

32.

'I think one of those might be hers.' I point in the direction she showed us. 'Over there?'

The woman nods. I grab the parents and we move in the direction of the security boxes. They are stacked four

239

high. Each of them is about a foot and a half square. We walk down the line and see the grey boxes looking solidly permanent. Locating number 32, I see that there is a combination on it. Thankfully, it's not a key.

I peer closely at the box. There are dot marks along the edges of it. I point excitedly. 'Look! Barbie marks.'

I take out the crossword puzzle again. What would grandma be thinking? What numbers would she use?

'What is the combination?' Dad asks.

I shush him. I don't mean to be short, but I need to think.

'Maybe we should try those numbers from your missing space pages,' Mom suggests helpfully.

'No, there are too many numbers.' I point to the lock. 'This is only a three number combination.'

I stare at the lock pleading with it to reveal its secret. I can almost taste the success. Then, suddenly, I remember the clue this morning. *The White Man will bring your case before the court.*

40/61.

Four, six, one.

Tentatively, as if reaching out to see if a wire is electrified, I touch the combination and enter the numbers. Looking back at the others, I smile and pull up on the handle.

Click.

Yeeeees.

Exultantly, I open the door and inside there is an attaché case. I pull it out and hand it to Dad. Making sure the rest of the locker is empty, I scour the inside just in case Grandma has decided to leave anything else, but it is empty. I hug Shime, then step back awkwardly.

'What are you grinning at?' I squint suspiciously at Dad's widening grin.

'Nothing, oh, nothing,' Dad says trying to play it cool.

'Come on,' I say pulling Shime's hand. 'Let's get home so that we can figure this thing out.'

Like déjà vu all over again, we stand around the Weismann's kitchen table. The attaché case, dark brown and dusty, lies inert under the bright kitchen lights. The leather is dry and scarred, an old wineskin holding valuable contents.

'Go ahead, Jeri,' Dad says. 'You open it.'

'I was hoping someone would say that.' Gently, I reach for the case and pull it towards me. Unbuckling the clasps, I look around one more time. The suspense is delicious. Click. Click. I open it slowly and everyone seems to crane forward.

Only two objects.

A Barbie leg and a photograph. The leg, I get. It's always been a play on words. I pick it up. There is a word written on it. *Jedanascie.*

I hold up the photo and show it to the others. 'Who is this?'

They are all frowning. 'I was expecting it to be a photo of Eichmann's lair or treasure trove.'

'But who is it?

Miriam leans forward. 'Hans Frank.'

'And he is?'

'Another Nazi butcher. Governor General of Poland during the war. Very nasty.'

241

'But why him? What is Grandma telling us?' I look at the picture; the man's face is rigid, unsmiling and his hand is extended in the Nazi salute.

Dad takes the photo from my hand and holds it up in front of his face. He even examines the back before giving an old-fashioned 'A-ha!' He points to the multiple sets of Barbie fingerprints. 'I guess this makes it authentic.'

Suddenly Mom starts laughing. 'Oh, Iris, you sly woman you. Or should I say, you sly dog.'

'What?' I ask.

'Hotdog... Frank.'

To be entirely honest, Hans Frank is not a name that comes to mind when I think of Holocaust. It's not even a name that sounds like a mass-murderer. I say it aloud. Hans Frank. Hans Frank. When I look at the picture of Frank, I see cold, agate eyes, thinning hair and a chubby face.

'What did he do?' I ask.

Chaim breathes deeply and then blows his cheeks out, then steps back and runs a hand through his hair. 'The implications of Frank being involved in this are far reaching. It changes the parameters, certainly. I mean, if we were talking simply about Nazi hunting, Frank wouldn't even be in the picture.'

'Why not?' I see that his eyes are very troubled.

'Well, for one thing, he was executed after the Nuremberg Trials. For another, his role was different than military men.' He pauses and then restarts. 'Okay, okay. My dates might be off slightly, but they'll be close enough. Hans Frank was in with the Nazis from the very beginning. He was a lawyer working closely with Hitler. Some even claimed that at least one of Frank's children was one of

242

Hitler's illegitimates. Obviously, if you see a picture of any of his children, none of them look like the Fu...' He stops and reddens. 'I'm sorry, the Germans called him Führer, but here in Israel, we call him something different.'

'Don't worry about my ears,' I say.

Chaim continues. 'After Poland is quickly and efficiently conquered by the Wehrmacht, Hitler installs Frank to be the Governor General. Although not a politician, he is effective in managing the Nazi government transforming Poland from a peaceful, Catholic nation, into an adroit mass murder machine. Within Poland's borders alone, five million people were killed. Estimates are that sixty percent were Jews. Eichmann may have been the Architect, but Frank was the Builder.'

'Sounds like the Devil,' I mutter.

'He was.'

'Why would he be important to what we're doing?'

Chaim pauses to think. 'Yesterday, when we were working through the clues, you mentioned something about a piece of artwork - a Raphael, I think. Frank would be the natural person to investigate if so.'

'Yes,' Mom broke in, 'during our own research, we saw that the Raphael, along with many other invaluable pieces of art were stolen and stored in Poland. The last I heard hunters were looking for that treasure buried in a railway somewhere.'

Miriam nods. 'I heard that too, but also that artwork might be underneath a chapel somewhere in Silesia.'

'Or,' Chaim concludes, 'these works of art may have been destroyed just to spite the rest of humanity.'

I lift up the Frank photograph. 'Is there something special about this picture? Do you know anything about it?'

The adults all look at it, but they shake their heads.

I flip the photograph over and study Barbie's fingerprints distractedly. 'So, where do you think we are going next? Do you think Poland?'

'It's a possibility,' Dad responds and takes the photo from my hands. 'But Poland is a very big country. Auschwitz, maybe? It might be a needle in a haystack.'

'Shime,' I touch his arm, 'what do these letters on Barbie's leg mean?'

Shime takes out his phone and types them in. He smiles and nods. 'Eleven. *Jedanascie* is the Polish word for 'eleven.''

'All right,' I state with firmness. 'I assume the remaining limbs will have numbers on them too. Maybe a combination?'

Everyone nods. 'Good. Well, I suppose we'd better dive into Hans Frank then.'

Time to work.

A week passes. So much has happened and yet so little.

I have been thinking about Maximus. She must be lonely for us. We video messaged Dongle who was surprised and happy to see us once he figured out how to connect to the call. Dongle seems happy. He showed us around both of our backyards. It is June and the grass is beginning to get crispy, but Dongle has watered ours so that it is only dusty green rather than brown. Maximus was in the background and when Dongle brought the phone to her, she seemed very pleased to see me - or at least that's what I want to think.

Over the course of these days, I've had the bittersweet pleasure of switching houses. I got to spend three days at Saba and Savti's house. They are wonderful people, talkative and generous. They took me to the market to buy some souvenirs and try the coffee. They have been taking many pictures of us. Yugi and I are the screen saver on their computer now.

As I sit at the kitchen table of Savti and Saba's house, I feel the early morning sunshine on my legs. The kitchen doors, multiple panes of glass, crisscross the light. I enjoy the sight and feel of the morning, but something has changed. I don't know if it's a metamorphosis, a butterfly moment, a caterpillar twisting out of its old body, or if it's just me feeling uncomfortable in my old skin.

Saba and Savti are outside puttering in the garden like Dongle does. In many ways, they are just like Dongle and Margery: content in retirement, enjoying the things they like and worrying less about the things that don't really matter. Saba looks up from his weeding, sees me and lifts a hand. I suppose it's strange for him, akin to having a young, unrecognizable specter living in the house with them. I wave back at him when suddenly, my phone rings. It's my app for international Wi-Fi calls.

'Good morning, Mom,' I say, but I'm surprised to see Yugi's face pop up on the screen.

'Jeri!' He shouts. 'I figured it out!'

I sit up in my seat. 'Figured it out? What do you mean? What is it?'

'The clue. The one on the back of the picture.'

'They were just fingerprints, weren't they?'

His face is split by a grin. I can see the adults huddled over the table in the background. Shime is standing by them, but he is looking over Yugi's shoulder into the phone. 'They were Barbie fingerprints, but they were also a shape.'

'What shape?'

He adjusts the camera. It shakes. 'We scanned some copies of both the picture and the back. There was nothing else in the case that we could see. We looked for a secret compartment, nothing. But then from the fingerprints, I got this crazy idea.' He paused waiting for me to get frustrated.

'Dammit, Yugi, just tell me.'

'Okay, okay, don't snap your bra.' My face reddens as Shime smirks in the background. 'The fingerprints looked like connect the dots. While the adults were trying to figure out what the 'secret message' was, I took one of the scans and started connecting them.' He held up a picture but it was blurry.

'I can't tell what it is, Yugi. You're shaking the camera too much.'

He holds it still and an image materializes. 'It's a dragon.'

That's exciting. 'What does a dragon have to do with the mystery?'

'The adults figured that out a while ago - actually, Shime did.' I see Shime give a thumbs up behind Yugi. 'Here, I'll let you talk to him.' *Thank you, Yugi*, I thought. Yugi passes the phone and Shime's face enlarges.

'Hi.'

'Hi, back,' he says.

He clears his throat and stares at me through the phone. 'When Frank was installed as Governor General of Poland, he was given privileges, not just of power, but also wealth. It seems that when he and his wife, Brigitte, along with at least two of their children, moved to Poland, they took up residence not in a home, but in a castle: Wawel Castle.'

'I remember reading about that,' I say.

Nodding, he unconsciously itches his nose. It's cute. 'Inside Wawel Castle, Frank was able to 'acquire' priceless works of art from the Polish National Museum - Da Vinci, Rembrandt and Raphael. Supposedly, he hung some of them behind his office desk to impress dignitaries.'

I try to connect the other dots before Shime reveals the answer. 'Frank helped build the concentration camps. Auschwitz was one of them, right?'

'That's right, but get this,' Shime said as Yugi's face appeared just behind his head sticking out his tongue and crossing his eyes, 'I think we figured out the 'foul' man also. Your parents did anyway - it doesn't work as well trying to translate it from English into Hebrew. The word 'foul' is in parenthesis so when my mom read it out loud, your mom heard it differently. Her mind went to 'bird man.''

Mom yells out from the background. 'That was me! I still got it!'

Muted laughter.

'So who was the 'fowl' man?'

'Eichmann. We were on the right trail all along. After he escaped from the Allies, he went into hiding with the name Eckmann. He did some jobs, working for a farmer and then, before leaving for Austria, worked in a little town in Germany where he was a chicken farmer.'

''Fowl' man.'

'That's right.'

I stared into his eyes. So beautiful. 'What does the dragon have to do with anything?'

'There is an old Polish myth about a dragon in Krakow which terrorized the city and demanded that a young virgin be brought out to feed him. As the story goes, the king offered a reward that whoever could rid the community of the dragon would receive his daughter's hand in marriage.'

'Ugh,' I say, 'women as sheep for the slaughter.'

'You're more right than you know. A poor farmer in the area, Krakus, took a sheepskin and filled it with sulfur and something else and set it in front of the dragon who ate it and immediately became so thirsty, it flew down to the Vistula River and drank so much that it exploded.'

'That's funny.'

'Here is the ... I can't remember the ... the...'

'Moral?'

'No, something else.'

'Kicker?'

His face glowed and he smiled. 'Yes, the kicker of the story. The dragon statue is placed outside Wawel Castle and one of the entrances is said to have the dragon's bones hanging above it.'

'Wawel Castle. That's where Frank was living.'

'Exactly.'

I roll my neck. 'I guess we get to go to Poland.'

His eyes darkened. 'I have to let you talk to your parents about that first.'

'What is it?' My heart drops, but he is already moving toward my mom who is holding out her hands.

I can see it in her eyes, or at least somewhere between them. She looks pinched, halfway between a smile and a grimace. 'Good morning, Jer. How are you doing at Saba and Savti's?'

'Fine, Mom.' My grandparents are leaning on hoes talking to each other. Saba is wiping his forehead with a handkerchief. Savti's colorful, floral dress has mud on the seat. I wonder if Saba and Savti have ever done exciting things in their lives? 'Now, what happened?'

Chapter 27 Down:

She sighs and looks behind her, but the rest are still poring over the table. 'They're here.'

'Who?'

'The CIA.'

'What? But how did they find us? Didn't we cover our tracks?'

Mom shakes her head. She speaks slowly. 'They're the Central Intelligence Agency. Do you think a family of four could actually outsmart them?'

'But you guys are former spies. You've got to know some kind of techniques, right? Can't you like erase your tracks?'

'This is real life, Jeri.' My mom's face tightens.

'Wait, wait. So how do you know they're following you? Maybe you're just paranoid.'

'We were in the service for a long time, sweetie. We know. Even the Weismann's have noticed. There was a couple walking outside the house today. We saw them a few times in different outfits.'

'What do we do now?'

Mom's face takes a turn towards sadness. 'We'll have to leave as soon as possible.'

'Are the Weismann's coming with us?'

'No, Jeri. We can't put them at risk.'

'I think we've already done that.'

She shakes her head again. 'It's not possible. And the logistics for seven people traveling and staying together would be too cumbersome. We thought about leaving you and Yugi here with them, but we know how adamant you are about seeing this through.'

Suddenly, I realize that I'm only *half* as adamant as I was last week. I've met this new family, new friends, new feelings and a good segment of me wants to stay. Then, I think of Grandma and Grandpa, Dongle and Margery, all the people who suffered because of the Nazi monsters/CIA villains. I chide myself. 'So when are you picking me up?'

'Soon.'

'Okay.' I feel my emotions beginning to rip like a sheet from top to bottom. Happiness and amusement give way to frustration and annoyance. I know that fear and anger are about to come. As I disconnect from the call, my eyes fall upon my grandparents who have returned to their normal life, planting and uprooting. A time to be born, and a time to die. There is a season for everything. As they move back and forth through my vision in the windowpanes, it seems like a silent home movie. I see them from afar and I find that a tear has formed in the corner of my right eye.

There is never enough time.

Chapter 28 Down:
Done without rehearsal (9)

Leaving. Every day is a departure from something or someone, from the people who made me who I am, or the events that have transformed me. This one feels very, very different, though.

Our bags are packed, breakfast is eaten, passports are in hand. We stand awkwardly outside the Weismann's house. They are driving us in separate cars to the airport. Goodbyes are difficult and strange. Shime stands with his hands in his pockets, his shoulders are ratcheted up by his ears. I can see he is not happy. He argued long and hard about accompanying us on the journey, but to no avail.

As we stand there, shuffling our feet and pretending to laugh, my mom's face changes and stops, frozen.

'What is it?'

'Don't turn around, but our watcher is at the corner.'

If ever you want someone to turn around, the best thing to say is, 'Don't turn around.' All the kids immediately follow Mom's gaze.

Yugi even goes so far as to point. 'You mean that guy over there?'

'Yugi! Don't look!'

'He's not looking at us anymore,' Yugi says.

I watch the man on the corner. He is about thirty yards from us. He is a middle-aged man, in his forties, I think. Even from this distance, I can see that he is good looking. He has a strong jaw and a shadow of beard growth. He has a phone in his hand texting someone.

He looks up again. 'Hello, Mr. Spy!' Yugi shouts out and waves at him. The man looks up and frowns.

'Yugi,' my Mom hisses again. 'Stop it!'

'Why? Maybe if they know that we know, they'll stop following us.' The man looks one more time and Yugi pretends to make a rifle with his arms and pretends to shoot the 'spy' with a *pchew* sound.

The man turns away from us and out of sight. Mom bends down in front of Yugi. Face to face, her eyes wide, she prepares to give him the what's what, but before she can start, Dad puts a hand on her shoulder.

'Beryl, it's okay. They obviously aren't trying to hide it too well.'

'Then why would they do it?' Mom asks straightening up again. Yugi exhales. He had been holding his breath in preparation for a tongue lashing.

Dad shrugs. 'I suppose we'll find out eventually.'

For a few moments, we stand in silence looking between one another. Each face seems etched with varying emotions. I can tell that the Weismann's are worried about us; Shime is frustrated; Yugi is excited. My dad seems resolved, while my mom seems to be holding back. Nobody knows when the next time we'll get back to Israel.

Yugi rides in the car with Shime and me. I would have preferred having the last minutes alone with him, but my parents insisted. They had some 'adult things' to talk about.

As we pull into the airport, I look at Shime and see that the muscles in his jaw are jumping. I reach out and touch his hand. He grabs it. Thankfully, Yugi does not say anything. He is busy staring out the windows at the Jerusalem airport. Shime swings his car in behind Chaim's. We open the doors and begin to unload our luggage. Inside

Chapter 28 Down:

Dad's suitcase is Grandma's attaché case. Who knows if we will need it again?

Goodbyes are not fun. I hug Chaim and Miriam. They bend down to embrace me and kiss me on the cheeks. They attempt to do the same with Yugi, but he squirms away from them. Shime has resumed his hands in pockets. I stand in front of him, waiting, heart beating, hoping that he'll take his stupid hands out of his pockets. Finally, he does. He spreads his arms - it's awkward, like I hoped it wouldn't be - and I hug him. I can feel his heart beating hard; whether this is from nervousness or from pain, I don't know. He bends down and also kisses me on both cheeks. My hand follows to where his lips were and I blush. I look into his eyes and find a promise of something, a reconnection, I hope. Yugi is sticking a finger into his mouth and making a gagging noise. I don't really care.

'It was nice to meet you,' I say in Hebrew.

He looks shocked.

'Saba and Savti have been teaching me a few words.' I am pleased that I said it right.

'The pleasure is all mine,' he responds.

I laugh and wipe a small tear. *Where are all these stupid tears coming from?* 'I don't know what you said.'

'Let's just say, I'll find you again.'

'Promise?' I whisper.

'Okay,' Yugi says loudly, 'now that we've got that out of the way...' He claps his hands. 'Come on, people, we've got a long journey on a very bouncy flight ahead of us.'

The adults laugh and I try to, but I can't.

Shime releases me. I let him go.

Here's to the next leg.

My knuckles are just loose enough now that blood returns to my hands. How people do this for a living is far beyond my understanding, but as soon as we landed, I feel like I can breathe again. Yugi was fascinated by the landscape as we flew over it, but I chose to keep my eyes fixed directly ahead staring at the video monitor which was logged in to the flight path. Each minute seemed to pass slower than the last, and every time we hit an air pocket, I had to swallow a scream. Eventually, when we entered Polish air space, I glanced across Yugi's body out the window. I was surprised at the countryside. I thought Poland would be something like Oklahoma - wide swaths of green and nothingness, flat, unbothered by a need to grow upwards. But the beauty from the air astounded me. Hills, forests and even mountains appeared in the distance. Everything was green and blue, whether tree to sky, or pasture to lake.

Shakily, I get to my feet. The pinging-unbuckling-seatbelts noise has barely stopped before I am surging to the front of the aircraft. It's hard to imagine a worse feeling than the panic overtaking a person when they are, or feel, trapped. My dad calls out to see if I'm okay, but I simply raise a hand in response and call out that I will see them in terminal. A few passengers grumble that I'm jumping the line, but once they see my face, the redness and sweat, they don't say anything. Impatiently I wait for the flight attendants to 'unlock cabin doors.' One of the flight attendants, a young woman in a navy-blue uniform and white handkerchief tied around her neck, eyes me as if I'm somehow now going to hijack the plane, but my panicked look stops her. She asks if there is something that she can do but I swallow twice and breathe rapidly. 'Just open the door.'

Thankfully, she does.

Briskly, I walk the gangway and situate myself just outside the roped off area. I lean over and gulp deep breaths of air. I thank God that he didn't make me a bird. I walk slowly away from the meeting area. As I face the wall, I tent myself against it and stare at the floor praying that we'll stay in Poland for a couple of years.

I feel a hand on my shoulder and I jump. It's my dad. 'You okay?'

'No.'

'Do you need a drink of water?'

I shake my head. 'Why is it that when children are struggling a parent's first instinct is to get a drink of water? What does that actually do, anyway?'

'Gets your mind off your panic, I think.'

'Well, a cold glass of water is not going to do that for me today. But thanks for asking.'

'No problem,' Dad responds.

Yugi is standing next to Mom scanning the crowd. Every few seconds he says, 'Is that a spy?' to which Mom responds. 'No, and don't ask me again.' After Yugi does this four times, Mom says, 'Yes.'

'Really?'

'No, all the spies are in the bathroom changing out of their fake airline clothes. Make sure you look for janitors now, especially ones with big beards, okay?'

The sarcasm is lost on my brother who is indeed looking for cleaners with big beards.

'Are you ready to go, Jeri?'

I pump my arms against the wall a few times as if preparing myself for a dive into the deep end and then push

255

away. 'Anything to get us away from the airport.'

Moments later, we arrive at the baggage claim. Our carousel is still empty and motionless. We wait beside it until Yugi points. 'Mom, there's a spy!' We turn and see a cleaning man with a large beard picking up trash and putting it into his cart on wheels.

'I was kidding, Yugi. We won't see any in the airport.'

He is disappointed.

Our bags finally arrive on the moving carriage; we grab them, extend the handles and begin making our way out of the airport. Nonchalantly, I turn around and look behind me. The cleaning man seems to be talking to himself.

Fortunately, my parents have made reservations in downtown Krakow. Like the scene from above, Krakow is an explosion of color and light. The buildings, centuries old, fulfilling my dreams of European architecture, are immense and astounding. Although the streets are busy, the air is remarkably fresh as if infused with excitement and energy. I see others like me craning their necks to gaze at living history.

I am humbled. In my desperate desires to travel, I had never thought of Poland. When anyone says, 'Think of the most exotic place in the world,' my mind doesn't leap to - *ah yes, Krakow*. The name sounds like something in a Batman movie. No, I hear Paris and Rome, London and Venice, Athens and Barcelona. Krakow, not so much. As we drive, I see billboards for tourists in English, but I also notice the incredibly difficult pronunciation of Polish places and words. The best one I saw - Wrzeszczewice. I don't even know where to begin other than to think someone sneezed and this is what came out.

The hotel transport van pulls up outside our accommodation, a blocky, squat building with narrow windows. A green gabled roof covers it all. We pull the bags from the back end of the van, and after checking in, we ride the elevator to the sixth floor. Yugi is excited that there is a swimming pool, but Mom warns him to check that excitement.

The clues are spread out in front of us. I had, upon entering the building, gone to the racks to gather tourist maps. We spend some time circling different spots that we'll probably need to go to.

'For sure, we're going to Wawel Castle.' I point to it on the map.

'I have no idea what we're looking for, but I'm sure something will come up,' Mom responds.

'My guess,' I point to the brochure of the castle, 'is that we'll need to dig up another one of Barbie's legs.'

There is a silence between us. 'Mom, when did life begin to change for you?'

'What do you mean?' She watches me trace my finger on the map.

'I mean, when did you start *feeling* like an adult. Do you remember when that day was when you thought, 'I can't go back to Mom and Dad's. It's not their job to take care of me anymore?''

Mom snorts. 'There are many days, before seeing myself in the mirror, that I think I'm still a girl. I'm going to wake up and suddenly I'm warm and comfortable in Jerusalem, surrounded by everything I know and love.'

'Do you regret leaving?' I ask quietly.

She leans into me nudging my shoulder with hers. 'Not once. Not ever.' Her eyes glow with intensity. 'I miss leaving childhood and the comfort of it sometimes, but my life is infinitely better now. I have you and Yugi and Dad and all the things I need. And now,' she pats the table twice in front of her, 'we've got a new adventure. I haven't felt this alive in years.'

'Why did you leave Jerusalem?'

'Because my new life is much more important than my old.'

I wait a second before asking the next question. I know it's been on all our minds. 'Are you worried about the people who are following us?'

Her eyes cloud. 'Yes. A little.'

'What do we have to worry about?'

Mom walks to the window overlooking the city. 'That's the worrying thing, Jeri. We just don't know what we need to fear. Once you poke a hornet's nest, you never know how many stingers are coming your way. So far, their interest in us has been relatively benign other than breaking into our garage.'

'Oh, is that all.' I tried to lighten the mood.

'I'm not taking this lightly, Jeri. I worry because...' I wait for her and see that emotions are tumbling and twirling inside of her, '...you haven't had the easiest life growing up.'

'Mom, please, my life has been so boring.' She looks hurt. 'Okay, so boring isn't the right word, but I haven't really had a chance to spread my wings. This trip is the first time. If you think about it, doing this together is exactly what we needed to catapult me into adulthood.'

She sighs and turns back to the window. 'Maybe I just want to hold on to you as a little girl for a while longer.'

Chapter 28 Down:

I begin to understand the weight of parenthood and the daily tug-of-war with responsibility, emotions, teaching and loving that comes with raising children. Perspective is incredibly hard to find, but now that I'm at the base of the Mount Adult, I can see how they might worry. It's a long climb upwards, and even though they've taught me well, you never know what kind of footholds will show up... or crumble underneath.

I watch my mother's face as she stares through the glass. She seems pale, altered by the strain. Somewhere between Israel and Poland, a crow has etched furrows in the edges of her eyes. As she ponders the streetlife, the outdoor noise is muffled, a symphony of double basses, truck and car engines trying to bulldoze the streets. Shouts and whistles, strings and horns, blare and blurt, but it is all just background noise to what is going on inside our heads.

'Why did you ask the question, Jeri?'

'As much as you like to pretend otherwise, and I love you for it, I'm not normal.'

'Jeri...' Mom turns, wanting to move towards me and my mountain. She wants to keep me from climbing it, I know.

'I'm not bitter. It's just the way I tick. I get overwhelmed and irritated quickly. Without thinking, I say things I probably shouldn't.'

Mom sighs. I know that she wants to speak again, but this time she lets me finish.

'All over the world, I find that people my age and a little older are finding different ways to blame everyone and everything else for why they don't get what they want. We get blamed for being entitled and brattish and maybe even a little precious at times, but I know that eventually, we all

259

just have to get over the fact that we can't always have what we want.'

'So, Mom, since my weird and awkward graduation, I've decided that I'm not going to let other things control me. I'm not going to blame my mistakes on someone else. Whatever success I have, I recognize that I didn't do it on my own, and whatever failure occurs, I recognize my part in it. Either way, I win.'

There is a tear in Mom's eyes. A jewel of emotion. 'Welcome to adulthood,' she whispers.

I feel like I just clipped in.

Unfortunately, my parents only rented one room with two double beds. As always, Yugi and I have to share a bed. What he does in his sleep is beyond me: it's a mixture of pole vaulting and driving a cement mixer. The kid never stops moving. Somewhere in the middle of the night, I hear him mumble something like, 'Hey, can I get a big snack... mumble mumble...my kidney!' I understand that he's still prepubescent, but wow, the kid is in a full out sparring match with it. When those hormones hit him, I'm standing very, very far back.

After breakfast, we load up our travel info into the YMCA attaché case and take a taxi from the hotel to the castle. Our driver, a local with an immensely bushy moustache, is quite happy to practice his heavily accented English. He is wearing a t-shirt and blue jeans. When he sees our faces and hears our American accents, he is hoping for a few extra zlotys.

'Good morning!' the driver sings as he puts the van into drive. 'Where you like to go today?'

'To Wawel Castle, please.'

Chapter 28 Down:

'Aaah,' the driver says with pleasure. 'Good choice. One of best spots.'

I lean forward from the back seat. 'Tell us about it. What's interesting?'

He gives us an overview from its beginnings - As far as I can tell, he says something about Casimir the Great and Wenceslaus, which makes Yugi start humming the Christmas song. As we approach the city center, he relates the castle's medieval history and the artwork that used to hang in it.

'Masterpieces,' he said and kisses his fingers like an Italian blessing spaghetti. 'Draperies, paintings, even a sword.'

Yugi interrupts the man. 'What about a dragon? We heard there was something about a dragon?'

The man winks in the mirror at the young boy. 'You are dragon slayer, no?'

Yugi shrugged and smiles. 'I dabble.'

'You, little knight, would have struggled with great Smok.'

'That's a weird name for a dragon,' Yugi says.

'You would not say to his face,' the driver responds. 'Smok was monster dragon. They say no weapon kill him. What you call this?' He pounds on his shoulders.

'Scales?' I say.

'Yes, yes.' His 'yes' sounds like *yeus.* 'Of course, scales. Smok, he eat people, swallow them one bite.' The driver makes a gulping sound which makes me cringe. I can see his Adam's Apple moving up and down. Like my father's, it's far too prominent and his moustache looks like a pipe cleaner for his nose.

He retells the story of the dragon and Krakus, a poor shoemaker. I zone out knowing the conclusion, but

Yugi is enrapt, not only because the local is telling the story, but because he is listening hard to overcome the accent. I can see that Yugi is trying to form the words in the same way as the driver; his lips are pushed out - *Krakus. Krakus. Krakus.*

'What does the dragon have to do with the castle?' Dad asks.

'Well,' the man steps on the brakes and honks the horn at the car ahead. He mutters under his breath and then apologizes to the family sheepishly. 'Sorry, my language.'

'We didn't understand anyway,' I say. Mom and Dad exchange a glance and smirk.

'Smok is part of legend of castle. A few of bones hang over door of castle. True, true.'

'I think you're pulling my leg,' Yugi responds doubtfully.

'I not pull anything of yours. You see when you get to castle. Smok guarded castle and all treasures until Krakus kill him.'

'Can I ask you another question?' Dad asks.

'Of course.' The driver looks in the mirror and without indicating changes lanes. There is a cacophony of angry horns. He makes a sign with his hand but refrains from swearing this time.

'What about the Nazis.'

The driver frowns and crosses himself. He spits to the side. 'Nazis.'

'Can you tell us what happened?'

'It was my grandparents who were here - good Polish people. Tough, strong, you know? They never do *anything* wrong, then one day, this *kurwa*, Hitler and his beady-eyed little *szkodnik*, Frank, take over castle - right there.' He points ahead at Wawel hill in front of us. 'He tear down all good Polish things and churches and buildings.'

'We have heard of him, *rzeznik Polski,*' Dad responds. *Butcher of Poland.*

'You speak my language?' The driver asks in Polish.

'A little,' Dad says. My eyes are wide. Mom is smiling too.

Suddenly, she leans forward and asks something that sounds like *wrinrisiizil brakkszi Frank rzeznik frlish Eichmann czykepeloski.* I stare at her, dropped jawed that she has formulated whatever sentence this is in another language.

The driver almost loses control of the car. 'Who are you?'

'We are tourists,' my dad continues, 'but ones who want to clear up a few wrongs from the past also.'

'What you want to know?' He stares suspiciously into the back at Mom and us two kids. We have no idea what's going on. Where did my parents get this ability? It's like they got lost in the Matrix and suddenly stuck that thing in the backs of their heads to learn Polish.

'We want to know if Eichmann and Frank ever met.' Mom says in English.

His face hardens. '*Yeus.*'

'When?'

The driver does not know how much to say, but his jaw twitches. He pulls up to the curb. We are not yet to the castle.

'Just before war ended. Eichmann came to Krakow. They say he help move precious valuables, paintings and other things.'

Mom and Dad look at each other.

'Where did they meet?'

The driver points forward. 'Wawel.'

We leave the cab and Dad pays him and leaves a tip. The man accepts it grimly and leaves without saying goodbye.

We stroll towards the castle. As one from small-town America, seeing a castle is as amazing to me as finding a wild giraffe roaming Oklahoma. There is nothing petite about this place, from its bulwarked walls to its thick towers. From the outside, it appears like a large complex of dormitories: a few are dark brown, others are white, but as we enter the gates, a complex, multi-colored world is revealed.

The cobblestone path which leads into the castle complex is wide and beautiful and opens up to a courtyard of green. A few trees grow indiscriminately dotting the landscape. It appears as if there is no horticultural plan. In the center of the castle complex is the cathedral. Its patinated spires dominate the skyline above. In front of the cathedral is a bell tower, the spire held up by both white and red brick. Circling the castle are other red roofs.

'Can we just stop here for a moment and recap what just happened in the car?' I hold my parents' arms arresting their movement forward. We stand in the shade of the buildings. 'How many languages do you speak and when did you learn them?'

They look at each other. 'You mean individually or combined?'

'Considering you both speak Polish, let's go with individual.'

'I'm not as good as your mother,' Dad says, 'but I've got five under my belt, or at least in the conversational sense.'

'I can speak eight,' Mom says, 'but they have gotten progressively worse since living in Oklahoma. It's not like there's a large calling for Arabic or even Serbian there.'

I'm flabbergasted.

'It's one of the family gifts.'

'Then why do I struggle so badly with Spanish? Why can't I speak that? I mean, a lot of the words are even the same.'

'*Porque tu eres una idiota, Jeri,*' Yugi pronounces my name as 'Hairy.' Mom and Dad both laugh.

'Shut up, Yugi. I can translate that.'

'How about we get back to Poland,' Mom says.

'Yes, why don't we, Mom.' I am frustrated now. All the language ability seemed to have landed on Yugi's narrow shoulders.

We walk forward together as a family, but also as distinct, separate individuals. All the trust that Mom and I had built last night feels fundamentally rustier. Climbing this mountain isn't going to be quite as easy as I thought. In corporate silence, we journey down the cobblestoned path and begin reading maps and signs. First, we enter the cathedral. Even though there are only tourists in the cathedral, I have this feeling that I'm in a holy place.

As we wander throughout the grounds, it becomes immediately apparent that Grandma could have hidden the next clue anywhere. Without some luck, we might be here a very, very long time. I watch Dad and Mom peruse the various exhibits. My parents do not display any frustration. They actually seem to be enjoying themselves, to be learning something different.

We eat lunch in one of the small cafes. Most things seem to be relatively healthy which is good. After finishing the meal, I grab everyone's trash and take it to the plastic trashcan with a swinging door. On the other side of the trashcan is a tall man, a priest, obviously. He's wearing a clerical collar and a strange hat. It kind of looks like a muffin tied up on top of his head.

'*Gin dobre.*' The priest says to me and smiles.

'I'm sorry,' I stammer, 'I don't speak Polish.'

He spreads his hands magnanimously. 'No matter,' he replies in English. 'How are you today?'

'I am fine. What is your name... uh... your lordship?'

The priest's laugh is strangely high pitched for a big man. Unnatural. 'Father Wlocaw will be fine. Or, if that's too hard, Peter is fine.'

'Nice to meet you, Peter,' I say. 'Are you the archbishop?'

'That, my young friend, would be an unwanted miracle.' He opens his hands. 'No, I'm simply the rector of the chapel. I help with worship services for the community on Sunday mornings.'

'Interesting,' I say, but I'm not really interested.

'Are you visiting Krakow for a while?' he asks.

'No. Well, I actually don't know. We're kind of being spontaneous on this trip.'

'You're with your parents?' He leans down slightly as if to hear me better.

I point to them. Dad has Grandma's attaché case on his lap. He is resting his forearms and chin on it. 'My Mom and Dad and my brother Yugi.'

'That's an interesting name,' he says.

'He's an interesting boy.'

Peter clears his throat. 'Have you explored everything?'

'No, but we've got a few more days, too.'

Chapter 28 Down:

'Would you feel comfortable introducing me to your parents? Perhaps I could offer my services as a guide around the castle.'

This could be a great twist of fate. 'Yeah, okay.' He follows behind me.

I stop at the table and my parents look up at me quizzically. Yugi's face is scrunched up in a weird frown. 'Mom, Dad, Yugi, this is Peter. He is rector of the chapel.'

Dad stands and shakes his hand. They are about the same height, but the clergyman is about fifty pounds heavier. 'Nice to meet you,' Dad says in English.

Peter repeats the process with Mom and Yugi. Mom smiles but Yugi looks at his hand as if he touched something slimy. 'In talking with your daughter, I wondered if you would like a tour guide around the castle.'

'Why yes,' Dad says, 'that would be wonderful.'

Mom and Dad stand and Yugi plants himself behind them. Tugging on Dad's sleeve, Yugi pulls his head down and whispers something to which Dad says, 'No, Yugi, he is not.' I'm pretty sure he asked Dad if Peter was a spy.

Throughout the afternoon, Peter takes us through the wide-open courtyard topped by white balustrades with beautiful cream-colored arches. Peter shares some of the earliest history of the castle and takes us into various rooms offering tidbits of trivia that the guidebook does not. Other tourists watch and begin to follow, which makes Peter smile. Soon, he has an entourage hanging on his every English word. Someone in the back asks him if he speaks German, which he does, and begins to give his impromptu tour in both languages. I am extraordinarily impressed, and I vow that when I get back to Oklahoma, I'm going to start learning at least two other languages - Hebrew and something else. And I'm going to stick with it, too.

Now that we have a larger group, we move slower. We decide to separate from the group. Just as we are about to leave, Father Peter points above him. 'Last thing, Jeri. Here are the bones of Smok the great dragon.' All eyes, faces and phones are immediately pointed upward. When we look down again, Peter is smiling. 'Smok cautions you to beware. There is danger in and outside the castle. And where the dragon is, there is the dragon's lair.'

Yugi clears his throat. 'Your Holiness, where is the dragon's lair?'

Father Peter peers over his glasses and puts on a face. His voice lowers dramatically. 'Below the castle, young man. In the caves.'

'Thank you, Father,' Mom says, 'we have to go. We appreciate your help.'

'God be with you on your journey,' he says. 'You never know what you might find when you're not looking for it.' I have a strange premonition that his words will come true.

Chapter 29 Across:
Added unnatural hues (4)

We move out of the pack and into the bright courtyard. The sun is still shining, reflecting everything. I squint; my eyes have not yet adjusted. In the grass beside us are the ruins of an old building. They look like bleached bones, perhaps of Smok himself. Moldy and pitted, it seems as if the earth is trying to absorb the remains of the building. I wonder if this is what happens to human bodies once they are laid to rest.

Dad and Mom are facing one another while Yugi has run around to the entrance of the ruins to peek into the various nooks and crannies. Below us, I can see the blue ribbon of the Vistula River as it twists and turns on its way to the Baltic Sea. The city seems locked in a cosmic struggle between the past and the future. The present is the umpire trying to decide which direction the city should go. For my part, I love the past. The future is full of fear and worry. I look toward the southeast, or what I think is southeast, and see a large white building. I take out my map. It is probably the Oskar Schindler Museum. If we have enough time, I would love to see it. There are so many...

'Excuse me,' I hear a voice behind us. I turn and see an older woman standing beside Mom and Dad. She is wearing an enormous, flowered muumuu. Her hair is dyed an odd color - it's hard to explain what hue it is. It's caught somewhere between purple, blue and green. It makes me feel kind of queasy. For a moment, I don't even realize she introduced herself in English.

'Can I help you?' Mom asks.

'What's in your case?' She points at Dad's hand.

'That's really none of your business. No offense.'

The woman laughs and bends over slapping her knees. Her blurplereen hair hangs loosely and almost touches the ground. Unsure of how to proceed, Dad motions with his head that we should leave, but the woman stands up quickly.

'I know you,' she whispers shaking a finger. 'She told me you'd come.'

'What are you talking about?'

'You know,' she says touching her nose. 'Barbie.'

Our nerves are on edge. Yugi is still playing amidst the bones.

'What do you know about it?'

The woman circles my parents. It's like she's made out of water. Her face is wide and full of life, but insane. She's making weird motions with her hands.

'We've been waiting. Watching all these years. One of us was going to be here for you.'

There are multiple spontaneous murmurings in my mind, but the first one that arises is: *Which one of the people talking inside your head is speaking to us now?*

'You might have to explain things a little better to us,' Mom says.

The woman dances around. She's like a hippy but hippo-ish. Scanning the crowd, the woman pops in between my parents and puts a hand on each of their shoulders. 'I will, but you'll have to come to our house.'

'Okay,' I interject standing directly opposite the dancing hippo, 'maybe you should be moving along now.'

The woman's face freezes. 'It's an act,' she says in a low voice. 'Truly, Iris told me that you'd eventually come and that I should give you what you needed.'

I am startled but recover quickly. 'What is it?' I ask.

'I don't know.'

'Where is it?'

'I can't tell you yet.'

'How do you know we are the ones you are looking for? Maybe we're the others...?'

The woman's face turns hard. 'You don't know them.' She pointed at Dad's briefcase. 'You were to bring your case before the court. You have the case, here is the court of the kings - Stanislas. Casimir. Wenceslaus. Great unmentionable kings of Europe. Iris said I should look for someone carrying this case.'

'How do you know it's this one?'

'I see her fingerprints all over it..."

We all look at the attaché case. 'I don't see anything,' I say.

'You're not looking very closely, are you?' the crazy woman responds.

Mom's face hardens. 'It's fascinating that you know Iris and that you actually have an idea about what is going on, but unless you give us something solid, we'll just be moving...'

The woman squeezes my mom's arm hard. My mother reacts in a way that I never would have expected. She spins quickly out of the old woman's grasp and prepares to strike. The old woman, amazingly, moves just as quickly as Mom. They stand facing each other.

The old woman looks around. 'We can do this here and draw the attention of everyone, or you can come to my house and I'll share everything with you.' She drops her guard. 'Please.'

My parents face each other. Yugi comes bounding up. 'What did I miss?' Then he looks at the wildly dressed lady. 'Are you a spy.'

Her eyes twinkle. 'How did you guess?'

'Finally,' Yugi declares with a sigh. 'It's about time.'

We glance around the courtyard. A few people are recording the strange woman on their phones.

We walk across the lawn, the woman dancing and leaping in front of us. I am so confused. Outside the main entrance, we turn left and walk down the hill. She has stopped cavorting and now briskly walks in front of us. I can't take my eyes from her hair and dress. The shapeless costume hides the fact that she really isn't very big, and I also see that she's not as old as I first thought. She must be in her late 60's.

We find an open place in the shade of a tree by the Vistula River. A few park benches contain random people: an old man feeding the ducks and geese, a young mother on her phone, while her small son chases pigeons in front of her.

Suddenly the woman turns around. 'I'm sorry for all that up there,' she says. Her eyes are bright blue and blazing with intelligence. Pulling off her wig, she ruffles her short, gunmetal grey hair fluffing it up. 'Certain disguises require certain roles.'

I am astonished how much the change of hair transforms her appearance. Then, she pulls the muumuu over her head and smiles at my jaw drop. She is thin and fit. Her arms are muscular and sinewy strong.

'Who are you?' Dad asks.

'My name is Geraldine Dresser. I'm English, but my grandparents were German.'

'How do you know Iris Walker.'

'Don't forget Walter,' she says waggling a finger. A smile stretches across her face. 'I always thought he was so cute. And you, Kevin, you've really grown up.'

It's Dad's turn to be shocked. 'Yes, we've met before when you were young. You won't remember it - we were in Germany working on the Wall. I had to disguise myself most times. You'd remember me as Christina Menzel.'

'Oh my, gosh!' Dad exclaims. 'That was you? You look nothing like...'

'I'm good, right?' Geraldine laughs wildly.

'But... but... why the act up there?' He points back to the castle.

'People lose interest in crazy after a while, but lurkers? Not so much. I, or some of my associates, have been patrolling the castle for many years. Iris charged me with protecting something very important for her, something that would come to light when I saw the attaché case. When you showed up with this morning, I knew exactly who you were and I'm so happy to have found you.'

'Tell us how we got to this place. How did this all come about?'

Geraldine's eyes cloud over and she looks out over the Vistula River. 'For many years, our division had been working on Nazi war secrets, hunting the old bastards down, rousting out sympathizers and chasing down leads to Nazi loot. No one was better than Iris. I remember watching her from a distance - she could charm anyone and everyone to give them just a few more bits of information. As we were closing in on one of the most important finds, we slipped.'

She sighed deeply. 'It wasn't really Iris' fault, it was just an accident, but they found her and Walt and made them talk. Her cover was blown and so was mine.'

Geraldine seemed sad. 'Fortunately, they didn't kill her, but she had to leave. When she did, she asked that I

273

would watch and wait for the time. 'Be patient,' she said, 'someone will come later - it may be a long time - but when they show up with the attaché case,' Geraldine pointed at it, 'you will give them something for me.'

'What is it?' I ask.

Geraldine shakes her head. 'Do you trust me yet?'

Before we say anything, Yugi pushes forward. 'Yes, absolutely.'

'Then come with me to my house - out of the spotlight. Even now, there are people watching us.'

'You can see them?'

'No,' she said, 'but my body can feel when things are... off.'

She does not speak on the walk to her house but leads us, walking twenty paces in front. Carrying her dress and wig, Geraldine looks like a fit old woman out for her afternoon exercise. Mom and Dad are speaking softly in front of us and it frustrates me that they are speaking in another language which I don't understand. Which one of the five is it? I can't tell if it's Polish. Maybe Russian? So weird.

Entering a street lined with old houses, trees perched in the front yards, boughs branching over the paths, we follow her as she turns up a lane. She allows us to move past her and the gate she is holding open, and then peeks back down the street. Confident that no one is following us, she urges us toward the house. The front lawn is unkempt. There are toys and broken objects littering the grass. The porch has arches which reveal dirty, ripped furniture padding.

'Props,' she says and grins.

After unlocking the door, she ushers us into the house. Our eyes are met with a modern marvel of comfort.

Chapter 29 Across:

It is spotlessly clean. In the furnished living area, sofas and furniture sit facing an old stone fireplace. A basket of wood is waiting for a match. The walls are covered with relics - black and white photographs, youthful faces staring out at the viewer. They are full of life and excitement. The women are beautiful and they stand next to handsome men.

In one snapshot, the photographer must have been lying on the ground shooting upwards under two women who are standing side by side gazing up and out. The bright sunshine causes them to shield their eyes with open hands. Scarves are tied around their necks and the sweaters they wear hug their curves. Lipstick has been applied liberally and even though the picture is black and white, it wouldn't take a great deal of imagination to believe that these two are magazine models.

I know that the woman on the left is Grandma and I assume the woman on the right is Geraldine. There is no mistaking that smile.

Geraldine neatly folds her dress and lays it over one of the chairs. 'Tea or coffee?' She asks.

'Yes, please. Coffee would be nice,' Mom says. We are all still slightly shellshocked by what has happened.

While Geraldine brews a pot of coffee, she tells us to have a wander around. Yugi takes this to heart and immediately moves through every single room in the house. Mom, Dad and I go into the kitchen with Geraldine.

'Kevin,' Geraldine's voice rises above the noise of the brewing coffee, 'how are your parents?'

Dad tells her about them. Geraldine shakes her head. 'I miss them.'

'So do I,' Dad responds.

'So many good stories.' Geraldine's nostalgia makes her humph.

'What kinds of things did you work on together?' Dad folds his arms and leans against a tall white cupboard.

Geraldine continues to ready the mugs. The pot is beginning to hiss; the water is almost ready.

'We met in 1982. We gathered and sent information mostly, but Iris always kept a dossier on something special. She never told me what it was, but when that day came, I assumed it had something to do with artwork, is that right?'

Mom and Dad nod. 'Why wouldn't Mom - Iris - just have you follow up the trail?'

'Couldn't,' Geraldine said and turned away toward the steaming coffee pot. 'My cover was blown. If I would have continued, the Nazis would have turned me over to the Polish authorities.'

'The Poles don't know you're here?'

Geraldine shrugs. 'I assume so. But I'm so old and inconsequential, they probably believe me to be safe.' Her wry smile belies her true abilities.

'People tend to think that about o... er... mature people,' Dad says.

Laughing, Geraldine hands steaming mugs of coffee to each one of us and then holds one in her own hands to blow on it. 'I've had good years. But, I don't think they actually know it's me at Wawel. I can hide pretty well, don't you think?'

'That's for sure,' I say.

Yugi comes running into the kitchen and almost slides across the floor. 'Wow, Geraldine, you've got some amazing things. I love your toy soldier collection! And those tanks! Are they German?'

'Yes,' she says, 'but... wait a minute... Tell me your names.' She points at Yugi and me.

'My name is Yugoslavia, but you can call me Yugi.'

'I will. And you are...'

'Jeri. That's short for Jerusalem.'

'How did you get those names?'

I blush. 'Well, my parents have an affinity for places that they've been before.'

'The toy soldiers...?' Yugi says impatiently. His face is lit with expectation. Freckles speckle his face and his blue eyes sparkle. He has two large front teeth, almost rabbitish, that shine in the bright light.

'Ah, yes, Yugoslavia...'

'Yugi.'

'All right. Well, Yugi, those toy soldiers are English troops from World War II and that tank, that's German, and it's made out of aluminum. No plastic in those things. My parents gave me those as a reminder of what we had to overcome - German might with English... pardon me... Allied brains.'

'Cool,' Yugi smiles. 'Can I play with them?'

'Yugi, no,' Mom says.

'Of course,' Geraldine intones. 'They're toys.'

'Thanks!' Yugi runs out of the room and stumbles over the carpet almost falling to the floor.

Mom and Dad shake their heads.

'Now, where was I?'

'You were telling us about how we got here.'

'Ah, yes. Years ago, your parents were whisked from Poland under the cover of darkness, but not before they could drop off something for the owner of the attaché case. Now that I've found out it's you, Kevin, I'm even happier. You were such a handsome young man.'

'Were?' He laughs.

'Aach, we all grow older and less beautiful, but we get better, I think.' She touches a finger to her temple. 'We know things.'

'What was it that she left you?' I ask.

Geraldine's eyes twinkle. She takes another sip and smiles behind the lip of the cup. Steam floats before her eyes. As she swallows, she turns and leaves the room. When she returns, she's holding a metal tube – it looks like a blueprint case.

'I've never looked in here before.' She hands the blueprint case not to Mom and Dad, but to me. As she bends down and offers it to me, it seems very much like the passing of a baton.

'How do I open it?' I ask.

'I don't know,' Geraldine responds and stands back to cross her arms.

It takes me a few moments. The ends turn, but they aren't screwed on. The case seems like a puzzle in itself.

I am nervous to have everyone watching me.

I look closely at the case and then I see it.

Barbie's fingerprints. I look up at Geraldine who sees that I've figured it out. Twisting the lid, I turn it until the two sets of fingerprints line up. Then, turning it upside down, I do the same on the other end. Suddenly, both ends loosen and pop off. The adults move in closer and we look inside. Whatever it is, it is made of paper.

Suddenly, a shadow passes in front of one of the living room windows. Like shades, or demons, there are suddenly two or three more.

'Into the living room!' Geraldine yells and grabs me. We all dive into the next room when voices begin shouting. Before we know it, the front door crashes open and we are swarmed by black hooded figures.

Chapter 29 Across:

Menacingly, they scan the rooms with weapons drawn. We have all hidden behind chairs in the living room. Yugi appears from the back room, his hands over his ears. He looks incredibly scared. The men turn their guns toward him and suddenly, my world is completely and utterly turned upside down.

Cue the heavy metal music.

The adults come out of nowhere. It's as if they've been planning this. Their movements are coordinated and each one of them goes after one of the men in black. *Fwiiip, Thwerp, Schmock.* As I watch from my perch on the floor, my dad has disarmed one of the intruders with a swift movement of his hand. A sweep of the man's leg puts him on his back before he can realize that Jackie-frickin'-Chan-Dad has just shown up. While my dad pulls out his inner jiu jitsu, Mom goes all Black Widow on her guy. His gun clatters across the room before he can recover. Suddenly, she wraps her legs around his neck and sends him flying backwards across the room. The man crashes into the wall and lies still. Similarly, Geraldine breaks into action. I can't believe a woman so old can move so quickly. Within seconds, and I mean that, literally less than ten seconds, they have disarmed the intruders.

Yugi is in a state of suspended animation. Mom is leaning over the face of a very startled man, her finger is in his face. 'Don't you ever point a gun at my son.'

I've never seen her snarl before. Well, I've never seen her disarm someone before, almost break their neck and land on her feet either. Dad has gathered up the weapons and distributed one to Mom and Geraldine. My mind is spinning so rapidly, I can't quite comprehend anything and the only words I can string together to form even a semblance of a sentence is, 'What in the world was that?'

Mom stands up and pushes her hair behind her head. Geraldine still has her gun trained on the soldiers.

'What?' Mom asks.

'WHAT IN HEAVEN'S REALM WAS THAT?' My shouting has a wee bit of hysteria to it.

'Muscle memory,' she laughs. One hand is holding a gun and the other is on her hip. They are breathing deeply, but don't seem to be injured in the least.

'Geraldine,' my dad says, 'do you have any zip ties?'

'Top drawer, left side of the kitchen.' As you do, if you're a spy. I mean, everyone has a stash of zip ties in their kitchen utensils drawer. Like duh.

Dad motions for me to get them. In a trance, I glide to the kitchen, but once I get there, I'm so shocked that I almost forget what I'm supposed to be getting. There is broken glass on the floor. It crunches under my feet. There is a small bag of zip ties tucked into a drawer with ladles, whisks and cake-decorating spatulas. The surreality of the event leaves me speechless and as I return to Dad, I mutely hand them over to him. Quickly, he ties the men's hands behind their backs and their ankles together.

Looking over his handiwork, he steps back. 'Do you recognize them, Geraldine?'

'No, but I recognize their style. CIA - not special ops, lower level. Maybe guys that have been out for a while. A little slower.' She slaps one of them on the stomach. He flinches. 'This one's even got a gut.' She leans into his face. 'How's it feel to get beat up by an old lady?' She cackles.

Maybe I was right in the first place. Maybe she is a little bit more than crazy.

Chapter 29 Across:

I look at Dad as he steps back from the men. His bald spot is glowing in the dim light of the late afternoon sun. 'There are probably more coming,' Dad says.

'You guys need to get out of here,' Geraldine's face shows worry.

'Come with us.' Mom says.

'I can't. I don't want to jeopardize anything. Besides,' she scratches her head with fingers on her left hand, 'I need to interrogate the bastards who sent them.'

'Are you sure you can handle it?' Mom asks.

Geraldine snorts. 'Get out of here. Someday I'll read about it in the papers, I'm sure.'

'After all these years and you never get to see what's in the tube you protected.'

'Such is the life of a spy.'

We leave one of the strangest situations in our lives where an old woman holds three agents at gunpoint.

Our hotel debrief is going to be out of this world.

We walk away from Geraldine's house quickly. Every ten steps, it seems like at least one of us is looking over his or her shoulder. When we reach our hotel, we take the stairs - we don't want to be trapped in the elevator.

When we open the door, our room has been turned upside down. Our bags have been emptied onto the bed; our clothes are in disarray, shirts, underwear, pants, and a couple of bras are scattered across the beds. The cupboards are open. Just like when our house was ransacked, I feel violated and unsafe. Instinctively I cross my arms and cover my chest.

My parents' faces have hardened. Fortunately, everything that we needed for the journey is in the briefcase and in my backpack.

'Mom... Dad...?' Yugi's whimpers.

'It's okay, Yugi,' Mom says. 'We're all right.'

Still in a state of shock, I feel my blood refuse to attend to certain parts of my body. My extremities feel numb, and I am lightheaded. Even my lips feel like rubber bumpers.

'Can you help me understand what just happened?' I ask the two of them. 'No more half-truths - Yugi and I have a right to know.'

Dad points to the chairs in the room where Yugi and I sit down. Mom and Dad sit next to each other on the bed, on the clothes, staring at us like kids who are in trouble. The roles are reversed - the parents must tell us exactly what they've been hiding.

'The real work of what we've been doing, in Israel, in Herzegovina, in Poland, among other places, takes place mostly behind a computer. We have rarely ever been in the field - mostly because we have you. We didn't want you to be put in danger.' Dad breathes deeply. 'Every once in a while, I had to go on a mission.'

'Mission impossible,' Yugi whispers. My dad gives him a look, one of *silence would be the better option.*

'I told you that I worked in an office because that would surely cause for less questions.'

'What else did you lie to us about?' I ask. As I look at the baggage strewn about them, I feel like this is the new state of my reality.

'Jerusalem,' Mom says lovingly, 'half-truths are necessary. Lies are imperative sometimes.'

'But truths are certainly easier to recover from. At least I can trust that what you say is genuine.'

Mom looks hurt.

Chapter 29 Across:

'Look, Jeri,' Dad says as he grabs Mom's hand, 'for the rest of this trip and at least for the foreseeable future, we will attempt to reveal everything that we can.'

'What is that supposed to mean?'

'We can't tell you everything. It's just part of the job.'

'Okay,' I say tapping the arms of my cushioned chair. 'What can you tell us about your training? What can you tell us about the years we don't remember? How did you get these 'skills?''

'Standard CIA. But we,' he motions to Mom also, 'had some extra training. Because we wouldn't be working with... uh... munitions as much as special ops, we needed more hand-to-hand combat skills.' He smiled. 'Let's just say, there aren't many fights that your mom and I would lose.'

'That's so cool,' Yugi says. Dad smiles and Mom frowns. Dad frowns.

'So really, why is the CIA, *your employers* after you? Us? Why are they trying to harm us?'

Mom leans forward and reaches out for my hands but pulls them back. I can't reach out for her yet. 'We think it's the Raphael.'

It is quiet in the room save for the ambient noise from the outdoor street. The chair creaks as I get up from it. As I pick up the cylinder, I sense that something important is about to happen, like a crack is about to form in the foundation of a building.

I reach into the tube and pull out the large piece of paper.

I was hoping it would be this.

'It's a map!' Yugi exclaims. 'A treasure map!'

'Let's not get overexcited, Yugi,' Dad says, but I can see that he is already overexcited. His eyes are lit up like a

283

Christmas tree and he's already leaning into the table where I've placed the map. 'All right, what do we see?'

'It looks more like a blueprint than a map,' Mom says. She touches the surface of the paper lightly, as if fearful it might crumble.

'Yes,' Dad says, 'but there are no distances written along wall edges - no piping, no ductwork.' He waves a hand along the straight lines of what appear to be buildings.

'How do you know this?' I ask.

She responds without looking up. 'I've seen a lot of schematics over the years.' *Who is this woman and what has she done with my housewife mother?*

'What are all these other lines?' Yugi asks. Obviously, there is a reason to have a grid placed over the top of whatever map it is.

'Maybe it's a grid to help us systematically search?' My eyes are caught by the even distribution of the lines.

'Yes,' Dad says, 'but that kind of search would take forever.'

I turn the map slightly. It is about eighteen inches square. 'What are these buildings?' I highlight them with my finger and turn to Mom. 'They aren't labeled.'

Mom squints and turn her head. She looks at me and then at Dad. 'This is the Castle from above. Look, here is the entry way; here is the cathedral, the bell tower, the residences, the meeting rooms, the tombs.' She puts her finger lightly on an object in the middle. 'Here are the ruins. The ones you were inspecting when we met Geraldine. Do you remember that, Yugi?'

'Yes.'

'So how do we know where to start looking?' I ask. 'Do we just start near the gate and make our way forward?'

Dad shakes his head. He is frowning. 'We don't know what we're looking for, Jeri. That's the problem. We're missing something. Some piece of information that will unlock the map for us. A key, of sorts.'

'Where do we find the key?'

Silence settles around us.

'Maybe,' Yugi says slowly, 'we go back to the clue before this one - the Barbie prints on the back of Hotdog's photo. Maybe we were supposed to find something near the dragon before actually using this map?'

'That's a great idea, Yugi!' I exclaim and almost make the mistake of hugging him. 'Remember what the priest told us? The dragon's lair is under Wawel Castle. We should start there.'

Quickly, Dad opens his phone and finds the website for the castle and dragon's lair. 'We've got one hour. Supposedly the entrance to the lair is on the courtyard side of the Castle. You buy a ticket and descend into the belly of the dragon's lair.'

'Come on!' Yugi shouts. 'Let's go!'

Our fright from the near-death experience with guns and scary men has almost left us. But as we look around the room, we realize that we must do something about our current situation. Quickly, we pick up the clothes and stuff it into the suitcases. While they are cleaning up the room, I hide my phone above the TV and press record on the audio memo. If someone breaks in again, we may have at least an opportunity to hear who it was. I don't have enough video space on my phone to record the whole thing, so this will have to do.

Yugi packs our essentials into the briefcase, all the things that we cannot do without, the clues for the journey, our passports, money - we now have begun to live and feel like real life spies, I think. Mom calls a taxi and a short while later, we are back where we started.

Wawel Castle.

We pay our entry pass into the cave. Frustratingly, it took a little bit to work out. The machine did not accept paper notes, so Yugi and Dad ran off to find some change. It's funny, until I've seen him jiu jitsu some CIA agents, I've never noticed the fluidity with which my dad moves. He's always seemed like just kind of a normal, middle aged, male-pattern-balding accountant. But now that I know the truth, I can see it in how he carries himself. Mom and I stand by the entrance to the dragon's lair. Her eyes are scanning everything and everyone.

'What do you see?' I ask.

'Almost everything. It's exhausting, really - to always be on the lookout for danger. I rarely look for movement. It's better to check for the spaces between things, for people standing still, reading a paper or pretending to enjoy coffee. Sightseers that stop to tie their shoelaces behind me or even tourists reading a map. The ones that are moving,' she shrugs, 'are usually the ones you don't have to worry about. It's the ones who have stopped...'

I try it. There are kids playing and adults having an argument. Non-threat. A beautiful couple, lie almost on top of each other on a blanket near the shelter of a tree. Not a threat.

Dad and Yugi return. Yugi is holding the coins as he runs to the cave's entrance. He is unbothered by the lurking danger. There is something breathtakingly simple about him, something daring and pure. He looks up at Dad, hero-worshiping, grin spread across his face, and I notice a pulsing goodness about him. I've never really thought about his innocence before.

Dropping the coins into the slot, Yugi accepts the tickets and we begin our descent into the underbelly of Wawel Castle. Small strip lights help us on our way down. After fifteen feet of descent, the temperature drops rapidly and I feel a chill come over me. The sweat that had been part of the cooling process above is now part of the chilling process below. I rub my arms.

The descent takes longer than it should because a slow-moving procession is in front of us. There is an older couple blocking us as they tend their grandchildren. Frustrated, I want to shove past them, but it would do no good. There are a dozen people below them clogging the stairway at various intervals.

The cave smells damp and musty. The limestone appears greasy. The lights reflect the combined moisture of water in the cave and the condensation of breath. I notice that I am beginning to breathe a little bit faster, not from effort, but from claustrophobia. I should have known after my plane experiences, that confined, inescapable spaces are a recipe for disaster. We are going down into the earth and there are tons and tons of rock, dirt and soil just waiting for the next small tremor to shake it all down on top of us. I can feel my chest constricting slightly. Are we running out of oxygen? What happens if someone shuts the door at the top? What if it starts raining and the cave begins to fill up? My mind races ahead to pretty much every claustrophobic-worst-case scenario and it's there that I tread water.

'Jeri,' Mom eyes are concerned. 'Are you okay?'

I hadn't realized that I had stopped. I nod. 'No,' I squeak.

'Are you claustrophobic?'

My voice is pinched. 'Maybe.'

'Do you want to go back up?'

I see the entrance has been completely swallowed by the mouth of the dragon. I realize that this is not a dragon's lair, but it is the dragon itself and we have been ingested. There is no way out. We are Smok's afternoon snack.

'Umm... I don't think I want to climb back up, but maybe if we can move a little faster on the way down, that would be more helpful.' My eyes are wide. Smok's esophagus...

'Excuse me,' Mom says to the less-than-speedy elderly couple in front of us. 'Do you mind if we pass? My daughter...' She points to me as if apologizing for me.

The elderly gentleman stares at us as if we've asked him his multiplication tables. He has wide eyes and his pupils are dilated. Thin white hair flutters gently in an unseen downdraft.

'No speak English.'

Suddenly, Mom switches to Polish. He shakes his head. Then, Russian. His eyes light up. *'Da. Da.'* He smiles. Mom rattles off a couple of sentences in Russian and I am astounded how quickly she can bounce back and forth between them all. He and his wife move to the side and he gruffly calls out to his grandkids. They respond. As we step past them, I ask her what she said.

'I told him that you were about to puke.'

Thankfully, we reach the bottom of the stairs and I feel relief course through my body. The cave is relatively open. Its small side-caverns are lit and it feels like we've moved from the beast's belly to its lungs. Alveoli-like crevices puncture the limestone walls. The lighting has a greenish tinge, somewhat like my face, I would guess. We gather near one of the alcoves and make our plan.

'As we said before, we're not sure what we're looking for, but something to do with the map. Maybe a small tube. Heck, I don't know. Just be creative.' Dad's face is excited.

'Aye aye, Cap'n,' Yugi salutes Dad as they are swallowed deeper into the belly. Mom and I start near the footsteps.

Taking my time, I read some of the plaques on the wall, it is interesting to note that Smok's lair was used both as a pub and a brothel a few centuries before. It is a fascinating place and I wish we could take our time, but suddenly, a voice calls out from the exit. I am not sure what it says, but I assume that it means the dragon's lair is closing.

Hurriedly, we check through the last of the accessible rooms, and I feel a sense of dejection. Either this was not the place or we didn't find it. The lair manager has moved behind us and is guiding us like sheep towards the exit in the back. On one hand, I am thankful that we are going to be ejected out the anus of the dragon, but on the other hand, disappointed.

A few tourists have stopped just in front of us to sign the visitors' book. I really like visitors' books. People love to write in them, to share where they are from. I'm not sure why there is such a sense of pride about where you come from, other than people look at your home and say, 'Wow, you've really traveled a long way to be here? Ooh, that's an exotic destination - Canada!' I search through the book hoping to find long lost Nazi names or famous people, but I find none of them. Just as I am about to move to the end so that I can sign it, my eye falls on a strange entry from 2012:

9/13/12 Bar~~b~~ara Perambulator What a great pen! L~~o~~ved the light! 17 ~~O~~klahoma, U.S.A.

Oklahoma? Barbara? 'Mom!' I hiss, 'Come here! I think I found it.'

Mom hurries over. 'What is it?'

I point to the entry. 'Barbara Perambulator. Barbie Walker. 17? That's not an address. Letters crossed through? Come on, that's got to be a clue for our book. And look at the comment! If that was a normal person, why would they gush about the pen and the light?' I pick up the pen and notice that there is a light on the eraser end. I push it. It has a bluish hue. *Odd.*

Mom grabs the pen from my hands. It is attached by a chain to the small desk, but she turns the light back on and shines it over the page. Suddenly, the page glows with hidden letters. It is a black light!

'What is that?' I ask.

'It's a message. Flip through the pages quickly.' Mom holds the light on the pages. As we are scouring them, the lair manager approaches us from behind and speaks in Polish to us. Mom replies without turning. 'Just a moment.'

'I'm sorry, Ma'am, but we're closing.'

Mom's voice changes. It's weirdly sultry. 'Hi. We're really fascinated by this book and if you would just give us two more minutes, I'd really appreciate it.' She smiles suggestively and licks her lips. The man backs away slowly.

As the words appear on different pages, I use Mom's phone to write them down. *Use the pen. Find her. Get the map.*

We gasp together. 'That's it! Jeri. Now, when I distract the guard, I want you to rip the pen off of its chain. We'll take it with us.'

'Got it.'

Mom wheels to face the guard who is watching her suspiciously. Mom has become someone else. Her words drip with honey, and I can see that her body is moving like a... My jaw drops as I watch her. She has touched the security guard's arm and is stroking it, touching it, testing the density of his biceps. Embarrassed, it looks like he wants to pull away, but his face has flushed. He is tall and lanky, probably closer to my age than hers, but when he sees Mom's obvious attraction to him, I can see that he is already pushing his chest out a little farther. His eyes are locked on hers.

Mom is giggling unabashedly at something witty that the young security guard has said. Her voice echoes throughout the chambers; it is loud enough to cover the sound of the pen being yanked from the desk. Quickly I put it into my pocket. Just as I secure it, Dad rounds the corner and sees Mom flirting with the guard.

'What the heck?' I hear him say under his breath. Grabbing his arm, I spin him back toward the exit.

'She'll explain when she gets out.' I call out over my shoulder. 'Mom! It's time to go.' Mom pats the young guard on the cheek and turns swiftly from him. Her face, exultant, has returned to its normal maturity. Amazing.

After leaving the cave, we see that we are on a set of dirt steps taking us downwards. I look up and see the castle rising high above us. As we descend the steps, Mom and Dad are whispering; Mom excitedly explains the reason for her subterfuge. Dad starts laughing. Along the wall are more bones hanging from it - dragon bones, they say. A sign next to them reads:

> *Krakus, a Polish Prince*
> *Ruled 730-750 A.D.*
>
> *Here is the cave in which he killed the dragon. He settled at Wawel and founded the city of Krakow. This inscription was made by Stanislav Jablonowski, prince of Prussia and captain of the Polish army artillery.*

'That's pretty cool,' Yugi says. 'I didn't really think that dragons were real. I thought they were like the Easter Bunny and Santa Claus.'

I roll my eyes at him. 'Don't believe everything you read, Yugi.'

'Whatever. I want to believe in dragons, so I will. It's just like you believing that you're in love with...'

I throw him a toxic look full of promised fists and kicks.

Mom and Dad approach. 'All right, all right,' Dad calms us, 'let's get back to the hotel and see if we can make some sense of this.'

When we return, Yugi keys the card into the room and we breathe a sigh of relief that nothing has been rifled through. Yugi goes into the bathroom while the rest of us huddle around the table again. Dad opens the briefcase and pulls out the map and unrolls it like a scroll. Flattening it on the table, he places books on the edges to keep it down.

Mom holds out her hand. 'Pen.'

Reaching into my pocket, I extract it and hand it to her. 'Well, here goes nothing.' Clicking the pen, she runs it over the map. For a moment, my heart leaps to my throat. There are no hidden words in the buildings. Quite by accident, she shines toward the edge and a word flashes.

'Mom, shine it back over here.' I point to where I want it.

Suddenly, a message emerges. What was once invisible text is wrapped around the map. It reads. 'Open the book. Find it. You'll remember its address. Seek and ye shall find.'

'Address?' I look at Mom and Dad. I frown.

Dad cups his chin in his hand. 'I'm not sure.'

'What about,' Mom says slowly, 'the address from the book.'

'The puzzle book?'

'No, from the visitors' book. Do you remember what it was?'

I nod. 'Yes, seventeen, Oklahoma, U.S.A.'

She smiles. 'Seventeen. Puzzle seventeen. Look for crossed out letters, just like the visitors' book.'

I pull the Barbie crossword puzzle book from the briefcase and quickly open it to puzzle 17. Yugi has now finished in the bathroom and I can smell both soap and hand sanitizer. Thankfully, he's decided to wash his hands. That doesn't always happen. They crowd around me, pressing in to look over my shoulder, or around my arm, in Yugi's case.

We are delighted to see that on page 17, there are letters crossed through on various clues - six of them, to be exact.

3 Across: A cardinal direction.
E is crossed through
11 Across: Shoemaker
H is crossed through
13 Across: Mindnumbing
B is crossed through

293

18 Across: Make an ~~h~~onest woman
H is crossed through
19 Across: Be~~d~~evilment
D is crossed through
24 Across: Po~~p~~eye's eye apple
P is crossed through

We write the crossed-out letters and reference them similarly to the first time we explored the various explanations of the crossword puzzle book. Attempting to arrange the letters in any order doesn't work. Two 'h's in a word is infinitely difficult in English. Mom attempts to go through the languages that she knows but cannot order the anagram to make any sense.

For some reason, we always think that solving clues is going to be easy. I mean, if Grandma would have intended for them to be easy, she would have just made an 'x marks the spot' to show us...

Holy Moses.

X marks the spot.

'Dad, let me see those clues.' He hands the paper we wrote on and the Barbie crossword. 'Okay,' I say, 'what is this a map of?'

'It's an aerial view of Wawel Castle,' Mom says.

'Yes, but why are there parallel and perpendicular lines crossing it?'

'An electronic forcefield?' Yugi offers.

'Not likely,' I say. 'Wow, I usually see these in math class.' They look stupefied. 'It's a grid.'

'Look.' I point at the clues. 'This is not about the clues nor is it about the answers, but it is about the numbers. Notice,' I point to 3 across, 'if we think of the y axis as numerical and x axis is alphabetical, we can mark out where these clues will be on the map.'

I plot them out on the map and then cross reference with the actual map of the castle I got from the hotel.

3E = Crown Treasury and Armory

11H = Lost Wawel

13B = Sigismund Bell Tower

18H = Ruins

19D = Royal Tombs

24P = Sandomierska Tower

'Wow,' Mom says. 'I don't know what to say...'

'How about, 'Gee, Jeri, that's highly impressive. I think we'll buy you a car when we get back.''

'What kind of car would you like?' Mom asks, a smile playing across her face.

'Are you serious?' My heart leaps to my throat.

'No, but we can certainly talk about you inheriting the Camrillac. Dad and I are in the market for a new one.'

I make a *pshhhhew* sound and turn back to the grid. 'Tomorrow, when we head back to Wawel Castle, these are the places we'll start.'

'But where are we supposed to look?' Yugi asks.

'Grandma will tell us. She has all along.' My heart is sure, but my mind less so.

'What time does the castle open?' Dad asks.

'Just a second, I'll get my phone.' I walk to the TV and grab my phone. I'd forgotten that I was recording. I thumb it on and start the recording. I start replaying the audio. I fast forward. About half an hour before we returned, there is a sound. I return the play to real time. Voices, faceless whispers are in the room.

'G, look in the bathroom.' Silence. 'I didn't find anything. They must have taken everything with them.' Whoever is in charge must be frustrated. 'Have you looked under the beds? The tube must be there.'

Suddenly, we look at each other. We know that voice.

Geraldine Dresser.

Chapter 30 Across:
The product of mass and velocity (8)

'What in the world?' Mom's hands are on her hips.

'Are you sure that's her?' I ask.

'Play it again.' We do it four more times and each time we are more certain.

'How is that possible?' My mind is reeling trying to understand the intricate webs we're pulling from our faces. 'She even told us that she and Grandma were in the CIA together.'

'When Grandma was forced out, maybe Geraldine was kept in to be a decommissioned set of eyes in Poland?' Dad suggests.

'She must have looked into the tube and tried to figure it out,' I say. 'Why didn't she just find whatever it is that we're looking for?'

'It's the same as us. She couldn't have possibly known where to start looking or what she was looking for. It would take years to scour the place.'

'She probably was,' Mom added. Yugi has taken a seat in a vacant chair that's been pushed back. His feet swing back and forth under him. An outsider might think he was bored, but I can tell that his mind is working furiously.

'But then,' Yugi says as he stares at his swinging feet, 'what was that Kung Fu back there at her house? Why would she beat up her own men?'

'I don't know, Yugi. Maybe she was faking it.' I don't really have an explanation.

'I hope we see her again someday to ask. She seemed so nice.' Yugi popped his hands against his cheeks.

'I hope that we find what we're looking for so we can get out of here.'

There is nothing to be done until the next morning, so we pack our essentials back into the briefcase. We order room service and spend the rest of the night discussing what might be on the grid. What was Grandma wanting us to find? Where was she taking us next?

I hear voices in the middle of the night. Because my nerves are so keyed up, I feel like I'm not even remotely getting a decent night's sleep. My eyes flare open and I can see Yugi sleeping next to me, or at least I see his butt near my face. As I quickly arrive at total consciousness, and adrenaline pours into my bloodstream, it feels as if I can see in the dark, hear in the dark – anything. The whispers coming my direction, thankfully, are not from intruders, but from my parents. I think about moving, but guiltily, I want to hear what they are talking about.

Mom's voice. 'I feel like we're in Oz.'

Dad's voice. 'It's surreal, yes.'

'What do you think is going to happen?'

Silence. 'I think our luck is going to run out relatively soon. But it's still so... exciting. Do you remember this feeling?'

'Yes,' Mom giggles. There's quiet and suddenly I'm quite aware that they are making out. Totally gross. I get that this little adventure might have been nostalgic for them, but come on, your kids are in the room. I want to speak out, *Get a room,* but they already have one. More rustling. I reach out to Yugi and I pinch his butt really hard. He cries out and proceeds to sleep talk/sleep whine.

Chapter 30 Across:

'There's a place nut shadow... buppa, will you try the wings?' I hear Mom and Dad stop what they were about to do and chuckle.

Mission accomplished.

The taxi arrives at eight fifteen and drops us off at the base of the castle, right outside the exit to the dragon's lair. I want to go back in and look through the visitors' book one more time, but I'm afraid Mom's lustful security guard might be stationed there looking for his previously chained blacklight pen.

Dad carries the attaché case as we walk through the front gates.

While Dad keeps watch, Mom, Yugi and I begin to search every square inch of the third ruin. We check for loose rocks, loose dirt, anything to point us to Grandma's mind. Yugi and I are on our hands and knees scrabbling about. Dad is trying to distract anyone else from noticing what we are doing. After half an hour, I notice on the southeast corner, just where it seems to show on the map, there is an 'x' on one of the rocks. It is nondescript, but still visible. Without calling attention to Yugi and Mom, I scrape away the excess dirt around the 'x' rock. My heart leaps as the stone pulls out and an inner recess is revealed. I reach my hand into it and my fingers close around something small and cylindrical.

It's an aluminum container about the size and shape of a cigar tube.

'Mom,' I approach her and she turns. I hold out my hand and show her what I found.

Her eyes light up. 'Kevin,' she says softly and sharply. Dad turns around and enters the ruins with us. His eyes scan the surroundings for danger.

'What did you find?'

Mom twists open the tube. Inside is a rolled-up piece of paper. It has yellowed from age but is dry. Unscrolling it, we are disappointed to see that it is blank.

'What's that about?' I ask.

Mom turns the tube over in her hand in case there is a clue on it. But there is not.

'Wait a minute,' Dad says. He puts the attaché case on the rock and opens the clasps. They click and he pulls the lid up. Pushing aside the clues, the Barbie leg and arm and the mirror, he holds up the blacklight pen. Clicking the light on, suddenly, a paragraph of words appears.

Invisible ink.

'This isn't the time to read it, not yet. We'll read them at the hotel.'

'Good idea,' Mom says.

For the rest of the morning, we split up. This time, I go with Dad and Yugi goes with Mom. Mom and Yugi take the far end, to the royal armory and treasury. Yugi wants to see royal weapons and money. Dad and I take the royal tombs. There are different sections to the tomb: monarchs and princes, presidents and leaders. The clue is in the 'Bards' Crypt' which contains the remains of famous poets. But it also contains a plaque commemorating Frédéric Chopin, the great composer. His heart was taken from his body and buried here. Next to his plaque is a loose stone where we find the clue.

After scouring the tombs, we buy tickets to ascend the Sigismund Bell Tower. As we read on the way up, it takes between eight and twelve people to ring it. The bell weighs almost eight hundred pounds. It is an awe-inspiring sight, but it leaves me feeling slightly empty.

Chapter 30 Across:

The clue is lodged at the very top of the tower. Even after we find it, Dad and I stand along the edge overlooking the courtyard and out to the Vistula River. Though cloudy, it is amazing to see the elegant beauty of the river. Winding from here to there between soft cliffs, the Vistula is a snake investigating the land. Around the next bend, it must be testing the air with its tongue. I look up at my dad; his forearm is propped on my shoulder. It's just me and my dad and that's a good thing.

This is not a moment to hurry away from. Even in my youth, I am fully aware that time with my dad, is limited. There are always pressures of work and bills and recreation and this and that, but there is rarely a pressure to depressurize, to unloose the valve that turns all people and all relationships into strained and stretched composites of contented people who enjoy the small things in life. Here was a small thing, standing on top of a bell tower in Poland - well, that's not entirely accurate: this is *not* a small thing. Two months ago, standing on top of our porch with him would have been considered a big thing. Now, to stand in Krakow, Poland above a cathedral, an ancient castle, overlooking a glittering river, this *is* a *big* thing.

My dad's face is serene, beatific. He is smiling broadly, something that doesn't happen regularly in Oklahoma. I don't think it's simply because we are in Poland. I think a large part of it is that we are on the precipice of a different phase of life. For what seems a speckle of time, we stand, father and progeny. Without warning, he taps my shoulder.

'Come on, Squirt. Let's get the rest of these and get out of here.'

As we descend the steps, I run my hand along the stone wall. It is cold and smooth and feels as if the years

301

have worn away all the sharp edges. This passageway is a cold and foreign place threatening to erode the sharp edges from me. I hurry down the steps not just because I want to leave, but every transition, and every sharpening, is painful. I exit before my dad. Although the light is not brilliant, the transition from darkened stairwell to outdoors sunshine hurts. I shade my eyes with a hand. My dad does the same as he exits. When our eyes adjust, we can see Yugi and Mom jogging excitedly across the open courtyard. Rapturously, expressions of delight, they approach. It is as if we have all become younger versions of ourselves - except Yugi - and nothing can ever take that away from us. I see the wind blowing through their hair, clothing swept out behind them; this is the life of which we always dreamed.

I look at Dad and he shrugs. 'I'll race you.'

'You're on.' We can see Mom and Yugi streaming for the Sandomierska Tower. It's our turn to chase them.

Dad and I sprint from the Sigismund Tower. He is faster than I, but there is one thing that no dad ever outgrows: the desperate desire to take care of his kids. He overtakes me and then slows so that I can catch up. It is frustrating that I cannot beat him without his help and yet I am grateful that he waits. Eyes turn towards us, quizzical eyes, questioning why four strange people are running across the courtyard. *What are they running to? What are they running away from?* Finally, just outside the main gate, Mom and Yugi see us. Yugi finishes the last distance to the tower's entrance and places a hand on the wall. 'I won!' He shouts, and of course, for a boy his age, everything is about competition and victory. The mere fact that he had a fifty-yard lead means nothing. Only finishing first is important.

Mom and Dad stand beside each other. They are breathing hard, but not overtaxed. Even though they are jubilant, I can see that they have not let down their guard. Like partnered police officers, they stand looking in opposite directions.

'Did you find the other tubes?' I ask Yugi.

'Yeah, and we found them faster than you.'

'Dad and I stopped for a coffee first because we didn't want to listen to you moan and cry when we found this last one without you.'

'Whatever,' Yugi says, but looks up to Dad for confirmation. 'Did you, Dad?'

'I have had coffee today, yes.'

His noncommittal answer satisfies Yugi's curiosity that I am, in fact, lying. 'Well, let's find the last one.'

'You two go ahead,' Dad motions with his hand. 'Mom and I will watch from down here.'

Yugi and I bolt into the building. He is faster, but I am bigger. We take the steps two at a time. By the time we reach the top, I have outpaced him. I can see his face sours with frustration. 'You cheated.'

'Don't be a sore loser,' I say. 'Pouters are painful.'

We scour the tower. 'Where did you find your cylinders?' I ask.

His eyes are faced along the wall searching every rock. 'The first one was in the armory. That's a really cool place. There was this sword. It was so cool. Supposedly it was sent to Canada during World War II so that the Nazis wouldn't take it.'

'Fascinating.'

'And then we went to this other building, I can't remember what it was called, but there were some amazing rooms in there, decorated with all these old... I don't know the right word...'

'Trappings?'

303

'Yeah, maybe, but the furniture was really old and the drapes were this thick fabric. It took us a lot longer to find it in there because we didn't know what floor the cylinder would be on. Thankfully, Grandma didn't hide it quite as hard as some of the others. It was in the bottom of a wall.' He squints, his gaze no longer at eye-level but above it. 'Where did you find yours?'

I tell him about the tomb and the tower.

'Did you see any dead people?'

We have made a full circuit of the room when suddenly, Yugi points three quarters of the way up one wall. 'There's a small 'x,' Jeri!' Unfortunately, it is out of our reach.

I put my hands on my hips. 'I guess there are two options, Yugmeister. Either we run back down the stairs and get Mom and Dad to reach it for us, or I lift you up on my shoulders...'

'Fine,' he says, 'bend down. I'll get on your shoulders.'

I bend down and pick him up. He is heavier than he looks. And sweatier. I grunt and lift him upwards. For just a moment, it feels like he is going to go feet over head, but we gain equilibrium. I walk him over to the segment of the wall and he strains to reach it.

'Can you get it?' I ask. Already I'm beginning to feel the strain on my shoulders and back.

'A...l...m...o...s...t.' After a few scratching, failed attempts, I feel his hand pull on something and the weight is released momentarily.

'I got it!' He shouts and then leans to the side.

'Yugi!' I shout. I know he has overcompensated and we're going to crash down onto the floor. It happens in slow motion. By the time we both hit the wooden floorboards, our momentum has slowed enough that both of us know we'll have nothing more than a couple of bruises. We tumble apart from each other. Yugi comes up laughing, holding the tube in his hand. He raises it above his head, a triumphant victor and then his face falls.

Geraldine Dresser is standing in the doorway.

'What do you want?' I ask.

'Jeri, it's me, Geraldine.'

'I know who you are.'

She takes a step towards me, and I twitch. I'm looking for a way out.

'What's wrong? What happened?'

'We heard you, Geraldine.'

'I don't know what you're talking about.'

'In our room. We know you were in our room.'

Geraldine's face hardens. 'You don't understand.'

'Exactly. We don't understand. You helped us escape from some very bad people and then a few hours later, you've broken into our hotel room. What were you looking for?'

'Jeri... you'll have to calm down.'

'I will NOT CALM DOWN! You're the enemy.'

'No, Jeri I'm not, listen,' she holds her hands up in surrender. I take a step back. 'I want to - no, I need to tell you a few things that I couldn't share yesterday.' Her eyes soften. Her hair hangs limply around her shoulders as if it's too tired to stay upright.

'Go ahead,' I say.

'We need to go back to my house.'

'What? So you can fake an ambush again?'

'That wasn't fake.'

'What was it then?'

'Please, Jeri, Yugi.'

I look over at my brother. His eyes are wide and I can tell he is very frightened. 'Tell us.'

'Not here. There are too many other eyes and ears here.'

'I don't know if I feel comfortable going to your house. Why should we trust you now?'

'Because you have to.'

'No, we don't. We can just scream. Right Yugi? We can just scream.' He nods, but I'm not sure he could make any noise at the moment.

'Please don't do that,' Geraldine says, 'They won't be able to hear you anyway.'

'Why not?'

'Because I've already had them... escorted to my house.'

'WHAT!'

'Jeri, don't scream. Please.'

'What did you do to them? You haven't hurt them, have you?' Yugi's eyes are round with terror. He is beginning to whimper.

'No, we haven't hurt them. Please, just come.'

I look at Yugi. He nods bravely.

'Okay,' I say, 'but you realize we can't possibly trust you.'

'I understand. All will be revealed. I promise.'

We walk back down the stairs. It was an interminable walk to her house.

We enter Geraldine's house again. The front door has not yet been fixed, but the glass has been swept up. Signs of struggle have been replaced with makeshift tranquility: a doily covers the coffee table again; an umbrella stand is moved into the perfect position behind the door. The wooden table remains resolute in the dining area.

I look at Geraldine who has beckoned us to enter and I see Mom and Dad sitting on the sofas in the living area. Across from them are two serious looking men in polo shirts and khaki pants. They are both large men, broad chested with thick necks and wide hands. The man on the right has a full head of brown hair and a thick moustache. His partner has a receding hairline, but his skull has been shaved. Neither man looks at us when we enter. Their eyes are trained on my parents whose hands are tied.

'Come on, kids,' Geraldine says, 'go sit by your parents.' We rush to them. Tears come to my eyes.

'Are you okay?' I ask Mom.

'Yes. Just a little shocked. I can't believe we didn't see them.'

I look at Dad. I notice that he no longer has the case.

Geraldine perches herself on a stool between all of us. As she leans forward, I am still shocked at how well she moves.

'Let's be candid, shall we?' Geraldine's face is impassive revealing nothing. None of us say anything. 'Although I was truthful about many things yesterday, I must say that I was... reticent to share everything.' She spreads her hands out and smiles. 'Old habits die hard.'

She takes a deep breath and leans back on her cushion and crosses her legs. She seems comfortable and enjoying this position of power. 'Twenty years ago, Iris Walker and I did indeed work together on a few *special* things for the CIA. Espionage was only a small part of our responsibilities. On the more benign side of the work, looking for priceless things was what Iris and I did.'

'If we're being totally honest, it only took a day for me to open the cylinder that she left. I truly thought that the Raphael would be inside, that she would have trusted me to keep it. Of course, as we all know now, the map was inside and it meant nothing to me. To search the entire castle grounds for something would have been a waste of time. But I did it anyway. I wasted my time. After we were removed from the CIA - that part was true - I regularly went to the castle to nose through all the dusty old places, like a mole, I guess,' her nose scrunched up.

'I would probably be the best tour guide on site.' Geraldine's face hardens. 'If Iris would have let me, we could have found the painting, sold it and lived the genteel life of retirees - she and Walter could have moved back to whatever backwater town they wanted, and I could have returned to London.'

'But she didn't trust me. I was hurt. I guess I shouldn't have been. No one makes friends in this business, but somehow, Iris was able to find both friendship and love and I,' her face disintegrates into something different, something weird, and she looks at the brutish man to her side, the one with the brown moustache, 'was able to find neither. I've been stuck in Poland waiting - waiting for something and someone who may never come.' There is a pregnant pause which gives birth quickly and loudly, 'But... here we are. The Walker family and me.'

'What about the goons beside you?' Mom asks.

She doesn't look at them. Shrugging, Geraldine changes her attention to me. 'You know, Jeri - my parents used to call me that - Geri. I never really liked it - too mannish, I think.' A hint of a smile plays across her lips. 'You know, you and I have more things in common than just our names. You are bright and strong willed. It will take a strong man to rein you in.'

I think briefly of Shime. 'Why do I need to be reined in?'

'That's the spirit,' Geraldine laughs and pulls her seat closer. She is sitting almost directly in front of me now. It feels like we're about to take the world's weirdest family picture. 'I'm sorry to have double-crossed you like this, but it's the way of the world. If you want something, sometimes you have to take it.'

I can feel my jaw harden, but I'm very frightened. 'Why not solve all of this and share it like you wanted to with Grandma Iris?'

Geraldine's lips purse and she shakes her head. 'So young, so naive. Jeri, that's not the way the world works. You have no bargaining power.' She taps the attaché case next to her. It looks like a villain's pet in a Bond movie.

'If you let us go,' Yugi suddenly interrupts, 'we'll let you live.' His lower lip is trembling.

Leaning forward on her cushion, Geraldine smiles wickedly. 'Oh, that's precious, my little boy. You've been watching far too many movies, I think.'

Suddenly, without warning, as Geraldine's head tilts toward her legs, my mom leans backward into the sofa and kicks Geraldine in the face. Her head snaps back and she lands on one of the men. My dad, intuitively sensing Mom's movements, leaps forward and even though his hands are hogtied behind his back, he head butts the other guy. The chair flips over backwards and they both go head over heels into the fireplace. The man's head hits the floor. My dad cannot stop his momentum and continues into the hearth.

Simultaneously, Mom has jumped on Geraldine. They are scuffling around the floor. I am too shocked to do anything. I am not a superhero. I am not a secret agent. I am not skilled in the fine arts of war making. Mr. Big Moustache reach for his gun, but it is lying six feet away. He sees it, but so does Yugi. They scramble for it. Yugi suddenly darts forward and grabs it. Unsteadily, he aims it.

The man stops and holds up his hands. Everyone else in the room stops struggling.

'Okay, little boy,' the man says as he moves towards my trembling brother. 'Just take it easy. I know that you do not want to shoot me. That would be a terrible trauma for anyone, much less a six-year-old boy.'

'I'm not six, you moron. I'm ten.' His quaking hands make it difficult to hold the heavy gun leveled at the agent.

'Of course you are.' His voice is calm. 'Now, just hand me the gun before someone gets hurt. Gun shots make a lot of blood, you know.'

'Like duh,' Yugi says softly, 'I've seen Rambo.'

The man moves forward slightly. Yugi takes a step back.

'Just hand it over.'

'Yugi,' Mom says, 'don't give it up.'

'Should I shoot him?' Yugi asks.

'If you have to,' Mom says.

Yugi's face turns a different shade of green, somewhere between pistachio and lime yoghurt. The man takes another step. Yugi points the gun at the man and pulls the trigger.

Chapter 30 Across:

The report is so loud, it feels as if my own head has exploded. My ears are ringing and I see that Yugi's face is shocked, not because he pulled the trigger, but because the recoil was so great, he has staggered backwards. The man he fired at looks similarly shocked. Fortunately for him, Yugi has never shot a gun before. The bullet ended up somewhere in the ceiling.

'Okay, little boy. Let's stop messing around.'

Yugi's face hardens. Now that he has broken the seal on his gunslinging, his hands stop quaking. 'One more step and the next bullet is a wiener shot.'

The man flinches as Yugi has indeed aimed the gun at his privates. 'Relax, kid. We can work this out.'

'One more step and you can say goodbye to Mr. Willie.'

He pauses. In the movies, guys seem to be willing to take one in the gut, the leg, the shoulder, but when it comes to a man's best friend, they get all concerned.

'Jeri, go get the other gun.'

In spite of the circumstances, I laugh nervously. Quickly, I go to my dad and the other man who is still groggy. I notice that my parents are sitting on the chests of their adversaries. I reach inside his coat pocket and grab the gun. I fumble with it, almost dropping it. Dad smiles and shakes his head. Blood is running down his cheek and into his shirt. *Good Lord, I'm holding a gun.*

'Jeri,' Dad says, 'go throw it out the front door before you shoot someone. Then, run to the kitchen and get a knife and cut Mom and I loose.'

I hold the gun as if it's a dirty diaper, open the front door and toss it outside. I cringe thinking that it's going to spontaneously shoot like they do in the movies, but it doesn't, thankfully. Running to the kitchen, I grab kitchen scissors and hustle back to the living room where Yugi Wayne is still threatening the bad guy's family jewels. Taking a wide birth, I snip Mom's zip tied hands. Freed, she rubs the blood back into them and rises off Geraldine whose face has transformed into utter fury.

'You do realize that we have people everywhere?'

Mom bounces once on her chest which causes Geraldine to grunt. Mom sidles towards Yugi.

'I got this, Mom,' he says.

'You did a great job, Yug, now I'll take it from here.' Disappointedly, he hands the gun to Mom. I have already freed Dad from his restraints.

'Kevin, tie them together.' Dad nods and goes back to the kitchen where, of course, we already know where the zip ties are stored. After the three have their hands tied behind them, Dad then ties all six of their hands together.

'We'll find you,' Geraldine says.

Dad shrugs. 'Whatever.' It seems like a highly deflating response. He should have said something cool.

Finally, the four of us stand together. Dad grabs Geraldine's phone.

'Who are you calling?' I ask.

'The Polish police.'

'Try saying that really fast ten times,' Yugi says and then tries it. *PolishpolicePolishpolicePolishpolice.*

'Not now, Yugi,' Dad says.

'Why are you calling the police?'

He smiles. 'They'll be very interested in finding three foreign agents here in Krakow. I wouldn't be surprised if they find themselves in a considerable amount of trouble.'

'And jail,' Yugi adds.

'There's that,' Dad finishes the call. 'All right, let's get going.'

'Wait, can I do something?' I have an idea.

'What is it?'

I run to the kitchen where I saw a permanent marker. Going back to the goons, I right three words, one on each of their foreheads. They shake their heads trying to get me to stop, but it only smears the amount of black ink on their faces. It looks pretty funny.

We are spies.

'You were right, Yugi. You are a spy hunter.' His chest puffs out.

Mom grabs the case and we leave the house. Dad throws the guns into a trash can.

Chapter 31 Across:

Hanging around suspiciously (9)

We escaped the city by renting a car. While pausing at a roadside rest area, Yugi explores the trees and the bushes, we open the tubes. I think we all needed an urban break. At the picnic table, we open the briefcase also and are thankful that everything remains intact: puzzle book, photos, pen, Barbie mirror, map and six tubes, amputated Barbie limbs.

The six pieces of paper from the tubes fit together like a puzzle. Mom flashes the pen on the papers, and I hold my breath. They are full of handwriting. We lean in.

'That's Mom's handwriting,' Dad's voice is hushed.

'Write this down.' Mom begins to read the letter.

Dear finder,

Well done. I wondered if anyone would be able to put it all together, so it seems that we - you and I - have an affinity for looking outside the box. I hope you enjoyed your time in Jerusalem and now in Krakow. I thought the dragon bit was quite ingenious, don't you think?

I hope you got to meet Geraldine, too. She is a good friend and I miss her. Maybe she has regaled you with stories of how we met. She always seemed fond of Walter, too.

Much of me thinks I should write in code where to go next, but I think it's important that I do not do so now. In the annals of world history, sheer evil should be revisited so that we never duplicate it. It does no good for subsequent generations to attempt to change or erase the past by tearing down statues, translating less than desirable parts of history in order to feel better about themselves.

Chapter 31 Across:

Germany, for the most part, has not attempted to erase its story, but there are some who would desire to see it repeated. I hope that you have not encountered them yet.

Now, we are coming to the sharp end of the stick. It's time to drive it home.

Auschwitz. That's where the next leg is. I've given you a 'leg' up where to find the next clue already.

Inside number 11, you'll find Frank's journal. It will detail some, if not most, of the atrocities which occurred at Auschwitz and especially Birkenau. When you read it, it will also show that Frank and Eichmann met in the Dragon's lair where you found this pen. The transfer, as far as I was able to tell, was made to conceal the painting from the Polish authorities.

When you read the journal, you'll unfortunately understand how deeply ingrained evil is in this world, and the spite for humanity that comes from racial arrogance. I felt dirty when I read it, so beware.

Follow the trail. Frank to Eichmann. Eichmann to....

I'm sure it is him.

Barbie.

Auschwitz is seventy-five kilometers from Krakow. For some reason, I was hoping it would be a lot longer; longer so that we would debrief and de-breath, take a break from running. My body, mind and spirit have been on high alert for so long that I have a headache. During the drive, I read my parents whose grim faces bespeak a high level of stress. I want them to say something, anything, really, to shatter the silence around us. Even Yugi is quiet. He stares out the window, chin cupped in hand, pondering the grey

315

sky and the fact that his life has irretrievably changed from boy to young adult. This trip through history has altered his reality, both of ours, and I wonder if he wants to go back to the innocence of the past. I do.

After parking, we pay our admission price to enter the Auschwitz complex. It leaves a strange taste in my mouth that we are buying a ticket to see the world's most efficient engine of murder, as if somehow it was an amusement park ride.

We approach the front gates. Under the despairing sky, clouds threatening to release their sadness, we witness the banal nature of the way both the past and the present appear to 21st century humans. A crowd of young people has gathered, couples in their twenties, hanging on each other's arms, staring into cameras, taking selfies, smiling. I loathe their smugness, their freedom, the irresponsibility of our contemporary world treating tragedy and horror as self-amplification. A woman stands next to her hulking boyfriend; she is wearing a tight striped body dress and he a muscle shirt. They are both tanned, and she is heavily made up. She leans into him, he puts his arm around her and she clicks, clicks, clicks the camera on her phone getting just the right shot of them standing in front of the Auschwitz entry sign behind them:

Arbeit Macht Frei - Work will make you free

and I want to confront them, to shout at them in their beautiful clothes and their healthy bodies, their hale expressions of joy; I want to fling spittle in their face as I say, 'HOW DARE YOU! HOW DARE YOU DEFILE THIS UNHOLY SACRED SPACE!' I want to scare them and their entitled healthiness and remind them that 1.5 million people were slaughtered here, right behind them. Their ghosts still sing eerily between the reconstructed cell blocks. Their screams still echo underneath the grey clouds. These victims, these erased lives, do not want to be photographed, only remembered. How dare you!

Mom has already begun to cry. Silent tears, dew of mourning, glistening and dropping uncaught to the ground. Her people - our people - all of them, Jews, Gypsies, Poles, Czechs, homosexuals, handicapped individuals - we all belong to each other - are burned or buried here.

Suddenly, I am not sure I can go through with the tour. I look up at my dad and see that he, too, is frozen in disbelief, not just at the callous nature of the spoiled few, but that we are entering a space which leaves no one unchanged. To our left is a cadre of older women, Jews, I think, who cover their mouths, eyes wide with grief. Underneath the sign is another young woman posing for her friends. I am overcome. I am undone. What is wrong with us?

Work will make us free, and yet we know, that work never makes people free; it only enslaves them to something else, to the tyranny and dominance of world power. For the people who suffered in Auschwitz-Birkenau, it was the Nazi war machine; for us today, it is the enslavement of the false dream of affluence. We are enslaved by the thought of money, not relationships. As we stand under the sign, I cringe at the thought of the people who were brought here on chugging trains, herded as cattle into cars, freezing and frightened, desperate for air and warmth. I cringe at the thought of them disembarking the train, being separated out, randomly chosen for execution or work; women and children, aged and infirm on the left, men and able bodied on the right. Those on the left summarily murdered by gassing, or execution, or any other

317

unmentionable form of mitigated death. How could they stand it?

And perhaps the Nazis, the SS, were never sane to start with. Perhaps something in the cultural arrogance of the German people who had been shamed and embarrassed after the first world war, caused them to lose a grip on their collective conscience. When Eichmann plumbed the ancient depths of hell, he rose with blueprints of Auschwitz.

We enter and are silent. Yugi knows that this is not a place for common conversation, and the only thing we hear are the sniffs and controlled sobs of modern-day mourners who cannot cope with the past. For the first time in years, I cling to my mother's hand and she to mine; Yugi's knuckles are white as he holds tightly to Dad's arm and buries his face in his side. My parents cannot and will not release each other. We must do this as family.

At this moment, I realize that everything else that we've done on the journey is meaningless. Grandma has brought us to this place to show us what is priceless and cannot be redeemed. All of the clue-solving, all of the running, even the painting itself, has no merit in comparison with what we will experience and learn here. It feels as if this is the center and yet lowest part of our journey, and here at Auschwitz we find the incomparable and immeasurable worth of humanity and our desperate need to strive to live together, without prejudice. Our priest once said: 'There is no Jew nor Greek, slave nor free, male nor female, for we are all one. There is neither gay nor straight, frightened nor fearless, black nor white, for we are all one.' His face was wrapped up in emotion and I wondered what had happened in his life that caused him to be overwhelmed. 'You have to understand,' he said with his hands planted squarely on the pulpit, 'Jesus doesn't call us to be the best person we can be, the Superman, he calls us to be a selfless servant, willing to die to oneself, so that all can know true freedom in life.'

It is for this moment, this death-walk through Auschwitz, that his words resonate now. We wander slowly, deliberately stopping at every post and every sign. Even though we are quite sure that Frank's diary is near Block 11 - the number that was tattooed on Barbie's severed leg, the number on Barbie's house, the number in Barbie's note - we avoid it and the death wall positioned next to it. That will have to come last, even if it is a few days later. This cannot be hurried, for it is here we will be reminded of what the future must look like.

We stand in front of a room. There is a glass panel which separates us from one million men's jackets.

We stand in front of another room. There is a glass panel which separates us from an assortment of striped prisoner outfits. We see photos of emaciated faces and bodies, some stripped bare in death, bones protruding, black and white and grey and yet somehow I can't help but put living flesh on them, thoughts and hopes, laughter and love. I feel my chest constrict. Photos of children, kids my age and younger, stare out at me, pleading with me to do something.

Do something.

I realize that my mother has released my hand and I feel cold. I reach forward, hand extended, but I cannot get behind the glass which separates me from these, my people. They are gone and I am here, watching from the outside...

319

I imagine that I can make it, keep hold of my tenuously trembling self, emotions quaking and shuddering, until we stand in front of a room where there is a glass pane which separates us from...

Two tons of human hair.

I fall to my knees. No longer can I see clearly through my tears and yet they seem to magnify what is behind the glass; shorn hair no longer looking human, but animal. Because of time and the elements, everything has faded, not just the color; the world has turned grey and black and white. All joy has been monochromed.

I see a small braid of hair at the front, a little girl's curl, and I am rent asunder. I sob. I know that I have never cried this hard before in my life, yet my parents do not touch me. They recognize that every person, regardless of age, must come to grips with Auschwitz. To be comforted is to miss an opportunity. And so I cry supervised, yet alone.

Each one of these children, these women and men, these disembodied souls, must be collectively remembered by that which was shorn from them, not just their hair, but their life.

For what seems an eternity, I contemplate my own complicit role in the way that humanity continues to be torn apart and I apologize to God for my ignorance. I vow that somehow, whatever the outcome of our journey, whether we find the stupid painting or not, I will dedicate my life to making things better for others.

Chapter 31 Across:

The tears subside and I find that I can almost stand. It is in this finality that Mom and Dad reach down with a hand to hook under my arms and help me up. I look gratefully at them, but I realize that my own tears have brought theirs down also. Yugi looks frightened and does not understand - why is the hair there? Dad tells him that the Germans had uses for the hair... He leaves it at that.

As we walk, we see rows and rows of bunkhouses, thousands and thousands of people remained there for a day, a week, five years. Some survivors said that they didn't know if they should pray for death or life, because they knew that if they lived, it would be a living death. They could never forget those who had been slain at Auschwitz.

We walk to the far end of the camp which overlooks a green field, new life, grass and other flowers which have forgotten that their ancestors were trampled under the feet of Auschwitz's slaves. The green is a heresy - nothing should be growing here.

And yet, the green is a promise of life, that we can and must move forward. I take a few deep breaths. I close my eyes and feel the slight rays of sunlight on my face. It is warm and cool at the same time.

'How are you doing, Jer?' Dad asks quietly.

'I... I... wasn't expecting this. I wasn't expecting to feel this way - I thought I could view it all clinically, stay distant, you know?'

He nods. 'It's impossible.' He points behind them. 'Even the ones who were taking pictures at the beginning have either turned and left or have stopped recording their steps.'

I notice that too. It's a good thing.

'We have to go back,' Dad says as he puts an arm around my shoulder. 'We have to see it. Grandma requires that we finish.'

The crematorium and the Death Wall. 'I don't know if I can do it, Dad.' My voice falters. 'It's too hard. It's too much.'

'Jerusalem Walker,' he says softly, his voice resonates with tenderness, 'we do this together. We won't let you go.'

I nod and know that I am ready to spill the last of my tears.

We pass the solitary bunkhouses, the workspaces, and tread the same ground that soaked up the blood of so many people. What was once mud and slop is now a covered path. I wish they had left it the way it was and not tried to beautify it, and yet I am grateful that they have made it even slightly easier for us.

Now we must confront that part, the place of execution. It is there that we will contend with the aggregate evil of malevolent world. Some have stopped to hug or to close their eyes to the inhumanity of everything. I shouldn't be angry, but I am. We, as humankind, have been closing our eyes to injustice far too long. Though we cannot erase the past, we can write new sentences for the future.

Without knowing how we got there, we see the sign for Block 11. As we draw near, the signs describe crimes without comprehension. I am devastated to read that along the Death Wall the blood ran so deep that the soldiers often went crazy from looking at their boots. Some committed suicide. There was a quote about Rudolf Hess that said he could not stomach the gore. Thus, he developed the gas chambers where he rounded up Jews and Gypsies, political prisoners and babies, up to six thousand per day, and loaded them into the showers. Their corpses were dragged out and burned in the crematoria.

All the posters we read create images, vibrant and horrific pictures in my mind which I cannot uncreate. I weep again as I imagine the unimaginable; I place myself in the line of women forced into the confined space of the gas chamber - of course I had heard rumors, dark and horrible rumors, that these were not showers. My bladder and bowels release with fear as the screaming, the keening begins. I cover my ears not wanting life to be over, and yet wanting this sound to be done, and then... the slow hissing from above, the Angel of Death lowering...

Angel of Death.

I can't help it, but my mind has leapt to where it shouldn't have, and no matter how much I feel I should remain in this present moment, I understand what Grandma was telling me.

The Angel of Death - Josef Mengele. Who, or what, else could it be.

From the beginning, this is where she was taking us: The Angel under the Cross - Mengele. Somehow and somewhere, Mengele and Eichmann must have met.

'Mom and Dad,' I say quietly, 'we have to find the journal and go.'

'You figured it out too, didn't you?' Mom says and smiles sadly.

'I can't say his name.'

'Don't worry about it. Come on, let's go.'

Surreptitiously we approach the Death Wall. We look around, a few people are loitering behind us, but no one really wants to stay and certainly no one wants to touch. But we do, and within seconds, we see that at head height, there is a loose block with an 11 scraped into it.

Dad quickly reaches up and pulls the objects out. Grabbing the book and the Barbie leg, he replaces the brick.

Everything is back to normal.

Normal - it's what I always wanted, but I can never be that - not ever again.

We return to Krakow. Once checking in to a new hotel, we all take showers; each one of us spends at least twenty minutes in the warm spray washing away the accumulated anguish of Auschwitz. Cleansed, we huddle around the table with Frank's journal. Mom has translated some of it – fast-forwarding through parts relating to numbers sent to camps - and then to his interaction with Eichmann near the end. It seems that Frank somehow knew that Eichmann would be able to slip through the Allied lines.

At the end of the journal is an inserted piece of paper, a letter with recognizable handwriting - Grandma Iris'.

I'm not sure I can keep going. The painting is trivial compared to what I've unearthed along the way. But to bring you along this far and leave you would be unconscionable.

The intention of what we do is not for money, it's for memory. When you write this down someday, do not sugarcoat. Tell the truth. Tell them everything.

It's time for you to go back to the beginning. Back to the start of it all.

Find him.

He will help you.

Donald.

Chapter 32 Across:
Not paying attention (9)

The flight from Krakow to Chicago was subdued to say the least. Although my anxiety for flying was still evident, I found that in comparison to the train ride from Auschwitz, I am able to cope. Our shock at seeing Dongle's name was overwhelming - just one more time that Grandma and Grandpa have pulled the wool over our eyes. I mean, I knew that Dongle was friendly with Grandpa and Grandma, but come on - he's in on this whole thing?

By the time we near Tulsa International Airport, we are very tired and very jet lagged. During our trip across the Atlantic, we had seats next to each other, but I would have been happy if Yugi would have sat by himself. He put his feet across the rest of us and it became quite apparent, quite quickly, that he may have been wearing the same socks the whole time.

As we descend into Tulsa, I feel a strange sense of foreignness. We've only been gone a couple of weeks, but in that time, I met my maternal grandparents, fell in 'like', flew to Poland and experienced the depths of the Holocaust. In essence, I am a very different fifteen-year-old than when I left.

When the pilot tells us we can turn on our phones, almost everyone's device starts to ding, beep, quack, toot and play music. To be honest, I had forgotten my phone, really. It was good to use as a camera and a voice recorder, but I did not miss text messages. Somewhere along the way, I realized that there was no substitute for conversation.

Yugi is humming into the plastic window. Since our family excursion to Auschwitz, he seems to have grown up.

'What are you thinking about?' I ask Dad.

'Hmmm?'

I repeat the question. His eyes are glazed over.

'Just wondering how life is going to be different.' He smiles. 'I'm pretty sure I'm going to have to find a new job.'

'You can always teach jiu jitsu.'

Fortunately, he laughs. 'What about you, Jer?'

'I was just wondering how we can spend our lives with our eyes closed, oblivious to people. We're always so self-centered.' I pause and search his eyes. 'Did you know about Dongle?'

'Donald? No.' He huffs once. 'I thought I was pretty good at spying, but I guess not.' He snorts. 'My next door neighbor.'

'Grandma did a good job of hiding things right under our noses.'

'You can say that again.'

I hear the thump of the luggage bays being opened and realize that I've moved so far past my fear that the descent did not even move my heart rate. It could be that I'm so tired I don't even remember who I am.

After disembarking, we stand by the luggage carousel. It only takes five minutes or so for our baggage to come round. Dad kept the briefcase with him the whole time. It was searched both times because of the cylinders, but they were not confiscated. At the carousel, Yugi finds our baggage and attempts to pull it off, but he is not quite strong enough, so we do it together. I thought he would slap my hand and say, 'I can do it,' but it seems as if he has outgrown that, too.

'Well,' Mom sighs, 'let's go find Donald.'

Chapter 32 Across:

Waiting outside by the curb is a difficult thing, but eventually we see Dongle's behemoth rumbling forward. He parks in front of us, opens the door and walks around. He doesn't look us in the eye - it's almost as if he knows something is up. He nods to Dad and they hoist the luggage into the back of the car and we hop in.

As we begin driving, Dongle turns off the radio.

'So,' he says slowly, 'how was the trip?'

No one knows who should answer first. Everyone is tired but also reticent to begin this difficult conversation.

I lean forward and put my head on my forearms between the front seats. 'It was incredible, Dongle. Jerusalem was awesome, we got to meet... some great people and then we flew to Poland. Have you been to Poland, Dongle?'

His cheeks redden and he clears his throat.

'Because If you haven't, it's an amazing place with incredible history. Some amazing World War II things to learn - we even went to Auschwitz and learned about different Nazis like Adolf Eichmann and Hans Frank and even Josef Mengele. Have you heard of Josef Mengele?' His discomfort actually makes me feel better because it is a release for some of my anger towards him. 'These guys must have had some amazing secrets of things that happened during and after the war. Imagine what it's like to have secrets,' I say. 'Secrets that you can't tell anyone else - not even your next-door neighbors.'

I hit the right nerve. Dongle presses on the breaks and veers to the side of the road. The turnoff for Interstate 44 is in front of us but he pulls up short.

'Okay, Jeri,' he says looking in his mirror at me, 'get it all out.'

'How could you have kept it from us? I thought we were friends. We're neighbors.'

His hands grip the steering wheel. 'What did you want me to say? By the way, Walkers, your parents and I did some pretty shady things in the 70's and 80's.'

'You're a spy,' Yugi says simply.

Dongle shakes his head. 'I'm retired, Yugi. I'm your neighbor, Donald Berry. I take care of your lawn and your pet possum.'

'But you lied to us,' I complain.

'I didn't *lie* to you,' he counters, 'but if it makes you feel any better, I do have a guilty conscience about withholding information from your family.'

'It seems like everyone in the world is a spy,' Yugi proclaims ponderously. 'We're all looking for other people's secrets.'

'Ain't that right.' Dongle's voice seems strained.

'Grandma wrote that we are supposed to ask you for help, as if there is some information you have that will help us.'

Dongle glances in his rearview and then side view mirrors. 'Do you mind if I drive while we talk?' He pulls into traffic and speeds up quickly. 'Look, when your grandparents moved all of you to Oklahoma, I owed them a favor. They basically saved my life while we were in South America and I told them that if there was ever anything that I could do, I would do it. So when she asked me to look out for you, I bought the house next door. I've even installed a security system for you while you were gone. They've been back, you know.'

Dad turns toward Dongle. 'Who was back?'

'The people. I guess they're still looking for something.'

328

'But we took it all with us. And we brought it back here - in this case.' He taps it between his legs.

Dongle's face is impassive, but I can tell that his mind is furiously working out what to share next. 'You didn't take everything.'

'There is something else in our house?'

'No, it's not in your house.'

'Where is it then?'

He waits and then speaks. 'It's in mine.'

'What? All this time you could have helped us?' Mom leans forward and lays a hand on Dad's shoulder.

'I promised your parents that I wouldn't get involved until the right time. You needed to see for yourselves; you needed to understand with your own eyes the kind of things your parents were doing, the risks they were taking.'

'Well, somehow we survived.' Dad is not happy.

'Then how did you know about everything. The CIA. The people who were after us?' I demand.

'I can't tell you. I'm sorry, Walker family, I just can't tell you. It wouldn't be safe for any of us.'

'Donald,' Mom says as she looks at his driving profile, 'we haven't been safe for a long time. Just tell us.'

'I can't. It's not the right time.'

'When will that be?'

'It... that... I don't know,' he stammers. 'It's just not right now. When we get back to the house, I'll share with you what your grandma wanted me to, but to be honest, I don't have many answers. You might have to tell me about everything you learned on your trip.'

'It feels like it will be hard to trust you right now,' Mom says.

329

He takes a deep breath and sighs. 'Do you trust Iris?'

'Yes, of course,' Mom responds.

'Then transfer it to me. Eventually, all will be revealed. You have to understand Beryl, Kevin, that we can't give up all our secrets.'

'All right,' Mom says leaning forward also, 'at least let us know how they saved your life.'

Our turnoff from 44 onto 81 south is approaching and he signals to change lanes. 'In 1969, we all were stationed in South America.'

We were searching for escaped Nazis and the trail led us to Argentina. The ratline across the Atlantic always seemed to end up in one of these dictatorships. Mengele lived on an estate in the country guarded by dogs, henchmen with machine guns, you know the type. But he was always afraid - always. After the Mossad nabbed Eichmann, he went into hiding, but not before he and Eichmann met. Iris and I, we found out where the meeting was supposed to take place, but unfortunately, I was stopped by the police on the way to the meeting. We were so close to getting them.'

I was taken to the Buenos Aires jail, but a few days later, Iris found out and freed me. I knew that they were going to torture me, but somehow she convinced them that I was in the wrong place at the wrong time - a bumbling tourist.' He stopped. 'She could convince a paint salesman that wallpaper was a much better investment.'

'How did I never know this about my mother,' Dad mutters.

'Don't beat yourself up, Kevin,' Dongle says. 'There are a lot of things that I don't understand either.'

Chapter 32 Across:

'So you've been watching us for how long?' Mom asks.

'Since you moved to Duncan. It was all orchestrated by Iris, but then...'

'Then her mind started to go...' Dad filled in the blank space.

Dongle gives Dad a look but doesn't say anything.

We are nearing Duncan now, but I don't necessarily feel a sense of relief. We're home, yes, but Duncan seems to have grown smaller, like leaving a fishbowl to swim in the ocean and then back to the fishbowl again. The signs are the same, the roads have familiar names, but the streets seem smaller, less functional as if I am not able to drive them anymore.

The last ten minutes elapse in silence. We are all caught up in our thoughts wondering whether our previous world has changed too much to adapt to. Or is it the other way around? We see our house. Its two-story structure does not seem imposing, but it looks like a head sticking above the ground, eyes of windows, mouth of door, secrets unspoken behind black shutters and locked locks. The voiceless questions continue as we unload the car. It is very warm out. And humid. The rest of the family takes the luggage to the house while I run around to the back. Maximus is hanging on her branch. Her eyes are closed. Running up to the cage, I bend over to look in. One eye opens and then shuts. Either she has forgotten about me, or she is not very happy about being left behind for the last weeks.

'Hi girl,' I whisper.

She contemplates me with bemused sleepiness. 'I've got to help unload but I'll be back later.'

After unloading and unpacking, Mom puts on a load of laundry, Dad checks the mail, Yugi airs out his room which is very hot and stuffy. It feels as if we have silently slid back into our routine. We have agreed to meet at the Berry residence just before dinner, though.

When the clock chimes six, we are dressed and ready to go over. Dad carries a bottle of wine - keeping up appearances, just a friendly get together. We have taken both a shower and a nap and are feeling somewhat refreshed. We knock on the door and Dongle answers. His face is a mask of control.

Dad hands him the wine bottle and he holds the door open for us to enter. Mom enters the kitchen and greets Margery with a hug. Margery, after the embrace, pushes her back and happily claps her hands lightly in front of her chest. Dad is the last one through, but Dongle stops me in front of him.

'Kevin, would you mind if I talked to Jeri.'

Dad's eyes narrow, but he does not decline. He nods at me.

We move into their living room which is surprisingly similar to Geraldine's. This thought shocks me. *Could Geraldine and Dongle be conspirators? What if his source of information has come directly from their mutual connections? Are they planning to double-cross Grandma?* An antique table sits in the brightly lit front room. Four chairs are positioned on each edge. A china cabinet is planted in the corner. Antique dishes and cutlery decorate the inside. Mirrors plate the back side and I can see our smaller forms reflected in it.

'Jeri.'

'Donald.'

'I know this must be...hard for you, but...'

'Dongle, before you begin, I just want you to know I feel a certain amount of hurt about this.' He winces. He is taller than I, and as he looks down, I can see the sadness and a desire to tell me something.

'I'm sorry. Truly, I'm sorry.'

'How much does Margery know. About you. About all this.' My eyes move around the room, over him.

'Nothing. It's torturous to hide it all, but she knows nothing. She thinks I've always been gone on business trips.'

'She never suspected anything?'

'Not that I know of.'

'Not exactly the basis of a great marriage.' I don't know why I want to hurt him, but I do.

'No, no it's not,' he responds softly. His shoulders droop. 'But every marriage has various sacrifices that have to be made. Mine was to my country and the price of it was a fractured home life.'

'Dongle, what did you want to tell me?'

He nods and then moves to the ancient oak desk. Opening a drawer, he pulls out an envelope. I see that Grandma's handwriting is on it. My name is written on it. *Jerusalem*.

Handing me an antique letter opener in the shape of a sword, I insert it and open the envelope. In true Barbie form, there are no words, only five fingerprints on the piece of paper. Two to the upper left and three below and to the right of that. I show it to him.

'What is it?'

I can see that he recognizes it. 'What does it look like?'

'Barbie marks.'

He flinches. Something about her name has set him off. 'What is it?'

'Connect the dots.'

'I'm not in the mood, Dongle.'

'Do it,' he says fiercely. 'You've come this far, you've grown, I can tell. Don't give up.'

I look back at the picture. 'It looks like a pan.'

'You're close.'

'The Big Dipper?'

'Extremely warm now.'

'I don't know, Dongle!' I'm frustrated, fatigued and tired of having the wool pulled over my eyes.

'It's the Southern Cross. It's a constellation.'

'Yeah, so why is it important?'

'That, Jeri, is all I can tell you. I don't know everything that you've been through nor everything that you've done. But think. You've been sent to me for a reason, Iris must have thought it important. Think. Think!'

I shake my head and grind my teeth. At this point I feel like giving up. I've seen enough and experienced enough to last a lifetime. I think back to the clues. Why would Grandma leave me a clue about the Southern Cross?

Cross.

Angel beneath the Cross. It was capitalized - it's the name. The Angel of Death under the Southern Cross. Startled, I look up at him. 'I've never seen this constellation before. Where can I find it? Which part of the sky?'

'You won't find it, Jeri. Not unless...'

'Unless what? Do I need to escape the earth's atmosphere?'

'No,' he says gently, 'only the northern hemisphere. The Southern Cross is only seen below the equator.'

'South America.'

He nods. 'South America.'

'We have to go there.' My mind is spinning. We've just returned from the Middle East and Europe and now we'll have to get on a plane and fly for God knows how long to... 'Where was Mengele?'

'Argentina.'

'Dammit.' I say. *Why couldn't he have escaped to Mexico?*

'Take the paper and talk it over with your parents. Whatever you do, be careful.'

'Like duh,' I say. 'Why do people always say that?'

He shrugs. 'It seems appropriate.'

His eyes stray over my shoulder. I turn. 'What is it, Dongle?'

'They're here.'

A man and woman sit in the front of a car; he is eating something, a doughnut, maybe, and she is drinking coffee. I can't see their faces too well, but they look like they have settled in.

'We'll take care of them later,' Dongle says. 'Let's go get something to eat.' He stops but then puts a hand on my shoulder. 'I'm not asking for you to forgive me yet, but someday, I hope we can be friends. When all this is over...'

'We'll see.'

The meal passes quickly. When we finish, I get up to help with the dishes, something that I very rarely volunteer to do, but I notice that Margery was pleased that I offered. I stand next to her drying the dishes while she prattles on about the news from Duncan. She is pleased that Donald had fully recovered from his attack. Still nervous about a recurrence of the event, Margery tells me that thankfully, the police have gotten to the bottom of it.

As the night wears on, some of the uneasiness erodes and dissipates into the conversation. Margery is effusive in bringing us up to date on the gossip. Dongle watches from his perch at the foot of the table, his elbows prop up his folded hands, his mouth hidden behind them, but his eyes follow the words closely. Something has happened to his eyes, something deeper than I know. I wish I knew.

Yugi gives an abridged version of our travels. Although it is dangerous to allow him to narrate the adventure, he has been briefed on how much and what things he can share. Any reference to the painting, Barbie, clues, etc... has been censored, and if he dances too closely to that edge, I have been allowed to tap his leg with my foot. A few times, especially when he nears the Auschwitz story, I nudge him, but generally, he is good.

'My goodness,' Margery exclaims as she holds a hand to her heart, 'it seems like you're a little young to be traipsing around a concentration camp.'

He shrugs. 'There were kids who were there a lot younger than me who never came out.'

We all recognize the horrible truth to his statement and let it be.

'But the flights, Margery, so much fun!' It's as if a switch has been flipped and his face lights up like a Christmas tree. 'We were so high in the sky, way above the clouds!' He uses his hand to demonstrate a plane soaring above the earth. 'Vroom, vroom. One time we dropped a ways and Jeri got all freaked out. I think she peed her pants.'

This time, I kick him hard.

'Ooooww!' He whines. 'You didn't have to kick me.'

'Okay,' Dad says and pats the table. 'I think that's a sign that perhaps jet lag is taking a bite out of our happiness. Berrys, thank you very much for your hospitality and for taking care of the house. We really appreciate it.'

'Our pleasure.' Dongle reaches out tentatively to each of us, but we are reluctant to embrace him.

As we exit the house, I am aware of the darkness awaiting us. Even though we are only steps from our own front door, it feels as if a menacing presence waits for us just beyond the limits of the streetlights. We descend the steps and I look back; Dongle and Margery are standing side by side, arms around each other, a normal elderly couple waving goodbye to their children and grandkids, and yet I wonder if it's all been a sham. Have the Berrys been watching out for us or just watching us?

Out in the street the sedan still sits. My eyes linger on it and then move away. I can only imagine what the two people, the stalkers, are thinking. I hold onto Mom's arm a little tighter as we walk the last steps home.

A voice. *I know that voice.*

Of course, I know that voice; it belongs to my dad, but it startles me nonetheless. Sitting upright in bed, *Wham!* I ram my head into his chin. I wasn't aware that he was leaning over my bed.

He stumbles backwards and grumbles. My head hurts now that I've given myself a morning concussion.

'What was that?' he asks bewilderedly.

'I... heard a voice and someone pushing me. Must have been a bad dream.'

Dad shakes his head and moves to the door. 'That was me. Get dressed. We're going shopping and you're driving.'

'Hooray,' I mumble sarcastically.

After dressing and brushing my teeth, I eat breakfast. While Mom and Dad argue about the shopping list, I visit Maximus. She sees me coming and stirs. I've brought some scraps from breakfast and even snuck a raw egg. Mom doesn't think it's such a good idea to feed her eggs. If she gets a taste of them, she might go looking for them, to which I respond that she's not a shark - she won't go looking for manflesh.

I open the lid and Maximus stretches her back like a cat. I reach out an arm and she climbs slowly. Her claws scratch my skin - I'd forgotten that feeling, and when she finally wraps herself around my neck, her tail curls around the front. It feels like I'm wearing a strange, calloused necklace.

Stroking her, we walk toward the side gate. I haven't asked Dad if I can bring her, but once he looks into those beautiful brown eyes and ugly white and brown face, pink nose like a greasy gumdrop, he won't be able to resist having her in the car. I'm sure of it.

As my dad approaches me, I can see the strain in his eyes. Black circles ring them, and his shoulders seem hunched. Dad stops his descent on the steps when he sees Maximus. 'No, Jeri, he's... she's not coming with us.'

'But Dad,' I complain, 'she's lonely. She doesn't want to be back in her cage. I'll stay in the car with her while you do the shopping.'

'That's exactly why I don't want her to come along. I want you to help me.'

'We'll take Yugi. I'm sure he'd love to do the shopping with you.' He gives me a look, *Yeah right.*

Chapter 32 Across:

'Come on, Dad, please?' I don't often pull the whiny voice, but this feels like an appropriate moment. He hesitates. 'Just look at this face,' I touch Maximus' snout with my hand which makes her pull away, 'is this a face you could say 'no' to?'

'Quite easily, actually.'

'Dad.' It feels as if I'm petulantly bouncing up and down.

'All right, Jeri. Fine.' He puts up an index finger as he walks away from me. 'But she stays in the car when we shop.'

'But...'

'Your choice, Jerusalem.'

'Fine,' I respond tersely, but I'm happy because I get to have a normal day in the car with my pet possum.

Dad is already sitting in the car when I get in. As I stoop, I try to extract Maximus from my neck to hand her to Dad, but she is reticent and wraps her tail tighter around my neck. Her claws dig into my shoulders.

'Maximus!'

Dad rolls his eyes. Finally, I pull her from me and hand her over. Dad accepts the possum with disdain. It is apparent that neither one views the other with affection, but hopefully they'll tolerate each other at least while I'm driving. I situate myself behind the steering wheel, adjust everything - it's obvious that Dongle has taken his role seriously and driven the car a few times. I look over at my dad who has allowed Maximus to crawl up his arm and wrap around his neck.

'Oh, that's so cute,' I say and reach out to touch her.

'You find this pleasing?' Dad cringes. 'She smells like garbage.'

339

'Don't talk about my sister like that.' I reach out to her, scratch her under the chin.

I reverse down the driveway. Looking both ways for cross traffic, I accelerate into the street and notice a new car parked just up the street.

'That's them.' I point out the window to the car, but Dad is fussing with the possum

'What?'

'The car that Dongle was talking about. The Stalkers.'

'Are you sure that's not just a neighbor's car?'

'How many people drive sedans in Duncan?' Most everyone drives pickups or SUVs.

'True.' I pull over, put the car in park and open the door.

'Where are you going?' Dad asks.

'I'm just going to go look in the car.'

'Jeri, don't.' Dad opens his door and rushes to stop me, but I'm halfway across the street already.

Just as I reach the door of the sedan, Dad grabs my arm. He's about to stop me but I rap on the window before he can.

'Hello?'

They look up with faux surprise.

I knock on the window again.

The man behind the steering wheel opens the window. 'What do you want?'

'Who are you?' I ask.

'What's it to you?'

'I'm inquisitive by nature.'

He frowns and shakes his head. 'Why does your dad have a possum around his neck?'

Dad's eyes are wide. 'How did you know he was my dad?'

'He looks like you. Er, you look like him.'

'Move along,' I say. 'We don't want transients parking in our street. Too many drugs already.'

'Do we look like drug dealers?'

'Maybe not, but why are you parked on our street?'

He looks at his partner who nods. 'All right, we'll move on,' the man responds.

'You do that.' My dad is totally speechless. Unconsciously, he is stroking Maximus.

Dad and I walk back to the car and get in. I sit behind the wheel and watch them.

'I can't say that was actually a smart thing to do,' Dad says.

'Why not?'

He blusters. 'Generally, in the world of espionage, it is better if your enemy believes they have the element of surprise when you know they do not.'

'Why?'

He leans down slightly and points out the windshield at them. 'If I can see them, I know what they are up to; if I cannot, I'll always wonder.'

'I'll remember that next time.'

'Come on,' Dad says. 'Let's go shopping.'

We slowly drive past the stalkers. I toot my horn twice. I am gratified to see that they are frustrated.

We turn left and head towards the grocery store. Dad has taken out his phone and is working something into the screen. 'What, uh, are our plans, Dad?'

'Hmmm?'

'What are we doing?'

'We're going for a driving lesson and then shopping. But, I was thinking we could stop and see Grandpa and Grandma too. Grandpa might like to know how we got along overseas. We can pass on the greetings from Weismann's also.'

'No, I mean, what are we doing? Are we going to finish this thing or not? What about South America?'

'Yes, we'll... find it.'

'Why did you hesitate?'

Because he can't look at me, he appears incredibly guilty. 'I... I might... stay back...''

I almost slam on the breaks. 'Why would you say that?'

'Well, your mom can handle herself and it's probably safer that she goes alone.'

Now, I do slam on the breaks. Maximus hisses. 'What do you mean, 'by herself?''

'Jeri, be reasonable. You both did a great job in Israel and Poland, but South America may be a whole different kettle of fish. I think...'

'Not this again!'

'I realize this is not what you wanted to hear, but you and Yugi are still very young and to be perfectly honest, outside of a Disney movie, do you think kids really should be engaging in this kind of stuff?'

'Why not? This is what we do! We're always trying to figure out who is lying to us. Who else is perfectly suited to paranoia? Teenagers!'

He raised his eyebrows. 'Fair enough.'

'Beyond that, isn't it best if we all stay together where we can take care of each other?'

'Yes, Jeri, but I have to think about Grandpa and Grandma also. Who is going to look after them? What if the agency tries to get at them to get to us?'

I grind my teeth. I know that Grandpa would want us to go. 'The nursing home will take care of them. That's their job. It's not like the CIA can go waltzing in there with their badges and say, 'We'd like to bring in one of your dementia patients.''

He is quiet. I know that I've hurt him, but I can't help it. What he is asking is patently unfair.

'I'm sorry, Dad, but this, from the beginning, has been a family affair. Even the crossword puzzle book is my forte.'

'We'll see,' he says quietly and motions to the road in front of us.

As I reacquaint myself with driving, Dad says little. He is lost in the surroundings. Duncan seems to have shrunk; the stores seem smaller, the streets are a Hotwheels car track. Everything about the place they reared their children has changed. Duncan no longer seems like a comfortable place. After a while, Dad directs me to drive to Pine Point nursing home.

'What are we going to do with Maximus?'

'She'll stay in the car.'

'But it's so hot.'

'Jeri,' my dad snaps, 'you wanted to bring her.'

I can feel myself sinking into a grouchy place. I frown at him, but he's had enough of my petulance. As we pull into the parking space, into which I purposely park badly to frustrate him, he places Maximus in the backseat. Maximus does not seem to mind in the least. She stretches out on the fabric, claws puncturing the cushions like hypodermic needles. I crack the windows to let the hot air out and then we walk apart, separated by mood and mission.

As we enter Pine Point, I recognize that the air conditioning smells as it always does, of disinfectants, bleaches, flowers and elderly people. There is something mothbally about walking to the nursing home that aways sets my mind on edge.

A new nurse greets us, takes our temperature, and makes us sign in. She doesn't know that we are related to Walter and Iris until we sign our last name.

'Oh, they'll be so pleased to see you. They haven't had any visitors for almost a month.'

I feel my father cringe as if somehow the guilt of my grandparents' loneliness falls squarely on his shoulders. Right, left, right and we are almost there. The hallway, as always, is packed with the nation's pickled history. Wanting to stop but unable, I see so many recognizable faces, names that are on the tip of my tongue, and for a moment I feel like what they do: to see someone and just not quite know who they are, like grasping for a rope, dangling, dangling, tantalizingly close, but... nothing.

Grandpa Walt stands near the large hallway window. He is staring outside. The light fills every piece of his face; it looks as if he is absorbing it, swallowing it. There are so many other things dying in his life that for a moment, I wonder if the light is the one thing that he can still hold onto.

'Grandpa!' I run to him. He turns around as fast as he can and when he sees me, his face is transformed by a smile. Holding open his arms, I run into him and encircle him. His smell is different, but familiar, like putting on a coat that you haven't worn for a while.

'Hello, Jeri,' his voice low and welcoming.

'Hi, Dad,' my dad says and stand behind us. 'How are you?'

'Oh, well, you know...' he shrugs and leaves the sentence dangling like that very rope of recognition.

'And Mom?'

He looks down at me and smiles sadly. 'How was your trip? Did you ... see anything?' He waggles his eyebrows.

'Grandpa, we found...'

'Jeri, maybe we should all go for a walk.' Dad says. 'Would you like to get outside, Dad? Maybe we can take Grandma too.'

'I'm sure they'd make an exception just this once.'

We go into their room and are greeted by darkness. The shades are closed, even those over the bay window where Grandpa likes to sleep. Grandma is standing by the bookcase, staring at the books. She is mumbling words, phrases, 'not that one, never that one.' A hand, white and worn out, rests on the shelf touching each one of them. Perhaps there are people in these books that seem even more familiar than her family.

'Hi, Grandma.' I move next to her, but she does not respond at first. Then, she turns, but her eyes are vacant. I don't know any other way to put it, but she smiles. Her face is a complete question mark: who are these people? Why are they here? Where am I? And yet her mind has not forgotten how to smile. Something deep inside of her understands. Maybe it is the same place that reminds her how to speak, how to cry, how to keep her heart beating.

'Hello, so nice to see you little girl. What's your name?'

'I'm Jeri.'

'That's a beautiful name.' She reaches out and touches my face like she's touching a flower. There is a

345

struggle, a tug of war, between what was and what can't be again. I wish I could pull her back to us out of the darkness.

'Come on, Grandma,' I touch her arm, 'let's go for a walk.'

She looks around at Dad and Grandpa. Dad shifts from foot to foot. Grandpa, though, sees this every day, every moment, the woman he loves has become the woman he lost, and now what is left is a dying coral reef of memories.

Grandpa takes her by the hand and we follow them out of the room. Slowly, they walk, the pair of them. Even though they will be warm outside, they are dressed in long pants and sweaters. Grandma's hair is done nicely.

Left, right, left.

The new nurse, by her name tag, *Eloise*, smiles at us, but I feel like it's somewhat patronizing, as if she's really thinking, *Those poor things.* Once signed out, the four of us exit into the heat. Pine Point does not smell of pine trees, but of dust and smoke - one of the male nurses has chosen a patch of sidewalk forty feet from the front door to feed his addiction, but the smoke has wafted back towards us. Birds twitter above and around us, free and floating, stressless and without care. I am not jealous of their flight, only their freedom. Every person is bound by something, chains of regret or circumstances. Even though I am yet young, I sometimes feel the cords of despair uncoiling from the depths of time to catch at my feet.

'Grandpa,' I say, 'I brought Maximus!'

'Maximus?'

'Yes, don't you remember? My pet possum.'

'Ah, yes. Of course.'

The Camrillac is halfway in the shade but it's too hot for Maximus to be inside. I ask Dad for the keys and I manually unlock the car. Reaching into the backseat, I allow Maximus to scrabble up my arm.

'Well, isn't that nice,' Grandma says when she sees Maximus.

I'm happy that she noticed. 'Grandma, this is my pet.'

'Mmm, a pet, yes. Nice puppy.'

Maximus growls at her but she doesn't notice. Already she is walking away from us, away, away, slowly away, moving down the sidewalk. Dad and Grandpa share a look and Dad hurries after her.

'Do you want to hold her, Grandpa?'

'No, no, that's all right, Jeri. You hold it.'

'How has she been, Grandpa.'

'The same. Very much the same.'

'Do you ever wonder what she would be like now if she never got dementia?'

A strange, wry smile crosses his lips - something trembles inside of him, and I can see he wants to say something but cannot.

'It is what it is.'

There are cracks in the sidewalk, crevasses filled with decaying cement, but every once in a while, a clump of grass or a lonely dandelion has accepted the challenge to give life a try. I put my hand in the crook of his elbow and feel his strong, sinewy arms, granite-like. He pulls my hand closer to his side. 'Everywhere we went, Grandpa, in Israel and Poland, we met a few people who spoke the best things about you and Grandma. The Weismanns, even a lady named Geraldine Dresser.'

He stops, startled. 'Who did you say?'

I repeat her name. He swallows hard.

'She knew you both.'

347

He nods and speaks slowly. 'What did she say to you? What did she want?'

I tell him what happened in her house, the interaction and the fight.

Grandpa is stunned and horrified about Geraldine's behavior. 'I can't believe it, Jeri, but I am glad that you're okay.'

'We have to keep going, Grandpa.' My eyes focus on Dad who is pointing to various things for Grandma.

'Jeri, Geraldine Dresser is not who she says she is.' He is speaking to me, but his eyes are focused ahead on his wife and son. 'She... she was...'

'What is it, Grandpa?'

His throat needs clearing, obviously. I can see is Adam's apple working furiously to dislodge whatever trouble is clogging up his ability to speak.

'Geraldine is a Nazi. Through and through.'

'What!'

'She was one of the three in the room that day, the one where Grandma had to... give up her secrets.'

'Wait a minute. She told us she was CIA.'

Grandpa takes in a deep breath, holds it and then exhales. 'She was, but she turned.'

'At first she seemed so nice...'

His wry smile pulls up one side of his face. 'No one is as they seem. Not in the spy game - not in life - you can be anyone, anyone at all - a kind old woman petting her lapdog; a Russian anarchist, a militant, space archaeologist – it's all about practical deception.'

'I guess I never thought of that.'

'Geraldine Dresser is as close to pure evil as you will come to. She's not right up here.' He points to his temple and taps it.

Chapter 32 Across:

'What should we do?' My voice pleads with him to give us the correct answer. Maximus has shifted towards my ear. It seems as if she, too, wants to hear what Grandpa has to say.

'It's a three-team race, I guess: us, the Neo-Nazis and a division of the CIA.'

'Why don't we just work with the CIA? Aren't they the... how do I put this... the best of the worst? If we work together, maybe we can find it before Geraldine and the Nazis.' Maximus yawns broadly. I can see her pink nose and mouth right next to my eyes. Her tiny needle-like teeth are exposed.

'Think about it - if we assist the CIA and the painting is found, what will you all get out of it?'

'We'll split the sale proceeds in half.'

He smiles sadly. 'Your innocence is beautiful, Jeri. The Walker family will get nothing except a handshake and the knowledge we've helped make a down payment on another war. Always another war. The merry-go-round never stops.' His voice trails off.

'So we do this on our own.'

Grandma and Dad are ten yards from us now and his voice is low and hard. 'Jeri, you must be observant. Be careful. Like I said, few things in life are ever as they appear.'

Dad takes Grandpa and Grandma back to their room. I can tell that Grandpa has to take a deep breath before reentering the building. The nursing home, for all its shiny exterior and happy little bushes and happy little windows, is a place of darkness and disillusionment. To live there - or more to the point, to exist there - is a test of will. For

Grandpa, who has watched the last years of his life pass outside his window like a never-ending stream, a mirage of time, this place is a battle against a broken spirit. Grandma, on the other hand, seems comforted by the return.

As I stand by the side of the car, Maximus clings to my neck and watches over the street. My spatial awareness has never been better. I notice things that I never have - license plates, signs, noises and smells which aren't quite in line with what we should expect from Duncan. My eyes are drawn across the street and for a moment, I think that I see the dark sedan from this morning. My heart skips a beat. Maximus senses this and raises her head slightly.

Without warning there is a sound, a low rumble, a deep, coughing sound as if the earth has a hairball. Maximus constricts her claws into my skin and I wince. As I wonder what the noise was, two things happen simultaneously:

First, the sedan suddenly pulls from its parking place and screeches down the street narrowly missing cars and pedestrians.

Secondly, my phone rings. It is Dongle. *That's weird.*

Just as I am about to answer it, I see my dad running out of the front doors of the nursing home. His face is apocalyptic, revealing the end of something. In his hand is his phone; it is held out from his arm as if bringing it near his face will singe him.

'Jeri! Get in the car! NOW!'

I am frozen to the spot. I've never seen him scared like this. Never.

'What is it? Dad?'

He rushes to the driver's side of the car and pulls up on the handle. It is locked and he almost pulls the handle off. 'Jeri, unlock the car and get in. Hurry. Hurry. Hurry.'

I take the keys from my pocket and unlock the door. Quickly, Dad takes the keys from my hands. As he starts the car, I notice that my phone has stopped ringing.

'Dad, you're scaring me. What happened?'

The Camrillac peels out of the Pine Point nursing home. 'Jeri, something bad...'

'Was it the noise?'

'You heard it?' He turns the corner without stopping at the sign. The wheels leave rubber contrails on the asphalt below us.

'Yes. What was it?'

His jaw twitches.

Instead of taking ten minutes to get home, it took us three. When we turn the last corner down our street, the one that has always contained our home and our lives, our past and our future, we see everything has gone up in smoke.

Literally.

As we approach the remains of what used to be our house, I find that my vision has started to narrow, blacken - *so this is what it feels like to faint?* To stay conscious, I stroke Maximus. She is not particularly pleased by this as I was rubbing her fur in the wrong direction. She scrambles up onto the seat behind me, watching, sensing the destruction in our lives.

Our house is on fire. Not only is it on fire, our lovely home has been decapitated. Pieces of our roof, our rooms, our glass and mortar are strewn across the lawn, sidewalk and street like bone, hair, blood and flesh. Through the windows of our car, I can see things, I can feel things - our house is writhing in pain; the front door an open mouth, a maw of raw terror. Like Edvard Munch's famous painting, it screams at us, at whomever is nearby - this is very frightening.

My dad has already leapt from the car, the door of the Camrillac still ajar. The pinging sound is incessant, more noise, more catastrophe. I can feel Maximus begin to shudder. I reach behind me to grab her. For some reason, I can't get out of the car. I cannot step over, across and onto the pieces of my childhood.

Sirens sound, wailing, keening, the cry of the bereaved. Ahead, firetrucks turn the corner and rush to the site of the nightmare. Firefighters, clad in heavy yellow gear, helmets glinting in the sun, stream out. They are an army of yellow ants scurrying, hooking up hoses, rushing to communicate, hurrying to establish a plan of attack. For them, they are always prepared, but never fully ready, for the irrepressible ringing bell calling them to action. This is what they were trained for: to fight the ravenous dragon's all-consuming fury.

Our house accepts the streams of water, the pressured hoses training torrents at the base of the inferno, through the windows, into the rafters, attempting to slake the dragon's thirst. I can only watch helplessly. I want to help but I can't.

I'm just an odd little girl with a possum on her lap.

I see my dad standing at the edge of the heat, close enough to feel our home's pain, yet far enough away not to be injured. Behind him, I see my mother, Yugi, Dongle and Margery watching. My mother is covering her mouth with one hand. From this distance, I see that she is crying. Dongle has an arm placed around her; strangely I'm conflicted about this. Because of his deception, he seems an inappropriate savior.

Chapter 32 Across:

The fire continues to rage; the fight for our house goes on. Firefighters know that this is a losing battle - it was lost before they even arrived. They knew it. By the slouch in their shoulders, the shaking heads, it all adds up, yet they soldier on. Their task is to prevent the spread to other houses. In this heat, the Berry residence could be added to the conflagration, so they fight. The hoses make a loud hissing sound. There are continued shouts. A crowd has gathered to gawk. Most have their phones out recording the cremation of our history, and I wonder, with an utter sense of revulsion, if this is what happened at Auschwitz. These people standing by, these onlookers, looking on, thankful that they are not personally affected by the tragedy. Their unwillingness to help, multiplied by their smugness, their desire to post this video on their social media pages, makes me furious.

Ultimately, the rage sends me over the edge and I thrust myself from the car. I run at them. Maximus is still on my shoulder, ever present, ever comforting.

'WHAT'S WRONG WITH YOU!' My shout startles the social media warriors and they turn their devices towards me. One of the women, a girl in her twenties, appears startled. Of course she is surprised; her videography has been interrupted. No one does that. How dare I.

They don't respond. None of them. Most of them return to cinematography, but their eyes are trained on me. They are mute, senseless, creatures of habit and of entertainment. They care nothing about feelings or sensibilities.

'Didn't you hear me?' I shout again. 'TURN THEM OFF! TURN THEM OFF!'

One of the men looks ashamedly at me and silently stops the recording and puts his phone down. The rest do not.

I move in front of them. I dance before their cameras. 'Don't you see? This is our life. It's going up in flames! Everything is burning. Put down your phones.' I point over to my family standing on the lawn. 'We're suffering enough. Don't just stand there. Go help them!'

As one, their heads swivel towards my family. Their faces register no emotion, no reaction. They do not move. They cannot - they have been conditioned to watch, to record, to comment from afar, but certainly not to act.

To make matters worse, my eyes catch movement farther up the street. A man and a woman stand, a duo who look suspiciously like the agents who have been watching the house, binoculars held to eyes. I am inflamed even more.

I am my house.

I am on fire.

I feel as if I have exploded and pieces of what used to be me are smoldering on the ground, smoking, vestiges of life and what made me.

But inside, I feel very much like a phoenix, and something grand and gallant is rising from the ashes.

Let this be now - I am a new Jerusalem.

Chapter 33 Down:
Characterized by conflict (9)

It is no insignificant thing that we made it to Buenos Aires without major incident.

After booking our tickets online, we still had plenty of money left from Grandpa and Grandma's generous account, so we bought new clothes, new suitcases, new everything and placed them in a corner of the Berry house to await our departure.

Thankfully, the necessities for our trip, our passports, the clues, essentially my backpack, had been placed inside the family safe before we had gone shopping that morning. After the explosion, it took us a while to find the safe. When given the go ahead to sift through our cremated home, we found the safe deposited safely in the basement. It was too heavy to carry out, so Dad opened it in situ. Our hearts were in our throats as the blackened door creaked outward. Fortunately, the fireproof safe lived up to its billing and the contents were left unaffected. Pulling out the passports, Barbie's limbs, the mirror, the clues and especially my crossword puzzle, we were thankful we had everything we needed.

Once again, Dongle drove us to the airport. This time, though, there was no conversation. Repeatedly, Dongle glanced in the rearview mirror, paranoid that we were being followed. I asked him about it, but he shook his head and said he was just being cautious. I could tell he was worried, though.

About halfway to the airport, I summoned the courage to ask him the question I had wanted to since we returned.

355

'What's your part in all this? You worked with Grandpa and Grandma, but not with Geraldine Dresser?'

'I've only heard her name spoken. I've never met her.'

'What do you know?'

'Very bad lady. She's been working to support the Neos for a long time.'

'Why doesn't the CIA just... you know...' I left the thought hanging, as if the CIA was truly in the business of assassination.

'This isn't the movies, Nosebleed. You can't just go around... you know...'

'So Grandma sets you up as our guardians? Is that right?'

Everyone was listening. I was certain that Dongle had already told my parents everything, but it was going to be interesting for them to hear how he explained it to me.

'A long time ago, your grandma told me she was on to something really big, something that might change the world. I know she didn't trust many people, maybe not even Walter - she wouldn't have wanted to place him or you in danger. She could trust me, though, because I was part of the security team, her sounding board. When she connected the dots between Eichmann and Frank, at first I didn't believe her. It seemed far too easy - high ranking Nazi officials handing off stolen merchandise.

'She didn't tell me everything, of course. And it was wise that she didn't.' Voice quiet, Dongle took a deep breath. 'The CIA coerced me to spy on them. I adored Walt and Iris and I wanted to help, but when the CIA wants something, they get it. So, I was left with twisted arms and twisted loyalties. I gave the CIA bits and pieces, and I kept your Grandma's secret close, but it tore me apart to have to spy on them at all.' His lower lip trembled. 'I'm so sorry.'

Mom reached forward from the back seat and patted his shoulders. 'Don't beat yourself up, Donald. It all turned out for the best.'

'Best?' He shook his head. 'Your house has been blown up. You've lost everything.'

'Donald,' Dad's face is generous, 'we have each other. Everything else...'

'I know, replaceable,' Dongle interrupted, 'but...'

'Not to keep beating a dead horse, Dongle, but what kinds of information did you pass on about *us*?' I had to hear it all from him.

'Updates, mostly. Because you guys never really entered the garage, there was nothing really to say. Yugi was throwing balls against the walls of the house, and you, Jeri, were hanging up laundry, or your parents were watching movies at night after you two had gone to bed. You were just a normal family trying to do normal things.'

'What about when we found the clues in the garage?'

Dongle's face turned stony. 'When you started poking around in the garage, I assumed you found something, so I had to... call them. They sent over a few agents to dig through the garage. That night, when Yugi startled them, I watched because I wanted to make sure you were safe. Good Lord, I laughed so hard when Yugi shouted at them, 'Freeze, Suckers.''

'That was pretty good, wasn't it, Dongle?' Yugi had been listening intently.

'What about the night you were stabbed.'

'That was Geraldine's group, and they weren't nice about it. I'm lucky to have gotten away with just a friendly little scar.'

Silence ensued, but I couldn't help breaking it. There were still too many question marks.

'What are our chances of figuring everything out, Dongle?'

He shrugged and flicked his blinker. Taking the offramp to the airport, the car slowed. 'You might figure out the clues, you might find the place, you might do everything right, but a lot of time has gone by. You're probably too late. These people have too many resources. They can find anyone on the planet at any time. I'm sure they are tracking us right now. Phones are terrible things.'

Without thinking, I touched the device in my pocket. It felt strange, an oblong piece of hardware, alien and evil.

'Thank you, Dongle,' I patted him on the shoulder. It could have been taken as a patronizing gesture, but Dongle reached up with his right hand and touched mine.

'No, thank you all. I'm very sorry. I should have told you. I should have.'

Dad stared out the window, unresponsive. The veracity of Dongle's statement hung in the stifling air of the car.

After he dropped us off and wished us luck, we waved to his truck as it drove away. By the time he passed us, he was already on the phone. I hoped he wasn't talking to the CIA.

I learned a lot on the flight to South America.

It's hard to quantify the Angel of Death, a doctor of Auschwitz. Mengele represented everything wrong with the Nazis. He was said to have whistled while he worked. As the trains rolled into Auschwitz, he would stand at the front of the line, smiling, licking his lips as he flicked a finger one way or the other: to the left was living death, camp life, to the right were the gas chambers. His decision was one based on sight, which ones could work and which ones could not.

He also had a thing for twins - specifically, identical twins.

He performed the most sadistic experiments.

Many Germans claimed ignorance. Some metaphorically picked their fingernails, poking at the dirt underneath, while the crematoriums burned white hot behind them.

It was better not to know. It always feels better not to know.

Mengele was blamed for everything.

Strangely, Mengele escaped by sheer luck, really. The Allies were looking for the security squads, the Waffen SS. When they found Mengele, he did not have the blood type tattoo on the back of his upper arm.

He had been far too vain for a tattoo.

They overlooked him and his gap-toothed smile and his thick black hair and soulless eyes and his vile contempt for human life.

After escaping the Allies, Mengele lived a comparatively simple existence in Germany until he felt the threat of Nazi hunters. Strangely assisted by the Red Cross and the Catholic Church, Mengele found his way to South America, living in Argentina until the Nazi hunters found him.

Somehow escaping their net in Argentina, he settled in Paraguay where he died in a swimming accident in Brazil while on vacation. One his many aliases, Wolfgang Gerhard, was placed on his headstone. After a later exhumation and subsequent testing, it was proved that Mengele, the Angel of Death, was finally dead.

Somewhere along the line, though, Mengele must have had his hands on the Raphael. There is no other reason that Grandma would have positioned him so neatly in her crosshairs.

The plane descends into São Paolo, South America's largest city. Even though we have now been in large cities, I'm shocked by this Brazilian metropolis sprawling below the wings of our airplane. The vastness of the city, even though smoggy, is impressive. Stretching almost one hundred kilometers, São Paolo seems like it should be a more tropical version of New York, Paris or Shanghai.

We call a taxi which weaves through dense traffic, horns, screeching, voices - similar to Jerusalem or Krakow - but multiplied by something *alive*. Where Jerusalem seemed to be perpetually tan and Krakow stony grey, São Paolo is electric blue. Something about it makes me want to dance.

After reaching the hotel, we spread out on our beds. We have been over the notes so many times, studied the pictures, memorized every detail, that I am tired of them. As we strategize one last time, I can hear the city beginning to tune up. The drums begin in the background, and I feel my foot tapping to the beat. I am unable to control this movement. The other three look at me, Dad down at my foot, Yugi frowning, Mom's eyes widened.

'What are you doing?' Yugi asks.

'What?'

'Stop moving.'

'You're one to talk, always wiggling.'

'Oh yeah?'

Chapter 33 Down:

'Kids,' Mom tries to placate us, 'it doesn't matter.'

We make plans to take the train north out of town and then rent a car to take us the rest of the way to Caieiras, a suburb where Mengele lived on a farm. As we scan the photos, there is a picture that Grandma has taken of Mengele with a guarded gate and German shepherds. Two young men are standing in the front yard. In the photo, Mengele is lifeless, still. A cigar dangles from his lips. He is looking away from Grandma's camera - something down the road has caught his interest.

Yugi is yawning by the window looking past his reflection into the street below. I join him. Revelers are preparing to dance. Beautiful, bronzed women, Amazons, truly, are wearing white tops, sleeves draping precariously on their shoulders. The dissonance of their white tops, brown skin and black hair is exceptional, and I can't help from admiring the fluid way with which they move. They are made of the ocean, the tides, crashing waves and swirling water. The men, rhythmic and powerful, wearing khaki pants and button-down shirts, move as effortlessly as the women. Life is swarming, turbulent, like foam dancing on top of moving water. I want to go down there, not to dance, but to feel it, to be part of the current, to feel the ebb and flow as it eddies by me.

'Are we going down there?'

'No chance,' Dad says.

'Please, Dad. Take us. Let's go. Let's be tourists. Just tonight.'

'It's too dangerous.'

'But...'

'Jeri, we didn't come here for a vacation. We have a job to do.'

I can feel the frustration in my jaw. 'But what if this has all been a wild goose chase? What if the Agency or Geraldine has already found the painting? Then what? We'd have wasted the experience.'

'Jeri, we wouldn't be able to keep you safe. There's too many peo...'

'Safe? When has this ever been about keeping us safe?' My blood pressure rises. 'Look at what we've done together already, and somehow we're still together and alive.'

'Jeri, calm down.' Dad's hands are out in front of him and this infuriates me.

'I don't want to calm down. I want to lose control. I want to stop thinking about this thing - for one night. Don't you get it? We're in Brazil. BRAZIL! You might be used to this, but I want to be like them!' I point down to the swelling miasma of people. There are so many in the streets now that it looks as if the alleys are alive, dolphins, sharks, eels, writhing and twisting. My voice lowers and I point to the table in front of us. 'I want to live free of this, of Eichmann, Frank, Mengele, Nazis, Raphael, everything - I want to feel it.' I close my eyes; the throb of the city is just outside the window.

'Well, maybe...' Mom hesitates.

'Yes! Yes! C'mon, Mom, put on a sexy outfit and come dance with me.'

'I'm not dancing,' Yugi crosses his arms.

'Good. Stay up here. You wouldn't understand anyway.'

'No, if one of us goes, all of us goes.'

'But I don't want to,' Yugi pouts.

'Sorry, Champ. Jeri gets to choose.'

Chapter 33 Down:

Mom's face lights up furiously and she pulls me by the hand to the bathroom. 'Okay. Come on, let's do it the right way.'

After dressing, we lean into the mirror together. 'If we're going to do this, we're going overboard.' She colors her eyelids with blue and orange. I copy her. As I look in the mirror, I'm not sure whether to laugh or be impressed. The transformation is so strange, complete. Mascara, some rouge on the cheeks and lastly, lipstick. Mom chooses dark red, almost blood red. She has the look of a piratess, or a prostitute - maybe it's kind of the same thing. I choose blue. At first I wonder if the color will make me look frigid, but once combined with the rest of the outfit, I realize that it is a good color on me. I'm kind of...

'You look entrancing,' Mom says.

I stare at myself. I've never thought about myself that way. Over the last two months, my arms seem to be more toned and even the skin around my neck looks tighter, healthier.

'You look great, too.'

We look at each other in the mirror. 'Should we go show the boys?'

Suddenly, I'm hesitant. It's one thing to be in the dark, dancing in the moonlight, but another thing to be scrutinized by brother and father. I suck in a deep breath. 'Okay, here goes nothin'.'

We open the door and Mom goes first. I can hear dad wolf whistle. His appraisal causes my mother to laugh and spin around. Her skirt is small. I look down at mine.

'Come on, Jeri,' Mom motions with her hand.

With very little confidence, I stick my head out the door.

'Holy hypothermia!' Yugi exclaims.

363

'Ow!' Yugi complains. Dad must have ruffled his hair hard.

'Come on, Jeri,' Dad calls out. 'Let's have a look at you.'

'No.' I'm tempted to wipe off the makeup, to replace the imposter's clothing and makeup with something more appropriate. Blue jeans. A t-shirt. Maybe a chastity belt?

'I'll come in then.'

'NO! That's even worse. Just give me a second. I'll come out.'

One more deep breath and I turn off the light to the bathroom. Maybe a little less ambient light will disguise me.

I step through the doorway and turn. I can see it in my father's eyes. Something is different - something goes atilt.

'Wow.' He says quietly.

"Wow', like, I'm a weirdo, or 'wow' like, I'm impressed.'

'The second one,' he says. Something has happened to my dad, a change in perspective and he is wrestling with the fact that the metamorphosis is finally catching up with him.

I blush. 'Thank you.'

'Are you cold?' Yugi says looking at my blue lips.

'No, stupid. It's lipstick.'

He makes a *pbbbbbst* sound.

Yugi is wearing his gaucho outfit, something he thought was cool while we were in Argentina, but now that we're about to go out in public, he looks... stupid. The outfit is replete with a black, wide-brimmed hat, white shirt with a red bandana tied around his neck, grey pants and cowboy boots.

I snicker.

'What's so funny?' He looks down at his clothes and spreads his arms as if he is bowing.

'Nothing.'

'Enough, you two,' Dad approaches Mom who spreads her arms and curtsies. Then, pulling down on one sleeve she looks over her shoulder coquettishly.

'*Ven aqui.*'

'Rahr rahr,' Dad responds.

I want to gag.

'Let's go!' Mom twirls herself under Dad's arm and pulls him out the door. Suddenly, neither of them are afraid of what might happen, only frightened of what might *not* have happened. Dad sends Yugi back to put our belongings in the safe. After doing so, he bounces back to us looking somewhat like an Italian gondolier.

As we walk through the front doors of the hotel, the music assaults us. Somewhere in the middle of the street, drums, congas, a bass, trumpets, and brass, blare, blurt and thump. People are shouting, laughing, drinking - this is a party. This is something we *don't* have in Duncan.

But here... This is an alien world where movement signifies life. There is a dense, tangible, silky sexuality about the place, not a meat market like a college bar, but a raw, abrasive and overwhelming confrontation between desire and happiness. Young and old alike squirm through and around each other. Women shake their hips; men move in rhythm behind them - it is not obscene, just fun. Mom pulls Dad into the stream and they are dragged away. Mom motions for me and Yugi to enter too, but we don't know how to dance. Little Yugi appears incredibly vulnerable in his little gaucho costume with his hands hanging limply by his sides, his narrow shoulders hunched.

'Come on, Yugi. Live a little.' Once we are in the middle of everything and everyone, the darkness covers us while the music consumes us. I see women around me, hips and legs moving, hands raised in the air, and I try it. It's delicious.

'What are you doing?' Yugi shouts above the music. I ignore him.

'I'm going back to the room,' he turns to leave.

'Yugi, just stay with me for a little while longer. I don't want to be by myself.' Mom and Dad are separated from us by four other couples. Mom is wriggling up and down Dad's body. His hands are on her arms. They are transformed by the night and the music - they seem young and immune to everything we've come from. Tonight, they can't remember we've lost our home, our belongings, our safety. In this place and time, the past is erased and there is only – now. The music suddenly switches. It's a fast, pounding beat. Women scream while the men shout and raise their hands in the air. Jumping, everyone jumping at the same time. I join in.

'Jump, Yugi, Jump!'

'I'm not a dog.'

'Just try it.'

He jumps once and glances around self-consciously. Nobody cares about him and his little gaucho outfit. No one cares about anyone else. This is the way that dancing should be. He jumps again, and somewhere the smile creeps out from his bandana and sits on his face. He jumps and raises one hand in the air and then, without warning, he is hooked. I no longer have to convince him of anything. Yugi has caught the rhythm of the night. He looks like a little bouncing pirate now and after he caroms into a few people who laugh and point at him, he understands that they aren't laughing at him. They love the fact that a little boy has lost his inhibitions.

This is our moment. I love him, but I don't know why. Tonight, we are just two kids on a journey. Maybe that was always the intention of music, why the Ancients created instruments, to sing songs of meaning and of temptation, so we could forget how small and separate and isolated we are from the cosmos. Music connects our souls to the stars, maybe.

On this night, I choose to surrender to life. While Yugi absorbs himself in jumping, his red tie has bled into his neck, and he looks as if he has been garrotted. I laugh and tilt my head back. The dark of the streets gives way to the twinkling stars above - just a few can be seen, a few peek between the folds of the universe to wink at us. *Why do you make such a big deal of such little things? Why don't you just live?*

Someone gently nudges my shoulder. My eyes are caked shut and my mouth has a gluey film caking it. One of my eyes has the temerity to open and find the person who has disturbed my beauty sleep.

'Jeri.' It's my mother. It looks like she has slept upside down. Her hair is a mess, sticking up from the right side of her head. Lipstick is smeared, mascara is stuck in clots to her eyelashes and her eye shadow seems to have drifted up onto her forehead. What was once sexy is now decidedly not so.

'Wow, Mom, you look great.' My voice is gravelly. I stretch my hands above my head.

'Thanks. It's time to get up.'

'What time is it?' I groan.

'Noon.'

'What?'

'You heard me.'

'Weren't we supposed to be on the road by eight?'

She snorts and puts a hand in her hair. 'We were out on that road until three. I'd say we're doing pretty good.'

Yugi and his resolutely immobile behind is perched once again less than a foot from my face. Ugh. 'Where's Dad?'

'He's in the shower. I just ordered room service. I don't speak Portuguese, but I think I ordered eggs.'

'What, you don't speak every language in the world?'

'Very funny.'

I pinch Yugi's butt and he flinches.

'Jeri,' Mom warns.

Yugi sits up rubbing his eyes like a baby. The sight of his stained neck makes me laugh. 'You look like a murder victim.'

'Shut up, cage fighter.'

After breakfast, we make our way to the train station. It should take us two hours to get through the city where, at our last stop, we will pick up a rental car.

As we ride the train northwards, Yugi's face is pressed near the plexiglass window. His breath fogs it up and he is drawing pictures in the latent mist. It disappears quickly, too quickly, so he blows again recreating the world of his imagination as the Brazilian cityside rushes by.

Mom and Dad are huddled next to each other. The briefcase, our constant traveling companion, looks much the worse for wear. The brown leather is ripped and the handle has been duct taped back together, but we felt like this was a lucky charm that we needed as we traveled.

As the apartment buildings, businesses and shopping stores morph into small cafes, Mom and Pop grocery stores and small pubs, I can feel my attention resetting. We arrive on the northwest side of the city in the suburb of Perus. A man is supposed to meet us with our rental car. I'm not sure why we didn't get one in the city, but Dad said it would be easier to navigate the countryside as opposed to the congestion of city traffic.

When, the train comes to a juddering stop, Yugi's forehead knocks against the window and he rubs it.

'Well, here we go.' Mom's nervousness is apparent.

A man stands near the station. His eyes are fixed on us, and I feel suspicion and anxiousness. In his hands, though, he is holding a sign which reads WAKLER, but we're pretty sure that means us.

Dad gestures to the man in threadbare clothes. His beard is scraggly, and his hair looks as if it has had only a passing relationship with a shower and comb. His broken English is held together by enough nouns and unconjugated verbs that we can at least make out what he is hoping from us.

'You come. I auto.'

The man takes us to the parking area where he smiles and stands beside what could be considered a car... I think. Yet, I am more concerned about his teeth, or lack thereof. Those that remain are stained red, or brown, or something in between.

'Money?'

Dad hands over the correct amount. The man pockets it and hands over the keys. Our rental car is yellowish with chickenpox rust spots. The seats are a mixture of fabric and insect microhabitat. Because the license plate hangs to the bumper by wire, I wonder if the license plate is bogus or if the car is just that rickety.

We open the doors, and simultaneously our heads are repelled by the odor. *Whoa.* It smells like a whole family of possums have feinted in there.

'Holy crackerjack!' Yugi pretends to retch. 'What is that?'

Curiously, the smell is less eau de colon as it is a strange mixture of cigar smoke, body odor, camphorwood, gasoline and mothballs. The interior has been ineffectually tainted by a long since euthanized, scented pine tree which hangs from the rearview mirror. The man who rented the car to us smiles weakly and lifts his thumbs to us.

'All good, cowboys?'

On the road from Perus to Caieiras, Yugi and I alternate staring out the front window to the back windows, spotting different kinds of plants and animals, each punctuated by a thwack on the arm, 'Look at that!' Every time we traverse tractor-tire ruts we make an *aaaaaaaaaaaaaah* sound which jiggles and wiggles in our throats as if someone was pounding on our backs.

Changes in the road surface signal our arrival into Caieiras. We pass hotels with ritzy facades, Catholic churches with inspiring steeples. I feel a sense of wonderment that out in the middle of nowhere, there is a place of respite away from the manic world. Kind of like Duncan, maybe, but better.

'Where are we going, Dad?'

His eyes follow me in the rearview mirror. 'We're going to meet someone.'

Yugi is as surprised as I am about this revelation. 'And that would be...?'

'Eduardo Montanez.'

We wait for him to explain, but Mom takes over. Her forearm rests on the seat back. 'Eduardo is a friend of Grandpa and Grandma. When they came here in the 70's, Eduardo was their guide.'

'Guide to what?'

'To Mengele's estate, or hideout, or prison - it's all perspective.'

'He lived here?'

'Right up until his last days.'

Mom turns back to follow the map with her finger. She tells Dad to turn right, and then after a few more intersections, she points to the correct left. We drive up a slight incline and finally stop at a hacienda near the terminus of a dead-end road. It is not large, but mostly hidden by trees. Curved archways, stucco siding and slate tiles give it a sense of expansiveness. Dad parks the car and turns off the ignition.

The car doors screech open. The cool and humid afternoon air is, literally, a breath of freshness. I can smell new things, green things; I hear the birds screaming at us. No need for a guard dog or an alarm system. A few good parrots will do.

As we walk along a gravel driveway, two 'guard' dogs, ponder us confusedly. One is black with a grey face, salt and pepper whiskers, and the other of similar age but tan with a waggly tail. They both raise their heads at our approach but lower them soon after we pass them.

The screen door screeches open and an ancient, stooped man steps out, leaning on a cane.

'*Ola.*'

My mom nods. '*Como voce esta?*'

His grin widens even further. It appears as if he is attempting to straighten, to stand taller, to see us.

'Welcome to Caieiras.' He speaks in English, but it is heavily accented.

'Thank you.'

'You are just in time.'

'For what?'

'Afternoon snacks.' Without waiting for us, he turns back to his front door, opens it and walks back inside.

We follow.

The man, who I assume to be Eduardo, is wearing a woolen sweater and tan corduroys. Neither looks to have been laundered recently. Actually, Eduardo doesn't seem to have been laundered either - his stubbly chin hair has breadcrumbs in it. His hands are stained with oil and mud.

My eyes adjust to the dimly lit interior. The rooms are sparsely decorated with furniture; everything seems worn out, tired, exhausted from sitting, from collecting dust. Above the hearth, an antique clock ticks, one second per click, back and forth, back and forth, the pendulum swings monotonously.

'Please, sit down.' He points to a table in the kitchen. There are four chairs and five people. 'Please, please.'

We rake another chair across the floor and sit. His cane makes a thwopping sound as the rubber tip attaches itself to the linoleum and releases. Returning to the table, he brings steaming mugs of coffee. Yugi sees and smells what it is, wrinkles his nose and pushes it away from him.

'What, you don't like coffee?'

'No way. Do you have any Coke?'

'No, but I've got some lemonade.'

'I'll take that.'

While he scrounges for lemonade, he speaks over his shoulder. 'Your father, Walter, he said you were coming.'

The old man turns back to us with four pieces of burnt toast on a stone plate and bowl of jam. My stomach rumbles. Even though the toast is charred, I feel like I can eat whatever he puts in front of me.

'This is all I have,' he apologizes, 'but I think it will do.' He settles into the fifth chair. 'So.' The release of breath is like a grunt. 'I am Eduardo Montanez. Your parents and I, we met many years ago in this house.' As I listened, I was unaware that I had taken a bite of my toast, but I could taste the carbon in my mouth, so I put it down.

'I remember the first time I saw Mengele, and I thought to myself, 'He looks like you or me, a common man and a common face,' and yet he was evil,' Eduardo pointed to his eyes.

'The neighbors, they say he came from Argentina or Paraguay.' He spits spitefully towards the floor, 'Fascists. We here in Brazil, we love people.' He spreads his arms wide as he says the word 'love.'

'But this demon comes from the south and puts on his rancher clothes and grows a thick moustache. He looks like Stalin to me.' Both of his hands rest on the crook of his cane, but his eyes are alight.

He raises a finger and then rises slowly. Walking into the living area, he returns with a photo album. 'I have been caretaker of Mengele's estate since before he died in 1979. I praised God,' he points up to heaven, 'when I heard the monster was finally dead.'

'Wait,' I say as my hands tap the table, 'you're the caretaker? Haven't you looked through everything? Why

373

wouldn't Grandpa and Grandma just tell you what they found? Why put us through all this?'

'I guess she thought it best not to trust anyone.'

'Do you know what we're looking for?'

'No. No. I have always known it had something to do with Nazis and Mengele, but now that most of them are dead, it does not really matter, only that there is justice.'

'When did you talk to Walter last?' Mom asks.

'Three weeks ago. But before that, it had been many, many years - decades. It was a surprise to hear his voice. He sounds very old.'

'I bet he thought the same about you,' Yugi interjects.

Mom is about to reprimand him when Eduardo cackles. 'Yes, yes, *Senhor*. I am old, but not dead. I have heard about your grandmother. She was a beautiful *wooman*.'

'Please go on with your story, *Senhor* Montanez,' Dad encourages.

'Please, please, my name is Eduardo - Eddie.'

'Okay, Eddie.'

He opens the photo album. 'Mengele was always afraid. He would pace the grounds, stand in the tower with his binoculars always thinking the Jews or Americans were right around the corner. And yet,' he purses his lips, 'he would still go on his holidays, to the beach, back to Argentina, even to Germany once, I think. It was a long trip.'

'While he was away, I tended the house, but guards patrolled the grounds. They marched, like little Nazi puppets. They let me inside the house to tidy up. I was just a servant from the village, you see. I pretended to be simple. But I watched everything, the guards and the servants, the animals, the weather. Then, one day, your grandmother shows up. She was good at pretending. She watches me, sees me and finally tells me to come to her, which, of course, I do because no one resists Iris Walker.' He chuckles.

'She asks me if I know who lives in the house.'

"Of course, *Senhora,* of course I know who it is."

"Do you like him?"

'I am wary, but I say, 'He smells."

"What does he smell like?"

"He smells like a Nazi."

'Then her eyes narrow. 'If you get me into the house, I will erase his odor from the house."

Eduardo's eyes glint. 'I like this woman very much, so I let her into the house while I stood guard for the guards.'

'What did she find?'

'Nothing, as far as I know, except the location,' his voice lowered, 'of Josef's safe.'

A safe.

'Will you take us to it?' I ask.

He smiles at me. His face is kind, but I'm still wary. 'Of course, *senhorita.*'

'Well, let's go now.' I push back the chair with my legs.

'There is no rush, little one, no rush. The safe remains... safe.' He motions back to the photo album. 'There are some things you must see first.' He flips through the pages. We see the face of the monster come to life, from middle age, a gap-toothed somber monster, to elderly demon, portly and wary, with paranoid eyes. 'Here, this is the estate. And here,' his finger turns the page, 'here is his wife. I'm told that she was his sister-in-law. Sickness through the whole family.'

He turns the page again. We all collectively gasp together.

'What is it?' Eduardo asks.

Mom puts a trembling finger to a very recognizable face - a very young one.

Geraldine Dresser.

'You know her?' Eddie questions and we nod.

'How do you know her?' Dad asks.

Eduardo shakes his head. 'A very evil woman. Mengele's mistress.'

'Whoa.' I wasn't expecting that.

'I want to show you one last thing,' Eduardo's voice croaks. He licks his finger and turns the page to the end of the album. Behind a scenic, picturesque photo, he pulls out another. 'One of my most priceless treasures.' He hands the picture to Dad whose mouth twists into a forlorn expression.

'My Mom and Dad.' He runs his own fingers over their faces as if somehow he can touch what they used to be. They and Eduardo are standing along the edge of a cliff, hands over shoulders, Grandma in the middle.

'It was a beautiful day.' He pondered the photo, then continued. 'When I recently received the phone call from your father, he told me that I would get another letter in the mail.' He rises from his stool and walks slowly to the kitchen counter. He opens a drawer and retrieves a manilla envelope.

'It was sent to me, but inside I found another envelope with your name on it, Kevin.' Eduardo hands the package to my dad.

Dad takes the inner envelope out and opens it. His face turns white.

'What is it?'

From the envelope he pulls out an object.

The remaining Barbie arm.

'What is it?' Eduardo asks.

'I think,' Dad holds the plastic limb in his hand, 'it is the last clue we'll need.' He points to the arm. The number *31* is written along the forearm. Dad reaches down to the suitcase and opens it in front of Eduardo. Retrieving the other pieces of Barbie he lays them in front of everyone.

'Fingerprint hand. The numbers '4' and '11' and '31.''

'We've already used them, haven't we?' Yugi asks.

Dad's face is amused. 'Think, Yugi. What are these numbers for?'

'The Barbie crossword?' It would make sense - everything else is in there.

Dad shakes his head. Mom's face lights up with realization. 'The safe. It's a combination.'

'That's what I'm thinking.'

Eduardo's eyes are alight. 'We're going to the estate.'

Eduardo produces a jagged, corroded key from his pocket. It looks like a fossilized shark tooth. Inserting it into the lock, he turns it and the mechanism inside crunches. Obviously, it has been a long time since anyone has entered the property. Limping over to the security panel, Eduardo punches in the numbers and the alarm is deactivated.

Inside the estate, everything had been left as it was when Mengele died. Furniture has been covered by drop cloths. Photos which used to be on the wall have been put back.

'When he lived here,' Eduardo speaks in a whisper, as if voices would disturb the ancient, malevolent spirits still in residence, 'he went by the name of Peter, or *Senhor* Pedro, as he wanted to be called. Everyone thought he was a nice man, courteous - guarded, yes - but towards the end, he wanted to be around people. He would go into the town, or even the city, to eat and drink with people. Many of them, of course, were people from his past. Maybe some Nazis, I don't know.'

'Here is his sitting room and library.' It is a dark place with shelves full of leathered, dusty books written in different languages. 'He would have his afternoon siesta and then come in here to drink his coffee and talk. Sometimes he would even speak to me. Not about his past, but about what he was thinking. One time he slipped. He talked about the Fatherland, as he called it, and the time of the war.'

'Once, in this room, he sat beside the window staring out into the trees, and I asked him if he needed anything. His face was strange. 'I want to show you something,' he said. I was still a young man, perhaps forty years of age, and he was an old man, in his sixties.'

Eduardo motioned with his finger for us to follow. We wove our way through the furniture and turned down a long dark hallway. Turning into a bedroom, we encountered an old four-poster bed situated in the middle of the room. At the foot was a chest, and underneath the chest, a carpet.

'If you move the chest and the carpet, you will find what we are looking for.'

My heart beats rapidly. I'm so excited I feel as if I'm going to explode.

Chapter 33 Down:

Yugi pushes aside the chest with a grunt and then rolls up the carpet. Underneath is bare wooden floor.

'Go ahead,' Eduardo encourages him, 'open it.'

'Open what?' Yugi frowns.

He points to Yugi's side. 'There is a small knothole there. Put your finger in and pull. It may be stuck. It's been a long time.'

Yugi pulls with all his might. Finally, four attached floorboards lift and underneath them, in a darkened hole, is a large grey safe.

A safe. And there is a spinning combination lock on the front.

'Why didn't Grandma open this herself?' I ask Eduardo.

'We didn't have time. I snuck her in here to show her, but she said she'd have to return later.'

'That was a long time ago.'

'Yes. But she never came back.'

Yugi reaches into the space and turns the safe's dial. Slowly.

I have never felt this kind of impatience before. Up until this point, everything in my life has been less meaningful, even my brief interaction with Shime.

4.

11.

Twist. Around one whole time. Yugi sticks out his tongue. Expectantly, we wait. If this isn't the combination, we have journeyed here for nothing. I have that feeling, just like before the end of a test, there is a niggling suspicion that I missed something. And even though I know my answers are correct, something makes me distrust my preparation and ability.

379

As Yugi clicks in '*31*' he looks up at us. There is a bar next to the wheel which must be turned to unlock the door. This bar is a metaphor for adulthood, I think. All the spinning combinations of adolescence, all the numbers and confusion, are just white noise at the end. Inside us is a treasure waiting to be unlocked. During adolescence, we search for the hidden clues, hidden meanings in relationships, in life, in ourselves. We take notes and we make decisions to prepare us for this moment, this bar to be turned, but until it actually cracks the safe, we wonder...

Yugi's hand reaches for the bar and we hold our collective breaths - even Eduardo. He is licking his lips and rubbing his fingers together as if waiting for a gift.

Grasp.

Click.

The safe's door swings upward and outward. All of us unconsciously huddle over Yugi. Unfortunately, it is not what we hoped. There is no painting - no rolled up tube - only documents, files, old pieces of paper, manic scribbling, and a few photos. Yugi pulls them out and hands them to Dad who holds them disconsolately in his hands. He, just like the rest of us, hoped that this adventure would end here.

We walk back to the table in emotional tatters. It seemed like everything had been tied up in that moment. Plopping back in our chairs, Dad puts the contents of the safe on the table.

'There wasn't even any money in there,' Yugi complains. 'Only stupid papers.'

Mom takes one in her hands and starts to read. Her face turns ashen.

'What does it say?'

'These documents... they... they...'

'Are you okay?' Suddenly I'm worried for her.

'They detail the experiments. The experiments on children. Twins.'

Dad shuffles through the photos and stops. His hand begins to tremble. He sets one in the middle of the table and our world is turned upside down. It is a picture of three people:

Josef Mengele.

An unidentified man.

And a very famous portrait of a Younger Man.

The Raphael.

On the back side of the photograph, there is writing. It is in Portuguese.

'Can you translate this for me?' Dad asks Eduardo.

'Of course.'

'*On this day, I give to my good friend and colleague, Klaus, this priceless...treasure... May it remind him of better days as it did me when I...* what is the word... *helped to rid the world of the Jewish plague.*'

'Who is that man?' Dad asks pointing to the man on the right.

'You mean you don't know?' Eduardo replies incredulously.

'No.'

'That's the Butcher of Lyon. Klaus Barbie.'

My vision shrinks to a pinhole. Everything spins, upended turning, a kaleidoscope of colors, thoughts and emotions.

Barbie.

Quickly, I dig through Dad's briefcase and find the very first clue.

'Remember this?'

Dear Whoever You Are,

I assume the book has guided you to me, so let it continue to do so. One never knows what kinds of numbers and words one might find inside.

In my house, one finds all sorts of things.

I also assume that you are on the yellow brick ratline that I was, but if you are not, I suggest putting this small piece of history safely where you found it and go about your daily business.

Now, to work...

Just follow the path. Follow my prints.

Visit the White Man to the first leg of the journey.

He will bring your case before the court.

The White Man will speak of the hotdog man whose story will send you to the second leg.

The connection made between the hotdog man and the 'foul' man who fled.

There you will find the Angel beneath the Cross.

At that intersection, the union place...

You will find me.

Finish the book, where I was unable. Pieces of me still remain.

Love,
Barbie.

'We've solved almost everything - the last things: 'There you will find the Angel beneath the Cross - Okay, that's Mengele, but the intersection, the meeting place. You will find me.' I shake my head and hold it in my hands.

'We've always assumed that Barbie was Grandma, but Grandma knew it was Klaus Barbie. *You will find me.*'

My grandmother's brain is incredible.

'Why didn't she just come out and say it?' Yugi asks no one and everyone at once.

'Grandma must have had her own reasons for being so secretive,' I said.

'I would guess,' Dad leans forward and takes the clue from my hands, 'that there were too many smart people after her and the painting. Maybe it was the only way she could help someone, us, thankfully, to wend our way through to the end.'

'Do you think we're near the end?'

'Yes, I do.' He looks at Mom who reaches her hand out to him. He grabs it and shifts his attention to Eduardo. 'Where is this place?'

Eduardo squints at it. 'I do not know.'

There is nothing in this picture to signify exactly where the exchange might have taken place. We'll have to do some digging.

'Thank you, Eduardo,' Mom says to the old man.

He leans back in his chair, crosses his hands on his belly and sighs deeply. 'You are very welcome, my friends. I think I can now die happy.'

Chapter 34 Down:
Hypnotising (11)

We return the car to the man with the bad teeth. He welcomes it home as if it were a long-lost mule. He pats it on the hood.

The train ride back to the hotel is one of whispers and sidelong glances. Every moment, we suspect that Geraldine's strange face will pop up above the seat behind us like a malevolent Jack-in-the-box.

Back at the hotel, we shed our clothes and take showers. Yugi is not entirely happy about this turn of events, but after that car, we all need to wash off the smell. Dad has situated himself at the table with Mom, the articles of Mengele's safe are positioned in piles. Mom and Dad translate the papers for us, but I know that they leave much of it untranslated because the sheer horror is too much to imagine.

Meanwhile, I connect to the hotel's Wi-Fi and begin to dig through the life of the Butcher of Lyon. I write some notes.

Nikolaus Barbie - born in Germany, Bad Godesberg, 1913. Wanted to be a priest, or at least study theology. Terrible family life - brother died young, Barbie joined the Nazi party. Sadistic. During questioning would routinely torture people for pleasure whether guilty or not. Stationed in Lyon, France as part of the Gestapo, the German secret police. In Lyon, was active in unearthing subversives and uprooting Jews. 1944, at Izieu, Gestapo discovered a secret farm enclave *of 44 children. They were packed onto trains and sent to Auschwitz-Birkenau. None were ever seen alive again. Captured by the Americans after the war, instead of execution, Barbie trained CIA operatives and ratted out Nazis in hiding. Barbie was tried twice in France, in absentia, for crimes against humanity, but was stashed by the CIA in Bolivia where he remained unrepentant about any of his crimes, even to the day he was extradited back to France. There he stood trial a third time and was remanded to prison for a life sentence. He died in prison in 1987 of cancer.*

As I continue to search, it becomes patently clear that the Nazi's needed each other even after the war. Whether they felt guilty, or their ubermenschen arrogance desired only those who shared the same ideals, they continued to meet. To talk about the good old days. One of the stray pictures shows Barbie and two young boys standing by the ocean. In the background is a younger woman, face turned away, perhaps the mother of the boys, just an innocent bystander looking out over the vast, intrepid seas. I see Barbie's face and I want to hate him. I want to feel something vengeful so that I can destroy him, but it is very hard. It's very hard to hate someone you don't know. The little boys' faces are turned towards each other. They are not identical, but I recognize something about them - is it their eyes? Is it their cheeks? I can't figure it out.

The hotel room is quiet. Yugi has curled up on our bed with his game. He has seen and heard enough.

So have we all.

The city of São Paulo wakes at dawn. Slowly, noise rises above the horizon of its consciousness. As the businesses begin to crack open their doors, the traffic moves blood-like through the arteries and veins of the streets. São Paulo rouses, arms and legs stretch, the blood moves faster, the yawn of commerce draws breath into the people and the Brazilian cultural song rises from the heart.

I wake slower than the city. My parents are both up standing by the window, cups of coffee are steaming near their faces. They are quiet.

'Good morning,' I say.

'Good morning,' they respond identically and then, like twins, both take a sip of coffee.

'What were you talking about?' I ask them both.

'Life. Where we're going to live when we get home.' Dad's voice is tired.

'Aah.' I haven't really given it much thought, but kids don't, normally. They don't think about bills, insurance, getting the car serviced or what's on the shopping list either.

'What's the plan?'

Mom turns while Dad stares out the window. 'We look through all the clues again, see if there is anything we missed.' Her voice is low, as if she's trying to maintain a level of calm. 'I want to go through the Mengele papers. No, that's not right - I *have* to go through the Mengele papers.'

'Do you think the answers will be there?'

'I hope so. If not, we're going to have to fly to Bolivia.'

I gulp.

'What are you staring at, Dad?'

Chapter 34 Down:

His face is illuminated in the window, the aura surrounding an angel face. The creases around his eyes have deepened. This adventure has been good for the soul but hard on the body. 'There's somebody out there.'

I get that dropping sensation in my stomach, like when I'm on the plane, a greasy, sugary feeling that neither feels good nor tastes good.'

'Who is it? Is it Geraldine?'

He squints. 'I can't tell. The sun is reflecting off the windshield of the car, but I've been watching for about an hour. There's two of them at least. The one in the passenger seat went to get coffee half an hour ago. He carried an extra with him and passed it into the car.'

'How do you know it's *them*.'

Dad turns back to me. 'They're white.'

I join him at the window. He points at a car about two blocks away. My eyes catch movement further up the street - not so much movement, I guess, but something out of order. There is a man, a native, dark skinned and black haired, leaning against a red brick wall. Standing still. I remember Mom's words when we were in Poland - *It's not the ones who are moving you have to worry about, it's the ones who are standing still.* He is wearing a Panama hat. Under his arm is a newspaper and in his other hand he holds a take-away cup of coffee.

'What about that guy, Dad?'

'Which one?'

I show him. 'Do you think he's just a local waiting to read his paper?'

'It's too cliché to be real.'

Furtively, the man stares over his cup of coffee at the car *we've* been watching. It feels weird that we're all observing each other but no one is doing anything. The

387

man's head rotates across the street. Underneath a canopy, there are two sets of legs sticking out from under the table. Unfortunately, we can't see their faces.

'He just nodded across and up the street.'

'Where?' Dad peers through the glass and squints. I point.

'There.'

His face is tense. 'I was worried this might happen.'

'Is it them? Is it Geraldine?'

'It could be.'

'So what are we going to do?'

'Maybe it's a day to relax a little? We'll take the train again, go to the beach? How does that sound?'

Suddenly, Yugi's head pops up from the bed fully awake. 'Beach? Beach!' He raises his hand. 'I choose today!' He scrambles from the bed. His scrawny white legs are a blur of activity as he rushes around the room. With a flourish, he throws on a t-shirt and then stomps into the bathroom to put on his swimming trunks. He returns moments later with arms spread wide. 'Ta da!'

'You know, Yugi, here in Brazil, the beaches are swimming trunk-less.'

'What?'

'Naked.'

'No, they're not.' His voice is hesitant, hoping that I am not serious.

'You'll see. In a little while, you're going to see a lot more of the human anatomy than you ever wanted.'

His face pinches. 'All right, moron, let's see how comfortable you are exposing your body.' He crosses his arms and nods.

I was just pulling his leg, but I suddenly realize that I put myself in the situation. 'No problem. I'm perfectly comfortable in my own body.'

Yugi snorts. 'Yeah, right.'

'We're not going to a nudie beach.' Dad has moved away from the window and situated himself near the suitcase. He takes out his colorful swimming trunks and then throws Mom's to her. Hers have polka dots. Dad chucks mine to me, but they are not the ones that I wore to the swimming hole. I decided on our trip to the store to get a bikini - yes, this is a weird new thing, but I'm stepping out into the world. I know that I'm going to wear a swim top over it, but hey, it's the thought that counts.

This is not the way I assumed the day was going to go, but a day at the beach is infinitely more enjoyable than staying inside the hotel studying our notes. We know them so well, but we need a mental break to unlock the last clue. We've got to find the intersection.

After locking the door behind us, we pad down the hallway in our flip flops and swimming suits. Our second set of clothes is stashed in my backpack. Yugi bounds in front of us turning frequently to hurry us up, his hand flopping with impatience. 'C'mon, c'mon!'

As Oklahomans, we don't get to see the ocean that much - actually never - except the one time we went to Florida. I remember sitting on the shore, toes dug into the sand, listening to the sound of the perpetual waves, and wondering if there was anything more beautiful in the world than an ocean.

The tram ride to the beach is short, but it seems long - very long, not just because we are impatient, but my little brother spends the entire trip twitching like an electrocuted frog. First, staring out the window, then hanging on Dad's arm, then holding on to the pole, then pretending to press the emergency stop button while looking back at us and giggling. Was I ever like that?

I see the ocean in front of us. I am transfixed already.

We disembark and begin the trek to the beach; we are slowly drawn by its mesmerizing vastness. I smell the sea air, the acrid seaweed, exhaust fumes and fish. Fast food wrappers whip alongside the sidewalk in front of us. Cars, booming with bass, zoom next to us.

Once we reach the sand, we take off our flip flops. Yugi has done this quickly and thrown them at my parents who stoop to pick them up while he bolts to the water's edge. His bare feet flick sand up behind him. I am slightly more restrained, not because I want to be, but now that I'm an adult, I must act more adultish. This is true only until the moment my parents decide that they are not adults and scream down the sand after Yugi. How embarrassing.

I stroll to the beach, head held high, above this low-class frivolity.

For the rest of the day, we alternate between frolicking in the waves, staving off sunburn by liberal applications of sunscreen and lying on our blankets to reminisce about our adventure.

Around mid-afternoon, I check for signs of covert ops and notice a bronzed man and woman lying side by side on towels fifty yards to our right. There is nothing truly suspicious about them, per se, but thirty yards beyond them is a different couple who seems to be watching them.

I nudge my dad. 'I think they're here?'

'Who?' He has been lying on his back, his eyes closed behind aviator sunglasses.

'The CIA.'

He lifts his head. 'Where?'

'Behind and to the right. And then behind them is someone else - could be Geraldine's people.'

Dad doesn't turn, but he takes out his phone, turns the camera on and reverses the image to look over his shoulder. He pretends to take a picture of me. 'I see them.'

Mom and Yugi come running up from the ocean. Yugi splats in front of me sending a cascade of sand over my skin and blanket. I hate the feeling of sand stuck to sunscreen. 'Yugi!'

He grins and digs through the food. The sand on his hands mixes with everything including the sandwiches. I hate sand in my food even more than on my skin. We eat without speaking, but it is hardly silent. A few small children excitedly run and splash in the waves. A woman in a very, very small white bikini which may cover six percent of each breast and even less of her caboose walks in front of us speaking very loudly into her phone. Drowning out every other noise is the sound of the surf crashing against the shore. It is at times like these that, despite the seasoning of sand in my sandwich and sunscreen, I wish we could stay here for weeks - just the four of us, even Yugi.

After we finish eating, Yugi announces his need to 'drain the main vein.' He and Dad stand, brush the sand off from their swimming suits onto my water bottle - hooray - and then walk off towards the bathroom facilities. Mom is lying on her back propped up on her elbows surveying the ocean. She appears ten years younger. Her skin is beginning to brown, and the sunscreen makes it glisten.

As I watch her, I can't help thinking again about the places we've been and the things we've done. Israel, Poland, back home - our house blowing up, here in South America, even Yugi trying coffee for the first time. It wouldn't surprise me if...

Something trips over in my mind.

Intersection.

When we were in Caieiras yesterday, Eduardo made a passing comment about Mengele traveling into town to have coffee. He wanted to meet people. We've been following Grandma's clues the whole time, but we've missed one word.

That.

That intersection. Not *the* intersection. I recite the clues again. Two words above it are capitalized.

We need to find what's at the intersection of Angel and Cross, and I'll bet my very last dollar that what we find at that intersection is going to be a place of great importance. I take out my phone and find Google Maps and I input the two roads in Portuguese. My heart beats faster than I ever thought possible.

Holy Moses.

Suddenly, there is a noise behind us. Dad is sprinting towards us. A look of abject horror is spread across his face. He is shouting and waving to us. My gaze is drawn quickly behind us. Both sets of watchers have sprung up on their knees. The woman behind us is on her phone.

'They've got him!' Dad shouts. 'We have to go!'

My heart sinks.

'What happened?' Mom asks. 'Where is he? Where is Yugi?'

Dad attempts to explain. 'I was waiting for him in the bathroom, when suddenly a man pushes me into a stall and jams the door shut. I hear Yugi shouting and struggling and even as I yell, whoever shoved me into the stall took Yugi and ran. I pounded on the jammed door until it opened, but it was too late.' We race to the street and hail a cab. Dad gives him the address of our hotel.

Chapter 34 Down:

Our heads are huddled together in the back seat. Dad's face is set like stone. 'Whoever has him, I'm going to kill them.'

'But how will we find him?' I ask.

'They will contact us.' Dad picks up his phone willing it to ring.

At the hotel, we pay the driver and run up the stairs to our room. As Dad is unlocking the door, I turn to Mom. 'Shouldn't we call the cops?'

'In any other situation, I would say we should, but we don't know anything about the police here. There is a good chance whoever did this has some friends high up.' She's on the verge of tears. 'We'll just have to wait.'

Dad curses as the door refuses to open, but when it does, we see that for the second time, our room has been ransacked. And to make matters worse, the safe has been broken into and everything is gone.

It feels as if there is nothing we can do. Dad calls Grandpa and tells him what has happened. As Grandpa speaks, we watch Dad's face as he listens to the reply. He nods a couple of times, says, 'yeah,' and then hangs up.

'He's going to contact some old friends. People he can trust.'

'Do you think *she's* got him?' I don't need to add Geraldine's name.

We feel the vast emptiness and quiet in the room. We are alone. Where Yugi's voice should have been shouting and giving us a play by play of how amazing his day was, the taste of the salt in his mouth, the grit of the sand between his toes and how much he loved making castles, there is only a wispy memory.

'I think I figured out where the painting is.' I say softly.

They both look at me sharply. 'What?'

'Just before...' I couldn't add the words *Yugi was taken*, 'you know... my unconscious brain must have been working overtime when I thought about the clues again.'

'We don't have them,' Mom says softly.

'I know, but I have the clues memorized.'

'*In my house, one finds all sorts of things.*

The White man Will speak of the hotdog man whose story will send you to the second leg.

The connection made between the hotdog man and the 'foul' man who fled.

There you will find the Angel beneath the Cross.

At that intersection, the union place...'

They wait for me to continue. 'Okay, we followed the trail of people - from Frank to Eichmann to Mengele to Barbie. Those are the people, but I missed the important part - where the last two met. Eichmann and Frank met in Poland, Eichmann and Mengele met in Argentina, but Mengele and Barbie met here, in São Paulo.'

'Yes, but where?'

'At *that* intersection.'

'Which intersection?' I can tell Mom's stress is making her frustrated.

'At the intersection of Cross and Angel Streets. Look.' I point to the capitalized words. 'And you'll never guess what's at that intersection... at *Rua Cruz* and *Rua Anjo*. It's a cafe called...'

Dad figured it out. 'Union'

I nod. '*Uniao Local* - Union Place.'

Chapter 34 Down:

Dad takes a deep breath. It feels as if the last word has been placed into the correct blank space of the crossword, yet there is no sense of satisfaction. Until Yugi is back with us, it doesn't matter.

'Okay,' he tries to smile, 'good work, Jeri. The information will come in handy when they call.'

As we peer out the window together into the blinding sunlight outside, the phone suddenly rings. Startled, Dad almost drops it. It is a private number. He puts it on speaker.

'This is Kevin Walker.'

'This is your son's captor.' A man's voice, accented, tumbles from the phone's speaker. Mom's face crumbles and she puts a hand over her mouth. Her eyes are wide with fear.

'We want our son back. Now.'

He has an accent. German, maybe. 'You have information about the whereabouts of a very expensive work of art.'

'We have clues, yes.'

The voice chuckles malevolently. 'You used to.'

'You bastards. You broke into our room, took everything and then kidnapped our son...'

'Easy, Cowboy. You don't want your son to become Serbia and Croatia.'

The thought of my brother being broken is almost too much. But the fact that this man is making a joke of it makes me boil. My dad suddenly becomes deceptively calm. 'Tell us what you want then. If you have all the clues, certainly you should be able to figure them out.'

'Alas,' the bodiless voice intones, 'we do not have the time.'

'And...?' my mother speaks impatiently.

'Tell us where we can find the painting and we will meet you there - with your brat.'

I can tell my dad wants to rip his face off, but he controls himself. 'We'll find it and then make a trade.' If we tell them where it is, we lose all our bargaining power.

There is silence while the bad guys deliberate. Finally, the voice speaks again. 'You have three hours. If you haven't contacted us by seven o'clock, we will begin... doing what Uncle Klaus taught us.'

'How will we contact you?'

'You won't,' the voice says simply. 'We will contact you. Good luck.'

The phone call ends. The conversation has hardened my parents, solidified them and returned them to their days of espionage.

'What do we need to do?' I ask.

'We have to find a car. Then, we'll drive. You know the place, Jeri?' I nod.

'I'll call Dad and tell him what's going on. Beryl, you pack what's left of our things and find the nearest car rental.'

'Got it.'

Now that we are all busy, it feels easier to move. Within ten minutes, Mom has secured a vehicle for us. I pack our meager belongings into my trusty backpack, and we leave quickly. My eyes fall on the empty suitcase and for the briefest moment, I have a sense of loss about losing the Barbie crossword puzzle. I had come to think of it as my last remaining connection to Grandma.

Why couldn't she have made this easier for us?

Instead of *wanting* to find the painting, we *need* to find the painting.

Chapter 35 Across:
Producing vapor (8)

Less than a mile away from *that* intersection, I begin to feel nervous. I hope beyond a shadow of belief that my intuition is correct. We round a bend in the road and see a road sign which reads *R. Cruz* - Cross road. I see my dad's eyes in the rearview mirror. He nods in encouragement and we accelerate. As I watch the map on my phone, I see the street names approach and finally *Rua Anjo* shows up.

'It's up here in three streets.' I point in front of us.

Hearts pounding in our chests, Dad slows and we finally see it.

Uniao Local.

It is a ramshackle building with open wooden shutters badly in need of paint. The veranda's supporting beams are chipped and gouged as if a herd of cattle had stampeded through and roughed them up. A few tables are occupied by locals who are drinking. Almost everyone is smoking.

Dad parks the car and puts the keys in his pocket. 'Let's get our boy back.'

I've never seen my parents look so tough. I walk between them feeling myself prepped for a battle in which I cannot possibly help other than to locate the painting.

Inside the bar, the cigarette smoke is not quite as heavy, but there is still a haze. Other than the electric cash register and credit card machine on the counter, the interior is much like an Old West bar. The walls contain old black and white photos and some paintings. Above the fireplace is an immense mirror. I can see our reflections in it. My face is tired and pinched.

An extraordinarily beautiful woman is preparing coffee from a very noisy machine. Waiting for drinks is a middle-aged couple standing close to each other. My dad steps in front of them. When the man is about to protest, he takes one look at my dad's face and steps back.

'Excuse me,' he says to the barista.

She glances over her shoulder but ignores him. My dad slaps his hand down on the wooden bar. The sound booms through the room and all other conversation stops. The middle-aged couple takes another step back from our family.

'Excuse me."

The barista appears frightened. She has left the steaming coffees on the grill of the machine.

'I'm not going to hurt you,' my dad says in a quieter voice, 'but I'd like to talk to the manager.'

Her eyes are wide with fear. 'I no English.'

'*Hablas Español?*' She nods. '*Necisito hablar a su superior.*'

She nods again and hurries along the length of the bar to a staircase. A banister of stained dark wood runs to the second floor. Climbing the steps quickly, she raps on a door. While she waits for an answer, I scan the bar. Although movement and conversation has stopped, music still plays through overhead speakers. I take a closer look at the walls lined with black and white photographs. There is no one I recognize. Perhaps they are all local heroes.

Behind the bar is a twin mirror to the one over the fireplace and I noticed movement in it. Faces approaching the swinging door. Faces I've seen before.

Oh no.

Geraldine Dresser and her henchmen.

'Dad. Mom. She's here.'

Chapter 35 Across:

They, too, see Geraldine in the mirror and as she pushes the door open, we turn around to meet them. Like gunfighters squaring off, we are prepared to see this thing through to the end.

'Where is he, Geraldine?' Mom asks.

She smiles knowingly. 'Your son is safe. Barely.'

'I thought you were going to call us?' Dad's fury is barely contained.

'I just said we'd contact you.' She spreads her hands. 'Consider yourself contacted.'

At this point, I am standing behind my parents, but I want to know things. I want to know how it ended up like this. 'How did you get out of Poland? How have you been following us? Did you blow up our house?'

'Child,' she says condescendingly, 'it would take much more than *you* to stop *us*. But if you must know,' she shrugs, 'we have friends in higher places than you.' She stops to inspect her fingernails.

'And the house?'

'A sign. We didn't want to kill you, but accidents happen.' A smile spreads slowly across her face. Like rats scurrying from a sinking ship, the middle-aged couple, along with the other patrons, streak for the door.

There is movement behind us. At the top of the stairs, the manager is descending the stairs with the barista in front of him. His moustache bounces just under his nose.

'What is the meaning of this?' He asks authoritatively.

Geraldine barely glances at him.

'I said, What is...'

Geraldine's henchmen pull back their jackets to reveal guns. Suddenly, I have this incredible need to

399

urinate.

The manager and the barista turn tail and run back up the stairs, slamming the door behind them.

'Where is our son?' Mom asks.

'He is close. Nearby.'

'Bring him to us and you can have your painting.'

I'm surprised. *Does Mom know where it is?*

'Interesting.' Geraldine moves forward to stand just out of Mom's reach. She knows that my mom is dangerous. 'And where is it?'

'Yugi first.'

Here is the standoff. Geraldine's eyes sparkle with malevolent glee; my mom's are darkened with hatred. Geraldine snaps her finger and one of the henchmen speaks into his cufflink. As much as I don't want to think it, my brain says, *Dang, that's so cool.* We wait. Finally, there is shuffling outside. I can see small feet beneath the door and Yugi bursts through. He has tape across his mouth which I guess isn't really that surprising. He runs to my mom who rushes halfway to him also and she embraces him. I want to do the same, but I'm rooted to my spot in fear.

Mom gently rips off the tape. Yugi winces but doesn't cry.

'Hi, Mom. I'm sorry for getting caught.'

She hugs him again.

'Fair is fair,' Geraldine's mouth moves back to the grin. 'Where is it?'

Mom stands up and pushes Yugi behind her. Now, a lioness, it's almost like she's turned into the predator. Geraldine's face falters slightly. 'It's on the far wall.'

'How do you know?' The Englishwoman's voice is distrustful.

'Because we've been following the clues for months. Instead of random terror, we use our minds.'

Geraldine's eyes smolder with rage. 'You have not even begun to understand terror. The Führer would be proud of us.'

Mom snorts. 'Hitler was a moron and his disciples, Frank, Eichmann, Mengele and Barbie - idiots. Cowards. They couldn't wait to save their own skins.'

'They needed to survive for the Reich.'

Mom sneers. 'Spoken like a woman who isn't strong enough to stand up to them.'

Geraldine strikes quickly, like a cobra, slapping my mother across the face. Mom's head snaps to the side, but I can tell that the pain has galvanized her. 'Is that the best you've got?'

Now it is Geraldine's turn to sneer. 'I will show you what the disciples were prepared to do, Nick.' She holds out her hand and one of the men approaches, bends over and produces a vicious looking bowie knife from a sheath tied to his ankle. He hands it to her and she wields it menacingly.

'When Herr Barbie used to *encourage* his enemies, one of his favorite tricks was to cut off pieces of fingers, one knuckle at a time.' She paused to let this tidbit of history sink in for effect. She clucks her tongue sympathetically. 'It's too bad it usually takes just one knuckle - if I want it to go quickly, the thumb goes first. If I want to... enjoy the process... let's start with the pinky.'

'You don't scare me,' Mom says.

Geraldine shakes her head. 'I am not talking about you.' Her knife points at me. 'I think Jerusalem will have looser lips.'

401

My eyes roll in fear. Very much do I feel like Maximus now and I wish that I could simply pass out. As she moves toward me, my dad steps in front. Faster than the eye thinks possible, my dad's forearm is sliced open. He stifles a cry. Mom attempts to overtake her, but similarly, she has opened a gash in my mother's left arm. Blood is flowing freely. My parents attempt to staunch their wounds while simultaneously protecting us.

Geraldine shakes her head. 'Nick. Enzo.' The goons move in and grab Yugi and I away from our parents. We struggle, but are no match for these two behemoths. Our brief time in Poland has implanted the memory of these men deep within my brain. Whichever one has me smells like deodorant and French fries. He grabs me around the waist, takes me to the bar and splays my hand on top of it. He grunts in my ear. 'Either hold your hand out, or she'll lop it off. Then, we'll just move to your brother.' I gag.

I'm confronted with two equally bad options. Both of my parents are bleeding profusely next to me. My mom is now crying and my dad is struggling to hold himself back.

'Okay, okay!' Mom shouts. 'I'll tell you.'

Geraldine holds a hand up to her ear. 'I'm sorry. I'm hard of hearing. I can't quite hear you.' She moves closer to me. Brandishing the knife, Nick or Enzo, whichever one it is, holds my hand out. 'I think one finger will be enough to make sure that you tell the truth.'

'Jeri!' My mom's voice is rising. 'Geraldine, don't do this! Don't do this! She's innocent.'

Geraldine whips around and faces Mom again. 'You Jews never get it, do you. You're never innocent. Many years ago, Josef showed me things. He showed me the beauty of the Aryan race and the stain of Jews, Gypsies, invalids and colored people. Josef was a tremendous man, a beautiful man, a passionate lover, and a truly progressive thinker who could change the world for the better. But Barbie had to get in the way. They met, and Barbie hid it for safekeeping.' She refocuses on my parents. 'But where?' For greater effect, she lowers the knife slowly downwards. I want to close my eyes, but I can't. I want to see my finger attached to my hand for the last time.

'Please,' my mom begs. 'Please don't.'

Geraldine grabs my wrist. Just as her body tenses, a gunshot rings out. It is so loud, my ears ring. Everyone twirls quickly and I have never been more shocked in my life.

It is Grandpa Walt.

But it is Grandma Iris who has a gun trained on Geraldine.

What in the world?

'Let them go, Geri.'

'Grandma?'

She smiles at me. 'Not you, Jerusalem. Geraldine.'

'So, I see your dementia diagnosis is somewhat premature.' Geraldine is frozen beside me still at the bar.

'It would seem that way.'

'Grandma?'

Grandma takes a deep breath. 'I had to, Jeri. I had to pretend. All these years - a nightmare, but it was worth it to keep you all safe.'

'But... you have dementia.'

Grandpa smiles. 'I told you she was a good actress. Even I was starting to wonder these last couple of years.'

'But why?'

'Because,' Geraldine interrupts, 'if she would have tried anything, tried to recover the painting, tried to expose

403

my comrades, we would have blown up your house a lot sooner. With you in it.'

I pull myself away from Geraldine and go to my parents. Grandma still has the gun trained on them. 'How long has our house had the explosives in it?'

Grandpa's eyes look sad. 'Ever since we moved into the nursing home. It was their control over us. But when they finally blew it up, we knew Grandma and I could finally get moving.'

'When did you get here?' I asked.

'About three days ago.'

'But how did you know to come?'

Grandpa nods at Dad. 'Your dad has been giving us updates, but he never realized we could actually help.'

Dad nods dumbly.

'You mean you didn't know?'

Dad shakes his head. He is as shocked as everyone else.

Grandma's face reflects the pain. 'I'm so sorry, Kevin, but it was for your own safety.'

'This is very touching,' Geraldine says as she steps in front of her guards. 'But where is the painting?'

'It's here. In this room.'

'Why didn't you get it all those years ago, Grandma?' Yugi asks.

'I couldn't do it without it being taken away. I was working for the CIA - the good ones, you know. The problem was that we all knew that this had something to do with Klaus Barbie. This whole fiasco was egg all over our faces. They wanted to make sure that the connections were not brought up again.'

'So,' I say, 'you just figured out how to hide the clues?'

Chapter 35 Across:

She nods. 'I knew it would be you, Jeri. I watched you grow up, and... and... the way your mind worked! I finally came up with the crossword idea when I watched you solving them at the nursing home.'

'We lost out on a lot of time together, Grandpa.'

'We'll have to catch up quickly then, won't we?'

'So where is it?'

Grandma smiles. 'It's in this building, this Barbie house, but I think you can figure it out.'

'But you know, don't you, Mom?' I ask my mother.

She shakes her head. 'I was bluffing.'

I feel the blood drain from my face. 'You're a good actress too.'

'Go through the clues, Jeri. What's left? What haven't you used?' Grandma's face is flushed as she puts a hand on my shoulder. 'Now, how about we find a very old painting.'

It still feels incredibly strange to have my Grandma Iris *compos mentis.* Her voice is strong and her movements are fluid. I see that Mom and Dad are watching her too. The amazement is writ large on their faces as we walk away from them.

I think back to the photos and my memory seems to sift through them one by one. There were pictures of Mengele and Eichmann, Mengele and his twins, Mengele and Auschwitz and some of the horrors of the place. Mengele and gas chambers. Mengele and...

Wait a minute.

There was a picture of Mengele standing with Geraldine and two young boys. Twins.

I wheeled to Geraldine. 'Your sons! You and Josef Mengele had twins together.' Geraldine remained silent, but her grinding teeth told the story. 'What were their names?'

Without thinking, Geraldine glances at the hulking brute to her side. 'Their names are Niklaus and Lorenzo.'

I look at the wall of muscle beside her - they must be in their mid-forties. *Good Lord, these are Mengele's sons!*

'Nick and Enzo.'

'I never wanted to name them that, but Josef would have no other. Barbie was a hero to him. Lorenzo was my choice.'

Nick's face is stony, but he nods. 'Josef Mengele is our father. We have waited a long time for this moment.'

I look around the room and suddenly I know. The walls hold the key to Raphael's young man. *In my house, one finds all sorts of things.*

In Mengele's house we found the photo of Geraldine, Nick and Enzo.

We have to find a photo that seems out of place.

'Not to hurry you, Jerusalem, but the odds are, the Nazis still have some supporters in the police department.'

Walking along the walls, I search the photos. Grandma's eyes are expectant. I can tell she wants me to hurry, but this is a seminal moment in my life.

'What are you looking for, Jeri?'

'A picture, or a photograph, maybe of Mengele, Geraldine and her sons.'

'That's a great idea, Jeri, but think. What clue are you skipping over?'

I think back to the letters, the crossword puzzle, the Barbie arms, the...

The mirror.

My eyes turn to the fireplace and my jaw drops. I look at her and tears fill her eyes as pride suffuses her being.

'Well, done, Jeri,' Grandma whispers to me.

Walking back to the wall Grandma and I stand for a few moments looking at our reflections. She is old and I am not, and yet somehow, we are twins, identical reflections from different ages. She is looking at me and I at her and I know beyond anything I've ever felt, an incredible sense of joy and accomplishment. Peering into the mirror, arms around each other, I am connected to an amazing woman who has suffered and loved beyond all expectations.

Then, there is a voice behind us. Yugi's. 'Jeez, you two. You're not that beautiful. Just find the stupid painting.'

My little brother, God bless him.

'You ready,' Grandma says.

'Yes.'

Together, we move closer to the mirror and each grab a candlestick.

'On the count of three...' I say.

Standing back, I find my reflection again, maybe for the last time as an adolescent. I see my youth melting away. I see everything - the way I used to be and the way I will be, because I'm standing next to my grandma.

'One... two... three...'

Simultaneously, we throw our candlesticks at the mirror and it explodes in a scintillating cascade of glass and light. Our images have been erased, but one face peeks at us from where the mirror used to be.

A fine young gentleman.

'We did it, Grandma,' I whispered.

'We did it, Jerusalem Walker.' Her eyes glistened. 'You filled in all the blank spaces.' Grandma pulls the painting from its place behind the mirror, pulls it carefully from the frame and rolls it up. Placing the painting in my hands, she hugs me. 'Take good care of it.'

Without warning, the back doors fly open and two men in dark suits, white shirts and sunglasses burst in with drawn guns. 'Freeze!' One of them shouts.

There is a whirl of action. I still can't get used to how fast my parents are. My dad and mom whip into a frenzy of martial arts moves. As soon as they are occupied, Geraldine, Nick and Enzo enter the fray and attack Mom and Dad from behind.

'Jeri, hide here.' Grandma leaps to action. Incredibly, she is strong and fit and she rushes to her husband's side. Nick bulrushes them and they sidestep. Nick ends up taking out one of the suited men. There is another shot. One of the suits has fired and hits Geraldine. She is holding the right side of her chest as she crumples. Enzo calls out and reaches her. Another shot and Grandpa is winged. The bullet clips his right thigh. Mom and Dad are limited because of the wounds in their arms, but they slowly position the suits in front of the door. Nick sweeps the leg of one and he goes down. Nick jumps on him and as his gun goes off again, Nick stiffens and his weight falls on the shooter.

The last suit attempts to hold everyone else off, but the melee roils out through the swinging doors. Like a good old fashioned saloon brawl, the action spills onto the veranda. I rush to Yugi's side and we chase out after them. The man who shot Nick cannot move his weighty bulk and he struggles underneath. Yugi, unhappy about being neglected, gives him the finger as we rush out onto the porch where we see that my parents and grandparents, bloodied and bruised are fighting the last suit. Knowing that it's a lost cause, the man puts his mouth to his cuff and runs down the street.

Across the street, there are a hundred people standing, recording the proceedings. Mom and Grandma look at each other. Grandma takes the lead. She begins to speak in Portuguese. *Wow.*

'Ladies and gentlemen. I'm sorry to have upset you like this, but you have been witnesses to a new movie being shot on location. The director,' she points back inside, 'is still talking to the manager, but he did not want any of the extras to know what was going on to preserve the reality of the show.' She raises her hands as if the victor of a contest. 'Thank you very much. Feel free to share with your friends.' Grandma walks down the porch and invites us to follow. She winks at me. I can't believe how quickly she has transformed herself.

The crowd begins to clap and laugh. A roar goes up and they begin moving back to the veranda. Grandma grabs her grandchildren's hands while Mom and Dad stagger towards the rental car. 'Which one is yours?' Grandma asks.

I point to the large white vehicle. 'Come on, get in.'

We race to the rental car knowing that we must leave quickly before the masses find two dead people inside. As we approach the vehicle, Dad winces and reaches into his pocket. 'You've got to drive, Jeri.'

'What?'

'Grandma is the only one not bleeding and she's going to have to wrap these wounds. It's up to you and Yugi to get us out of here. Very soon, some of the CIA's finest will be here. We need to get out of here!'

'What?'

'Stop saying that.' He throws the keys at me. I fumble them and then pick them up from the ground. I'm frozen.

'Jeri,' Yugi says, 'Chance of a lifetime. Come on, let's go!' His face is alight with excitement. 'It's like a real movie! Get in! Drive!'

He jerks me to the driver's door, pulls it open and shoves me in. As Grandma arranges the rest of the patients in the back, Yugi races around to the passenger door and leaps up onto the seat. How weird is it that he is not suffering any ill effects from his kidnapping? The kid is a machine. Buckling his seat belt, he bounces up and down next to me. I throw the one hundred-million-dollar painting onto my brother's lap and buckle my own seat belt.

Just as I am adjusting the mirrors, Yugi yells at me. 'We don't have time for you to get ready for your driving lesson, Jeri, start the car. We have to go!'

The car roars to life. This is vastly different than driving the Camrillac. The engine sounds like a grumbling lion. The steering wheel turns easily. The gear shifter is surprisingly easy to pull down. I put it into gear and push on the gas. Unfortunately, I was supposed to be going backwards, but I put it into drive. The car lurches forward and rams into the vehicle in front of me. Everyone in the back seat slams into the seats in front.

'Jeri!' Dad calls out.

'I'm frickin' trying my best, Dad!' I'm pissed now. I've never been in an accident before, but I've also never been an ambulance driver either.

'Just drive like we do in Duncan. Nice and easy.' Grandma is busily working on his arm while the other two wait for triage.

I slam the gear shift forward two notches and the car surges backward. I look over at Yugi who is smiling and still wriggling up and down. 'This is fun.'

Chapter 35 Across:

Successfully navigating the reverse and then forward into the street, I gun the gas which is much more sensitive than the Camrillac. The wheels make a screeching noise.

'Yeah, Jeri!' Yugi screeches with joy. 'You go, girl!'

I feel like a midget behind the wheel. We muscle down the street, slowly at first, but suddenly, I see that a car has pulled in behind me and is closing the gap quickly.

'I think they're behind us,' I say.

'Just keep going, Jeri,' Grandma says.

'You think?' I'm pretty angry right now. This is a real-life James Bond moment and I'm just a kid who's still on her frickin' learner's permit.

Safety be damned, I floor the stupid thing and it races down the road. I'm aware that, just like in the movies, at any moment an old lady is going to step off the sidewalk and she'll have a dog and she'll have to jerk it back and it'll go *ooork* and then a young mother will be pushing a stroller - a double stroller knowing my luck right now - at a crosswalk and I'll just about hit it and then for some reason we'll have to turn down a stupid alley that's waaaaaaay too small for traffic and a garbage truck will be backing in and I'll have to swerve around it and...

'Jeri!' Yugi shouts. 'You gotta turn!'

Unfortunately, the big vehicle turns slowly and suddenly, without meaning it, we are airborne. I've jumped the curb and we're now landing in a city park going forty miles per hour. I hit a trashcan, which figures, and narrowly miss a light pole.

'Where are you going?' Yugi shouts with glee.

'I don't know! I don't know! Dad just told me to drive!' I can feel tears in my eyes. I look in the rearview

411

mirror to see all their heads bouncing like bobbleheads as I drive over the grassy park.

Yugi picks up my phone and grins as he dials.

'Who are you calling?"

'I'm calling the cops, dingleberry.'

'I don't think you'll need to call them, they're behind us already!' I'm being followed by suspicious looking vehicles through the park, between trees, around fountains, over paths. There, ahead of us, near the intersection of main roads are the police.

Thank God.

In the middle of a grassy park, I slam on the brakes and stop the car. Everyone, me included, bounces forward and then backwards. Grandma smiles at me. 'You did good, Jeri.'

'Yeah, Jeri, you did good.' Yugi is holding up his hand for a high five.

I lower my head onto the steering wheel.

Chapter 36 Across:
Full of life and energy (7)

It was weird dropping Grandpa and Grandma off at the nursing home. The CEO stopped them on the way in and Grandpa, limping, made an excuse about wanting to spend some time away with his wife, which angered the CEO who then lectured Grandpa on how dangerous it was to take Grandma outside the confines of her safety. Grandpa's response was laughter and the words, 'Tell me about it.'

We plan to have two houses built in Duncan on opposite sides of the town. It wasn't that we didn't want to live next to each other, but distance still makes the heart grow fonder. Grandpa and Grandma decided to rebuild their house next to Dongle and Margery which made them very happy.

Grandma called some of her trusted friends in the agency to come get us out of Brazil. She also contacted the Mossad and dropped a hint that they had a gift for them. When the Raphael was turned over to the State of Israel, they humbly accepted the gift and promised that we, as Israeli citizens, would be welcome to tell the tale anytime.

Geraldine Dresser did not survive her gunshot wound. Neither did her son, Niklaus. I don't feel bad about their deaths. I try, but I can't.

A few days after our return, we gather in the park, Johnny Bing Bing's takeaway sitting on the picnic table in front of us. Now freed from her prison of acting, Grandma appears young and vibrant. Her hands, although deeply veined, are strong. As she relishes the taste of the Bing Burger and strawbingy milk shake, she smiles at me.

'Grandma, why didn't you just tell us where to go? Why all the cloak and dagger stuff?'

413

'Jeri, every good thing in life, every treasure you find, every treasured relationship you make, should be a beautiful struggle. You don't like to do easy crosswords, right?' I shook my head. 'If I would have made it too easy, you wouldn't have kept looking - none of you - you would have thought I was just a senile old lady making up stories. But because I made it difficult and took you on the journey, you were trapped.'

'But you were worried about us?'

'Of course,' Grandma said, 'but I know that your parents are quite good at taking care of you.'

I look down at Maximus who, instead of climbing up onto my shoulders, has laid comfortably in my lap. I stroke her under her chin, around her ears and she rumbles contentedly. Contentedly, that is, until Yugi pops a large brown paper bag.

What a smell.

I love this abnormal life.

The End